Robert Barclay

GREEN HARBOR

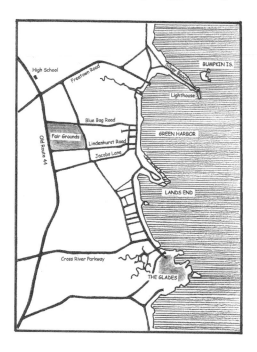

"Mr. Barclay's work. . .*sticks steadfastly to the old and abiding ethics about sex and family relationships. Those ethics seem to be either absent or minimal in the fiction I've seen during the last couple of decades. And while the competition focuses on dazzling images,* Mr. Barclay *takes us to the core of his characters. He doesn't avoid sexual realism either—he's completely modern in style yet traditional in content.*"

Robert Gover—Author & Editor

Safe Harbor

Robert O. Barclay

Cover design and cover photo by author. *
Map, title page art and interior graphics by author.
Author photo by Photographer's Guild of St. Paul, MN.

"Solitude" by Wheeler Wilcox—lines 5 & 6 quoted in chapter 31
"Apostrophe to the Ocean" by George Gordon Byron—lines 2—5 quoted in chapter 31.

* Front cover photo taken during Heritage Days August 4, 2000, is of the town pier in Scituate, MA.

Library of Congress Number: 2001091472

ISBN #: 1931646023

To order additional copies of this book, contact:
Beaver's Pond Press
5125 Danen's Drive
Edina, MN 55439-1465
1-952-829-8818
www.BeaversPondPress.com

Dedicated

To Jeffrey Lewis, a good and beloved friend. No one I know was kinder or more self-sacrificing. He was a staunch supporter of my writing and would certainly have been one of the first to read this new novel. He died too soon from complications of diabetes and will be sorely missed.

Author's Note

In my first novel, "A Gift Once Given", I chose Ocean Bluff for my setting. In this novel I used Green Harbor. Both really exist nearly side by side between Rexhame and Duxbury south of Boston. I borrowed the names because they seemed typical of the small towns that dot the Massachusetts coast—almost generic. Other than the names both communities are completely fictionalized.

I considered writing about a real town—I might have used Scituate where I grew up—written about real streets and businesses and beaches, but I decided that I couldn't do that objectively. The problem is I've lived too long in Scituate and my memories and impressions are tainted by the special circumstances of my own experience, and the reader might have found my observations suspect; so I decided that it was safer to take bits and pieces from real places and add or subtract details to make the setting fit the specific scene and character.

I hope my readers won't be offended by this imaginative slight of hand.

Acknowledgements

I spend hours alone, locked in my home office, pacing in front of my computer. It's a solitary work, but I love the process and the rewards when I finally get it right (that is when I have captured the subtle essence of a character or the perfect line of dialogue or discovered the secret of the scene that I have been wrestling with) are nearly beyond description. The effect is so powerful that it's become wonderfully addictive and I feel the need to come back again and again to the work even if no word ever ends up being published. Yet in the end I have to show the work to someone and get their objective feedback if the book is to be successful. And here I have been blessed.

Many people, both friend and professional, have been willing to offer their time and advice and it would be awful for me not to thank at least some of them. First my teacher Barbara Cockrell, who taught me the basics and gave me a better idea of what this novel ought to be about. Secondly, Robert Gover, my editor, who has been critical when necessary, but who has also encouraged me when I expressed doubts. The members of a local writer's group who critiqued parts of this work. Trish Cramer, our leader, Bob Metz, who also served as my copyeditor, Mike Jastrebski, who constantly reminded me to show not tell; Lori Eaton, whose talent and style gave me something to aspire to, Driene Hattingh (a native of South Africa) whose stories of her homeland constantly fascinated me. And a couple of newcomers Dan Ryan and Alissa Winternheimer. Special thanks to Scott Edelstein, author, agent, editor, consultant, and teacher at the Loft. And lastly Milt Adams of Beaver's Pond Press, a new friend and member of MIPA (Midwest Independent Publisher's Association) who has put a great deal of time and effort into the production and promotion of "Safe Harbor".

The Summer of 1985

Chapter 1

The sky, gray and heavy, hung low over the marsh and the sea's breath spread out in ghostlike fingers over the weedy pasture in front of Sam. The ankle-high grass felt wet and cold under his bare feet. At this early hour no one was stirring in the crowded cottages that were packed side by side along Blue Bog Road and only one home among a ramshackle line that ran straight down to the beach showed any sign of life. Coming from a narrow annex, attached to the house that was closest to the field, two blotches of light smudged the morning mist.

Sam stood alone under the drooping branches of a red oak. A single tree with a sixty-foot spread that grew on the crest of a hill on the northern edge of the field. Watching, Sam stretched his vision to pick out the dark silhouette of a truck emerging from the grayish fog. Leaving the narrow road to the south, this iron behemoth rolled out onto the field, flattening a thick tangle of cord grass and knocking over a patch of blue cornflowers. The wet ground gave way and the tires left clear tracks, which fanned out in all directions as one truck after another moved off to its assigned place. Shortly the dark figures of men descended from their lofty cabs and began to unload.

One truck stopped directly in front of Sam and another pulled up behind. When the driver of the first slammed his door shut the words Gopher Amusements & Concessions popped into view. Every summer this worn-out carnival traveled up and down the New England coast from its home in Penobscot, Maine, to Mystic, Connecticut, stopping at the smaller county fairs and working local charity events. But it was here today, to set up for St. Bartholomew's. This was the Gopher's last stop for the season, and compared to the other communities it served, this was the poorest.

Sam wasn't supposed to be here. He should have been at home with his mother; and if she woke up and found him gone there would be hell to pay. But he came to this field every year to draw whatever excitement he could from the jumble of sound and color that went into setting up the midway. He listened uneasily to the churlish shouting that passed from man to man. The ripple of muscle on the thick arms of one roustabout caught Sam's eye as he watched him wrestle with a bulky machine that resisted his efforts. The man gave a final grunt and Sam heard the piece snap into place.

The brightly painted trailer in front of him carried one of the rides. It was hard to tell what it was. At the moment all he saw was a mass of pipe and odd-shaped buckets tied together and chained down to the steel bed. Sam hoisted himself up on a low branch and with feet dangling, he bent over to peer through an opening in the bristle-tipped leaves. Several roustabouts swung the unwieldy pieces off the back of the truck bed and began to bolt the pipes together in a spider-like frame. At first their effort seemed fractious and chaotic, but as the work progressed he could see that every movement had a clear purpose. Two men had pulled off their shirts and showed off their sweaty backs—one ebony, the other darkly tanned. Both were tough and sinewy from constant lifting and he marveled at the smoothness of their actions as they pulled and dragged and locked the buckets into place with thick iron pins.

For most of the fourteen years he had lived in this beachside resort he had practiced this end-of-summer ritual. He supposed that it was a childish pastime and that someday he would grow out of it, but he wasn't looking forward to it.

◆ ◆ ◆

Green Harbor was an aging resort—crowded to overflowing in the summer and dull and empty the rest of the year. Even at the height of the season it was frumpy and unfashionable, a place where nothing important or exciting ever happened. Sam had seen little of the world beyond so there wasn't much for him to compare, but he was conscious of the fact that his life up to now had been pretty ordinary. Swimming in the sea, running roughhouse on a hot summer's day, playing softball with friends on the corner lot at Lindenhurst and Beachwood, watching a movie at the local theater on Main Street in Freetown, going to elementary school at Jenkins and later attending junior and now senior high at Southbridge. These and other mundane activities made up the extremes of his life—a rumor, some featherbrain scheme, a bit of skullduggery seemed like worldly excess.

He had a girlfriend, Winnie, Winifred Rowan O'Neill. She hated her first name and only Sam knew about Rowan, which her mother had taken from some ancient Irish ancestor. She was really more of a friend, who happened to be a girl, although when he was ten he did promise to marry her. But he hardly thought she would remember that; and if she did he was sure she wouldn't hold him to it. More than anybody else, she was his best friend. Of course Bruce, who had been around slightly longer and had been his ally through dozens of adventures, carried that title, but he had it by default. No matter how faithful Winnie had been, Sam just couldn't accept the idea of a girl being his *best friend.* Nevertheless, whenever he was in trouble or needed a confessor, Winnie was the one he always went to. That's why right now he was thinking that instead of being here alone sitting in the branches of this tree, he ought to be with her.

◆ ◆ ◆

Samuel Edward Stewart. It was a name that he had just begun to grow into. He often thought that it possessed a certain authority. Possibly some day it would appear at the bottom of important documents, but for now it was just Sam, which seemed a fitting title for a fourteen-year-old.

Growing up for Sam was a bugbear. He knew he had to do it, but he wasn't sure he was ready. If his friends could read his mind, they would laugh. He took everything seriously and in quiet moments of meditation (which usually came to him just before he fell asleep at night) he would have deep thoughts about the meaning of life. During one of these nightly sessions he came to the conclusion that there were certain privileges to being a kid. After all he was going to be grown-up for a long, long, time, maybe fifty/sixty years and he ought to enjoy childhood while he could. He thought he was pretty smart to come up with such an insightful idea, but he suspected too that such wisdom also demonstrated maturity, which was the very thing he was trying to avoid.

◆ ◆ ◆

A raucous clanging of steel jolted him from his hundred dollar ruminations and finding that he had closed his eyes, he opened them to a kaleidoscope of bright colors. A sign written in bold letters hung over the entrance—"THE OCTOPUS"—a proper name for a seaside amusement.

This one looked new; at least it didn't have the chips and scars that pockmarked the Ferris wheel or the layers of paint that had covered and recovered the horses on the carousel.

With the sun peeling back the fog he could feel the warmth of a day that was already too hot. Jumping down, he stretched his stiff legs, then sprang forward at an easy gait and headed down Blue Bog Road toward the beach. He kept up his steady pace until he came to Beachwood, then slowed to a walk as he approached his Aunt Em's house.

He spent a lot of time at Aunt Em's. It was his second refuge after Winnie. They both gave him a chance to talk about things that he couldn't talk to his mother about; And it was an easy way to escape from his father.

His Aunt Em was his father's sister. Born in the cast-iron bed that she now slept in, she had never left, never gone off to college, never married, and with her parents retired to Florida, she presently lived alone. Ten years ago they had moved to a trailer park in Gulfport, just south of Clearwater, and left her the house filled with its homey furnishings and its collection of common memorabilia. The house had been built in the twenties as a summer retreat for a middle-class family, but when the Stewarts bought it in 1946, they put in a furnace and converted it to year-round living. Only fifty yards from the water's edge, the house, worn and weathered by winter storms, was still in remarkably good condition. The cedar shingles had been bleached and silvered by salt air, but the newly painted sashes and trim (a dark forest green) made the cottage look neat and orderly.

Approaching from the road, the sandy embankment dropped away precipitously and Sam had to cross a long wooden bridge to reach the back door. He listened to the hollow sound of his feet as they slapped against the smooth boards. Grabbing hold of a knotted thong attached to a rusty bell he yanked it once to announce his arrival, then without waiting for an answer pulled open the screen door. The hinges creaked, and there was a twang as he stepped into the darkened interior. Hollering for his aunt, he continued down the narrow hallway and into the living room.

"Em, are you home? It's me, Sam."

The room was small and provincial, filled with an accumulation of bric-a-brac that had been collected by Em's parents. A storefront Indian stood guard at one end of a beach-stone fireplace, and a pile of split logs was banked steeply against the other. A floor lamp with a fringed shade hung over an antique Boston rocker, family pictures in ornate silver and pewter frames gathered on every flat surface and a pile of needlepoint pillows cluttered the sofa. As he moved into the musty coolness of the room he looked through the multi-paned windows and saw his aunt on the front porch. She was wearing green shorts and a fitted white blouse, and since she was looking out toward the sea she obviously hadn't heard his greeting. He shouted again through the open windows, and Em turned to wave. Then, moving swiftly, she made her way through the open doorway to embrace him. She had a slim, athletic figure, but the skin on her face, wrinkled and leathery from long exposure to the sun, made her look old. Of course Sam imagined that everyone over thirty was old.

"Sam, where have you been? Your mother called." It sounded like a reprimand, then she softened. "I covered for you, but you can't just take off like that, especially now. I told her you'd come over early this morning and fallen asleep on my couch; and that I would send you home when you woke up."

"How did you know? That I would come here, that is?"

"You always show up here when you're upset. So, explain yourself," she demanded.

"I went over to the fairgrounds to watch 'em set up. I know I shouldn't have done that without telling mom, but she was sleeping and she hasn't been doing much of that lately."

Em looked at him searchingly. She seemed undecided about how to handle this. "But you knew she'd worry when she woke up and found you gone."

"Yeah, I know. I just don't want to be there right now."

"Because of your dad?" she asked, gently touching his cheek. "He'll show up, sometime." Em said. If she intended to reassure him, it didn't bring him any comfort. His father had been missing now for five days—undoubtedly on a long binge—and whenever he drank, he came home ugly and abusive. Sam didn't want to be there. He couldn't protect his mother without getting slammed against the wall himself, and he couldn't stand to see what his father would do to her. He secretly hoped that his father was gone for good.

"I wish he were dead and buried," he said, expressing years of bitterness and frustration.

"Sam," Em cautioned.

Chapter 2

When Sam left he descended the sand-worn steps leading to the beach and walked stoically along the shore. Mrs. Eagan, his sixth-grade teacher, was out with her dog, an ugly little mutt that always showed its teeth and growled whenever Sam got too close. Otherwise the beach was empty. The fog had cleared, the bright sun shown above and reflected off a determined surf, and diamond-like sparkles of light bounced across the surface of the water as the wind moved it roughly toward him. He shuffled along, kicking at the sand, and occasionally wandering into the shallow puddles of water left by the retreating tide. The shout of a woman, chasing her little boy down the beach, caught his attention and suddenly a wistful image of his own mother leapt forward.

She had a biblical name, Sarah, which means princess, though nothing about her life suggested such a royal title. In his mind's eye he saw the youthful photograph that always sat on top of her bureau. The picture was old, the colors faded. Sarah stood alone under a rose arbor, the pink petals almost matching the color of her light summer dress. Her long, straight hair was not the dark auburn shade he saw now, but a bright orange. She had told him often of the grief that she had suffered because of her hair, and the teasing she got because of freckles that ran riot over her whole body during the summertime—how they gathered so thickly in some places that only a few spots of white showed through.

Nowadays that problem was under control, partly because she avoided the sun and partly because of the clever use of makeup. All that remained were a few tiny little dots that were too dark to be covered by makeup. They sprinkled the top of her cheeks and squeezed together in a narrow band that ran across the bridge of her nose.

Sam called her skinny. Her hair, bouncy and short, made her look almost like a little boy who needed a haircut. Her features were small and delicate with thin lips that often curved in a friendly smile. And there were shiny, bottle-green eyes below feathery brows whose wispy hairs were so light they didn't show at all unless she lined them with mascara.

Sam took in all these details, but his interpretation was affected by the fact that she was his mother. He might admit, at least some of the time, that she was pretty, but he saw more than her dark auburn hair and green eyes. He also saw her unhappiness, and he knew her weaknesses.

Besides being his mother, she was also his protector, especially when it came to his father; and Sam felt that she suffered greatly because of it.

The day his father had disappeared he'd overheard the two of them in the hallway downstairs.

"To hell with the kid," his father screamed. "You always put him first!"

Her answer was cautionary—almost inaudible. "He'll hear you." Which was foolish, because the house was too small for him to avoid it.

"To hell with him and to hell with you."

"You're drunk," his mother said as if she were apologizing for his anger.

"If you weren't such a bitch, I wouldn't have to drink!" The words slid darkly through the crack under his bedroom door, and Sam covered his ears, which muffled his mother's answer. A loud crash made him drop his hands and he heard the splinter of glass hitting the floor—a squeal of pain, like a small animal that had been wounded, then a sudden cold silence.

"Damn it!" his father cried out. "Don't just stand there like a friggin' dummy—scream, hit me, do something."

Nothing—just a quick sob then an abrasive scuffing sound as if something heavy were sliding down the wall. The front doorknob rattled, and when the door came back to slam into the frame, the whole house shook. Sam rushed from his room and stopped at the head of the stairs. Looking down he could see his mother sitting, back to the wall, her hand to her forehead. Broken pieces of clay from a Grecian urn, which normally stood by the entrance, littered the floor. Coming off the bottom step he noticed blood oozing from between her fingers. Apparently the urn had struck the wall behind and a jagged shard had sliced into her face.

Most of his father's abuse was expressed in vile and cutting language. He seldom hit her. Still, Sam wanted desperately to lash out at his father. He wanted to save his mother from the curses and obscenities that cut so sharply that if they had been knives she would have been bathed in her own blood, but he didn't have the height or the strength. One day that would change and he would put an end to his father's cruelty.

◆ ◆ ◆

A half mile down the shore, he turned up toward the dunes and followed the natural pathway between the high saw grass. Crossing

Beachwood Road and heading up Lindenhurst to the top of the hill, he opened the front door and called out to his mother.

"Mom, I'm back!"

He watched her descend the stairs like a summer storm, her expression clouded with worry and anger. She rushed toward him, then stopped suddenly at arm's length. Her hands were open as if she wanted to gather him to her, but something held her back. The wetness on her cheeks showed the intensity of her distress. He couldn't tell if it was because of him, or if some of it was his father—perhaps both. She pushed the tangled hair back from her forehead, then used the back of her hand to wipe away her tears. Stepping closer she grabbed his shoulders as if to shake him, but instead slid her arms around his neck and pulled him to her in a rough embrace.

"Sam, don't ever do that again," she chided, as she choked him in her grip.

"What was I supposed to think when I woke up and found you gone?"

He suspected that under different circumstances his disappearance wouldn't have mattered. "I go out lots of times without telling you," he reminded her.

"Well, you shouldn't."

"I didn't mean it, Mom."

"Didn't mean to go, or didn't mean to give me a heart attack when I couldn't find you?"

"Mommm!" he whined. "The *Gopher's* in town. I got up early to watch them unload the trucks."

"Is the summer so far gone?" she mewled, dropping her hands to the middle of his back.

"I start school in another week," he reminded her.

"Good Lord, it's all moving too fast—I can't keep up."

"Mom, what happened to Dad? Is he coming back?"

"I don't know," she said shifting her bare feet in the thick pile of the hall rug. "The police say they're looking for him, but with his past performance, I doubt they're looking very hard."

As Sam pulled away, he noticed the scab that had formed on her temple. He pressed his fingers gently against the wound. It looked well-healed, but she pulled back from his touch as if it were still sore.

"Does it hurt?" he asked.

She dragged his hand away and a blackness crept into her eyes, as if the sun had been swallowed up by a giant thunderhead. He supposed that once she had loved his father, but he couldn't see how. Certainly if she ever loved him that feeling had long since withered away.

"How can he do that to you?" he asked, breaking away from her embrace.

"He gets angry—he doesn't mean it."

"I wish he were dead."

"Sam. That's awful!" She sounded upset, but he couldn't help wonder if she didn't secretly wish the same thing.

"I hate him," he said, turning away.

"No—no," she said. Reaching out she took hold of his arm to turn him back to her. "Don't say that, don't even think it."

"Mom—I'm afraid," he said, pulling desperately at the bodice of her loose fitting dress.

"Afraid of what?"

"Afraid that I'll lose you too." Looking down he saw that he was dragging at her neckline, exposing the top of her breasts.

"How?"

"I don't know," he said, releasing his grip. "Afraid that he'll do more than just cut you . . .afraid that he'll kill you or drive you away."

"Oh Sam, I'm not going anywhere," she croaked, sweeping him into her embrace. She brushed her lips across the horn of his ear and stroked the back of his head. Then she pressed his face into the softness of her shoulder. "I love you too much," she mumbled.

As Sam stood there cradled in his mother's arms, he felt like a child. Normally he hated that feeling, but right now he wanted to be a child—her little boy.

Finally his mother let go and spinning him around pushed him toward the stairs. She gave him an affectionate slap on the behind and told him to: "Go clean up and change. I want you to come along while I go food shopping."

He took the steps two at a time and was soon deeply immersed in the stinging spray of a hot shower. She'd only given him a few words of encouragement and a hug, but it was enough.

Chapter 3

Twenty minutes later Sam came into the kitchen with fresh clothes on, slicking back his wet hair with an oversized comb he had found on the back of the bathroom sink. His mother was at the table writing a list. Just as he was about to interrupt her, the front doorbell rang. The chimes reverberated through the house, disturbing the sticky silence and shaking the cat loose from his nap on the windowsill. Coming into the center hallway and squinting down its length, Sam could see the silhouette of a man shifting nervously on the other side of the screen door. With the cat at his heels, he started down the hall and recognized the uniform of a state trooper. As he unhooked the door to let him in, the officer addressed him: "Son, is your mother home?"

"Yes," he answered.

"Would you get her for me?"

The authority in the officer's voice and the somber look in his eyes made Sam's blood run cold. Without hesitating he turned back toward the kitchen and called out to his mother. "There's a policeman here to see you." He heard the clatter of a chair as it crashed to the floor, then saw his mother come through the doorway and start down the hall. Sam moved to meet her, but she pushed him aside and begged the officer to step into the narrow vestibule.

"Are you Sarah Stewart?"

"Yes, officer," she answered, "is this about my husband?"

"Mrs. Stewart," he said, fingering the broad-brimmed ranger's hat he held in his hands, "we've found your husband's car on Route 44 in West Gansett, near Water Street. He wasn't in it. The car sideswiped a guardrail and went down an embankment, which made it hard to see from the road. There was blood on the steering wheel and more on the front seat, but the driver wasn't anywhere around. Then about twenty minutes ago some kids reported finding a body. . ."

At the word *body* Sam saw his mother's legs buckle. And as pale as her complexion was, her face turned paler still. The officer reached out to steady her. Backing her up, he forced her to sit on the hard bench that was built into one wall of the vestibule.

"Are you okay? Can I get you anything?" he asked solicitously.

"No, I'm fine. Tell me, why do they think it's Robert?"

"Well, there was no wallet, no identification, but the head injury fits the circumstances of the accident. And that *was* his car. The photo you gave to the police wasn't too clear and the copies we made were even worse. That's why I'm here. We need to have you come and make a positive I.D."

"How? How did he die?"

"It wasn't the head injury," the officer pronounced as if that were significant. "It looks like he left the car, walked about a half mile to the edge of an open field, and stumbled into an irrigation ditch. It wasn't very deep, but apparently he passed out and landed face down, then lay there until he drowned. A coupla kids found him. He wasn't looking too good, so . . ." The officer saw Sarah's lids flutter and her head start to wobble, then with a swiftness that caught him by surprise she fell forward and he reached out to catch her.

Sam thought the trooper might collapse under her weight, but he made a quick recovery and carefully lifted her upward until she was resting against the back of the bench. Then he spread her legs, brought her head forward and dropped it between her knees.

Now with his mother folded up like a rag doll a low cry crawled up from Sam's throat, but when it escaped it came out more like a bark.

The officer looked from his mother to Sam, and could see that both were in distress. Hearing a low moan he turned back to Sarah who was coming to and trying to right herself.

"Stop!" he advised, pushing his hand down firmly on the back of her neck to keep her from rising. "You need to stay put for a minute until your head clears," he added more gently. After a moment he helped her to sit upright, then instructed Sam to, go to the kitchen and get a glass of water.

Sam knew that his mother needed help, but he wasn't particularly clear-headed and that fogginess made it hard for him to move.

"Hey—*Waldo. A*re you in there?" the officer scolded.

"Yes," Sam answered, but he didn't sound convinced.

"Then help me out here. Go get your mother some water."

The sharp authority in the man's voice energized Sam, and he headed automatically for the kitchen. When he returned, his mother showed clear signs of improvement.

"Okay," the officer said as he took the glass from Sam's palsied hands. "Now who can we get to help?"

Staring blankly ahead, he could hear what this man was saying, but his words didn't seem to have any meaning. "What?"

"Snap out of it kid. I need an adult—a friend or a neighbor? Somebody who can help your mother."

"Call—call Em," he said, still disconnected. "She'll know what to do."

"Who?" the officer asked.

"Aunt Em. Over there," Sam said, pointing in the general direction of the kitchen, "there's a list of numbers by the phone."

"Now we're getting somewhere," the officer said, as he headed down the hall to locate the phone.

Sam continued to stand in the same spot as if someone had glued his feet to the floor. *It's my fault!* he thought. He knew that he hadn't killed his father, but he'd wished it and it'd come true. Besides there seemed to be a kind of luxury in wallowing in the blackness of his own guilt. It distracted him from the reality of what was happening around him.

Chapter 4

Em came and took over. Sarah alternated between long silences and short spurts that came out in one or two word sentences. Sam watched Aunt Em as she followed his mother from room to room. He saw his mother jockey a fragile antique Sheraton side-chair across the living room rug until she had pressed the back into the brocade drapes and couldn't move it any further. She tried to straighten a picture hanging over the dining room sideboard that wasn't crooked to begin with, plucked clean towels off the towel rack in the bathroom and tossed them in the clothes-hamper, flushed an unused toilet. Coming into the kitchen, she tried to make some herbal tea, but forgot to turn on the flame under the teakettle and couldn't seem to remember which cabinet held the cups. Em hovered over his mother, making sure that nothing she did was dangerous, fixing what she could, like turning on the gas to heat the kettle and pulling a tea bag from the canister next to the breadbox. As Sam watched all this, he became increasingly agitated. Why did his mother seem so disoriented and why did her actions seem so emotionally flat? She didn't cry, didn't get angry, didn't shout about the injustice or the idiocy of his father's accident. She never spoke a word about his father.

"Em," she said, looking into the refrigerator, "I need milk." Then pulling the carton from the shelf she popped the lid to sniff the contents. "It's sour," she said and turned to dump the lump liquid into the wastebasket when she would normally have poured it down the sink.

"Is Sam here?" she asked, returning to the refrigerator to poke absently at the leftovers.

"Yes, he's right behind me," Em said.

"Isn't he at your house?"

"No, he's right here," Em repeated and taking her by the shoulders she turned her to face Sam, but she still didn't seem to recognize him.

"He's always taking off when I need him most," Sarah said, picking at a loose thread on her sleeve and then going to the sink to get a washcloth, which she used to scrub a spot on the counter that only she could see.

"Should I call my dad?" she asked suddenly.

"Your dad's gone, Sarah.   He died over a year ago," Em explained, as she came up behind, and gave Sarah a hug.

"There'll be so many people and the house is such a mess," Sarah said, pulling free and opening the broom closet.   Pulling out a mop, she knocked over the bucket it was sitting in.

"We'll do that later," Em said as she carefully took the mop out of Sarah's hand and slipped it back into the corner of the closet.

For the next fifteen minutes Sarah circled the kitchen table spouting nonsense. "I ought to vacuum.   Those white drapes in the living room look awfully dingy."

"They're not dingy, they're beige." Em corrected.

"Maybe I should go and pick some tomatoes from the garden." Rattling the handle on the back door, which Em had conveniently locked, she asked: "Em, can you remember what I did with Sam's backpack? He'll need it for school."

"Sarah, school doesn't start for another week," Em said, taking her hand.

His mother stopped in front of a chrome kitchen chair, plopped down, and started reciting fragments from nursery rhymes. *"Here I am Little Jumping Ivan.   When nobody's with me I'm alone. . ."* she covered her eyes. *"I see the moon, the moon sees me. . .   Under the spreading chestnut tree the village Smithy stands. . ."* She made a circle above her head with her arms and hands as if she were forming the branches of the tree. *"A bird came down the walk, he did not know I saw."* Using two fingers she walked them across the tabletop.   Then, folding her arms across her chest, she started rocking back and forth, humming a child's lullaby as if she were comforting a baby, but all she held were her own soft breasts. And she squeezed these so tightly they threatened to spill from her blouse, which had come partly undone.

The lines in Em's wrinkled face deepened and her watery eyes were bright with concern. Sam, frightened, touched the back of Em's hand and asked, "What's she doing?"

His aunt didn't answer and that frightened him more. "Will she be alright?" Sam asked.

"Of course she will." Brushing his hand aside, she reached out to wrap her arms around him. "This is just temporary, we're all going to be fine," she said, rubbing her fingers between his shoulder-blades as if she were trying to rub away his concerns.

The kettle on the stove began to whistle and Em and Sam both jumped. Releasing Sam, Em hurried over to pull the kettle off the flame. She filled a cup with a tea bag already in it, gave it a perfunctory stir, then came back, slid the hot liquid across the table and waited for the smell of the steeping tea to catch Sarah's attention.

While Sarah sipped absently, the cat, who had gone missing after the trooper left, suddenly leapt into Sarah's lap. Pawing her skirt, to hollow out a bed, the black and gray tabby made one complete turn, then curled into a furry comma and began to purr. That noisy, outboard-motor purr broke into Sarah's subconscious and brought her back to the present.

"When are we going to Lakeville?"

"Lakeville?" Em asked.

"Yes. I have to go and identify Robert."

"Are you sure you want to do that?"

"I have to." Sarah insisted.

"Okay, but let me call ahead, and I'll do the driving." Em insisted.

"No, don't be silly, I'm fine," Sarah shrugged, then flicked her hand in a casual dismissal.

But once Em saw Sarah rise and walk erratically across the green linoleum floor she stepped in front of her and stole the keys off the hook before Sarah could reach out for them.

◆ ◆ ◆

When his mother returned with his aunt several hours later, she looked different. The closest thing Sam could compare it to was the gaunt expression of a man on the front page of the newspaper who had lost his house to a fire and was presently standing in the ashes. He couldn't even guess at what was going on inside his mother's head, but what he saw outwardly was telling. It filled him with apprehension, and when he reached out to touch her he was surprised to see that his hand was shaking.

"Sam," she groaned. Then taking his hand she spread his fingers and pressed them indulgently over her heart. He tried to pull away, but she held him captive and gradually his fear lost its edge and the blood stopped pounding in his ears.

He didn't know what to think, or what to feel. It was hard to cry and he certainly couldn't laugh; yet he needed desperately to do one or the other.

The house filled with people, and he heard the voices of friends and relatives as they swirled around him in a confusing blur. Sometimes they spoke to him, and he thought he answered their questions, but he couldn't be sure.

Eventually the day came to an end and the house got dark. Someone turned on a light in the kitchen and switched on another in the hall, then the other rooms began to light up. Except for the kitchen there were no overhead fixtures and in the other rooms only one or two lamps struggled to push away the gloom. The shadowy figures that danced on the walls closed in, and the heat and sweat of so many bodies mingled with the smell of stale tobacco and smoke and made the air thick and unbreathable. Sam felt as if the spirit of death itself had come to sit upon the roof; and he imagined that it was sucking the life from the house—drawing it up through the chimney in the corner and inhaling it into its gaping black nostrils.

At nine o'clock his mother put her arm around him and told him to go to bed. He climbed the stairs, went to his room, and took off his clothes a piece at a time until there was nothing left, then slid onto the bed. Sam pulled the cotton sheet over him, not because he was cold—the room was hot and stifling and the window-fan only sucked in more heat. He did it because he needed to feel protected. Lying on his side, he dragged the sheet over his shoulder and tucked it under his chin.

He was tired, but he couldn't sleep—couldn't close his eyes. The headlights from passing cars projected the crossed, window-mullions onto the ceiling and dragged them down the wall behind his bed. The dreamlike stupor that had shielded him from pain during the day deserted him now. It was replaced by a sudden sharpness that tore at his stomach and he felt like he was about to hurl. Guilt and confusion swept over him. He loved his mother in the passionate needful way of a child, and he wanted more than anything for her to be happy. Yet he'd watched her suffer over the last several hours and was utterly powerless to alter her condition or change the events that had caused it.

Eventually he drifted off into a dreamless sleep. When he awoke in the early morning hours, that same guilt and confusion rushed back to tear at his stomach, and he raced to the bathroom to find some relief, but nothing came up except dry heaves.

Chapter 5

Sam waited at the back of the Goddabout Mortuary and watched his mother while she kneeled on a long flat cushion and draped her arms loosely over the prayer rail. Head bowed; she spoke softly to the waxen profile visible just above the ivory ruffle that decorated the upper half of the casket. He couldn't make out her words, but even if he could, he was sure it wouldn't have helped. Unless she was praying for his father's soul, which surely must be damned, what could she possibly have to say to this man who had treated her so hideously?

Hiding in the shadows at the back of the room, Sam sat slumped in the middle of a row of folding chairs that were lined up against the chapel wall. He hoped to get through this without having to take the long walk to the ebony coffin that held his father's body. Even from this distance he could smell the flowers; the aroma was heavy, and pungent. Poorly arranged, the juxtaposition of color was garish and offensive. Sam wondered why flowers should be proper for a funeral. They seemed too beautiful to serve such a dark purpose, especially since they were also used for weddings and all sorts of other celebrations that were intended to make people happy. Then again, having been recently cut from some living plant, weren't they already dead, or dying?

In the midst of these gloomy suppositions, Winnie quietly took the chair beside him. She pushed her hand under his arm and wrapped it around his biceps. When she squeezed the muscle reassuringly, he turned to look at her and saw a hopeful smile. But what she saw in his eyes must have been foreboding, because her lips quickly straightened into a thin line and that hopeful smile disappeared.

Without saying anything, Winnie reached over with her other hand, and wriggling her fingers to separate his, she slipped her own between, locking the two together. Then she stood, pulled him up from his chair, and began to lead him reluctantly down the aisle. He didn't want to go with her, but he couldn't think of any argument against it. At first he resisted her pull, but she only pulled harder and her determination won out. Certainly there was a need to bring closure to this ordeal, but how would getting close to his father's body be of any help? Growing up, he'd had an instinctive desire to love his father and to be loved in return, but because that opportunity never presented itself (and now it never would) he was left with nothing but a feeling of emptiness. He wanted to forgive his father, or at least he thought that would be the right thing to do, but he couldn't. The whole idea of being this man's son seemed unnatural. All he could feel was reproach.

When Winnie eventually got him to the front of the chapel, she gently nudged him forward until he stood over the coffin. The first thing he noticed was the smell of perfume and powder, and underneath something that reminded him of paint thinner or lighter fluid. The body rigid, the hands folded, the gray suit pressed and clean but threadbare, the printed blue tie loose and crooked. Finally he looked at his father's face and he started to tremble. It began at his knees, then stubbornly crept upward. He folded his arms, pressing his elbows hard against his ribs, hoping to stop the progression, but the shaking continued. He thought: *I don't know this man.* Perhaps the fact that his father's eyes were closed, and he couldn't see the cruelty that generally was reflected there, fooled him into thinking this was a stranger—a man of peace—and not the man who had so horribly abused him.

Chapter 6

During this whole sorry affair Sarah had held herself together in a manner that showed uncharacteristic strength. Other than the initial shock, over these last two days she had handled the details of the wake and the funeral service and dealt with the problems related to Robert's family and his drinking buddies with a cool reserve that surprised her. Only once had there been any break in that cool self-restraint, and that slip came and went so quickly that Sam who had his arm around her at the time was the only one who had noticed. But when she stepped out of the limousine at the gravesite following the solemn service in the mortuary, it all started to come apart.

As Sarah made her way across the grass, she could hear grotesque sucking sounds as her pointed heels sank into the spongy ground. Standing near the flower-draped casket she fought for control and waited for the other mourners to gather around the gravesite. The minister bowed his head and asked for a silent prayer and her tears came—this time with such force that Sam, looking at her from across the open grave, stared in disbelief. Sarah struggled between sobs to get air into her lungs, and cursed herself for being so fainthearted.

The minister, unfazed, began to read from a small dog-eared book that rested easily in the palm of his hand. As his words spilled out into the powerful wind that pulled at the mourners' thin summer clothing, their heavy meaning tore down Sarah's defenses.

"For since by man came death, by man came also the resurrection of the dead. For as in Adam all die, so in Christ shall all be made alive. . .He shall save His people and he shall raise them up at the last day. . .and he shall judge them good for good and evil for evil." Except for the judgement of evil, the promise of forgiveness and salvation seemed empty and meaningless, and the words crackled in the air like hollow gunshots in the autumn woods. If she couldn't forgive him how could God?

The sharp ache in Sarah's heart cut deeper, and a watery weakness in her legs caused her to stagger and drop down onto one of the folding chairs that had been set up behind her. Breaking away from Aunt Em, who had been standing behind him with her hands resting reassuringly on his shoulders, Sam rushed to his mother's side, and bending over her, buried his face in her hair.

Sarah's tears were not for Robert. Last night she had talked to Sam until three in the morning and though she knew he didn't understand all that she had said, she made it clear to Sam that she wasn't sorry for his father's death. She had tried to explain to him that it was hard not to feel some kind of loss even if it was only for the years she had wasted. During their long discussion she wandered from memory to memory, searching for a time that she'd been happy, but she decided that only one good thing had come out of their union. Except for the few short years when she was a child, Sam had brought her the only real happiness she had ever known.

Reaching up, she placed her cold hand on the side of Sam's face and feeling the wetness of his tears, she used her thumb to gently rub them away. She knew that he wanted to be her protector the way she had always been his. But she knew too that he couldn't give her something that he still needed for himself.

Chapter 7

In the days following the funeral Sam found himself sloshing around in a dismal quagmire of remorse. While he was busy with the wake and burial and the reception afterwards there wasn't time to decide whether he was happy or sad, or if he felt anything at all concerning his father's death. Now, with nothing to crowd those feelings out, he was forced to face them head on. Winnie had tried to get him to deal with his grief when she dragged up to the front of the chapel and made him look at the reality of his father's death, and her effort was not unappreciated, but he wasn't ready—and even now he didn't want to dig very deeply.

Maybe that's why his friends kept trying to avoid him. Winnie was the only one who had shown any interest in spending time with him— the only one willing to put up with his dark silences. He rewarded her kindness by asking her to go to the Church Fair.

It wasn't an appropriate way to mourn his father's death, but his emotions had gone in both directions and he couldn't see any harm in trying to feel happy, even if that happiness was fleeting. He loved the fair; it was the crowning event of the summer. Besides, there wasn't any rule that said he couldn't run away from his problems, at least for a little while—and who better to run away with than Winnie?

◆ ◆ ◆

This was the last evening for the fair; at midnight everything would be packed up and trucked off to Camden, Maine, and the field would be left empty for another season.

Sam and Winnie turned off Beachwood and started to walk west on Blue Bog Road toward the fairgrounds. Winnie had on a pair of shorts that showed off her skinny legs and a large T-shirt which hung loosely from her shoulders and fell well below her waist. Whatever Sam had seen of Winnie's figure, even in a bathing suit, was angular and bony and generally that boniness was well-hidden by clothes that were several sizes too big. His costume wasn't any more exciting. He wore a threadbare oxford shirt with the long shirttail hanging out and the sleeves rolled up above his elbows. Below, he had on a pair of baggy pants that needed to be hiked up now and then, because the waist was an inch too big and he had forgotten to wear a belt.

They weren't walking arm in arm like girlfriend and boyfriend, but Winnie did stretch out her hand to take hold of his wrist, then crept down to lock her fingers into his. They kept the space between as if some invisible object prevented them from drawing any closer, but the touch of her hand was still important to Sam. The natural rubbing of her fingers against his as they walked, seemed reassuring, though he couldn't explain why.

As they moved down the street they skirted a couple of crabapple trees and stayed close to a line of stunted cypress while they tried to avoid the heavy traffic and parked cars. Nothing here offered any shade and they shielded their eyes from the setting sun whenever they looked toward the swirl of lights and the hurly-burly of the fair. Passing through the gate Sam paid for their admission and they headed for the Midway. The scene in front of them seemed almost surreal, and plunging into the crush of people, Sam's senses exploded. A pungent mix of dried animal dung and oily sheep's wool wafted thickly on the evening breeze as they passed the judging tent. Next came the stink of urine and wet cigarettes from the portable toilets. And lastly, the taste of salt and the peculiar aroma of popcorn, the smell of burnt cooking oil and foods seasoned with garlic and onions flooded Sam's nose and washed his mouth with saliva. He wanted to try them all, but he was anxious to get to the Midway, so they only stopped for a bag of popcorn and then moved on.

Sam and Winnie continued along a row of garish tents where carnival barkers encouraged them to throw hoops or darts, or race miniature plastic dogs up a grassy slope by squirting water at them. Ignoring these clever pitchmen, they pressed on through the crowd until they broke out into a circle of lights that cascaded across their faces and arms, and made constant changes in the color of their skin.

Here long lines of people queued up to wait for a ride that was bound to bring up whatever they had just eaten and spew it all over anyone who happened to get in the way. Sam and Winnie decided to wait until the lines got a little shorter and went over to an empty bench to sit down. Passing the bag of popcorn back and forth they watched the crowd. Sam noticed the people walking toward them came mostly in pairs. A young couple stopped across from them and the girl nuzzled her cheek into the boy's shoulder; another couple sat down on the other end of their bench and made sucking sounds as they tried to swallow each other with their slobbery kisses. The guy had purple hair and a dragon tattooed on his arm; the girl had almost no hair at all and wore a silver ring in her nostril. Winnie cupped her hands over Sam's ear and whispered loudly, "They need to get a room!" Sam laughed.

Another couple passed by, and Sam could see the guy's hand planted firmly on the right cheek of his girlfriend's tuckus. In fact, his fingers pinched her mini-skirt so tightly it rode up and exposed a narrow crescent of red underwear.

Sam glanced at Winnie, curious to see her reaction. Her eyes wide with surprise were glued to the guy's hand, but she didn't say a word.

More people came—some smiling, some laughing, some shouting obscenities. There were old women and old men, wrinkled and bent—and crying children, and sleeping babies, but even these seemed to come in twos. Sam began to believe that everyone in the milling herd was paired off and wondered: *Is this the natural order of things?*

"What?" Winnie asked.

Had he said that out loud? He didn't answer; instead he looked between the passing faces and noticed that they were sitting just a few feet away from the "Octopus."

"I watched them put that thing together," Sam said, pointing at the multi-armed whirligig pumping and dipping in front of them. "That was the day. . ." he stopped to consider what he wanted to say. "I never thought," he said, and paused again, "that my Dad would. . ."

"I know," Winnie cut in.

"It's like a bad dream, only I'm still caught up in it—and I can't seem to wake up."

"Sort of like getting on one of those rides over there and finding out that you can't get off," Winnie observed.

"Exactly!" Winnie was right. It did seem like some kind of crazy ride and that somehow he had to hang on until it stopped or at least until it slowed down.

"Well," Winnie asked, expectantly, "are we just going to sit here or what?"

"You're right, we're supposed to be having fun and this definitely isn't fun."

"So what d' ya wanna do?"

"How about that?" he asked, spreading his hands palms-up and framing the "Octopus" between them. Winnie simply smiled back in agreement. Taking her elbow, he guided her through the crush of people and they got in line.

◆ ◆ ◆

The padded buckets glistened under the fluorescent lights—red, green, yellow. . . The operator unhooked the chain that held them back and Sam and Winnie sprinted onto the wooden walkway. They circled anxiously until they came to a bucket that was bright orange. Sam squeezed through the narrow opening in the front and turning took Winnie's hand. When she stepped in, the bucket shifted, which threw Sam down onto the seat and Winnie landed on his lap. Both seemed befuddled and Sam panicked when his efforts to move her ended with him touching places that he had never touched before. And when he finally succeeded in getting her off of him Winnie slid to the opposite side of the bucket leaving a wide space between.

The low rumble of the motor rose and the clutch squealed as the operator engaged a lever on the control column. The bucket jumped harshly as the ride started and Winnie made a noise that sounded like a rabbit's scream. Turning slowly, the whole contraption lifted upward at a crazy angle that made Sam feel unbalanced. With the sucking and whooshing sounds of the hydraulics it plummeted toward the ground, then began to climb again. Spinning faster and faster, the buckets swung upward, then fell back. Winnie slid into Sam, then slid away until he came after her and they were slammed together again. The direction of the bucket reversed and Sam and Winnie both traveled across the seat to be thrown roughly to the opposite side. They were both getting sore from one bony hip grinding into the other. With each change—up and down, side to side, round and round—they collided and screamed. It was hard to tell if all that screaming made the ride any more fun, but it certainly helped to keep down the nausea that continued to rise in Sam's throat.

Winnie forced her hand behind Sam's back and wrapped her arms tightly around his trunk and he decided to do the same to her. This didn't stop them from being tossed back and forth, but at least they crashed into the sides as a single unit. Pressing her cheek tightly against his, Winnie continued to scream, until the motion slowed and the machine began gradually to descend toward the earth. As they circled slowly, neither one released the tight hold they had upon each other. When at last the bucket shuddered to a halt, Sam became suddenly conscious of how solidly they were attached. Only this time, for some reason, he wasn't as anxious to get himself undone.

At first he did nothing; then Winnie drew her face back until they were nose to nose and she looked him straight in the eye. Her pupils widened until they nearly blotted out the honey-flecked color. Part of this came from her excitement, but Sam saw something else too.

Winnie's mouth opened and her lower lip curled as if she was about to speak, but nothing came out. Then Sam thought she might kiss him—or did she expect him to kiss her? Winnie stared back at him for a long moment before she made any effort to untangle herself, and even then that effort seemed unhurried. It wasn't until she released the iron grip she had on his waist that Sam became aware of how he had hold of her. The fingers of his right hand were pushing into her ribs while the upper pad of his palm and thumb pressed gently into the soft curve of her breast—or at least he thought that was the softness he felt under his thumb. In all the time that they had known each other, he had never touched her in such a familiar way even during their occasional horseplay. It wasn't the boy/girl thing; not something connected with sex or hormones. For God's sake, Winnie was his best friend—he hardly touched her in any way.

Embarrassed, he withdrew his hand abruptly, as if he were pulling it off the superheated hood of his mother's car.

Winnie's reaction surprised him. She smiled coyly, and he thought he saw a certain telling glint in her eye. A tiny ripple in his stomach, which felt very much like the fear he'd experienced during the ride, made him slightly nauseous. Nervously he extricated himself from the safety belt, which had done very little to hold them down, and stood to extend his hand. Winnie hesitated before taking it and they stepped out onto the platform. Walking unsteadily they made their way past the bright cars and down the metal stairs until they felt the firmness of the ground under their feet. Those few seconds seemed magical, but as soon as they joined the milling crowd the magic disappeared, dissolving into the ethers of smoke and sweat and cow dung that filled the air, around them. And Sam wondered what, if anything, had happened.

Chapter 8

Reds, brighter than the apples in Mr. Finnegan's orchard, and yellows, more achingly vivid than the bus that picked Sam up every morning for school, covered the trees and the ground, and salted the road with thousands of points of color. The splendor of October was evident all around as Sam pedaled happily toward Southbridge. Winnie was supposed to meet him at the pagoda.

The curled multi-tiered roof of a pagoda (which had been copied after a real one just outside of Kyoto) served as the focal point for a beautiful Japanese garden. The idea came from Harrison Taylor Ford, a wealthy sea-captain who made his fortune in the mid-1800's, and then retired to a comfortable mansion in Southbridge.

Captain Ford had a special affinity for Asian art and turned his home into a kind of museum. He had some Korean and Chinese pieces, but the emphasis of the collection fell upon Japanese sculpture and seventeenth-century Japanese prints. He built the pagoda and the surrounding gardens, then established an endowment to maintain it. There was a plaque with his name on it—somewhere—but most referred to his legacy as *The Garden* or told their friends simply to meet them at *The Pagoda.*

Planted with Japanese cedar, bayberry, and Asian yew, and little bushes with white waxy fruit called snowberries, the garden was hedged in with a dense arrangement of trees and shrubs, including *sankokaku*—a red Japanese maple.

This was not a teenage hangout. The big people came at the end of the day or in the evening. He and Winnie always chose the middle of the afternoon because they knew the park would be empty and they could be alone. This particular meeting had been Winnie's idea. Coming here was always serious. Sometimes they talked, about the meaning of life—wondering whether or not God really cared. Sometimes they talked about the future—where they would go and what they would do once they were old enough to travel in the real world, outside of Green Harbor. Sometimes they said nothing and what went unsaid seemed the most serious of all.

Leaning his bike against a polished stone urn overflowing with dying pink chrysanthemums, Sam entered the garden and passed between two sixty-foot Chinese Scholar trees that were presently covered with three-inch seedpods. He followed the cobbled path, which led straight to Winnie. She was sitting on a thick granite bench facing the reflecting pool. When the sun was right and the water calm, the pool showed a sharp mirror image of the pagoda. Those were the conditions this afternoon: the air perfectly still, the surface of the water flat and undisturbed. Only one thing seemed out of place. Winnie, dressed in her usual vagabond fashion—baggy brown shirt, ragged pants and black socks—stuck out like an undertaker in the middle of a brightly painted circus.

Winnie heard Sam's footsteps on the cobblestones and turned to flash him a scintillating smile that ended with a peculiar twist.

"You're almost an hour late. What happened?" This didn't come as an accusation; she sounded fretful, and worried. She seemed to worry a lot about him lately. She could always read his moods and he had never tried to hide his persistent unhappiness. But today, there was something more.

It was odd how his father's death had made him sensitive to things that he had missed before. Every day he became more and more suspicious of something going on inside Winnie's head that would somehow affect their relationship—something important enough to affect the way they felt toward each other. In fact, he suspected that that was why she had invited him here today. He was curious, but he was fearful too of what she might say or what she might ask.

"I know, I know," he said, sounding exasperated, "I couldn't help it. Mom always finds something else for me to do. Especially if she can see that I'm in a hurry," he protested.

"Don't be so hard on her," Winnie cautioned. "After all, who else can she ask?"

"You're right—it's just. . .I don't understand, when my dad was around he never did anything, but now that he's gone, mom seems so lost. Maybe he did some good after all."

"I never saw it," Winnie observed. "Besides, is it really so awful to be needed?"

He couldn't help agreeing with the first, and he said so, but he chose not to answer the second. Instead, hearing the trumpet of geese, he cranked his head upward and watched four Canadas flying in a staggered line. They passed just above the treetops, and Winnie's gaze followed his as the geese stretched out their long, black-banded necks and constantly adjusted their formation. In an instant they passed beyond the curled roof of the pagoda, then turned and headed toward the southern horizon. "That was so intense," Sam said. "I swear, they were so low I could see the pinfeathers on their wings!"

"Righteous," Winnie said, and that one word seemed sufficient to explain the depth of her feelings.

"I love this time of year. I know everything's dying, but it goes out in such a blaze of glory. Of course, when the leaves are gone and the trees turn black and ugly. . ." Sam didn't finish.

After a moment Winnie asked, "How's your mother doing? I mean, is it better or worse now that your dad's not there?"

"It's hard to tell. She doesn't say much. The other night I got up about three in the morning and when I crossed the hall to the bathroom, I could hear her crying in her room."

"What did you do?"

"Nothing. I wasn't supposed to be there. Besides, what could I do?" Winnie didn't answer and he continued. "I can't imagine she would be crying over my dad, but something was wrong."

"Maybe she just feels lonely."

"How could she feel lonely? My father was never there!"

"You'll never know if you don't ask."

Sam put his fist to his mouth and scraped his teeth across his knuckles. "I can't." Winnie spoke in a whisper. "She needs to know you care."

"Course I care." Sam poked at a leaf that had just drifted onto the bench. "I just don't know how to tell her."

"Is it so hard?" she asked.

"I think about it all the time, but I don't know how to get the words out," he said, picking up the leaf and crumbling it between his fingers.

"Don't be such a wuss. Just say it." She slapped the hard muscle in the middle of his thigh to get his attention.

"Ouch," he said, swinging his legs away and crossing his arms protectively across his chest.

Winnie reached out to pull him back. "Sorry," she said. "What do I know? I still have both my parents. . ."

"And your dad isn't in the habit of beating on your mom," he said, with glib indifference.

"That really bites." Winnie said, spitting out the s.

"Sorry."

"My father loves my mother. I mean, they really have something, you know. Not that they make a show of it, but I've walked in on them a couple of times and. . ."

"Whooo-ey!" Sam exclaimed.

"Not like that!" she said, punching him in the shoulder. "They were just kissing."

"Oh," he said, with a note of disappointment.

"You're awful!"

"No I'm not."

"Admit it. You thought—well, I won't say what you thought."

"No—yeah, maybe."

"Yuck!" she said, punching him again, this time a lot harder

"Hey!" he complained.   Then Sam turned and shoulder to shoulder they stared straight ahead at the reflecting pond. The water lay flat and still—the air breezeless—the only sound came from the motor of a lobster boat far out in the harbor. After several minutes, Sam interrupted their quiet reverie with the sour observation that, "Life sucks."

"So, what's new."

"Okay, so it's supposed to suck." Sam admitted.

"You think you're the only one with problems."

"Who else?" he asked.

"Me."

"You?"

"Yeah, me. You think my life is *all that?*" she said, with an as if you care toss of her head.

"Well, maybe not great, but I thought you were crankin' it out."

"I am—most of the time." She pushed her raggedy hair out of her eyes, and gave him a sheepish grim.

"So, tell me about it."

"Why should I?" she asked, sounding a little peevish.

"Maybe it'll make me feel better."

"I doubt it," she said in the same tone. "Besides, why should I try to make you feel better?"

"You always make me feel better," he said.

Winnie laughed. "If you must know, one minute I'm ace-high, and the next I'm totally bummed out. A year ago I wouldn't have imagined that I could get so screwed up. I guess it really started to go haywire when I got into this tampon thing. . ."

Winnie stopped suddenly. He guessed she realized that she had just given away something personal and was waiting to see his reaction— only there wasn't any. There was no way he was going to touch the subject of her starting her period.

"Aren't you glad you asked?" She looked away, too embarrassed to meet his gaze.

"No," he said, then changed his mind. "Yeah—in a way—it sorta means that—you're normal. Not to say that you weren't normal—aren't normal. Arggggh," he moaned.

"Okay, okay, I get the idea," she said. "I'm as normal or as abnormal as the rest, it's just that you haven't been paying attention."

"No, I guess I haven't," he confessed.

"Sometimes I feel like the ocean or that tree over there," she said in a contemplative voice. "They're nice to have around, but otherwise they're not all that important."

"You're right, of course. I do take you for granted. But that doesn't mean you're not important to me. It's just that whenever I'm up to my eyeballs in muck, you're always there to pull me out. I've gotten used to that, and now I'm afraid it's all going to change."

"And if it did, what then?"

"I don't know. That's what frightens me," he said, touching her face, "Don't look at me like that, I can't explain. I just need you to be you."

"But I am me, and even if other things change, I'll always be me."

"You're wrong. You're already changing and there's nothing I can do about it," Sam said, pointing his finger at her nose as if he were scolding her.

"Outwardly maybe, but not inside where it counts. You forget I know you, all of you—there aren't any secrets between us—not any real secrets. No matter what happens—if we grow old and fat—I'll always care about you."

"You can't know everything," he insisted.

"No, but I know enough to guess at the things I haven't seen or heard."

"And if we're miles apart?"

"You and I are too connected. If you were in trouble I'd come and find you and you'd do the same for me."

"Winnie, you surprise me. No—no, I take that back; this is exactly what I meant."

"What are you talking about?"

"This—this ability you have to take the stuff that I see as so complicated and make it seem so simple. Whenever I get too serious, and try to make mountains out of molehills, you always set me down on solid ground again."

"Cut it out, Sam!"

"It's true," he said, as if he had just come to that realization. Then without thinking it through, he changed direction. "I wonder—I mean, this boy-girl thing—you know. Does that all begin by finding someone you can talk to, someone you're comfortable with and then—well—you sorta move on to the physical stuff? Or is it like an explosion; you meet and bang you're in love and you can't keep your hands off each other?" He hadn't asked this because he was feeling romantic, and he certainly wasn't looking at Winnie that way. He asked because he really didn't know, and thought that she might understand such things. "Or, or maybe it grows slowly and the bang comes when you suddenly realize that what you been feeling all along is love—real love."

Winnie didn't respond and when he saw that she had turned away he scooted forward on the bench and leaned out to stare at her. "Well?" he prodded. She dropped her chin demurely and began to scrutinize her hands. They were in her lap and he noticed she was pulling randomly at her fingers, first on one hand then the other as if she was trying to pop her knuckles, which she did sometimes. When he reached out and touched her shoulder, she swung around roughly to confront him and he saw that her eyes were bright and wet. The flush in her cheeks and a definite puffiness to her lips made her look sad and vulnerable. He couldn't tell why, but he felt the strangest stirring deep in his gut. There wasn't time to figure out what that meant because Winnie rose quickly from the bench and moved a few steps away, stopping at the stone edging that surrounded the reflecting pool. He stood to join her, and when he got to her side she dropped down on the edging and plunged her hand deliberately into the cold water. A line of ripples spread across the flat surface, bending the image of the temple and breaking it into a rolling line of distorted shapes.

Sam continued to stand next to her until she finally looked up and spoke. "You're too much, Sam. The next thing, you'll be telling me that you want to kiss me," she complained. In spite of her protest he felt that she wouldn't object to a kiss from him and yet he wasn't sure how he had given her such an idea.

He had known Winnie for so long that it was hard to think of her as a girl. At least he didn't think of her as the sort of girl he would want to kiss. Not that it would be so awful he supposed, but he thought a kiss ought to express passion and he didn't feel that way about her.

He knew Winnie was waiting for an answer, but he didn't have one to give. Instead, he reached down, took both her hands and pulled her up beside him. Again he saw that look (the same one he'd seen the night they had ridden the "Octopus"). It seemed as if she wanted to say something, but couldn't. She held his gaze for a few seconds; then fast as a frog catching a fly she touched her full lips to his, and fled from the garden.

Hot waves washed over his face and a sweet bubble rose from his stomach and escaped in a hiccup. The fever quickly cooled and he stood motionless, feeling suddenly disoriented and unfulfilled.

Chapter 9

$\mathcal{S}$oon it was Christmastime. Sam's first year without his father was an emotional roller coaster. Every act, every tradition renewed, reminded him of some Christmas past. And even though most of those memories came back to hit him like a punch in the gut, he felt a bewildering emptiness as if something meaningful was missing. Could it be that he was suffering over the absence of a man who had often made his life miserable and who had been especially awful during the Christmas season? The holidays always seemed to provide an excuse for his father to drench himself in liquor and go about the house spitting his words and crashing into the furniture.

Coming home one Christmas Eve, wearing a ratty white beard that was horribly askew, his father had sat beside Sam on the hall stairs and draping his arm heavily over Sam's shoulder he growled out a raspy "HO, HO, HO!" followed by an uncontrollable cough. The smell of alcohol and stale tobacco made Sam gag. He was only eight years old and he wanted to be anywhere other than under the weight of this man's arm. But he was afraid to move.

When his father released him momentarily to pull a brown bottle from his coat-pocket, Sam tried to escape, but his father grabbed him by the shirt-collar and spun him around. Standing, Robert shook Sam once like a rag-doll, then dropped him on the hall rug and stumbled out the front door. Sam knew his father wasn't Santa Claus, but still, after that incident he always got a little spaced out whenever he saw an ill-fitting red suit and a fake beard on a shopping-mall Santa.

That was the same year his father threw the tree out in the snow, ornaments and all. And later, when his mother went to remove the turkey from the oven, she found that the bird had flown the coop. His father had secretly taken it and tossed it out next to the tree. With memories like that, why should he feel any sadness over his father's absence?

Maybe it was because his father wasn't always drunk and on rare occasions he would get it right. Like the time he took Sam to Edaville Railroad in Carver to ride the old steam train around the cranberry bogs and see the Christmas lights. Or the morning Sam came down to find him still working to attach the handlebar stem to the frame of a shiny new bike. The same bike that he still rode everyday.

Sam decided that the holidays had always been traumatic, filled with uncertainty and distress, but in some perverse way that had become normal. All during the year the tension was muted and predictable, but at Christmas the level of tension rose dramatically until it became prickly and explosive. Now he felt that same familiar anxiety, but there was no justification for it.

His mother was affected too. Always full of plans for outings and pageants and carol singing, her efforts this year seemed flat and spiritless. In the past she had done these festive things—gone to these extremes—to counteract the ugliness that his father dragged into the house whenever he came through the door. But now that he wasn't there, his mother didn't need to emphasize the idea of peace and joy. Instead she approached each tradition with a lukewarm enthusiasm that soon deserted her. Unless Sam stepped in to finish what she had begun, the job went undone. That's why the lights were on the tree, but there were only three ornaments hanging from the branches. The rest sat on the floor in front of the easy chair, all neatly tucked away in their worn-out cardboard cartons.

Aunt Em came over when she could; came in full of hope and smiles, but failed to alter his mother's mood. Sam felt cheered by her visits, but he and his mother sucked away her energy, and Em generally left looking washed-out and depressed.

Sam and his mother took each day one at a time, until eventually the holidays were over. By New Year's Eve, both walked around the house looking stony and emotionless. There wasn't anything to celebrate, so they sat down on the couch at nine and watched TV till midnight, then went to bed.

◆ ◆ ◆

January and February blew by snowless, with bitter winds and subfreezing temperatures; but by the end of March as the weather moderated and the buds started to bulge on the trees, things began to change. During the next few weeks Sarah saw the crocus break through the black soil next to the back steps, the bright red throat of a barn swallow flashed at the feeder and finally the grass turned from a dirty brown to green, and with those changes the tiresome dullness of winter slipped away. There was something symbolic in the regeneration of life, and for the first time Sarah could see the possibility of erasing the images of abuse that had clouded her existence for so many years.

The first days of summer brought the heat of the sun and the infectious chill of the Atlantic. And now fully involved in her garden Sarah let her uneasy angst seep into the soil. Gloveless she used her fingers to bury the roots of a dozen young tomato plants and to press the dirt into little cone-shaped mounds.

In a few weeks the results of her labor began to sprout forth in lush green plants. The tiny tomatoes were round and hard and green, the cucumbers, prickly and wrinkled, stretched their bumpy fingers on the vine, and the lettuce put out broad full leaves that caught the morning dew and looked wonderfully fresh and succulent. She had already harvested half of the radishes and a second row had started to push up some ragged green leaves. Soon they would be enjoying tasty salads with her special homemade dressing poured generously on top.

The warm weather brought Sarah new life. Day by day, her somber face altered. Layer by layer, she let the brightness show through in her resurrected smile. It was a wonderful renewal. In fact, she wondered if it was more than just a renewal. Could this be the young woman who married Robert, or perhaps the rebirth of the little girl that had existed before she met Robert—before he'd beaten her down and molded her into a dowdy, submissive wife?

Sarah wasn't sure exactly how it had come about, but she had come back, and not just to her old self, but something better. In whatever manner, she had arrived at some resolution concerning Robert. And this was more than just a mental resolve; she seemed determined to eliminate every reminder of him. It started one day when she burned Robert's papers and photos in the fireplace. Later, she tossed out or gave away all of his old clothes. She kept this up until everything was gone. There was no guarantee that he might not still come back to haunt her, especially in her dreams, and she did have occasional nightmares, but for the moment at least, Robert had been banished, and she was happy.

She was talking to Sam again after a long dry spell in which neither was willing to discuss anything more complicated than the weather or what they would have for supper. Though their current conversations were often light and sometimes filled with laughter (something unusual in that household), they occasionally led to more serious matters, and one afternoon Sarah mentioned her plans for the future. In the past she never made plans that went beyond the end of the day or the end of the week. Now she spoke of her hopes for creating some positive changes in her life.

"Sam, I want to go back to school. I don't know what I want to do yet; I just want to learn. Maybe basic stuff like philosophy, or history. Oh, and reading, I want to know more about books—good books," she said, twisting a strand of her hair between her fingers and then chewing on the end. "Of course, I can't go full time; I've got to have a job!"

"Why?" Sam asked. He pulled his stockinged feet up onto the couch and pressed them affectionately into his mother's leg

"We don't have any money. Well, there's your dad's insurance, but that won't last forever."

"Are we broke?"

"No, don't worry about it, we'll be fine," she said. "Maybe I should get married again—course he'd have to be rich." She glanced at

Sam and smiled, then grabbed the remote and switched the station to the evening news.

◆ ◆ ◆

Sam knew she wasn't serious, but that idea—the idea of marriage—bothered him. Over the last year he and his mother had fallen into a routine. Suppers together, facing each other across the kitchen table. Watching TV, the two of them curled up on the couch. And even though they didn't say anything beyond: "Hey!"
"How's your day?"
"Fine."
"Got any homework?"
"Yeah, a little." He still liked knowing she was there when he got home from school. Usually he went to his room to study, but if he needed her for anything, she was only downstairs. Saturdays they went to the movies. Sundays they drove into Southbridge and had dinner at McNamara's, then afterwards sat over coffee (only one cup, a special concession to Sam as man of the house) and talked till late in the afternoon. If his mother married again, it would end all that.

The Summer of 1986

Chapter 10

June. Sam had just celebrated another birthday and at fifteen he was beginning to show more interest in the opposite sex. This was not something that came upon him all at once; he'd always had a healthy curiosity about girls—particularly about what made them different. But now there was a sudden urgency to satisfy that curiosity. This new awakening made him notice things that had slipped by him before. He even noticed some pleasant changes in Winnie. Always straight and skinny, she certainly didn't seem very feminine. She continued to be mostly straight and skinny, but now he could see a softness here and there, especially in her face, that sometimes made him think that she might actually be pretty.

Otherwise, the rest of her was still a disaster. Her clothes were too big and hung off her shoulders as if they were still on the hanger. She usually swam with just a T-shirt and shorts. Most of the time her breasts were invisible, but they showed all too clearly when she came dripping from the sea. The thin cotton material clung to her skin and stretched across two pointed bumps that weren't much bigger than a small orange cut in half. And her hard nipples, not at all boyish, stuck out fat and brown, and filled his soul with apprehension. Her bathing suit (when she wore it) was a long tube with ruffles on the top. It was old and threadbare, the color faded from too much saltwater, and it was inclined to bunch up in odd places.

In the past she had always presented a toughness that made her seem like one of the guys. When she was younger and smaller she played as hard as any and had more than a few fistfights in which she was the undisputed winner. She threatened to fight with some of the guys even now, but they wouldn't take her up on it. For one thing, she was taller than most, and for another, she was a girl. Even if she didn't act like it, they were aware of it; and besides, how would they deal with the embarrassment if they lost?

Presently, however, there were some cracks in this rough facade, and something more ladylike was beginning to emerge. The gangly walk that Sam was accustomed to had changed. Now he noticed a feminine smoothness that made him wonder. Her voice had lost its customary growl. True, she had always had to force that coarse sound, but now she couldn't seem to manage it as well, and whenever she got excited no amount of effort could suppress its girlish buoyancy. He was surprised more than once when she broke out into a giggle that rang with the same crystal tingle as the wind chimes hanging on Aunt Em's front porch. It was exactly the sort of sound he had been so critical of in the past. He still didn't like it, but coming from her it seemed less irritating. There were other things too: a subtle alteration in her mannerisms that at least suggested some delicacy. Once he thought he caught her wearing lipstick, though she rubbed the back of her hand across her mouth and denied it. Mostly, her conversations were confined to sports, but one day she started talking about the possibility of wearing a dress to someplace other than church.

Sam often stared at her, then had to turn away awkwardly when he realized she had caught him at it. Now when he saw her from a distance, and she smiled at him, he felt strangely embarrassed. He really didn't understand what was happening here, but if he could venture a guess he would say that she was pleased to know he cared. Certainly he cared, but somehow he suspected that her interpretation might be different from his own, and that idea made him uncomfortable. It forced him to rethink their relationship. Weren't they just good friends—best buddies—or could it be that they were something more?

◆ ◆ ◆

Actually, with all this brooding about Winnie, she wasn't the one who had created this urgency concerning the opposite sex. In fact, it was Jennifer who rattled his cage, spun him off on a carousel of lusty daydreams, and made him want *"to dip his wick into the warm, gooey depths of the honeypot."* He'd read this in a book somewhere. He didn't know exactly what it meant, but he had an idea and it sounded so incredibly sensual that it stuck in his mind and wouldn't go away.

Jennifer was the new girl in town. Her parents had moved into the cottage next to Aunt Em's on the first of June, and they would stay at least for the summer.

The day she arrived he spotted her on the open deck that hung off the front of her house. She called out to him when he passed by on the beach below. "Hello," she said while she leaned over the railing.

"Hello," he answered in return. She smiled, and he immediately choked. But before Sam could take the conversation any further he heard her mother calling her to come inside, (which was how he came to know her name). She turned and from the moment she disappeared into the darkness of her house, his secret yearning began.

For several days he didn't speak to her. Oh he knew she was there, and took every opportunity to watch her from afar, but the more he saw of her the more improbable it seemed that he would ever have the courage to approach her face to face.

♦ ♦ ♦

Until Jennifer came into his life his only sexual experience had been alone. Something done in the bathroom or when he got out of bed in the morning. When he was ten years old his mother had come into his room one morning while he was between PJs and underpants and caught him touching himself.

"Sam! Don't do that," she croaked, covering her face with her hands as if she'd just seen something unspeakable.

"Why not?" he asked, dragging the blanket up off the bed to hide his shame. He only touched it because the thing stuck out, and finding it hard and curiously sensitive, he wondered why that sometimes happened.

"Because it's not good for you," she said.

"Do you mean that I'll get sick?"

"No, you won't get sick—it's—it's perverted," she groaned, and her grim look made him feel ashamed all over again.

He was silent. He didn't know what *perverted* meant, but it sounded morbid.

"Just don't touch it," she said, in the same voice she had used to warn him about matches and fire.

His mother's reaction frightened him, and for a while he didn't even want to look at his penis (or his Willie as his dad used to call it). But by the time he was thirteen the temptation was too great and every so often he would succumb to a primitive need to diddle with the devil. Afterwards he suffered from terrible guilt, but it felt so good to spend a moment swimming in the slippery joy of his own being that he couldn't help himself. And if he prolonged that playful moment until the exquisite twitch of a thousand nerve endings suddenly exploded, the startling eruption that followed would send him soaring into a world of Mythological proportion. And when that eruption ended, leaving him adrift in the soft afterglow, he had to wonder about the wisdom of adults who considered this a mortal sin.

The real thing—the man-woman thing—was a mystery to him. Oh, he asked questions—asked his friends—and heard all their weird stories, but it seemed impossible to separate truth from fiction. A year ago those worries only scraped at the edge of his consciousness and occasionally heightened his curiosity. Now he was obsessed; sex occupied his mind every free minute of the day and kept him awake at night. He knew there was more to the business of falling in love than just the physical stuff, but he could see that it was sex more than anything else that was driving him to distraction.

♦ ♦ ♦

One afternoon Sam was sitting at the edge of the water letting the soapy backwash splash against his feet and swirl up around his outstretched legs. He was soaking in a shallow pool that had been left by the retreating tide. The water wasn't very deep, but occasionally a rogue wave would reach him, and the water would rise several inches before being sucked back by the undertow. Perhaps a quick dip in the cold Atlantic would have brought more immediate relief, but he was in a lazy mood, and getting up and pushing deeper into the sea was too much like work.

Suddenly he caught a flash of color as something moved into his field of vision. He turned to his right and saw Jennifer heading straight for him. Her lissome figure was clad in a royal purple bikini that was incredibly brief. Made from little cloth triangles, bound together with ribbons and bows, he felt sure that if it ever got wet it would fall apart.

Jennifer moved toward Sam with a smooth easy gait that defied explanation. He'd never seen bone and muscle function like that. The fluid motion fascinated him and he couldn't keep his eyes off her. He noticed a tingling sensation at the back of his neck, as if the hairs were being stirred by the ocean breeze, but there was no breeze. And as she came closer he recognized a distinct connection between what he saw with his eyes and a stirring down below. Not a disagreeable feeling, but he cursed himself for not having better control. Now with Jennifer standing over him a rapid flutter in his stomach made him feel as if he had swallowed a tiny bird and he wanted desperately to set the poor thing free.

"Sam, isn't it?" she asked offhandedly.

A throbbing at his temples made him open and close his eyes and his blurred vision convinced him that his whole body was under attack. Sitting there, in a warm puddle of water, he wasn't in any danger of falling over or stumbling or in some other manner making a fool of himself, but he didn't have to be on his feet to know that he was a mess. His mouth fell open and his mind told him what to say; yet he couldn't hear anything come out except air. As baffling as this was to him, it seemed to have no effect at all upon Jennifer. She didn't need an answer and wasn't about to wait for one. Instead, she continued without him. "Some woman up there," she said, pointing toward his aunt's cottage, "I think her name was Eve, or Ellen or whatever—says she needs your help and asked me to send you back."

Watching her discreetly from a distance, spending hours daydreaming about her, imagining the special things he might say to her when the opportunity presented itself was easy. But sitting there studying her feet, observing the fine white sand stuck to her ankles, following her long legs upward to the triangular patch that represented the bottom of her two-piece suit, was disabling. He couldn't move. Glancing upward from this angle exaggerated the size of her breasts, and he immediately dropped back down to stare at the soft whorl of muscle surrounding her navel. Even that proved too much, and he closed his eyes, hoping to make these potent images go away.

Before he could recover he felt a sudden disturbance in the air, and opening his eyes he saw the ripple of Jennifer's buttocks as she walked away. Apparently her job was done and since she had no further interest in him she simply dismissed him from her mind. What a disappointment this had been and how terribly deflating to his young ego. For days he had prayed for some excuse to speak to her and then when that opportunity presented itself he was defeated by his own ineptness.

She was already well on her way up the beach before he had organized his thoughts enough to move. He stood and waded into the sea until the water had reached his knees, then he splashed his body and swim-trunks to wash away the wet sand that was sticking to his legs and backside. When he was done, his swimsuit dripping, his skin wet and beaded, he scuffled up the beach to the stairs that led to Aunt Em's front porch, and taking the steps by twos he sprinted to the top. His sandy feet slapped across the shaded deck and as he stepped over the threshold into the living room his aunt stopped him short. "Where do you think you're going?"

"Coming to help you," he answered, confused by the obvious irritation in her voice.

"Well, you're not coming in here dripping all over my hardwood floors. Stay right there while I get you a towel and something dry to put on," she said. And leaving him, she headed toward the kitchen. He often changed here after swimming, so his aunt always kept some of his clothes in the laundry. Returning, she shoved a towel and a pair of camel-colored shorts into his hand; then, turning him around, she pushed him back through the doorway.

The front porch had a broad roof that extended a foot or more beyond the railing. Closed in by black screening that went around three sides there were several bamboo curtains, hung randomly, to help shut out the morning sun. But at this time of day the sun was behind the house and already falling toward the western horizon, which left the porch in cool shadow. "Change out here, and come in when you're done," his aunt ordered.

Even in the dimness of late afternoon, when the black screening tended to blur whatever objects could be seen from the beach, the porch didn't offer a lot of privacy. Which might have made changing pretty tricky if Sam hadn't had plenty of practice. He used his aunt's front porch often to get in and out of his clothes, and as a child he had even stripped off his wet suit in the middle of a crowded beach by simply draping a blanket over his head to make a kind of tent. In this case he wrapped the large towel around him well above his waist, and overlapping the ends, turned the navy terrycloth into a colorful sarong. Hiking up the edge he reached underneath and untied the drawstring of his swim-trunks. Next he tugged on the legs, until he wriggled the waistband past his hips; then took a few hard steps in place and watched the soggy material slip past his knees and plop down around his ankles. He pulled one foot loose, and used it to hold the swim-trunks down while he freed the second, then stepped clear. Still wrapped in the towel he patted the palms of his hands against his buttocks and legs, then turned to grab his shorts off the arm of the porch glider. He had one leg halfway up when the knot in the towel let go. Now, except for his shorts, which had only been pulled high enough to cover his right knee, he was naked. Hopping in a tight circle, he tried to jam his other foot through the second leg, but it was hard to keep his balance. Finally his toe caught the waist and plunged through opening. He yanked the shorts up, buttoned the top, and smartly slid the zipper home.

With everything safely tucked away Sam searched the beach below to see if anyone had been walking by. He saw no one, at least no one that was looking with any interest in his direction. Bending, he picked up the wayward towel and when he came back up he looked out through the dark screen to his right and spotted Jennifer. She was standing at the end of her deck leaning over the rail. Right now, she was facing away toward the sea, and seemed unaware of his presence. But he had to wonder what she'd been looking at a moment ago while he struggled to jam his leg into his shorts. And since the cottages along the beach were only a handshake apart, she might, literally, have seen it all. He was so disenchanted with his body; all the parts seemed elongated and out of proportion and the part he most wanted to hide seemed especially distorted. Somehow he thought it would have been better if he had caught her in the act—caught her gawking at him while his Willie dangled in the breeze, he would have been terribly embarrassed, but at least he would have known. This way he could only guess and the uncertainty was driving him crazy.

Sam watched Jennifer for a moment longer, but she never turned his way. Finally he stepped inside and hollered for his aunt. Wiping her hands on a dishtowel she sauntered in from the kitchen and started immediately to instruct him. "First I need to have you get those boxes in the corner over there upstairs and into the closet at the end of the hall. When you're done, come down to the basement and give me a hand moving some furniture. I had Grandma Stewart's sofa and chair stored down there, and that storm surge last February got in and ruined them. If you can help me carry them out to the road, Fred Berger says he'll come and pick them up."

"Are they really yucky?" he asked.

"Well, ya. But Fred says he might be able to save them. He'll have to strip off the old upholstery and dry out the frame, but. . ." Without finishing, Em turned away and headed for the basement, leaving him on his own. Wavering between his disgust of mold, and renewed speculation about what Jennifer had or hadn't seen, he decided to get to work

Chapter 11

The cottage was generally cool and comfortable. The windows to the porch were always open and a pleasant breeze swept in off the ocean. Today was different. The air felt hot, and the breeze, when it came, was light and ineffectual. The humidity made work of any kind uncomfortable and even though Sam wore only shorts and nothing else, he was sweating profusely. He worked sluggishly, moving the boxes upstairs one at a time, and in between he made frequent trips to the kitchen sink for water. Em had a variety of things in the house for him to drink, but water was the only thing that seemed to bring him any relief from the heat. And when he added a couple of ice cubes from the fridge it made the perfect refreshment.

With the boxes neatly stacked against the back wall of the closet, he made his way down the stairs and through the kitchen to a narrow hallway at the back of the house.

Opening a grainy paneled door he looked down at the rickety stairs leading to the basement. The light here was poor and he moved down the steps cautiously. Crossing the cracked cement floor he could see his aunt working in a dark recess that jutted out under the porch. She was pulling empty canning jars from a box, wiping them down, and stacking them in even rows on a wooden shelf. He quickly realized why she had come down here to work; the basement felt much cooler.

"The boxes are done, Aunt Em."

At the sound of his voice she gave a little cry and brought her hand to her throat. In her other hand she juggled the jar she was holding until it dropped onto the shelf and rolled to a stop against the wall.

"Sam, don't do that," she gasped. "I swear my heart stopped—and now it's beating like sixty! That kind of thing can take years off a person's life," she warned.

After she recovered, she came to him, took his wrist and led the way to the other side of the basement. The trip ended in a far corner under a framework of posts and beams that had been added to support the extra weight of the library, which stood just above. It wasn't really built as a library, but there were hundreds of books packed on makeshift shelves and stacked in crazy piles on the floor—a collection meant to satisfy Em's insatiable appetite for reading.

Aunt Em approached the couch and began to pull away the plastic she had used for protection. As she lifted the covering, a strong smell of rot and mildew wafted upward and Sam promptly pinched his nose to save himself from gagging.

"Sam, take those cushions off and toss them over there," she said, indicating a bare spot on the floor behind him. "It will make it easier for us to lift this thing without that extra weight." Following her instructions he picked up the end of a cushion and tried to pull it free. The damp cloth felt slippery under his fingers and repulsed, he snapped his hand away.

"Arrrgh, I've been slimed!" he complained, then laughed at his choice of words.

"Don't be such a wuss! Grab an end, and let's get this over with. Wait," she corrected. "Give me a minute to open the bulkhead doors so that we can scoot this thing outside."

While his aunt was busy tending to the cellar door, he made another try at the cushions. Using a broom handle he knocked them to the floor, then poked and prodded until they were somewhere near the spot Em had pointed out.

Em came back to scrutinize the situation, looking for the easiest pathway through the clutter that lined both walls. Then they each took an end and tipped the frame up so that it would clear the doorway.

Outside they followed a sandy path between the houses until they came to the embankment next to the road, then—feet sinking into the loose sand—they clambered up the steep incline. When they returned for the chair, Sam took the back end and Em grabbed the legs. Much lighter than the sofa, it fit easily through the door. Once both pieces sat by the roadside, Sam leaned against the shaky picket fence to enjoy the freshening breeze.

"Thank God we're done with that," he said.

"Sam," she cautioned. He knew that his aunt didn't approve of what she called inappropriate language, but he liked to think that he was praising God not cursing him.

"Do you really think that Fred can fix these? Look at the arm," he said, bending down and running his fingers over a black crack in the surface. "The wood is pretty wet and it's splitting along the grain."

"You're right," she said. "It doesn't look too promising." Sitting down on an old wooden box that was next to the fence, she assessed the damage and began to shake her head in dismay. "It's my own fault, that basement's a horrible place to store things, but without an attic I don't have much choice."

Sam turned to face the cottage next door and his thoughts quickly shifted back to Jennifer. He saw her feet pressed into the soft wet sand as she stood beside him reciting Aunt Em's message. He thought about how exciting it was to finally have her so close, and then he recalled her sudden dismissal. And now, with an achy emptiness churning in his bowels, a single word came to mind: *lovesick*. It seemed like a strange juxtaposition of words, but it certainly was an apt description of how he felt.

That led to a distressing image of Aunt Em's front porch and his embarrassing accident. He could picture Jennifer standing there watching him. In the past year he had suddenly grown tall: arms and legs too long, some muscle here, not enough there, and what showed in a bathing suit made him feel awkward and self-conscious. What didn't show—had so changed he was convinced that something had gone wrong--that he was abnormal. How would he face her? What would he say? And if she asked, *What'sup?*. . .he'd simple curl up and die of mortification.

Apparently his aunt saw the disturbed look on his face and asked, "What's up?"

"Nothing," he said, pressing his hand hard against the point of one of the palings, wondering if she had been reading his mind.

"You look like the cat who swallowed the canary," she said. "What's that cartoon?"

"Tweety bird," he said, but refused to answer the question about what was troubling him. Instead he folded his arms, leaned against the picket fence and looked down at his bare feet as he slid them deeper into the hot sand.

"Come on, out with it; what's got you so discombobulated?"

He didn't really know what that word meant but it made him smile.

"That's better," she said.

"It's too personal."

"So pretend I'm a doctor or a priest, whatever you tell me goes nowhere else," she said, winking at him as if they were involved in some kind of conspiracy.

"Well, if you must know, it's girls—or at least one girl. Have you seen—" he paused and nodded toward the cottage next door, "Do you know, Jennifer?"

"I didn't know her name, but yes I've seen her."

"Of course," he said, smiling with sudden comprehension.

"Sam, you fox! If you're interested in her, I've underestimated you," his aunt said, giving him a friendly slap on the wrist.

The blood rushed to his face. "Cut it out. I don't even know her. I mean—I know her name, but that's it."

"Soooo, what's holding you back?"

"Come on, isn't it obvious? You said it yourself; she's way out of my league. Besides, whenever she comes closer than fifteen feet, I get so rattled, I about die!"

"Well—at your age what do you expect?"

"I want to say something intelligent to her. It's just that every time I get close I panic. How do I talk to her without sounding like a putz?"

"Well, I know what they tell public speakers to help them overcome their fears. No—in this case that would be a bad idea."

"Why?"

"Wel-l-l-l," she said sounding squeamish, "you're supposed to imagine your audience is sitting there—naked."

"Oh sure," he exclaimed, "that would send me over the edge in a hot flash!"

"I told you it was no good."

"No good? It's awful."

"Sam, it's not as if you don't have any experience with girls. You talk to Winnie all the time and she doesn't scare you."

"That's not the same thing." He swung his head from side to side hard enough to flip the sweat off the end of his nose.

"No, not exactly, but she's your age, and she's attractive, well maybe not attractive, but she could be. You need to get hold of all those raging hormones long enough to start seeing Jennifer as a friend instead of a conquest," she advised.

"You don't understand at all, it's not a matter of hormones or. . . or. . ."

"Conquest." Em said, finishing his sentence.

"Yeah, and besides, there's a big difference between Winnie and Jennifer."

"Sam! You disappoint me. I understand that guys go for looks, but Winnie deserves better than that. One isn't steak and the other hamburger, you know.

"You're right, Winnie's great, but there is a difference."

"Yes, I suppose there is."

"I know that this girl thing is more than good looks. If I could only get to know her—Jennifer, that is. . ." He put his hand to his forehead and pushed away his sweat-sodden hair. "It's just that when I look in the mirror I see this tall, dorky kid, and I think, why would she even be interested? I mean she's sooo together."

"All I can say, Sam, is that she may not be as confident and unapproachable as she seems. I know I'm an old lady and times have changed, but people haven't, and when I was in school the most attractive girls generally had the most trouble getting dates. Oh, not because they weren't asked. There were plenty of wannabes, but they all had only one thing in mind and that was to get the girl into the back seat of their Chevy."

"I don't have a Chevy," he protested.

"That's not my point. Pretty girls like Jennifer always seem to attract the kind of scumbags who think they're God's gift to women."

"Oh," he said, as if he understood, but he didn't understand—not all of it anyway.

"Jennifer is probably desperate for some nice guy like you to come along and ask her out. So, buck up! Ask! At least say something more interesting than *hello.*"

"Yeah, I'll try," he promised, shifting his butt, which was getting sore, pressed against the pickets. "But what do I really know about girls? And when it comes to sex—whooowhee! I mean I've heard some of the guys bragging about the girls they've had, but that's a crock. Bruce and I talk, and he pretends to know it all, but I can tell he's makin' it up. So—how do I find out this stuff?"

"What about me?"

"Naw," he said with a futile wave of his hands. "Thanks, but that'd be too creepy."

"What can I say?" She threw her hands up in surrender, then reached out and poked him playfully in the stomach.

"Hey," he complained, using his hands to fend off her attack.

"Eventually you'll sort this all out, and if you get stuck . . ." She left the end of her sentence hanging in the humid air.

"It's not that there isn't a mountain of information out there," he said, "but it's not much use. Hell, if we were to go by the movies, Jennifer and I would've jumped each other the day we met. And I wouldn't even have had to get her name. But that's not real. I don't know anyone who's done that—not here in Green Harbor anyway."

"Is that what you're looking for?"

"No. I mean sure, Jennifer is hot, but I'm not lookin' to jump her bones."

"Good, I'm glad to see you're not just a knuckle-dragger."

"A what?"

"An ape. A Neanderthal," Em said, then changed the subject. "How's your mother doing?"

"Mom's okay. Definitely better now that she's gotten into her gardening." Then, looking his aunt straight in the eye, he said, "Did you know that she's going back to school?"

"She mentioned it, but I didn't know she'd done it."

"Well, she hasn't actually done it, not until this fall anyway."

"I know your mother's looking for work. She's already gone in for some interviews. Hopefully she'll find something before the summer's over," Em informed him.

"Why does she want to go back to work?"

"It's not that she wants to. Hasn't she talked to you about the money?"

"What money?"

"The insurance money. Your father had a life insurance policy. A chunk was used to pay bills and for the funeral; what's left won't last her much longer."

"Bummer," he said, beginning to experience some of the anxiety that must have been plaguing his mother.

"Your mom will probably kick me for telling you, but I thought you should know the score," his aunt said, folding her arms and turning her head away as if she knew more.

It had never occurred to him to worry about money. "Are we poor?"

"Not exactly. Life has thrown you a bit of a curve, Sam," she said coming round to face him. "And you're going to have to grow up a little faster because of it." Then as a kind of afterthought: "Who knows, your mother is still young, maybe she'll marry again."

Apparently Em saw this as a solution, but to Sam it was a threat. "Marriage!" he spit out bitterly. "Why would she want to get married? Has she said anything? Is there someone she's interested in?"

"Don't worry Sam, there's nothing imminent. Your mother got a bad deal. Robert wasn't any good from the day she met him, but all men aren't like that. After what your mother's been through she deserves a second chance. She has a right to find a little happiness."

"Haven't we always taken care of each other? Why does she need someone else?"

"You're not going to be around forever, and she might like to have something more than just companionship."

"Why?"

Em didn't answer. Instead she asked: "Why are you so interested in Jennifer?"

"Well, you know. I'm attracted to her." He stopped to think, "you're not saying—she couldn't—not at her age."

"Oh yes she could—and age has nothing to do with it. Look Sam, whatever your mother decides, I know that she'll come to you first, and when she does be generous."

"What do you mean?"

"I mean tell her it's okay even if it isn't." Em glanced at her watch. "Good Lord, look at the time. Your mother's probably been trying to call and we've missed her. I should have an outside bell, but like so many other things that need to be done I never remember it when I'm in a position to do something about it."

◆ ◆ ◆

Walking back through the house, Sam clumped down the stairs to the beach and headed off along the shore, using a route home that would keep his bare feet off the hot roads. He'd started his afternoon in a carefree effort to stay cool and had left his aunt's hot and tired, in a hapless condition, wretched about his inability to approach Jennifer and distressed about the prospect of his mother getting remarried.

MARRIED? No, he thought, it's not going to happen. There's no guy, and she's too busy to start looking for one.

Chapter 12

Wednesday, August 28th. Sarah was awake early this morning, lying in bed, worrying about her interview at the bank. Em had a friend, an employee for Freetown Savings, who told her about an opening for a new teller at their Southbridge branch. Hopefully, today would end the streak of bad luck that had kept Sarah from finding a job. At previous interviews she had been given vague excuses and ushered from the premises with promises about getting back to her—promises that obviously weren't real. She almost believed that some nasty little gremlin had cast a spell on her. Whatever the cause, each failure ate away at her confidence.

Sarah had no work experience. Other than babysitting and a few weeks as a senior counselor at Pontoosuc Lake Girl's Camp in the Berkshires, her only real job had been with the Gates Clothing Company in Freetown where she worked as a sales clerk until Sam was born. After that she chose to stay at home. It wasn't the popular thing to do; most women found some way to go back to work after their pregnancy, but she didn't want that. Robert ruled everything, and he insisted they needed the money, but on this one point she held her ground and he finally gave in. So interviews were something foreign to her. They made her nervous, and she felt like she was giving the wrong answers to the questions she was asked. These weren't questions about deep philosophical matters. They were just questions designed to get her to explain what her goals were. But she had no goals other than to get a job and pay her bills.

It had been another sticky night, and the ceiling fan gave Sarah very little relief. Only now in the dim light of dawn had the air cooled enough to bring her any comfort. The ugly sound of the alarm buzzed in her ear, and she reached out to find the button and turn it off. Reluctantly she slid out from under the sheet, and put her feet on the cool hardwood floor. After covering her body with a short terry robe, she pulled some clean underclothes from the top drawer of her bureau and padded barefoot across the hall. She'd heard the water running earlier and knocked on the door to see if Sam was out of the bathroom. The lock on the door had been broken for a long time, and there had been a couple of embarrassing accidents. When Sam didn't answer, she opened the door, switched on the light, and set her underwear on the stool next to the sink. Stepping over the wet towels on the floor, she tested the one still hanging on the rack next to the bathroom door, and found it was dry.

Sarah removed the dry towel and draped it over the shower curtain rail then took off her robe and hung it on an empty hook. Next she pushed the straps of her nightgown off her shoulders and when the brushed cotton stopped at her waist she teased the material past her hips and let the gown fall in a swirl at her feet. Reaching in, she adjusted the water to lukewarm, then stood under the showerhead and let the stingy spray hit her face. The water broke into tiny rivulets that ran down the front of her body, rushing along the inside of her legs and coming together again around her feet before it eddied into the drain. The force of the water felt pleasant and relaxing, and she concentrated on the spray as the prickly drops tickled her nose. After scrubbing her body, she let the washcloth fall at her feet and stepped back to allow the hard spray to strike across her breasts. Eyes closed she took a moment to enjoying the bracing power of the water as it pounded against her.

Arms loose, palms up, she let her spirit wander, dreaming of a time of innocence when the world had not come so hard upon her. She saw herself again when she was four years old, sitting in a tub while the warm water and soapy bubbles circled her tummy, her back arched forward, her head bent. She could feel her mother's fingers in her hair, working the shampoo into a rich lather. Occasionally a dollop would fall into the water in front of her; and squinty-eyed, she would reach out with her finger and try to grab hold of it. With this image came a wonderful sense of well-being, and she remembered what it was like to be loved and protected. But now that innocence was gone, and she had to face the reality of being alone. She couldn't help wonder how she had gotten from there to here, with a son to care for and bills to pay, a home to hang onto, and no job in sight?

An icy change in the temperature of the water woke her from her wishful dream and made her squeal. Then she fumbled with the single faucet handle and shoved it into the wall to cut off the flow. While the water dripped from her hair and ran into her eyes, she felt blindly along the top of the shower curtain rod until she located her towel. Mopping the wetness from her face, she stepped out and left a watery trail on the ruby red tiles as she rushed to the door and stuck her head out.

"Sam," she shouted, "did you just start the dishwasher?"

"Yes," he shouted back. "Why?"

"Because I was in the shower," she said. "Couldn't you hear the water running?"

"Sorry, Mom. Do you want me to turn it off?"

"No, forget it," she said with hapless resignation. "I've been in the shower long enough. But next time, pay attention."

She swung her head back into the room and bent down to retrieve the towel, which had fallen from her hand. With water dripping from the ends of her hair and fat droplets running down her body, she started to dry her legs. Facing the full-length mirror that was screwed to the inside of the bathroom door, she glanced up to see her bare form staring back, and straightening to her full height, she took inventory. A lot of damage had been done over thirty-four years. There was a little extra weight on her hips, and her stomach, once flat and tight, now had a distinctive bulge. After two pregnancies, the abdominal muscles had been stretched out of shape and she hadn't worked very hard to tighten them again.

Sam had been nine pounds. A big baby for her—a big baby for anyone—but then he was almost a month overdue. Becky would have been eight by now, if she hadn't died at twenty-one days. Sarah always wondered if her fall down the stairs halfway through her term had anything to do with Becky's untimely death. Still a painful memory, it no longer came with the same heart-crunching sharpness that it once had.

She decided she wasn't happy with her breasts. As a teenager she'd waited impatiently for those two bumps to grow into something bigger than two lentils and now they were shrinking again. On the plus side they were still firm; they hadn't gone south the way they did with so many bustier women, and she still had enough to fill out a dress so that it hung properly. She was carrying extra weight on her hips, but in all fairness that could be considered an improvement since it gave more definition to her normally straight waist.

She turned toward the pedestal sink and picked up her hair dryer. Running a brush through her hair, she combed it skillfully up and down, shaping and pushing until she had the fullness she wanted. Setting the dryer aside, she put on her underwear and made a hasty dash across the hall to her room. On a hanger behind her door she found the blouse that she had taken from her closet last night. It was white linen, sleeveless with cloth-covered buttons down the front, and on the bed lay a straight, bright coral linen skirt. After dressing she took a quick glance in the mirror over her bedroom dresser and was satisfied with what she saw. It wasn't fancy but it fit the way it was supposed to and it gave her a clean crisp well-groomed appearance that bolstered her confidence. Taking her white sandals in hand she descended the stairs and headed for the kitchen.

She was too nervous to eat, but she did pull a carton of milk from the fridge and drank straight from the container, which was not her habit. Grabbing her keys, she went in search of the folder that held her directions and a list of character references. Oddly she found it tucked between the cereal boxes in the pantry. Continuing out the back door, she slid behind the wheel of her car and backed carefully out of the driveway.

The trip into Southbridge wasn't very long and soon Sarah was jockeying her light blue Escort into a space behind the bank. Before getting out she gripped the steering wheel and offered a white-knuckled prayer. "Lord help me. And Lord, whether I get this job or not, please don't let me make a fool of myself. Amen." Grabbing a tissue from the box on top of the dash she wiped the perspiration from under her chin then dabbed at the mascara that had started to run from the corners of her eyes.

Opening the door to the bank, she felt a blast of cool air, and thought, at least I'll get a break from this oppressive August heat. Her sandals hit the hard marble floor with a hollow clicking sound that made people turn to see who was coming. Feeling suddenly conspicuous, she carried her folder in front of her as if she could hide behind it.

Approaching an oak railing she leaned over and tried to attract the attention of the woman who was sitting at the desk beyond.

"Excuse me, miss, is the manager in?"

"You mean Mr. McAulliffe?"

"Yes, I'm supposed to see him at ten."

"My name is Mary," the woman said, rising slightly from her chair and extending her hand over the railing.

"Sarah Stewart," she responded, shaking Mary's extended hand.

Mary glanced down at her appointment calendar. "Just step over to that gate," she said, pointing to a break in the railing, "and I'll buzz you in."

Hearing the noisy rattle of the latch, Sarah pushed against the gate and came through. Mary led her on a straight course between two rows of desks until they came to a large oak door with a pebbled-glass panel in the upper half. Printed in neat Roman letters across the center was the name Martin Harrison McAulliffe (an impressive title for someone so low on the executive ladder). Without knocking the woman opened the door and stuck her head in.

"Marty—I mean Mr. McAulliffe, your appointment is here," Mary announced. Then, turning to Sarah, she said, "Go right in, he's expecting you."

Sarah stepped inside and carefully closed the door. She kept her eyes on the man behind the desk, who sat busily scribbling some notes. He didn't look up, but simply asked her to sit. Glancing around the office, she saw an armless straight-back chair in the corner. She crossed the broad oriental carpet and clicked her sandals on the hardwood floor before she reached the chair and sat down. It wasn't very comfortable. First she crossed her legs, then uncrossed them, then finding that there was no place to put her arms, she folded them into her stomach, and when that didn't seem right she ended up extending her arms and clasping one hand over the cap of each knee.

Head down, Sarah pulled nervously at the cottony pilling on the hem of her skirt and waited. After a moment, she had the uneasy feeling that she was being watched. Afraid to look up and confront Mr. McAulliffe, she lifted her eyes coyly and discovered several locks of hair had fallen across her face so that she was able to peek out and observe him undetected. He was staring at her with an expression that was hard to decipher. It wasn't unkind—it might even have shown compassion, but it seemed to her that he looked wary—no, more than that, he seemed bewildered. And she wondered immediately if there might be something wrong with her appearance. Raising her head she openly challenged his stare, and when he realized he had been caught his face went through a curious cascade of color and she was surprised to see that he could be so easily flummoxed. But while she was enjoying this brief advantage; he quickly recovered, and when he stood and extended his hand she found him towering over her. Even when she rose and stepped forward his height was imposing and her newfound confidence evaporated.

However, he was not frightening. When her small hand slid into his, he gave a firm patriarchal grip, and though she couldn't say why, when he spoke she liked the soft timbre of his voice.

"Is it Ms. or Mrs.?" he asked.

"Mrs., please."

"So it's Mrs. Stewart then," he said, referring to a pink memo that he had picked up off his desk.

"Please. I would prefer Sarah."

"Sarah," he repeated. "My name is Martin McAulliffe." Then he came around to move her chair closer to his desk.

"Yes, it's on the door," she said distractedly as she looked at the floor around her feet. "I'm sorry, I came in here with a brown folder and I seem to have lost it." She realized that she had lost her resume. It wasn't much, just a copy of her application and a letter of recommendation (more like a note actually) from the lady who first told Em about the job. But misplacing it was irksome and made her feel klutzy.

"Is this it?" Mr. McAuliffe said, sweeping it up off the rug in the spot where her chair had been.

"Yes, thank you," she said, giving what she hoped was her best thank-you smile.

They both sat down and there was a brief silence. When Mr. McAulliffe didn't speak Sarah pulled a sheet of paper from the folder and handed it across the desk. It was the letter of recommendation, although she wasn't sure if it would do much good since she didn't know this woman very well. While he was busy reading, she took a closer look at his face hoping to find something—anything—that might make her feel a little more at ease. She was drawn immediately to his eyes. There was a softness there that reminded her of Dutch (the basset hound that she had grown up with). She thought that a peculiar comparison, but it was helpful. After all, how could she be intimidated by someone whose eyes reminded her of a long-eared lovable mutt?

He was obviously older, maybe as much as ten years. He had rugged features, with deep wrinkles around his eyes and mouth. At first glance he wasn't particularly attractive, but then as she had already noted there was something about his deep brown eyes, and there was a certain curl etched into the corners of his mouth that made him look cheery even when he wasn't smiling. She liked the appearance and movement of his large hands. And when his fingers accidentally brushed against hers, as he gave back her letter, it reminded her of the scratchy touch of her father's callused hands.

"Tell me about yourself," Mr. McAulliffe said, interrupting her thoughts. What surprised her was that his question didn't come across as an empty platitude; he actually sounded interested. So for the next few minutes she talked, not about anything profound: she just explained who she was, and what experience she had (or hadn't), and why she needed this job. Occasionally, Mr. McAulliffe would say yes or no, but mostly he leaned back in his chair with his fingers interlocked across his stomach and listened. Something in his manner, maybe the way he folded his hands, made her think of her grandfather. What was this? First her dog, then her father and now her grandfather. Could there be any significance to the fact that all of these, including her dog, were males? And more importantly, they were the only men in her life that she had ever trusted.

When she finished talking, Mr. McAulliffe continued to stare at her and she thought for a moment that she had lost him. Then he deliberately unwound his fingers and placing them on the edge of the papers in front of him moved them a little toward her and then pulled them back. "You know, Sarah, there have been a number of applicants for this job already, and frankly you're not as well qualified as some of the others. Can you give me any reason why I should consider you over them?"

His bluntness shook her. This was the sort of question that had sent her down in flames in the past. But this time all those soft images of her dog and her father and grandfather inspired an unusual confidence, and her answer came in a single word. "Motivation."

"What do you mean?"

She didn't know exactly, but she plunged ahead anyway. "I'm sure that the others who have applied are younger, and better educated. And I'm equally sure that they all want this job. But I want it more, and you won't find anyone willing to work harder to prove it. Frankly, I need the money. I have a mortgage, bills to pay and a son to take care of. . ." She stopped suddenly and looked to see if he was buying any of this.

"I like your argument. At least it's honest." He hesitated. "I'm tempted—well, that's probably the wrong word, but. . ." He left the _but_ hanging, and she held her breath. Then he started to rub his hands together as if to warm them, but it seemed more like a gesture of excitement, as if he were suddenly a little child anticipating Christmas and Santa Claus. "Let's give this a try. Would you be willing to work at this for—say—a month, and see how it goes?"

"Yes." She didn't say it very loudly or very firmly, but it was the best she could do when she could hardly breathe.

"Then we'll take a look—and if <u>you're</u> happy and <u>we're</u> happy, we can make it permanent."

"Yes," she said again, pushing the air through her teeth with a soft wheeze as if she were sighing.

"You can start tomorrow!" he said, demonstrating more of that childish excitement with his hands.

"Tomorrow?" she asked, a little uncertain.

"Is that too soon?"

"No—I mean yes," she stammered, a little shaken by how fast this was moving.

"It is too soon?"

"No, no! Tomorrow's fine," she said, this time more firmly.

"Then it's a date—I mean it's a deal. That is, you accept," he amended.

"Yes, well, until tomorrow then," she said, rising from her chair. She smiled, and he smiled, and Sarah tried to hold down the tickle of energy that mounted inside. It was only probationary, but she had a job!

"Nine o'clock," he said. "We open at ten, but I need to go over a few things and get you set up with Ada O'Connell, our head teller. Normally you'd train for two weeks at the home office in Freetown, but the circumstances here are a little different, and Ada will make a good teacher."

"Right," she said, thinking that she sounded too exuberant. Then she extended her hand.

Mr. McAulliffe took hold and shook it. But when she tried to withdraw her hand his solid grip prevented her. Suddenly he realized that she wanted it back and he let go.

Giving him a questioning look, Sarah turned to leave and dropped her folder again. Unthinking, she bent directly to retrieve it and heard the distinct rending of cloth as the seam of her straight fitted skirt ripped. She normally wore jeans or a loose-fitting dress and wasn't used to having her movements so restricted. Righting herself and swinging around to confront Mr. McAulliffe, she found him politely facing away looking out the window. She could see his hand to his mouth and his shoulders shaking.

Bending at the knees, she eased down to catch the folder with her fingertips, then put it behind her, to cover the tear, and backed toward the office door. As she rattled the doorknob, Mr. McAulliffe (still facing away) spoke again. "See Mary on the way out, and she'll give you some paperwork that you can start on this evening."

"Right," she replied, then sidestepped through the doorway into the outer office.

♦ ♦ ♦

After a few minutes, Mary stuck her head in the door.

"That was awfully sudden, wasn't it? Don't you have three more interviews today?"

"Shoot!" he said. "I forgot about that."

"So, where's the fire? Why were you in such a hurry to hire this girl?"

"You're right, I did act a little precipitously, but I had a good feeling about her."

"I'll bet!" she said with a smile.

"Okay, okay, enough of that," he said, losing his composure.

"What do I do about your other appointments then?"

"I don't know—try to reach them and cancel, will you Mary? Make up some excuse."

"That's easy, I'll just tell them the position has been filled. But—" When Mary paused, Martin looked up at her. "This isn't like you," she said.

It was true; normally he would have interviewed all the applicants and then spent a couple of days reviewing resumes and contacting references before he came to any decision. But something about Sarah attracted him, and he had to admit, at least to himself, that the attraction had little to do with the business of running a bank.

"Did you feel sorry for her?" Mary asked.

"Because she tore her skirt?"

"Did she?"

"Yes, just as she was leaving," he said. "It was only a small tear, but enough to expose her slip. At least I think it was her slip."

"Ohhh," Mary said, pinching her lips. "That's embarrassing, but it's not what I had in mind."

"What then?"

"Don't you remember, about this time last year—the accident on Route 44 in West Gansett?" He gave her a fractured look and she went on. "Robert Stewart was her husband. They found his body in a ditch near the highway. He'd fallen in and drowned."

"I'll be damned! I mean—I've heard the story, but I never thought—I never made the connection. Shh—oot, I hope she doesn't think that I was just being charitable."

Then Mary smiled and said, "Well, if it wasn't charity, it must have been her good looks." Martin brought up his finger in protest, but she didn't wait for his declaration of innocence. Instead she made a hasty retreat.

What am I getting myself into? he thought, as he leaned his backside against the edge of his desk and looked up at a Medieval print of Saint George slaying the dragon that hung on the inside wall.

Chapter 13

Following the long talk that he had with Aunt Em, Sam agonized over how to act. He still wanted to do more than just look at Jennifer, but he couldn't bring himself to take his aunt's advice.

In his special fantasy world, he couldn't really make any mistakes. Even if she caught him watching her from the darkness of Aunt Em's front porch, or through borrowed binoculars while lying in the tall grass or from the top of one of the sandy dunes, she hardly knew he existed, so why would she care? But being her secret admirer was one thing, spying on her was another matter. However much he tried to rationalize it the practice seemed perverted, but he couldn't help himself.

◆ ◆ ◆

Jennifer continued to appear on the beach in an assortment of bathing suits, some more revealing than others. They looked like the high-fashion stuff that showed up in the pages of *Vogue* and *Mademoiselle*. And compared to the K-mart knock-offs that the other girls wore she definitely looked more daring and sophisticated. Whether he was admiring her from a distance or up close, he appreciated the brevity of her attire; then berated himself for reacting to what he saw. He wasn't made of stone, and what he saw excited him. For the first time he knew what it meant to get all bent out of shape.

The sun had bleached her hair and turned her skin to a wonderful honey brown, which contrasted boldly against the new one-piece suit that she had recently started to wear. It was a bright white except for the red binding that rose in a V from the hollow between her breasts, then continued over her shoulders and plunged dramatically down her back until it ended in a narrow curve that fell low enough to suggest another sort of cleavage. And when she walked past, the thin stretchy panel covering her behind left very little to the imagination.

In spite of her appearance, Sam found it hard to believe that Jennifer was being deliberately provocative. But she certainly didn't dress the way she did accidentally; she had to be aware she was attracting lots of attention, especially from the guys.

One afternoon, while Sam watched Jennifer parade down the half-crowded beach, he noticed a young man, a stranger, watching her too. He didn't appear to be in Jennifer's path, but she suddenly headed straight toward him. As she got closer the sway of her hips seemed to get more exaggerated and the poor kid's jaw went slack. When the distance between had shortened to a dozen feet or so, she stopped, shifted her weight to one leg, then arms akimbo, she stood there staring him down. He tried to say something, but it came out as a kacking noise that made it sound like he was about to toss his lunch. Then she strode forward and stepped around him as if he were a skinny sapling that had suddenly sprouted up in her path.

Observing this sort of thing did nothing to calm the churning in Sam's gut whenever he got close enough for her to acknowledge his presence. But the worst incident happened on a Saturday, in the middle of a sticky August day while Sam lay on his stomach basking in the sun. As usual he was spying on Jennifer, who stood a safe distance away facing the sea. It delighted him to see the wonderful things the wind did to her hair as she squinted at the horizon.

Karl Kristian, one of the local jocks, came up unnoticed behind her. He was a real predator, the kind that bullied anyone who got in his way, and who had a reputation with the girls. Sam couldn't hear what Karl said, but her reply came back to him as an angry reprisal carried clearly by the wind. Karl looked as if he had just been cold-cocked, only he was still standing. He was not someone who lacked self-confidence, especially when it came to girls; and if anyone gave him trouble he quickly cut them down to size. So, Sam reasoned, if Karl couldn't handle Jennifer, what chance did he have?

Jennifer hadn't made any friends—hadn't tried to make any friends, male or female. She enjoyed the beach and the water, but every time he saw her she was alone. There was a coldness about her, a sort of protective wall that warned people to keep their distance.

Still, Sam believed that if he could just to get beyond that wall, beyond Jennifer's coldness, he would find a very special friend waiting on the other side. But he'd never have the courage to break through on his own he needed some kind of divine intervention—a miracle.

♦ ♦ ♦

As August heated up, and the summer drew to an end, his prospects for finding that miracle began to melt away. Then, on the Friday before Labor Day, Sam had a chance encounter. He was walking along the beach late in the evening. The sun had nearly disappeared beyond the trees behind the marsh. And suddenly Jennifer appeared from the shadows of an alleyway between two cottages. She wore a billowy blouse and shorts and the fading light coming from behind left her mostly in silhouette. Somehow at that moment, in that setting, she seemed less intimidating, and when she greeted him, there was a friendly softness in her voice that sounded inviting.

"Hey," she said. "What's happening?"

"Not much," he answered, before his fear had a chance to shut him down.

"Where're you headed?"

"Home." And he was going home, but only because he had nothing better to do. If he could have said anything else he might have captured her attention. He might even have found some excuse to join her.

Instead she said, "Go for it," then turned and headed in the opposite direction. She'd been friendly enough, she hadn't rebuffed him as she had the others, and yet he'd botched it. In two more days the summer would be over, she would be gone, and any excuse to get to know her would be gone as well.

◆ ◆ ◆

Labor Day came and went, school started again, and surprisingly Jennifer had not gone. Instead, while Sam was filling out his school ID registration card he looked over to see Jennifer sitting in the seat across from him.

He nodded and she nodded back, then he scrawled a note on a page from his notebook, tore it out, and passed it to her.

I thought you went back to the city?

Sam

She wrote on the bottom of his note and passed it back.

My parents thought the school was too dangerous.

Jennifer

He and Jennifer ended up in the same homeroom and they took English and biology together. He couldn't believe his good fortune. Thank God for the growing crime in the city.

Was this the miracle he had been hoping for? Probably not, but he <u>had</u> been given a second chance. All he needed now was figure out what to do with it.

Contrary to the scanty costumes that Jennifer had worn all summer, the clothes that she wore to school were not revealing but remarkably modest. Unlike her classmates she didn't dress in jeans and formless T-shirts. Her clothes were tailored and fashionable, and although short skirts weren't forbidden, her hemline was always at or below her knee. No pants—although she did make one exception. If she decided to ride her bike she wore a mid-length skirt (something called a culotte), which was clearly made of two parts that followed each leg independently when she walked.

This change in dress did not translate into plainness, in fact just the opposite: with all those seductive parts hidden, or only suggested by the sweep of her skirt or the drape of her blouse, she looked hotter than ever.

Although they now were thrown together in legitimate situations that required him to interact with her, it was hardly a gabfest. He only said what was necessary and did his best not to make a fool of himself.

To begin with, Jennifer didn't have any friends, but once she started school that changed. She quickly wedged her way into Green Harbor's limited social strata by befriending the three most popular girls. Every day he saw them gathered around her locker, waiting for her approval. That didn't surprise him. Jennifer's good looks and confidence were bound to bring her easily into the best crowd. But when she included Winnie, and pushed for the others to accept her too, he was thunderstruck. Winnie had never been part of the "in" crowd and at first he wondered if this wasn't some kind of cruel joke. But when he talked to Winnie about her new friendship, there didn't seem to be any evidence of such cruelty. Jennifer had apparently peeled back Winnie's rough exterior and discovered the sweet spirit hiding inside. Which shouldn't have surprised him, but somehow it did.

It was very clear that Winnie liked Jennifer too, but he knew that she wasn't comfortable with her other new friends. She hadn't liked them before, and she wasn't about to like them now. Interestingly, Jennifer seemed sensitive to this. He watched her defend Winnie against their sharp attacks, and when that didn't work, she planned things with Winnie that kept the two of them separate from the other girls.

Whenever he was with Winnie, she talked freely about the kind of stuff that went on between her and Jennifer, and he was encouraged. What Winnie shared made him less afraid of Jennifer, but other than the forced contact they had at school every day, any deeper interaction remained far too scary. Besides, he couldn't get past the porch thing—and when she greeted him one day with, "What's shakin'?" he imagined he saw something in her smile that made him wonder all over again what she might have seen that afternoon. It was irrational, but he could hardly act rationally when he was in Jennifer's presence.

To make things worse he couldn't help being a little jealous of Winnie. She had something he wanted so desperately, and she hadn't had to make any effort to get it. It didn't seem fair.

Chapter 14

$\mathcal{E}$m was right about attractive girls. Jennifer <u>did</u> have trouble getting dates. The decent boys were afraid of her, and the ones who weren't were just as Em had predicted. They were the jocks, the tough guys who had something to prove. The kind who have a reputation to maintain and who were generally looking for more than pizza and a coke at Sally's Cafe.

Whenever Jennifer was out of earshot, and especially in the locker-room, there was a lot of lewd talk about her. There seemed to be something about sweaty gym socks and jockstraps that expanded the male ego. If you wanted to be one of the guys you had to know the score—so you made up stories about the girl or girls that you had bedded. Jennifer was new, an unknown, a babe with a bod. She made an easy target, and the potshots they took were deadly. Words, like bone, plug, and boink peppered their conversation, and when they described her breasts they used euphemisms that were just as colorful.

Sam heard these things, but refused to participate. That made him more of an outsider, but then he'd never belonged. They called him geek and dork.

Between fourteen and fifteen nature had played some dirty tricks on him. Four inches taller, he'd built up some abdominal muscle and added strength to his back and shoulders, but his arms and legs were too long and his ribs showed too much. During the last six months, particularly down under, he had changed from boy to man. While most guys brag about size, it's always taken as an exaggeration, but Sam's new growth wasn't an exaggeration. In reality he showed barely an inch beyond average, but shape and color created the illusion of something much larger. At first he regarded this change as grotesque, one more fault in a long list of physical shortcomings. Later, he imagined that it might work in his favor—might actually help him to fit in, at least in the locker room where size seemed to count the most. He knew that the guys would never consider him a jock, but they might stop thinking of him as a so much of a geek.

He was wrong. The moment he stepped into the shower room on the first day of school, as soon as the other guys saw his advantage, they started to make cutting remarks. They tried out every insult they could think of and when they saw Sam's reaction they kept it up until Sam got into a shouting match with Karl and his friend Charlie and the coach came out of his office to shut them down.

They called Sam a mutant—a sideshow freak, and he believed them.

◆ ◆ ◆

Most of the girls mentioned in these locker-room harangues were strangers to Sam. He recognized some of the names, but couldn't necessarily put a face to them. On the other hand he knew Jennifer, at least he knew her well enough to realize that she didn't deserve to be denigrated this way, and would be terribly hurt if any of this garbage got back to her.

He couldn't deny that he had dreamed of her too. Dreamed of kissing her in some romantic setting—had even imagined her bare breasts whenever he saw her wearing a Band-Aid size bikini—but nothing as gross as the lies and perversions that were passed around the shower-room had ever crossed his mind. He understood that this sort of bravado was a guy thing, a ritual that separated the jocks from the nerds, but for the first time he realized that all this effort to be cock of the walk came at someone else's expense—someone who was powerless to defend herself.

As time went on Sam increasingly came to Jennifer's defense. He continually questioned their crudeness and his criticism was not well taken. After awhile, whether it came from bully or buddy, they all sought their revenge. The showers seemed to be the place that he was most vulnerable, and they didn't just shoot him down with words. Someone passing behind stung him with a wet towel across his backside. Another put Sam into a headlock and rubbed his fist hard into his scalp, giving him a painful *noogie*. While he was pulling his undershirt over his head, Karl's friend, Charlie pitched a half-used bar of soap at him and cracked one of his ribs.

At the beginning of the third week of school, Karl Kristian, who brutally ranked on Jennifer, and who seemed the most offended by Sam's criticism, gave him a body check that sent Sam crashing into his locker. And the following day Karl and Charlie, waylaid him as he left the shower.

"Hey kid, how's your girl?" Karl asked with a smirk.

"What girl?"

"Jennifer."

"She's not my girl." Sam said, immediately suspicious.

"Whatsa matter—she lose her lunch when she saw that donkey dick of yours?" Karl's nasal voice ended in a snort.

Charlie seized the corner of Sam's towel and yanked it out of his hands.

"Get him," Charlie said, snapping the stolen towel at Sam's middle.

Karl joined him, and Sam spread his fingers and flailed his hands to fend off the blows that were stinging his hips and thighs, and leaving long red welts.

"Cut it out!" Sam croaked.

"Hey, Charlie get my pocketknife, the geek wants me to cut it off."

"No!" Sam howled, full of rage.

"Why? You think any girl's gonna want that donkey-dick? That black crank would scare the hell out of her."

Mocking Sam, Karl grabbed the end of his penis and stretched it out in front of him. "This is what the girls want."

"Yeah, like that's not just as black and ugly," Sam said, surprised that he had the chutzpa to tell him so.

"At least I'm not a friggin' mutant!" Karl said, then took a jab at Sam's crotch.

Sam folded at the waist. "Don't be stupid!" he screamed, and his whole body began to shake.

"You fathead! Who you callin' stupid?" Karl took a second jab at him and when Sam swung around to avoid the blow he felt Karl's fingernails dig into the middle of his spine. The pain cut through him like a knife, but he chose to ignore it. Now facing Charlie he demanded that he give him back his towel.

"You want it?" Charlie said, taunting him. He held it at arms length and jiggled it in front of Sam like a chunk of bait. "Take it." And when Sam reached out Charlie snatched it away. A white rage burned behind Sam's eyes and he took a wild swing with his fist. When he heard the cartilage in Charlie's nose snap and saw the blood, Sam froze. Karl looked at Charlie who had wiped a handful of blood from his upper lip and all three stood perfectly still. When that stark tabloid sprang to life, the two took their revenge on Sam by driving him backward toward the locker-room doors. Someone standing behind opened the doors, and Karl and Charlie stepped forward, grabbed Sam under his arms, and dragged him out into the hall. Once they had cleared the sweep of the doors they dropped Sam on the creamy linoleum floor and ran back into the locker-room.

He pounded on the frosted glass and begged to be let back in, but Karl and Charlie ran a broom behind the door-handles to form a barricade.

Suddenly the fourth-period bell rang, and Sam heard the clatter of desks and the banging of doors as the students began to file out of their classrooms. The only hiding place he could find was a narrow recess where the water cooler stood. At least fifteen feet away, he bounded across the hallway, his Willie swinging ahead of him like some kind of phallic talisman pointing the way toward disaster. Back pressed against the cold tile wall, he slid down, pulled his legs up and wrapped his arms around his ankles. As the students spilled into the hall, he waited for them to discover his predicament and for the jeers and laughter that were bound to follow.

If only he had the guts to stand up and let it all hang out—literally—show Karl and the others he didn't care. But he couldn't get past the idea that Karl was right: that he <u>was</u> a freak, and the fact that everyone would see was too crushing. So he sat there like a dumb mule with his ankles crossed, knees tucked in, arms folded and waited for the onslaught. Consciously, he wanted to use every abusive word he could remember before anyone else could use them against him, but he didn't have the time or the courage to yell them out. Instead he prayed that fire and lightning would come crashing down from the sky and blast him into a pile of gray ash.

"Way to go, Sam!" one classmate shouted. "Crankin'!" called another. "How to get dissed!" said a third. "Hey Sam, is it turtleneck or kosher?" That last came from a girl, though he didn't recognize the voice. She likely wanted to know if he were covered or clipped, and the fact that she knew the difference—shook him. The entire ordeal lasted only a minute and a half before the coach came out of the locker room and wrapped him up in his starter jacket, but it might have been an hour for all the mental agony he'd suffered. He thought that his father had hurt him, but this hurt worse and he expected that it would last longer.

He began to feel that if he were going to defend Jennifer and then take all this abuse for it, he ought to know her a hell of a lot better.

◆ ◆ ◆

His mother heard the story which spread quickly through the town of Green Harbor and he told her more, though not all. Because she believed he had been a hero for defending Jennifer's honor (something he may have embellished a little) and because he had been treated so unjustly for it, she put up with him hiding at home through the weekend and let him miss the next two days of school before she forced him to go back.

Chapter 15

On Friday a week after the hallway fiasco, Sam came to school on his bicycle. His humiliation complete, he had invented an illness to explain to others why he'd stayed at home Monday and Tuesday. For the last couple of days he had chosen to ride his bike because it keep him off the bus and he could avoid embarrassing questions and comments. When he rode up the school drive this morning he saw Jennifer ahead of him on her own bike. He hadn't noticed that she had one during the summer, but it suddenly appeared once Jennifer's parents decided to stay through the winter, and she rode it almost everywhere she went.

◆ ◆ ◆

It was a warm September afternoon. Indian summer. The end of another school day. Sam came out of class in shirtsleeves with his sweatshirt stuffed into his book-bag, and headed for his bike, which was tucked into a small alcove between the assembly hall and the gymnasium. While he removed his lock, he saw Jennifer walking in the opposite direction. Her bike was lined up with the others in the rack at the front of the school. Slinging the padded strap of his book-bag over one shoulder, Sam straddled the seat and positioned the right pedal so that he could push off and start down the south side of the building. In his rush to be on his way, anxious to avoid even his friends, he started to pump the pedals faster. Just before Sam reached the corner of the main building, he heard someone call out his name. Not a casual greeting, but a strident warning, and he looked back to see who it had come from. When he brought his head around again it was too late.

Sam saw the impending disaster just moments before metal came crunching into metal, but there was no time to react. Now everything seemed to switch into slow motion, and the precise detail amazed him. As the edge of Sam's tire touched the spokes of Jennifer's front wheel, his own front wheel snapped at right angles to the frame, tearing the handlebars from his hand. The bike came to a jolting halt, and sliding forward off the leather saddle Sam came down hard on the crossbar. Letting out a primitive grunt, he rolled sideways off his bike onto the grass.

Instantly he grabbed his crotch with both hands, trying to find some relief from the crushing pain. Drawing his legs up to his chest, he started to roll from side to side, shouting: "Damn, Damn, Damn!" As he became more and more conscious of the pain he shut his eyes tightly and felt the tears squeeze out. He gritted his teeth and swore loudly: "Shit, shit, shit." It hurt so badly he had to wonder if that part of him would ever function again.

The front wheel of his bike had caught Jennifer's in the side just behind the fork. It mangled the spokes and spun her out of control, but instead of sending her forward, it flipped her off sideways. Sam heard a distinctive crack as she hit the granite curbing. There was a painful scream, not very loud, but high and shrill, and then silence. After that only his own hapless curses echoed off the side of the schoolhouse walls.

As the pain in his groin subsided Sam stopped rolling back and forth. Now, still curled up, he found himself facing toward Jennifer. She was sprawled on the sidewalk near the curb, holding her right arm and sobbing. It was difficult from his prone position to determine how gravely she had been injured. Forcing himself upward, he saw dark droplets of blood oozing from an abrasion on her arm. Where one side of her culottes had ridden up and exposed her leg other bruises began to show. She needed help, and he wanted to go to her, but his head throbbed from the torture of sitting up. Hundreds of sharp little needles stabbed at different parts of his body and when he removed his hands from his crotch in order to relieve this new pain, the old pain returned with a vengeance. There was no way that he could rush to her side and play the hero. He simply fell back onto the grass and gave up.

Within minutes a circle of students hovered over Sam and through a forest of legs he could see his science teacher, Mr. Sampson, running out the side door and sprinting toward the crowd. He came to Sam first, but soon discovered that other than the damage to the family jewels, which for the moment Sam was protecting with his hands, he seemed okay. For some reason Mr. Sampson decided to announce his findings to the curly redheaded girl who was squatting beside him. "Well, he took a mean crack in the balls, but he'll survive."

The girl's mouth dropped open and she said, "Ouch!" Then she smiled at Sam. He thought that she felt sorry for him, but there was no way she could understand the pain he was in. Suddenly it occurred to him, that this particular part of his anatomy always seemed to put him in the most embarrassing situations.

When Mr. Sampson stood up the girl rose with him and they both walked over to join the others who had gathered around Jennifer. What Sam could see of Jennifer now was caught in glimpses as her classmates shifted anxiously back and forth across his field of vision. He saw Mr. Sampson move her leg and a crimson spot bloomed on the hem of her culottes. When Mr. Sampson touched that spot, she yelled out. Cautiously lifting the blood-soaked material, he uncovered a deep gash that was bleeding heavily. Sam heard someone say: "That's going to need stitches." Then someone else said, "I think her arm is broken."

A quick vision of the accident replayed in Sam's mind, and he remembered the distinct snap of bone as her body hit the curbing.

Another teacher pulled up with his car, and with his help Mr. Sampson lifted Jennifer carefully and loaded her into the back seat. Then the two of them piled into the front, and with tires crunching against the loose gravel the car pulled away, heading presumably to the emergency room at Lakeville Hospital.

Chapter 16

It was after three o'clock, and Sarah sat alone working the drive-thru window. There were no cars idling impatiently outside, waiting. Only the rattle of dry leaves and sound of the breeze whispered through the outside microphone. The cramped booth hung off the northeast corner of the building, apart from the other tellers. Sarah sat on a tall stool busy sorting her checks, putting them in numerical order and separating them into groups, when suddenly the intercom crackled to life; Mary was paging her. "You have a call from your son's school." Her reaction was typical of any parent; she immediately assumed the worst.

Mary sent Ada to relieve her. Ada had been Sarah's teacher/trainer when she'd started a few weeks ago. Ada worked on a short fuse, which made her seem bitchy and harsh. But that attitude didn't affect Sarah. She had known some meanness in her life, and somehow she knew that Ada's anger wasn't evil, but only bottled-up frustration. Some of her co-workers referred to Ada as an old maid—others called her liberated. She was neither. She had told Sarah that she "would marry in a boinkin' minute, even if that meant settling for second-best" (her mother's words). And she knew who second-best would be if she could only convince him to ask. Sarah quickly found a kindred spirit in Ada, and the two became fast friends.

Ada squeezed into the narrow booth, and Sarah hustled back to Mary's desk to answer the call from school. Sarah picked up the receiver and pressed the flashing hold button. "Hello—yes this is Mrs. Stewart." She listened carefully as the principal explained the accident as he understood it, and reassured her that her son's injuries were nothing more than bangs and bruises.

The principal asked her to come and pick him up.

"Yes—yes," she assured him. "I'm not sure how soon. I have to discuss this with my boss." She paused to listen. "Yes." Another pause. "I'll do my best," she said and hung up. Clearly this wasn't very serious, and she was trying hard to remain calm, but it wasn't working. The thought of what might have happened still left her rattled.

Knocking on Mr. McAulliffe's door, she soon realized that he had been forewarned. Instead of a call to enter, Mary came through the door and motioned her inside. She stepped up to his desk, twisting her fingers nervously in front of her, and waited for him to recognize her presence. He made some mark or correction to the document in front of him, and then looked up.

"I understand there's a problem at school—something about your son?" Mr. McAulliffe said as he stood to face her. When his eyes met hers, she saw them waver timorously, and then fall to the blotter on his desktop. She followed his glance, watched him rub his fingers nervously along the edge of the blotter, and wondered: *why is he so affected? This is about Sam and he doesn't even know Sam.*

"Is he alright?" Mr. McAulliffe asked, with an unnatural firmness. His eyes circled upward around the room and came back to meet hers, and she thought it odd that he found it so difficult to look at her.

"Yes," she answered. "The school tells me there's been an accident with his bike, nothing serious, just some bruises, but they want me to pick him up as soon as possible."

"I understand; do you need to leave right away?"

"If that's possible."

"Of course it is," he said, again with that unnatural firmness. "Is there someone who can cover for you?"

"Ada's at the drive-thru now," she said. "Could I ask her to stay and balance out for me?"

"Sounds fine to me. On your way out, talk to Mary. Tell her what you're doing and she'll take care of Ada."

"Thank you, Mr. McAulliffe," she said, relieved that this had been so easy.

"No problem," he said lifting his hand from the desk and swinging it dismissively in her direction. "And please call me Martin."

"What?"

"I'd like it if you'd call me by my first name," he repeated.

"I'm not sure I can. I've always been taught to address my boss as Mr. or Mrs."

"So have I, but it seems too formal."

"But—isn't that the point?" Sarah said matter-of-factly.

"Yes, but . . ." He lifted his hands and shrugged his shoulders, in a gesture of surrender.

Sarah wasn't sure why this was important to him, but she didn't have time to discuss it. "Thanks again." She opened the door, then turned and hesitantly added, "Martin." He didn't answer, but she saw him smiling broadly as she pulled the door closed behind her.

♦ ♦ ♦

Driving to the school she thought back to Sam's last disaster, when he had cut his foot open on some broken glass that was half buried in the sand. Aunt Em had driven him home with a bath towel wrapped around his foot. When she uncovered the wound it looked a bloody mess and she'd ended up taking him to the ER for stitches. Before that he had cut off the tip of his finger while chopping onions. He was crying, of course, but she couldn't tell if it was from the onions or the wound.

Sarah supposed that Sam had no more accidents than any other normal child, but she couldn't help suffering along with him whenever he got hurt.

Now, trying to avoid some of that hurt, she took a mental detour; letting her mind switch back to Mr. McAulliffe (Martin) she wondered why he seemed so discomforted whenever she was around. He certainly didn't act that way with anyone else. And this business about his name—most of the other employees called him Mr. McAulliffe. Only Mary called him Martin or Marty, but the two of them had been friends for years; hell, they'd grown up together.

Martin had been a decent boss, and more than kind, but she often found herself a little unbalanced whenever there was any interaction between them. Sometimes dropping papers in his office or losing count when he stepped into her workstation, or worse—spilling her soda, or juice, or whatever liquid she happened to have in hand. She knew she could sometimes be clumsy, but not like this. And more than once something wet had ended up on the front of Martin's shirt or trousers.

Once in a while she would catch him staring at her. When she reflected on it, the look on his face reminded her of the boys in her junior high English class. They gave Miss Brunelle that same cow-eyed look whenever she was sitting at her desk or writing something on the board.

Miss Brunelle was fresh out of college, very young and very pretty and those seventh and eighth-grade boys were obviously ready to pop their cork over her. She supposed that they had just discovered that girls were good for something other than hitting—a sort of awakening. Except that they never seemed to notice the girls in the class. Instead they looked to someone older, someone unavailable. If Miss Brunelle suddenly caught them daydreaming, they came undone. And if she called on them—Whoa, Sarah thought, no way! Mr. McAulliffe's not some lovesick teenager.

Sam told her every day how special she was. He always had a hug for her when he got home from school, brought her tea at night when she was engrossed in her favorite sitcom, left silly notes for her on the fridge when he knew she was feeling down, said she was beautiful if she had on a new dress. But that was Sam. The idea that Martin might find her desirable seemed impossible. And if it were true, what was she supposed to do about it?

She consciously shook her head, making a little "brrrr," sound, and flipped her focus back to the problem of what had happened to Sam. The principal said he was injured, but seemed deliberately vague about where. Her first thought was a broken arm or a broken leg or a cracked head. He could be bleeding or unconscious, but if any of that were so, they would have hauled him away to the Emergency Room and she would be on the way there instead of heading toward his school.

◆ ◆ ◆

Twenty minutes later Sarah was driving up to the front of the building. She could see Sam sitting on the grass next to the sidewalk with his broken bike lying on the ground nearby. Seeing the twisted front wheel made Sarah wince, and she wondered what he had run into, and how he had escaped without some kind of major injury.

As she approached, she saw him struggle to his feet and walk toward the car with his legs slightly askew, and his slow bowlegged gait gave him away. Now she knew why the principal hadn't mentioned where Sam had been hurt. Maneuvering cautiously into the front seat of the car, Sam offered no greeting, he just made painful faces and groaned while he spread his legs and eased his bruised body carefully onto the padded seat.

Opening the hatchback, Sarah struggled with his bike; even with the back seat folded down, she couldn't get it all in. The front wheel, only partly attached, hung on by one nut. Taking a small adjustable wrench from a junk box that she kept in the trunk, she worked at the nut and pulled the mangled wheel free. Then she tied down the hatch with a piece of rope and left the fork and handlebars hanging out.

They rode home in silence. She didn't find out about the rest of the story until after they were in the house. And that only came in bits and pieces. Normally she would have dragged him into the kitchen and put him into a hard chair for such an interrogation, but being sensitive to his condition she couldn't do that. Instead they went into the living room, where he could sink slowly into the soft cushions of the sofa; then she started grilling him. When Sam got to the part about Jennifer's broken arm, Sarah worried as much about liability as she did Jennifer's well-being, but she didn't say anything to Sam. He couldn't tell her much more, other than the fact that Mr. Sampson and another teacher had taken Jennifer to the hospital.

Chapter 17

By four-thirty the pain had diminished to a dull ache and Sam was working hard to convince his mother to drive him over to Aunt Em's. Sarah kept asking why he wanted to visit his aunt, but he refused tell her. It became a 'just because' kind of argument, until finally he wore her down.

When Jennifer came back from the hospital that evening, with her parents, Sam was watching from the small window near Em's back door. The awkward reticence that had crippled his efforts to approach Jennifer in the past was gone, driven out by a dramatic sense of guilt and a powerful need for absolution. A careful examination of the facts might have helped to relieve him of some of that guilt, but at the moment he didn't want any relief. He needed all the guilt he could heap upon himself if he hoped to find the courage to walk across Em's backyard and talk to Jennifer.

Once he felt that Jennifer had settled in, he moved steadfastly out the back door and across the bridge to the road. Still too sore to walk with his usual stride, and fighting his fear, he pushed himself step by step toward his goal. After months of agonizing over how to meet her, and what to say, he was now standing at her back door compelling himself to ring her bell. He looked at his shaky finger and felt the plastic button vibrate, then heard a buzz from deep inside. Before anything else could happen Sam had to confront Jennifer's parents. Her mother opened the door and the sour look on her face made it clear that he wasn't particularly welcome. He could see Jennifer's father standing in the kitchen at the end of the long hallway. Even if he had never met them, they both knew who he was. They were fast friends with Aunt Em and recognized him as her nephew.

"Sam, isn't it?" Jennifer's mother asked, with hostile inflection.

"I don't imagine you're very happy to see me, Mrs. Hollypepper."

"You're right, I'm not." Cold and proper, she wasn't going to make this easy.

"I feel terrible about Jennifer. But it—it _was_ an accident."

"I know you didn't do it on purpose," she conceded, and her face softened for the first time since she had opened the door.

"Please! Let me talk to Jennifer," he said, putting his hand forward as if he were begging for a handout. "At least let me tell her I'm sorry."

"Wel-l-l-l," she said, looking toward her husband, who was at the sink washing dishes, "what do you think Jason?" Her voice thundered down the narrow hall. "Shall we let him in?"

He came from the kitchen, drying his hands on a flowered apron that was too small for his large frame. He stopped behind his wife and draped his thick fingers over her shoulders. "I suppose it's safe as long as he's not on a bicycle," he said.

Sam was about to explain that he couldn't ride his bike because the front wheel was bent, when he saw a broad smile spread across Mr. Hollypepper's craggy face, and he knew he that was being had.

Mrs. Hollypepper didn't respond to her husband's dry humor; she just took Sam by the arm, pulled him across the threshold, and directed him toward the stairs. "Go to the top and turn; Jennifer's room is the second on the right. Just knock before you go in."

As he started up, Mr. Hollypepper called after him, "Don't get too close, we don't need any more accidents."

Mrs. Hollypepper started to laugh, and Sam wondered what she found so funny. Glancing down over the railing, he saw her take a swipe at her husband's backside as they headed toward the kitchen. "Don't give him any ideas."

When he knocked, Sam heard Jennifer call out and invite him in. He opened the door slowly, feeling a little uneasy about entering her bedroom. She wasn't in her bed, but sat in a chair by the window with her heavy plaster cast resting on a pillow.

"This thing hurts so bad," she said. "They shot me up with a painkiller in the ER, but that's already worn off. I just took one of the pills they gave me—codeine I think—but so far it hasn't kicked in."

She nodded for him to come closer. The room wasn't very big and a few short steps brought him to her side. The dying sun lit the room with a soft light, and now that he was closer and could see her more clearly, she surprised him with a welcoming smile. He had expected anger and decided that perhaps this wasn't going to be so bad after all.

She wore a baggy pair of pajamas, which fit so badly Sam didn't think they could possibly be hers. They looked like her dad's, likely sacrificed because they would slip easily over her cast and bandages. The top had a V-neck and the right sleeve was rolled up almost to her shoulder. Someone had used a pair of scissors to cut the bottoms off above the knee, and a safety pin at the waist kept them from falling down. Though she was dressed for bed and probably didn't have anything on underneath, he didn't find that disturbing. The whole outfit hung on her like an old tent and the effect made her look small and vulnerable.

He came around from her side to face her more fully, and when he did, he saw the bandage on her knee. He stood there staring at the bulky wrapping.

"It took eight stitches," she said.

"Owww," he said, remembering the ugly gash that Mr. Sampson had uncovered while she was sitting on the sidewalk.

"I watched them push the needle through the skin. It was curved like a fishhook with a long black thread attached to it," she explained, and the mental image made him wince.

Sitting there with her arm encased in plaster and her leg buried in gauze and tape, she looked like she was being swallowed up by the bulky arms of the chair that surrounded her. Suddenly she seemed far less scary. Nevertheless, when he saw the damage he had done, he couldn't get past the idea that he was responsible.

Jennifer smiled and said, "Don't look so down. There may be a scar on my knee, but otherwise I'll be okay."

That did it. His throat tightened and he almost choked. She reached out with her good hand, and gently stroked the back of his wrist. "Take it easy," she whispered. Then she ordered him to sit, but there wasn't anyplace to sit. So he simply eased himself down on the floor next to the window and folded his legs Indian style. Still sore, the hard surface felt uncomfortable, but he decided not to complain. Being on the floor forced him to look up at her and the effect was humbling.

"Jennifer," he said, his voice full of anguish, "you look awful, you're all broken and bandaged, and—"

"Gee, thanks," she interjected. "Is that supposed to make me feel better?"

"No."

"Then why bring it up?"

"Because it's my fault. It's like I took this perfect thing and broke it."

Her lips parted, uncovering a row of straight white teeth, and a sweet sloppy smile spread from ear to ear. Her smile confused him—he was trying to be serious, and she looked clearly amused. "Don't be so dramatic," she said. "I'm not Humpty-Dumpty. And besides, I'm not the only one who got hurt."

"What do you mean?"

"Do you remember the girl who stood beside Mr. Sampson when he was checking you out?"

"Sort of."

"Judy Mackey," she said, "red hair? Anyway, I was on the phone with her when the doorbell rang," she said, tickling the telephone at her feet with her big toe.

The hair color clued him in and Sam could already guess what they had been talking about. He hoped that his stony silence would keep her from bringing up the subject, but she was not dissuaded.

"Are you all right?" she asked. "Is there any permanent damage—to—that is how's your wee Willie?"

The fingers of her good hand shot up to pinch the air as if she wanted to snatch those last words back; and that silly childhood reference made Sam's face grow hot and prickly.

"Uh—uh—it's okay. It's a little sore—not there—well, yes, there too, but . . . That is my wrist is bruised here, and here on my elbow," he said, touching both spots. Had he stopped at that point he would have been fine, but she had him so unnerved that he stumbled on: "and I—I'll have to wait for the swelling to go down—"

He stopped abruptly when he saw Jennifer's mouth drop. And when she laughed, her whole body shook. "Ouch!" she grabbed her broken arm to steady it. "Son of a—shit, that hurts!"

"Sorry," he said, though he wasn't sure what for.

"No, I'm sorry. Everything was fine until—until you said you were *swollen*." The last word came quickly and was full of S's as she started to laugh again. This time she was careful not to disturb her broken arm.

Sam's humiliation seemed unending. "That's not what I meant," he said, trying to save himself.

"I know it wasn't. That's what makes it so funny."

"Ha, ha." Sam offered, mocking himself.

"Don't get mad."

"I'm not," he said. At least he wasn't mad at her.

"Any injury like that has to be . . . that is . . . well you might— never mind," she said, then changed the subject. "So, Sam, what's your history? How did you get to be here in Green Harbor?"

"I was born here."

"Now, that's sad."

"Why?"

"You've gotta admit this is not exactly a happenin' place."

"No, I suppose it isn't," he said. "But then, I've never lived anyplace else, so what do I have to compare it with? What about you?"

"What about me?"

"Where did you come from. I mean, before your parents decided to move here?"

"I'm from Braintree. The big city—or at least big compared to here. There are two schools. I went to Northside. I miss my friends—I miss Digby," she said. And he watched her eyes cloud over as if she saw something that he didn't.

Sam wanted to ask who Digby was, but he decided he already knew. She had to have a boyfriend. Then again, maybe it was her dog. No, she would have brought her dog with her.

"I've met your aunt, and you've told me a little about your mom, but what about your father?" she asked.

"Don't you know?"

"Know what?"

"He died," he said without adding any detail.

"And?" she said, pressing for more.

"And—he fell into a ditch and drowned."

"Bummer." she gasped, her eyes wide with concern.

"Sorry, that was a cheap shot, dumping it on you like that," he said. Then tapping lightly on the edge of her cast, "this hurts," he said, "but someday it will heal, and the pain will go away. This," he said, slapping his hand hard against his chest, "this hurts all the time—a dull annoying ache that never goes away."

"I'm sorry."

"Don't be. I didn't like my father."

"I don't understand: if you didn't like him, why the does it hurt?"

"It's hard to explain. He was my father, but most of the time he was drunk; and when he was drunk he was mean."

He was still sitting cross-legged on the floor. At the moment he was staring down at Jennifer's feet. They were beautiful feet, long and graceful and still tanned, but he wasn't really interested in their beauty, he just didn't want to bring his eyes up to meet hers. Fearful that he might cry, he blinked several times before he felt it was safe to speak. "I never loved him. I know you're supposed to—but I never did."

"Can you talk about it?"

"NO!" He didn't mean that to sound so harsh, but he wasn't ready. "Not now anyway." He glanced up, and saw that she looked troubled. And when their eyes met she turned quickly to stare out the window toward the sea. At first he glanced that way too, and then slowly returned to gaze at her pretty profile. The dim light coming in through the window touched the front of her forehead, highlighting the thin edge of her nose, the curve of her chin and the long line of her neck. The rest blended into the growing shadows. For several minutes neither said a word. But that quiet was not entirely devoid of sound. He could hear her soft breathing, the creaking of the house, the rush of the ocean against the shore outside her partially open window. He felt the chilly breeze on his bare arms. His bony butt ached from the hardness of the floor, and his folded legs began to cramp. Jennifer didn't move to turn on a light and parts of the room began to disappear into the gloom.

During the months that he had shamelessly spied upon her, he had imagined she was some kind of goddess, beautiful, but cold and unapproachable. Now here in her room, he saw someone very different, someone almost ordinary. But that wasn't fair, because in spite of the plainness of her dress and the dullness of her fading features, she was far from ordinary. There was a noble quality in her posture as she leaned forward in her chair and when a spot of light hit the dark of her eye it sparkled like a bright jewel. She wasn't distant and inaccessible, but warm, and soft, and breakable; and he cursed himself for being afraid of her. All that time wasted when they might have been good friends.

"Sam, I'm glad you came," she whispered, without looking at him.

"Me too," he answered. The curl of the surf, the whisper of the breeze crept up on him in the darkness and set his mind at ease.

"I'm not afraid of you," she confided, after several minutes of silence.

"What?" he asked incredulous.

"I can see that I'm attractive and I suppose that's not a bad thing. But sometimes I wish it wasn't so."

"Not!" he challenged. "You're also talented—and smart—would you want to wish those things away too?"

"No, that's righteous stuff, but. . .be honest, would you be sitting here in my room talking to me if you hadn't broken my arm?"

He didn't answer right away. He wanted to tell her the truth, but he didn't know how she would take it. "Probably not—but not because I wouldn't want to."

"Tell me why then."

"Well—you know," he said, not able to explain his fears.

"No, I don't."

"Damn! It's because—I mean—ya, you're a babe and all that, but—that's not what kept me away. You—you—you're so together, so sure of yourself. It's scary!"

"For real?"

"For real!"

"Maybe so, but the guys I meet just see a face and a bod, and beyond that they don't give a rat's-ass."

"It can't be all that."

"But it is. You know that tall kid at school, the one with the bushy black hair? He's in our biology class."

"Karl Kristian? The captain of the basketball team?" He knew him, he knew Karl all too well.

"Yeah, that's him. Big. I mean, he's gotta be seven foot. Not bad looking. There's even a little muscle on him." She stopped, as if she were waiting for Sam to object.

"When I first met him, on the beach he came on like gangbusters and I dumped on him." Sam remembered the scene clearly. Her response had shaken him too.

"I made an enemy." She said, plucking at the front of her pajama top as if it somehow restricted her breathing. "At the time I could care less. But last week he cornered me in the hallway at the end of the east wing and pinned me to the wall. He planted his big hands on my shoulders so I couldn't move."

"What did he do?"

"Dirty, crusty things," she said, the pitch of her voice rising on the last word.

"Why?" Sam had seen him brag and strut in the locker-room, but he thought it was all puff and show. He never believed that Karl would actually try and do any of those things.

"Maybe because I kept turning down his advances and refused to go all weak and weepy when he told me what a stud he was and how he was going to make a woman out of me."

"That would definitely give him a hissy."

"A what?"

"Give him a fit—make him hysterical."

He watched her pick a loose piece of plaster off the edge of her cast and he shifted his position, stretching his legs in front of him—while he waited for her to continue.

"He—leaned in—and, and rubbed his. . .rubbed up against me, " she said. He heard a thin hard edge in her voice as if she were struggling to hold in her rage.

"What? How?" Sweet Jesus, he thought, as a black picture exploded inside his head that made him wish he hadn't asked.

At first Jennifer said nothing, she just sat there looking out the window, and the silence dragged on for so long he began to wonder if she was waiting for him to say something. Then suddenly she came back as if she had rushed back from the edge of a dark dream. The dimness of the room left her in silhouette and when she turned to face him he couldn't see her expression, but he did hear the quick anger in her voice. "Why? Why did he think he could do that to me?"

He couldn't answer, and when he didn't respond she turned away again, effectively shutting him out.

"I'm not like that," he said, looking for a way out of this dark impasse.

"I know," she said.

But wasn't he? Oh, he would never do the kinds of things that Karl had done to her, but in his imaginings—in his wishful dreams, he didn't exactly qualify for sainthood either.

"If I thought you were, I would never have let you come through that door."

"Considering that I just broke your arm, why <u>did</u> you let me in?"

"From the first time I saw you, I had the feeling I knew who you were—that I already knew everything about you. Does that sound crazy?"

"A little," he said. The word *everything* sparked his memory and filled him with a noisome anxiety. "Did you see me?" he asked.

"What?"

"Do you remember the day my aunt sent you down to get me?"

"I guess?"

"Later, when I was changing on the front porch—did you see me?"

There was a long moment while she considered his question then: "Ohhhhh!" And he could tell by the way she dragged it out that she suddenly understood what he was asking. "If you mean when you lost your towel. . . Yeah."

"And?" he probed.

"And nothing. I'm not a peeping tom."

"That's it?" he said, feeling oddly disappointed.

"Well, I saw enough to know you were naked."

"But that's it. You never actually saw. . .anything."

"Not really. Frankly, I wasn't interested," she said, then gave him an enigmatic smile as if she understood something he didn't.

It was the answer he'd been hoping for, but somehow it didn't bring him any peace of mind, and that confused him.

"What I meant to say, before we got sidetracked, is that when you walked in here a few minutes ago, I knew right away what you were going to say, and how I would answer. It was like being in a dream or a play and all I had to do was read my lines."

"Have you been doing that the whole time?"

"No, just in the beginning, and then it went away. But even after it went away, I felt different, as if I could do anything, say anything, and it would be all right. Have you ever had that kind of feeling before?"

"If you're talking about a sixth sense, or ESP yeah, a couple of times."

They were interrupted by a knocking on her door.

"Jennifer?"

"Yes, mom!" she answered impatiently.

"It's time for Sam to leave."

"All right," she said. "Give us a minute, okay?"

"One minute," her mother said. "And you're already on the clock."

Sam stood up and began to rub the cramps out of his legs. Jennifer switched on the lamp that sat on the table next to her chair. "Will you come again?" she asked.

"Yes."

"And not just because you feel sorry for me?" she postulated.

"No way!" he reassured her. "Well, I do feel sorry, but that's not why I want to come back."

The fact that his presence had disturbed her from the beginning puzzled him, but he also found it reassuring. And he liked the idea that she saw something fatalistic in their meeting this afternoon—something predestined in their accident. But he was especially pleased that she wanted him to come back.

"I'll be here tomorrow after school. Would you like me to check on your homework and stuff?" he added.

"Would you? Mom said she'd do it, but you know all my teachers and she'd have to track them down."

"Consider it done," he said, as he moved toward the door.

"Till tomorrow?" she said, giving him a playful wink.

He smiled, and tried to wink back, but it didn't come off. "You bet." he said, then slipped through the doorway into the hall. At the bottom of the stairs he found Jennifer's mom and told her he would pick up her daughter's homework for her. Then he let himself out the back door, crossed the yard and made his way around to Aunt Em's. All this was done with a lightness of spirit that was unfamiliar to him. He was happy, but he didn't know how to describe this kind of happiness, because he had never experienced it before.

Chapter 18

Sarah finally had a job. It wasn't particularly noteworthy, but it did require some intelligence, which helped to bolster her self-esteem, and her paychecks at least tended to slow the drain on what was left of Robert's insurance. Recently a new and strange emotion had overtaken her; she was happy—too happy. Sometimes she felt ebullient, filled with the sort of effervescent giddiness that wasn't real and that she knew wouldn't last. And it didn't last, but when those moments came she held on to them as long as she could.

She made fast friends of her associates, and became a favorite of the regulars who came to do business at the bank, which often meant her line was longer than the others. In spite of her experience with Robert, she remained relatively unsullied by the ugliness of the world around her, and it was this guileless quality that made her so easy to like. When she asked her customers how they were, they knew that she wasn't just being polite. She had a special gift for detail and from visit to visit she remembered names, remembered the things people said and picked up their conversations wherever they left off. It was uncanny, but when she listened to their stories and commiserated on their troubles, she gave her customers a genuine sense of importance.

Sarah was not manipulative, though with her remarkable abilities she might have been. She brought people under her spell so gently, and lovingly, that they were hardly aware she had captured their hearts. Even she was amazed. She clearly saw the effect, saw their willingness to surrender to whatever she suggested, but she couldn't see how she was responsible. All these people who claimed to be her friends served as a wonderful catharsis to her battered heart and like a soothing balm helped to mend her discordant spirit. She'd never felt so needed or so wanted in her life.

Martin also fell under her spell, although in the beginning he was reluctant to admit it. He was, after all, her boss, and therefore believed he ought to be able to resist her peculiar charms.

♦ ♦ ♦

Saturday, the morning after the accident, Sarah sat in the lunchroom nursing a lukewarm cup of hot chocolate that she had drained from the vending machine behind her. Martin sat with her at a table which was partially covered with used napkins, empty Styrofoam cups, and other debris left by those who had come and gone before them.

Sarah could tell that Martin wanted her to give him the details of her son's accident. But she didn't have all the details. Oh, she knew about the mangled bike, and Jennifer's broken arm, and it was obvious that Sam was deeply immersed in his own guilt. She did notice that he seemed happier when he got home from his Aunt Em's than he had been when he left, but she had no idea why.

Emerging from these thoughts, she realized that Martin was trying to tell her a joke, something that he'd heard the night before. "So this guy gives the $100,000 dollars to the priest and then another hundred thousand to the rabbi and a third to the minister. He tells them that when he dies they all have to a come to the grave and see that the money is buried with him. And when the time comes they all show up and drop an envelope into the hole just before the gravediggers fill it up. Then—then—. The priest told the rabbi. . .no, the minister asked the priest. . .damn." Martin started counting on his fingers as if that would help him get the story straight.

Sarah could tell that Martin had forgotten the punch line and his desperate efforts to remember made her laugh.

"It's not funny," he objected.

"But it is funny. Not the joke, but the way you're trying to tell it. Do it again."

"Do what? Tell another joke," she teased.

"Oh, go away," he said.

"All right," she said, and she started to get up.

"No, I didn't mean that. I meant leave me alone."

"That's what I'm doing," she said, and the more she teased the more addled he became.

Then she stopped and just sat there staring at him. It took a moment for her to realize that her staring made him nervous. He tried to lift his cup to his mouth, but his hand began to tremble, and he had to put it down before he spilled it. She pressed her fingers to her lips to hold back another laugh, but it leak out anyway, and she apologized.

♦ ♦ ♦

Damn it, he thought, how does she do that? It's those eyes. Putting aside her ingenuous personality, it was her eyes that always did him in. Heavy-lidded and full-lashed, with the transparent purity of a gemstone, her bottle-green eyes wreaked havoc with him whenever he was bold enough to search their depths. Mostly they were bright and positive, but on rare occasions there was a specter of sadness lurking just below their glassy surface. He saw only a hint of trouble and the mood quickly passed. For most these moments went unnoticed, but for Martin they lent an air of mystery to an otherwise uncomplicated woman.

"So, is your son all right?" Martin asked, trying to break the disturbing intensity of her gaze.

"Fine."

"Was he hurt badly?"

"No, just some bruises."

"How did it happen?"

"He wasn't paying attention," she answered succinctly.

She made him work hard for even the smallest fact, and he wondered if he had the right to ask. His questions had only served to bring those eyes to bear upon him again and his thoughts dissolved in a tremor of confusion. *God,* he said *under his breath, I'm at least ten years her senior; how can I let myself be driven to such distraction? My whole being seems to melt into a sophomoric pile of mush.* When he couldn't take it anymore, he dropped his eyes and studied the steam rising from his hot drink.

After a long silence, the sound of her chair scraping the floor startled him, and he looked up to see Sarah leaving the table and heading for the door. He couldn't think of anything to say to keep her there, and when the door of the lunchroom banged shut he put his head down on the table and banged his forehead slowly against the hard surface.

◆ ◆ ◆

When Martin's wife had died ten years ago he was sure no one would be able to reach him in that special way again. He had adopted that idea partly to protect himself from being hurt, and partly because he believed that God only allowed a man to love like that once in a lifetime. Now, whether he could or should love again seemed academic—there was no question in his mind that being around Sarah did things to him emotionally and physically that were beyond his control. Her smile, her presence, kept him off balance and upset the wobbly underpinnings of the simple life he had chosen to live.

Maria had died in 1976, the bicentennial year, a year of celebration for the nation, a time of incredible pain for him and his children. At the end of March, they had found the tumor in her breast, and by October she was dead. Passed away, gone to her reward, an angel gone home, resting with the saints—he had heard all those wonderful euphemisms and a good many others coming from well-meaning friends, but it hadn't altered the fact that she was no longer a part of his life, and it didn't help in the least to ease the pain or fill the emptiness of the bed where she had curled up around him every night for fifteen years. Now, when he reached out for her, only the coolness of the sheet fell under his hand. She had not ceased to exist—he was sure that she had gone somewhere: paradise, heaven, the spirit world. Sometimes he had the sense that she was only in the next room or around the corner. When he stood by the sink to wash the dishes or swept the dust off the top of her bureau or took linens from the hall closet, he could feel her, smell her— almost touch her. He was sure that she was nearby, and that someday he would see her again. But wherever she had gone, he was never happy with the idea that they couldn't be together now.

In the beginning he was certain that he wasn't going to make it. The loneliness seemed too debilitating, the ache too deep. If it hadn't been for his sons, he might have tried to join her. Not that he would have killed himself, such histrionics were not a part of his personality. But he <u>was</u> guilty of neglect. He didn't want to get out of bed in the morning, particularly if he had finally succeeded in falling asleep. Food didn't interest him, and work was something to be endured simply because it kept him from drowning in self-pity.

He suffered through each day until time put some distance between him and the event, and he literally grew tired of feeling sorry for himself. His children were still young, and their needs helped fill some of the emptiness. They also altered his career. He knew that they would require more of his time, especially now that he had to be both mother and father. So he quit his high-profile job in Boston and came out to Southbridge to manage this small branch. It put him much closer to home, and made far fewer demands on his time; and he used that extra time for his children. He didn't regret his decision, except that his children were grown now, and he was stuck at the bank in a position that would lead him nowhere. Still, even with no future, he had become resigned to his circumstances, comfortable with his routine, satisfied with its predictability. But whether he was willing to admit it or not, Sarah had disturbed that predictability.

He already knew that Sarah was important to him, but he hadn't made up his mind yet how important, or what he ought to do about it. It had occurred to him that he wanted to ask her out, not just for a cup of coffee, but on a real date: to a movie, or dinner, or anywhere that would put the two of them together in a place that was less restricting than here at the bank. But whenever he thought he saw an opportunity to ask, his position as her boss got in the way.

When he considered the idea of dating more carefully, he wondered: *do I dare?* The last time he had even thought of such stuff was in high school. Maria was the only girl that he ever seriously dated. Sure, there were a couple of girls before her, but Maria was the only one who put up with his ineptness. He probably wouldn't even have kissed her if she hadn't insisted on it.

He had gone out on a number of occasions after his wife died, agreeing to wine and dine several women (including one who was only twenty years old), only because his friends pressed him to do it. They had arranged those dinners and pushed those women on him, telling him that he needed someone in his life and that it was dangerous for a man his age to be alone. Really, he didn't know how it could be dangerous, or what his age had to do with anything, but he did agree that he was painfully alone. It was all done in his best interest, by people who loved him and who wanted him to be happy, but they just didn't understand that he'd had a wonderful companion and lost her, and he wasn't ready to find a replacement.

Because he didn't want to go in the first place, there was never any threat of rejection. If his date didn't like him, if they told him no thank you, it was a relief, not a disappointment.

That wasn't true with Sarah. What if she said no? What if she wasn't the least bit interested in him? Worse than that, he was her boss. What if she felt pressured to accept because of his position? Did that mean in order to date her, he would have to fire her first? That didn't make any sense, but then everything he thought or did lately, particularly when it came to Sarah, didn't seem very sensible.

When he saw Ada come through the door to the lunchroom, he knew that he had been in there too long. He stood and gathered up the coffee cups, put the napkins and paper plates in the barrel and went back to his office.

Chapter 19

On Saturday evening Martin went shopping at the grocery store on Main Street in Southbridge. He always picked up something to cook for Sunday dinner because he knew that at least one of his sons would come by to visit. Still suffering from the disparaging put-down he had taken that morning in the lunchroom, he wasn't in a very good mood. He didn't know if he felt dejected or rejected, but his efforts to build a relationship with Sarah seemed to be constantly frustrated.

He moved his carriage ahead slowly while he studied the top shelf looking for a brand of stew that he liked—well, he liked his own homemade mulligan stew, but since the boys had left that wasn't practical. When his carriage jostled lightly against another as he came to the end of the soup aisle, he didn't immediately react. He just gave an automatic apology. When he did turn to identify the owner of the other carriage, he saw Sarah smiling back at him; and his stomach started to flip-flop the same way the Sunfish did at Speckled Pond after he'd caught and then released them into the bottom of his boat.

Thank God he had both hands firmly wrapped around the handle of his grocery cart, otherwise he wouldn't have known what to do with them. He chided himself for acting like a silly schoolboy whenever Sarah crossed his path, yet he couldn't help chuckling over the fact that she could effect him that way. When he first dated Maria he had been full of youthful eagerness and when she aroused his passion he often became excited to the point of losing control. Once he even wet his pants. Not enough to show, but it was terribly embarrassing just the same.

This was different: he was older now—in control—immune from such youthful nonsense. Yet there was no denying that he had all the symptoms: sweaty palms, dry mouth, forgetfulness, and a bad case of the *clumsies*—spilling and dropping things that had never given him any trouble before.

He couldn't be sure of her feelings for him, but he could sense a connection between them—something strained and taut, like a thin strand of wire that if pulled too tightly would certainly snap. And it seemed that the tension rose exponentially the longer he was in her presence.

He greeted her brightly. "Well, Mrs. Stewart, imagine running into you here!" *I'm too happy and this sounds really lame,* he thought, silently berating himself.

"Was that meant to be a pun?"

"No," he said a bit too loudly.

"Tell me, how come you keep calling me Mrs. Stewart, when the other day you insisted that I call you Martin?"

"You're right, that isn't fair, is it, especially outside the workplace. So Sarah it will be. What are you doing here—Sarah?" he asked, then corrected his folly. "That's a silly question, since you have a cart full of groceries, you're obviously shopping."

"Yes, so it seems, and you too I see," she said, smiling.

"One of the mundane duties of bachelorhood. Not much fun, but it must be done." *Boring—why couldn't I be more original? It sounds as if shopping qualifies me for martyrdom.* Then, rushing blindly ahead, "Would you like to meet for coffee at Sally's Café? I mean—later, when you're done shopping?" He waited for the axe to fall.

"I'd like that," she said, giving him another of her pleasant smiles, "but I have frozen food, and milk, and I just picked up some fresh fish. I have to get them home."

"Oh sure—I understand. I have ice cream—of course I could put it back." *What possible difference would that make? Besides, one of the reasons I came here was for ice cream.* Still, he was desperate to salvage this. He was so close to something that at least resembled a date that he couldn't let it go. It might be a long time before he got a chance like this again.

"Tell you what," she said, interrupting his thoughts, "why don't you meet me at Sally's in about an hour. I'm almost finished here, and that should give me time to get this stuff home." Looking now at her watch, she said, "That would make it around eight, if that's okay with you?"

Okay? Okay? Martin felt his knees turn to water, and he tightened his grip on the carriage handle for support. He thought that she had used the perishables as an excuse to say no. Coming back with this invitation threw him. "Absolutely," he said, recovering. "It's a date," he added enthusiastically, then thought better of it. Again she surprised him.

"It's a date," she repeated, matching his enthusiasm.

When he looked at her face he saw an impish grin that made him feel like a mouse who has just taken the cheese, only when he heard the trap snap shut there wasn't any pain. She seemed to stare at him for much too long before she pushed away and started down a separate aisle to finish her shopping

Chapter 20

When Martin got home he worked quickly to put away the bread and can goods that he had bought at the store, and then stopped in the bathroom to make some minor adjustments, including a couple of swipes with his electric razor and a splash of after-shave. He would like to have showered and changed his clothes, but worried that he might miss Sarah at the cafe. Instead he pulled out his shirttail and hiked it and his undershirt up so that he could apply some deodorant then tucked himself back in before he hustled out to his car and drove off to his rendezvous with Sarah. Filled with anxiety, he suffered all the way there with a terrible case of heartburn.

♦ ♦ ♦

Meanwhile, Sarah found herself carrying out a similar routine in her own home, and wondering too how much time ought to be spent putting herself together. She came to the same conclusion as Martin: she wanted to look her best, but was just as antsy about not being late.

"Sam," she called out. She heard a muffled response from upstairs and realized he was in the bathroom. Coming up the stairs she heard the shower and suspected that he wouldn't be finished soon.

"I'm going out for awhile," she said through the closed door.

"Where to?" Sam bellowed above the cascade of water.

"Downtown. I'm going to meet a friend at Sally's."

"How long?"

"Oh, for heaven's sakes, you sound like my mother! I'll get back whenever, just don't get into any trouble while I'm gone."

"Okay, okay." he spouted, sounding impatient. She heard the pipes bang when he shut off the water and then the rattle of the shower-curtain signaled that he had stepped out of the shower.

"I'll call if I'm going to be late," she promised, just before she turned and headed down the stairs.

♦ ♦ ♦

Being a little closer to the café, Sarah arrived first. She pushed her way through one door, then a second, and stopped to looked around.

Martin wasn't there yet. This gave her the chance to decide where they would sit, and she picked out a booth at the back where it was dark and secluded. Perhaps the darkness would hide her hair, which stood out in frizzy disarray. She removed a small mirror from her bag and tried to apply some fresh lipstick. Lack of time and poor lighting made it impossible to put on any other makeup and she couldn't chance a trip to the powder room.

Once she had settled in, it occurred to her that Martin might see her choice differently. After all, this dull light might also be considered romantic. *So what,* she thought, *romantic isn't bad—is it?*

Sitting there, waiting, she started mulling over her relationship with Martin, if indeed it could be called a relationship. Up until yesterday she had only known him as Mr. McAulliffe, her boss. Considering his actions, or more correctly his reactions, whenever he was in her presence, she had good reason to believe that he had some feelings for her. But she could only guess at how serious those feelings might be. She found it difficult to imagine herself as the object of this man's desire—or any man's, for that matter. She had been told by one of her regulars at the bank (quite confidentially of course) that Martin would make a good catch if anyone could stir him to action. And it wasn't so disagreeable to think that she was capable of arousing Martin's interest. He was a good man, and his boyish awkwardness <u>was</u> endearing. Besides, it might be fun to try and arouse something more than just his interest. The colorfulvision this engendered startled her and she scolded herself: "Sarah Jane Stewart," she said in a low whisper. Then she saw Martin come breathlessly through the door.

He stood there for a moment, searching, and a sudden flash of disappointment descended upon his face when he couldn't find her. It was replaced by a fresh eager smile when she leaned across the table and waved to him. He moved swiftly down the crowded aisle and slipped into the booth facing her.

"You're so far back, and it's so dark, I couldn't see you," he said. "How did you come to pick such a remote spot?"

"I don't know. I guess when I came in and looked around everything seemed too noisy and crowded." She gestured toward the front of the café and Martin turned to hear the clatter of silver and china and the strident warble of the diners that he had just passed through to get to her.

"Besides, it puts us closer to the kitchen," she added as a waiter burst through the swinging door and banged it against the back of the booth behind her. She laughed and he laughed with her.

◆ ◆ ◆

In the middle of the table a single flame burned at the bottom of a cut-glass bowl. The flickering light illuminated Sarah's face, gave a warm luminescence to her pale skin and emphasized the freckles that crossed her nose and dotted her cheeks. Martin saw that the freckles were darker than usual, but thought they made her look like a little girl, and he let himself get lost in that puckish illusion.

He was studying her with such intensity that he didn't realize she was staring back at him with equal interest. The needful look in her eyes made him drop his gaze and rounding his shoulders he pulled his head in like a turtle hiding in its shell. For a moment he played nervously with his butter knife—shifting its position, then picking it up and wiping away an imaginary spot with his napkin.

Damn, she's done it again. Every time she catches me with those eyes, I melt into a puddle of mush. He straightened up in his chair, looked straight at her and blurted, "You look—great." He wanted to say gorgeous or incredible, but it seemed too presumptuous.

"Pardon me?" she asked, and he could see that his boldness had shocked her, but since he was already sinking in quicksand, he decided to risk repeating himself. "You look great. In fact you look incredible."

"Yes," she murmured, then paused while a ruddy bloom emphasized the bouquet of freckles across her cheeks. "Well—it's kind of you to say that, but the candlelight hides a host of imperfections."

"No, that's not so. And it isn't a matter of kindness—there are no imperfections."

She brought her hands to her face, clearly discomforted by his attention.

"I know my faults. . ." she said, her voice trailing off.

"We all have faults."

"I didn't mean it that way."

"What then?" he asked.

"I'm not sure if I can explain or if I want to." With her hands palms down on the table as if she intended to push herself away, her eyes stared past him into the crowd.

Sensing a sting of sadness in her statement he remained silent.

"My husband—my late husband, jeeze it sounds strange to say that, had a habit of pointing out my shortcomings."

"Why would he do that?"

"Maybe he thought he was being helpful—or maybe he just liked being cruel," she said. Then dropped her shoulders as if suddenly a heavy weight had fallen on her back.

"I'm sorry, I had no right to ask that."

"He told me I ought to be grateful."

"Grateful for what?" Martin asked, grinding his teeth.

"I guess grateful that he had condescended to marry me."

He didn't know how to react to this last statement. It was too disparaging.

In the void she reached for her glass of ice water and drained half of it away before setting it down again. When he looked at her now her skin had turned to parchment. Even the warm candlelight couldn't give it any color, and though the café was full of noise her silence disturbed him.

"All men aren't like that," he said, though he didn't know why. Was he coming to his own defense?

No—thank God!" She made it sound like a supplication. "My father was a good man."

"Was?

"His heart gave out two years ago. You remind me of him, and I can see something of my grandfather too."

"Oh?" He wondered if that were a good thing. "Do I seem *that* old?"

"Noooo," she covered her mouth to hide the smile sliding across her lips, "that's not it at all."

"Then what?"

"It has to do with mannerisms, the way you move your hands— that puppy-dog look that you get in your eyes—"

"When do I do that?" he interrupted.

She didn't answer; instead she took another sip of water.

"Do I have to answer that?" she asked.

"No, not if it makes you uncomfortable."

"Very!" was her only response.

But he couldn't leave it alone. "Can you at least tell me why I remind you of a dog?"

"Arghhh!" she said. "That's probably a poor analogy. But you do have a look sometimes that makes me think of Dutch."

"Who's Dutch?"

"Aw, you don't want to know." She waved her hand dismissively, and then tried to explain. "He was a big mushy basset hound."

"You mean the kind of dog that's so low to the ground that they trip over their own ears?"

"Exactly!"

"This gets better and better."

"No. Forget about the floppy ears. Dutch—well, it didn't have to do with how he looked. Dutch had been the runt of the litter. He was nearly two years old by the time my father found him and brought him home. I was four, and if I'd still been crawling the dog and I would have been attached at the hip. We grew up together. He lay at the bottom of my bed at night, and in the summertime when I didn't have any blankets he'd lick my feet, then crawl up beside me and fall asleep with his rump pressed into my belly. Which meant he took up most of the bed.

"Whenever I came home from school I could hear the clatter of his nails on the hardwood floor long before I saw him turn the corner into the front hall. Jumping up, he let me stroke his ears, then he'd drop to the floor and roll over—front paws folded, back legs spread wide—inviting me to scratch his stomach. And once I started, he made these squeaky little noises that sounded as if he were in dog heaven.

"Two days after my sixteenth birthday, I woke up and saw him stretched out on the braided rug under my window. I could tell from where I lay that he wasn't breathing. He was old, and he was in pain, but he loved me unconditionally, and when he died, half of me died with him." She stopped for a moment, staring blankly as if lost in that painful memory, then forced a smile.

All through her story her hands had been in constant motion: palm to palm as if in prayer, a finger to her lips to suppress a smile, scratching the table to illustrate how she treated Dutch, and finally her fingers crept across the table to cover his hand. "I don't know why I'm telling you this."

"I don't know either, but I think I'm jealous."

"Of my dog?"

"Yes."

"Why?"

"Think about it. He got to sleep in your bed, and lick your feet—then got rewarded by having you scratch his belly."

"You're incorrigible!" she said, trying to look shocked, but Martin was unconvinced.

"Sorry, but you opened the door."

"Yes, I did," she said, "and you came right on in." They both laughed. After a moment Sarah made a tent out of her hands and covered her nose, then looking warmly into Martin's eyes she asked, "Is it me or is this turning into a date?"

"God, I hope so."

"What do you mean?" she asked taking down her hands and sitting straight up in her chair.

Without any way of predicting her reaction, he decided to be direct. "Frankly, I've been mooning around for weeks trying to find a way to ask you out, and this is as close as I've come."

"I had no idea—well I. . ." she paused to suck in her breath, "it's—it's very flattering . . .but."

"But?"

"I'm not ready for this."

"Ready for what? I'm not proposing marriage."

"No. No, you're not."

"Then why can't we spend some time together and see what happens?"

"Because someone might get hurt."

"So? Everything about life involves risk. That's what makes it so interesting."

"I'm not any good at taking risks. I'm not equipped for it."

"Please! If you're talking about experience, I'm hardly a man of the world."

"No, that's not it."

"Then why not?"

He saw her slump and he studied the pained expression on her face; and the longer she remained silent the more he lost hope, until he saw a smile creep around her eyes and her thin lips parted. "Okay you win. But promise me, however we do this we'll take it slow."

"Absolutely!" he said. One of the butterflies in his stomach leapt to his throat and for a moment he was afraid to breathe."

"If I had any sense . . ." But she didn't get to finish. The waitress had finally found them, and asked if they were ready to order. He decided against coffee and Sarah said, "None for me, thanks." In fact, when he thought about it, Martin realized that he'd never seen Sarah drink coffee. Neither did he, but since everyone he knew had an addiction to the stuff, he had assumed . . . he still had a lot to learn.

Without referring to the menu he ordered a hot fudge sundae and Sarah did the same. Before the waitress turned away, Martin amended his order. "Lots of whipped topping. Oh, and how bout an extra cherry?"

"Me, too," Sarah echoed.

"See, you're already living dangerously," he pointed out, and Sarah laughed. Not the way she had before; this time it came from deep inside and was filled with latent sensuality. He hiccuped and tried to convince himself it was only gas. But he'd had this feeling before and knew that it had nothing to do with gas.

When the waitress left and they were alone again, they sat in strained silence, and Martin thought, *no matter where we go from here at least we've agreed to take the first step.*

The sundaes came, and they spent the next thirty minutes talking while most of their ice cream melted in the dish. This time they discussed lighter matters: likes and dislikes, the best place to buy lobster, the worst place for steak. He enjoyed books; currently he was reading Le Carre's *The Little Drummer Girl.* She didn't—didn't like Le Carre—she felt an affinity for Steinbeck, and other members of his generation. They both had a penchant for old movies, especially from the forties and fifties: romances with Tracy and Hepburn, the other Hepburn with Gregory Peck in *Roman Holiday.*

"Remember Cary Grant and Doris Day in *That Touch of Mink,* when they were in Bermuda and they kept showing up in that four-poster bed?" Sarah asked.

"And then they finally get married, and he ends up with the hives," Martin finished.

"This new stuff is too graphic," Sarah observed. "They always jump in bed together before they know each other's name and you have to figure out if you care."

"It's too quick and easy," he said. "In the old days they met, they fought, then they fell in love and at the end the doors closed, or the picture faded out, and the rest was left to your imagination. And if you had a good imagination that could be terribly erotic."

This led to speculation about what might be playing locally. "What do you think?" he asked. "It's almost nine, but we might get into a late show."

"Why not?" she said.

Calling the waitress back, Martin asked if she could find a newspaper, and she did. Poring over the movie section they soon discovered that "Murphy's Romance" was playing at the theater in Freetown. That was just a few miles away; if they left quickly they could get there for the last show at nine-twenty.

Sarah said she had seen the picture when it previewed at the Saxon Theater in Boston last September. "I went then, too," Martin chimed in. "We might have been there at the same time."

"I thought it was great fun."

"So did I," Martin agreed, and though he didn't say so, he couldn't help thinking that he would enjoy it much more now that he had someone to share it with.

Chapter 21

The gray Ford Tempo thrummed monotonously as it glided down the lonely two-lane road. The car's headlights picked out the trees and houses as they wound through the turns, and when the road straightened, Sarah watched the broken white line click by in a steady mesmerizing pattern. Staring out into the night she thought: How did this happen? I feel—I don't know how I feel. Content? No, it's actually much simpler than that. I'm happy. Happy to be in this car riding down this dark road, happy to be sitting next to this man, happy with the idea that he finds me attractive.

She had lived for so long in an emotional vacuum without any real sense of direction or purpose that the happiness she felt now seemed disproportionate—unreal. What was happening, what might happen next, was a mystery, yet she couldn't deny that she wanted these feelings to continue. Martin had only been a part of her life for two months and only in the last few minutes had he declared his feelings toward her. She had so little to build on. A chance encounter at the grocery store, and then later sharing ice cream and conversation at Sally's. Ordinary stuff really, but somehow something told her it wasn't ordinary. This was all so new to her. *Is this what happens to people when they fall in love?*

She could tell that Martin was a good man. She knew instinctively that he would never betray her the way Robert had. She was too young when she married Robert. It had been the wrong thing to do, a stupid mistake that had led to years of misery. But did she have any more wisdom now at thirty-four than she did at seventeen? Robert was the only man she had ever known. Well, she had known her father and her grandfather, but she had loved them and she hadn't loved Robert. Still, she had enough maturity to know that Martin wanted her. But so had Robert in the beginning, and she had been hungry for his love. Wasn't this the same thing? Wasn't she just as needy now? What made her think she had any chance of getting it right this time?

All these questions filled her with doubt and the more she doubted the more depressed she became. Why was she so hell-bent on tearing this apart before it had really begun? A moment ago she felt almost euphoric, and now she was driving herself into an abyss. Why couldn't she just enjoy this new feeling for at least as long as it lasted?

She sat back in her seat, pressed her head firmly into the spongy headrest, and forced herself to relax. She tried to banish her fears and uncertainty by breathing deeply and letting the air out slowly in one long whispering sigh.

◆ ◆ ◆

Martin stared straight ahead, concentrating on the road. Driving at night was always more confusing, even over familiar roads. Everything looked different and much of the surrounding countryside disappeared in the blackness beyond the reach of the headlights. After being so talkative at Sally's, Sarah seemed unusually quiet. He heard her long sigh, and wondered why—could she be having second thoughts? He could understand if she did. It would take time to test their feelings for each other. That knot in his stomach twisted again and rose to constrict his throat. He felt a palpable energy, a kind of electricity that tingled at the edge of his consciousness and created a special tension that was wonderfully familiar and exciting. When Maria died he thought that those feelings had died with her. Did he dare to awaken that spirit again? Did he have the right for a second time to experience that kind of joy?

Following Maria's death, he suffered such awful heartache, and it was a long time before that intense pain diminished to a level he could tolerate. Then, just when he thought he had it all locked away, an unguarded moment with a friend or one of his children, or something in a play or a book or on TV, would trigger his memory and the pain would come rushing back.

He did find joy in his two sons, but it was always tempered by the fact that he couldn't share it with Maria. Oh, he had no doubt she was aware, aware of him, and of Daryl and Stephen. In some way he was sure she saw and knew what they did each day and what they suffered. But, if indeed she could observe their trials through the veil that separated their two worlds, they weren't allowed to look back. They couldn't touch her, or hold her, or talk to her, and have the physical assurance that she heard and felt and cared about all the things that affected their lives. Now, with Sarah sitting beside him in the dark, the lights of passing cars occasionally lighting her face, he wondered if he could do it all again, suffer it all again.

Was he crazy to put himself in harm's way? And even worse, was he being unfaithful to Maria? No. If Sarah could bring him happiness, certainly Maria would wish him well.

As they drove down Union Street in Freetown, the interior of the car was flooded with lights from neon signs and bright street lamps. Approaching the stoplight at Exeter, Sarah looked around and said, "Don't we turn here? Isn't the theater at the end of the next block?"

"You're right," Martin said, switching on his turn signal. As they came closer, they saw cars pulling out of the parking lot from the last show, and knew that they had timed their arrival perfectly. Martin slipped out of the car and flicked the lock on his door before closing it, and then rushed around to let Sarah out.

◆ ◆ ◆

Sarah waited, wondering if she should expect him to open her door, or if she should pretend to be a liberated woman and open the door for herself. As a child, such things were just a matter of good manners, but nowadays all that seemed to be in question. While she thought this through, Martin opened her door and reached in. When her hand fell into his, she became aware of the bulky roughness of his fingers. There wasn't anything particularly stimulating about his touch, but she did find something easy and comfortable about the firmness of his grip as he pulled her up and out of the car, and that feeling carried with her as she hurried across the parking lot, still in his grasp. For some reason the warmth of his hand as it surrounded hers translated into a wonderful feeling of security. Glancing at the contour of his face and the curl of his smile, she was sure that being around this man could be very addictive. But first she'd have to overcome the irrational fear she had of being happy. Oh, she allowed herself to dabble in happiness—a little here, a little there, in an unguarded moment—but never for more than a moment.

◆ ◆ ◆

After he picked up their tickets, Martin bought a large bucket of popcorn and two sodas. Sarah had already gone ahead to find some good seats, and as he came down the aisle she waved. He saw their coats piled high beside her, and remembered the times Maria had done the same: staking out a place until he could join her. The vision came and went swiftly, but it shook him. Would Maria's memory come to haunt him every time he took Sarah to a familiar place or could he put her memory aside and not make unfair comparisons, which in the end could only be destructive?

Reaching the row of seats where Sarah was waiting, he excused himself as he climbed over a couple sitting next to the aisle and shuffled along until he was by her side. He scrunched down contentedly in the plush high-backed seat and got comfortable, and Sarah slid down in the seat beside him. The screen was a bright green and a printed message announced the rating of the preview they were about to see. They moved shoulder to shoulder and bumped heads as Sarah reached into the large tub of popcorn Martin was holding in his lap.

"Sorry," she mumbled with her mouth full.

How had he come so quickly to this cozy scene in a darkened theater, with no one occupying the seats immediately around them? He felt marvelously contented, though he was afraid to admit to himself that this was real. It seemed that once he'd gotten the courage to ask Sarah out, the rest had fallen into place with a suddenness that left him slightly giddy. As the movie began, he settled in and let the subtle humor of the romance that played out on the screen draw him in. When the drinks were finished and the popcorn eaten, Martin set the containers under his seat. Sarah happened to brush her hand across the top of his, and he immediately turned his palm upward to meet it. Sarah folded her fingers neatly between his, then dragged his hand down to rest upon her knee. And he was quite content to leave it there.

When the movie ended he brushed away some loose popcorn and gathered up their coats. Scooting between the seats, the two of them started to queue up the aisle, straining against the crowd to reach the side exit. Soon they were back in the car weaving from row to row, trying to find their way out of the parking lot.

From the moment they entered the car, they engaged in conversation. Mostly they talked about the movie they had just seen, comparing notes and sharing their opinions about the love that grew between the two stars.

"In the beginning I thought James Garner was too old for Sally Field," Sarah observed. "But somehow after a while that didn't seem to matter."

"They'd both had some tough experiences. She married a *child* who had no ambition and who ended up dumping her and his son. He had lost his wife—the love of his life. They both had good reason to be gun-shy, but then again they had to know what they were getting themselves into."

Sarah turned to Martin and said, "What about us? Do we know what we're getting ourselves into?" There was a gentle eagerness in her voice that demanded a truthful answer.

Martin took his attention off the road and gave her a long look. For what seemed an interminable length of time he said nothing. Then with rough conviction he said: "God, I hope so! This isn't some kind of a game, and it certainly isn't a movie where we can be sure of a happy ending."

"This is a new experience for me. I won't say I don't like it; I'm just not sure how to deal with it," she said, fingering her seat belt as if she were checking the safety net under a circus high wire.

"Let's face it, you don't know me. And for that matter, I don't know you."

"That's what worries me—once you know me better. . ." she said, looking at him with a frown.

"I'll see all the warts and wrinkles," he interjected. "But remember that works both ways." He tightened his grip on the wheel and pulled it to the right to make the turn into the parking lot next to Sally's.

"I know what I feel—what I have been feeling for the last several weeks— but I also know feelings alone aren't very reliable. Courtship," he said as he spotted her car, "is designed to help us find out about each other—the battle to discover 's each other's bad habits."

"Courtship," Sarah said. "Even the word makes me shudder. It's so old-fashioned and it practically screams commitment."

"So, we promised to take it slow," he reminded her, as he pulled his car into the slot next to hers. Shutting the engine off, he turned to look at Sarah and she looked back at him.

"Slow. . ." she agreed.

◆ ◆ ◆

Even in the attenuated glow from the streetlight, Sarah saw the wetness pool in Martin's eyes and when she thought it might spill over, she reached out to caress his cheek, then moved her finger along the orbit of his eye. A second tear oiled the side of his nose and her finger slid down to trip over his upper lip. Martin reached up with his hand and covered hers and Sarah jumped slightly from his touch. He rubbed the pads of her fingertips across the stubble on his cheek, then turned her hand over and kissed it. When he slid his arm into the curve of her back and walked his fingers up her spine, a tiny quiver pulled at her shoulders and her breath escaped in a low moan. After an awkward moment, her nose glanced off his and their lips came together. She let doubt and reason fly, and forgetting his promise to go slowly she pushed the tip of her tongue past the edge of his teeth and enjoyed the warm wet taste of him. She pulled away, then came back again, this time slathering his lips with warm spit and licking it off. A tiny contraction, a quick pull that tightened the muscles in her abdomen, caught her by surprise. It only lasted a moment, but it made her feel helpless and a little alarmed. Nothing had prepared her for this sudden arousal. Though she was not a child and certainly understood the connection, she had never felt this way before and was amazed at the urgent passion that rippled through her gut. She pressed her lips more eagerly against his, and Martin pushed back, then pulled away, gasping like a drowning man desperate for air.

Breaking the grip she had on his neck, they separated. "I love this," she said in a thready whisper, "but please let's stop. If we go much further . . ." She saw him smile broadly and his teeth contrasted brightly against his shadowy face. "Don't laugh. I guess I'm a throwback; an old-fashioned girl who still believes in being prudent."

"That's all right—you don't have to explain. When this evening started I hadn't expected it to end with a kiss, and certainly not a kiss like that."

"Was it so awful?" she asked, begging for his approval.

"No, not at all. It—it was wonderful. I just wish it had lasted longer."

Sarah felt the same way, which surprised her. She'd never had to rein in her emotions before. Any contact with Robert, even accidental, had been frightening—even repulsive. "Yes, I liked it too. But if it had lasted any longer it might have gotten us both in trouble."

"Hmmmmm," he hummed. "I haven't had that kind of trouble in a long time."

"Martin, you're terrible," she said, feeling justly indignant.

"Why terrible? You're the one who's been teasing the tiger's tail."

"I suppose you're right," she said. Looking down, she noticed the top of her blouse had come unbuttoned, and feeling suddenly exposed she quickly pulled the edges together, then wrapped her jacket up around her neck. "Maybe we should say goodnight."

"Must we?"

"Yes," she insisted, then slid across the seat and pushed against the handle until she felt the door give way. "Not that I want to," she confided. "But if I stay I'm afraid I'll be tempted to kiss you again."

"I wouldn't mind that," Martin said.

"Neither would I, but—" and before she could finish, he took her hand and drew her inward, then stretching across the front seat he touched his lips delicately against hers and released her. Because it was not passionate, but given gently, almost shyly, she nearly lost her resolve.

"That's not fair," she said as she stepped out onto the pavement.

◆ ◆ ◆

Driving home, Martin thought of the first kiss he'd had with Maria. After their third date they had come back to her house in his brother's '49 Ford pickup. When he pulled up to the curb only the misty edges of the front porch light filtered into the cab. That might have been very romantic, except there wasn't anything romantic about the rusty holes in the floorboard, the cracked windshield, the rips in the seams of the worn-out bench seat, or the long-handled floor shift that rose up between and kept them from getting too cozy.

They sat there and talked for nearly an hour. Maria was easy to talk to, and each of their previous dates had ended with conversation that lasted well into the night. He'd never managed to say very much to a girl before, in fact he hadn't managed much of anything before. With Maria it was different: whatever she said sounded exciting and whatever he said seemed just as exciting to her. No subject was off-limits—family, school, music, movies, even sex, though here both tiptoed lightly around the hard stuff (talking about having children, but not about how—about when to kiss and how long, but not who they had kissed or would like to kiss).

It was the sixties (the late sixties), and to use the common baseball metaphor, most guys would have been well beyond second or even third base by now. But he didn't know how to take the next step; he didn't even know what the next step ought to be. He was already so in love with her that he was afraid to do anything that might screw things up. And considering his past history (the fact that he seldom managed to get beyond the second date) he had good reason to be afraid. But it hadn't occurred to him that if he did nothing she would begin to believe he didn't care.

"Marty," she said. This was her own invention; she never called him Martin. "Is there something wrong with me?"

"No," he said.

"Don't you like me, then?" she asked.

"Of course I do," he answered, wondering what she was getting at.

"Then why haven't you tried to kiss me?"

"Uh, welll-l-l-l," he said, drawing out the word as long as he had breath because he couldn't find anything to add to it. It wasn't that he hadn't wanted to—but.

"Well nothing, either you want to kiss me or you don't. Whichever it is, you'd better get to it. Otherwise I'm outta here! And if I go, I won't come back."

Her directness shocked the hell out of him, but she was right. So he pressed his knee into the hard gearshift and leaned toward her. She scooted over to join him, but they came together off center and his lips sort of slid onto her chin. She didn't seem to be discouraged; instead, she came back for another landing. This one was better, but when he tried to press in a little tighter his knee popped the gearshift out and they started to roll down the street. She laughed heartily, while he stomped on the floorboards trying to find the brake and clutch and put the truck back in gear. This time he put it in reverse, which was up and to the left. That put the knob away from the seat and gave him a chance to slip one leg under the shaft. Now the knob was between his knees. But when he pushed against Maria, attempting to kiss her again, she fell back against the door and complained that the window crank was digging into her shoulder blade. It was a clumsy beginning, a comedy of errors that progressed from one calamity to another, but Maria wouldn't let him quit until they got it right.

Chapter 22

On the Saturday following the accident, Sam kept the promise he'd made to Jennifer. He came to her house, rapped his knuckles against the black frame of the wooden screen door and waited for Jennifer's mom, who greeted him with: "Oh, it's you."

At the top of the stairs he tapped timidly on her door. Then after a long pause heard the squeak of her chair, followed by the sound of her voice calling out, "Yes?"

"It's only me," Sam whispered hoarsely through the thin oak panel.

He stuck his head in, but before stepping through the doorway he took a moment to assess her condition. The pajamas she wore were wrinkled. They were hers—not her father's cut down—but they still fit badly. The sleeves were rolled and the legs had been tacked up with safety pins to keep her from tripping over the cuffs when she walked. The fact that she had no makeup on and that her hair stood up wildly in the back made her look exceptionally plain, but Sam didn't care.

"Come in," she said, sounding pensive. He pushed the door further into the room and stepped uncertainly across the threshold. Freshly showered and well-scrubbed, he had done his best to look neat and presentable, though he hardly thought that she would notice.

"Hi Jennifer," he said brightly, "doing any better today?" Inside, he bubbled over with anxious energy and excitement.

"It's hard to tell, the pain medicine is making me woozy, but I'm too chicken to do without it," she answered with a murmur of frustration.

"Is it bad for me to be here?" he asked, before closing the door behind him.

"No way! You're the only one who seems to care."

"What about all your friends?"

"Well—Judy Mackey called again last night, but that's it. I know it sounds like I'm complaining..." She paused. "Oh hell, I *am* complaining. So what! I feel neglected and miserable and I want someone to feel miserable with me."

"I'm here," Sam offered, letting some of his enthusiasm escape in a smile so broad it made his cheeks hurt.

"Yes, but you're so damn full of good cheer that it spoils the whole mood!"

"Sorry. I suppose I could pretend to be bummed out."

"No, you're fine, it's me. I just need to break out of this funk."

"Can I help?"

"I hope so," she said. Then, tilting her head to one side and squinting, "This isn't some kind of a guilt trip—I mean—just because you broke my arm?"

"No way!" he shot back. "Why would you think that?"

"I don't know, I guess I'm feeling a little insecure right now," she admitted, then changed the subject, "What do you want to do?"

"Cards."

"Are you serious?"

"Yeah, I thought we could play a couple of hands of poker."

Sam removed the clock and lamp from the small nightstand next to her bed and set them on the floor, then slid the nightstand over in front of her chair. He reached into his pocket and pulled out a handful of copper pennies.

"For money?"

"Of course," he said. Reaching into his other pocket, he took out a pack of cards and a zip-lock bag full of more pennies and dumped them out on the nightstand

"That's not fair," she said, curling her lower lip. "You've got tons of pennies and I have none."

"We'll split them between us."

"Do you always come prepared?" Jennifer asked.

"No. I just thought it would be nice to have something to do." Sitting on the edge of her bed he snapped off the rubber band, shuffled the cards, and started to deal.

"There's one problem. How do I hold onto the cards and play with only one hand?"

"Your fingers are free of the cast," he said, touching the plaster where it bridged her knuckles. "Can you use them at all without pain?"

"I think so," she said, wiggling them back and forth experimentally.

"Well, stick the cards in your right hand and use your left to pick up and discard."

"Sounds like a plan, let's see if I can make it work," she said as she attempted to pick up the stray cards that had fallen into her lap. At first her right hand wouldn't cooperate and she fumbled and spilled the cards back onto the table. She complained that it felt like she was playing the game back-end-to, and that she had to consciously remember what to do with which hand.

As the game progressed her pile of pennies began to grow, and he realized, that handicapped or not, she was good at this.

Sam's own cluster of coins kept growing smaller, and he started to hoard the newest and shiniest pennies, with the dumb idea that this would somehow change his luck. When he finally shoved the last of his pennies into the pot and bent to study his cards, he wondered how he could possibly win with only a pair of jacks. And when she dropped three kings on the table and scraped the last of his money into her stash, he groaned and slumped forward on the table completely crestfallen.

"I won, I won!" she said in a voice that sounded like she was jumping up and down.

"Aw-right, already—you don't have to gloat."

"Sorry. I guess I got carried away. But I've only played this once before."

"Oh great," he said, flipping the cards from his last hand in the air, "I not only lose to a one-armed bandit, but now you're telling me I've lost to an amateur!"

"Don't get all bent out of shape."

"I know, I'm being a jerk. It's just that after I won the first pot you completely skunked me."

"It's still your money," she suggested, pushing the pile toward him.

"I know it is, but I want you to keep it anyway. I played a rotten game."

"Fine," she said, and opening the drawer to the nightstand she scooped the money into it and quickly slid it closed. "Let's do something else. How about some music?"

Sam stood up and moved the table aside, thinking that she had accepted the money too easily. She might have argued with him a little so that he could enjoy the sense of being magnanimous.

With the table out of the way, he stepped across the room to a short bookcase. On top was a stereo. He studied the buttons for a moment until he found the one marked *power,* then switched it on. The function knob was already set for *tape,* so he pressed the *play* button and waited.

As the sound of a drum and the clear notes from a piano filled the room, Jennifer slid down in her chair, and Sam returned to lay down crosswise in the middle of her bed, face up, feet dangling over the back edge. When Lionel Richie sang the words from Penny Love: "The first time I met you. . .you looked so fine", Sam laughed softly. When Jennifer gave him a what's-so-funny look, he swallowed his laughter and his belly started to shake the bed.

Here he was in the same room with this girl who only a week ago seemed so beautiful and so far out of reach he could hardly speak her name. Yes, she was still beautiful—but she was no longer out of reach, and in those wrinkled PJ's her beauty was no longer intimidating. He wondered, after all those weeks of anxiety, how he could ever have been so afraid of her?

The tape ended with Diana Ross singing "Touch Me in the Morning," After five minutes of silence Jennifer broke into the quiet afterglow with a thorny question. "Sam, what are you thinking—I mean right here, right now, what kind of thoughts are plowing through your head?"

Jockeying his elbows under him he lifted himself up off her bedspread and looked at her aghast. *What does she want me to say? Is this some kind of trick to get me to reveal something weird?* Then, flopping back down, he groaned.

"Ooooh," she said, tossing her head back and staring at the ceiling, "I know it sounds crazy, but I need to know."

"Why?" he asked, hoping she would change her mind.

"I can see you over there lying on my bed, so close that if I wanted I could reach out and touch you. But I don't want to touch you; I want to get inside—well, not exactly inside—not literally. I want to know stuff that no one else knows, to uncover dark meaningful things that you wouldn't normally reveal. Tell me something you've done that you shouldn't have—something naughty or forbidden. Or tell me something you wish for that you could never get."

He heard all this, was horrified by the intimacy of what she was asking and decided that his supposition that she was safe and ordinary needed rethinking. He wasn't sure if she was saying this directly to him or if it was just wishful thinking that had slipped out unintentionally. He pushed himself up on his elbows again so that he could scrutinize her face, trying to decide if she were really serious. Her prolonged silence implied that she was waiting for an answer.

"You can't be serious!" *She might as well ask me to get naked right here in front of her,* he thought. As soon as that image leapt to mind, he remembered Aunt Em's front porch. Jennifer had already confessed that she hadn't seen anything ; that she wasn't interested. But maybe she'd seen more than she dared to admit and then denied it out of pity. He knew he ought to let go of this, but he couldn't shake the idea that Karl was right—that he was a freak, and that girls would find him repulsive.

"Look I'm not asking for some kind of lurid confession;" she said, "I just want to know what's important to you. And I don't mean the little things like your favorite color or whether or not you're afraid of the dark, or how many girlfriends you've had. . ." There was a pause, "Actually I might like to know about the girlfriends." Then, when he gave her a painful grimace, she laughed—not a mocking laugh, but something lilting and playful.

"Where do you get these ideas? Even Winnie doesn't ask me about stuff like this."

"I have this bad habit of saying whatever pops into my head," she explained. "My mom thinks I'm too bookish. That I fill my mind with all kinds of psycho-drivel. She tells me I'm crazy—loco en la cabeza." Taking the finger on her good hand she waggled it in front of her forehead in the universal symbol. "But when you get to know me better . . ." she stopped to jockey herself up in the chair.

"And I want to know you better," Sam said.

"But that's my point, how can we do that if we can't ask each other honest questions and get honest answers?"

"Too much honesty can hurt," he observed, shifting his eyes to the pineapple design on the top of her bedpost.

"It's not like I'm asking to see your Johnny—at least not today," she added with a smile. It took a second to realize what she meant, and when he did he hung his head over the edge of her bed and mumbled, "This is too weird."

"Let's make it easy," she said, ignoring his discomfort. "Tell me why every time I saw you last summer, you were staring at me as if I were something good to eat, and yet you never once came over and talked to me."

"That's not fair! I can't tell you that—well I could, but I don't want to."

"If you can't, you can't," she said, turning away and raising her nose to indicate her disapproval.

"Okay, I'll try, but don't be hard on me," he begged.

"I promise—Scout's honor, hope to die," she said, crossing herself, then added, "a curse on my mother's grave." The earnest frown that came with her pledge was followed by a crooked smile.

"Your mother's not dead," Sam protested.

"True, but if she were, I'd swear," she said, raising her hand as if she were taking an oath. "Besides, I've never been a girl scout either."

"Good grief!" he said, then lay quiet for a moment trying to figure out how to begin. "Okay—well—to begin with," then he stopped. "Well, the first time I saw you, you looked great. I mean I about fell over and broke my neck when I saw you leaning over your porch railing the day you arrived."

"But that's what I mean. I hate that."

"I know, but you wanted me to be truthful."

"Can't you understand how awful it is to be gawked at all the time?"

"No. Well, in a way, I guess I can."

"When people stare at me—when they give me that look—it makes me crazy." The word crazy made him think of Karl.

"You never told me what you did with Karl Kristian."

"What?"

"That day he pinned you to the wall?"

"I cracked him in the ribs with the corner of my three ring binder and when he folded I took off."

"Hooo-boy,"

"I know it was cruel—but it was the only weapon I had at hand."

"No. Painful maybe but certainly not cruel," Sam observed. "You had to get him off you somehow."

"How do you know I'm not cruel?"she asked, turning to challenge him.

"Because of the way you treat Mrs. Eagan. Nobody talks to her. And her dog Pepper? I mean jeeze—the little bitch is just plain vicious. Yet every morning when she goes out to walk her dog you deliberately stop and greet her. It's the only time I ever see her smile. And the first time you knelt down to run your hand over Pepper's head, I thought she'd snap you fingers off, but she didn't—it about blew me away!"

"So her dog likes me—big deal."

"No, it's more than that. Dogs have an instinct about people and it gave me hope that one day I'd be able get up the courage to talk to you."

"What were you afraid of?"

"A lot of things. You tend to shut people out."

"Do I do that to everybody?"

"No—well maybe to guys—mostly to guys."

"Does sex make a difference then?"

"Say what?" he asked in dismay.

"You know—the fact that I'm a girl and you're a boy."

"Yes, I think—I guess it does. A couple of years ago it wouldn't have made any difference. I didn't used to like girls. Except for Winnie, and she doesn't count—as a girl, I mean. Not then, that is . . ." He was having a lot of trouble, and Jennifer was obviously amused, but she didn't interrupt—didn't do anything to help him out. "Things aren't that way now, I like girls—well, certain girls—even Winnie, but she's changed. Well—not changed—it's just that she's a girl; of course she was always a girl, but she's different—arrrgh! This sounds stupid."

"No it doesn't."

"Do you understand what I mean?"

"Not at all. But if you keep on going maybe I can figure it out."

"Can't we change the subject?" Sam asked, extending his arms and locking his fingers together in a pleading gesture.

"No."

"Why not?" The room seemed to grow small and hot, and when he lifted his arms off the bed they stuck to the knobby spread.

"First tell me, why you aren't afraid of me now?"

"After I smashed into your bike and broke your arm, I felt awful. I had to get past my fear, and once I did, the idea of my being afraid of you seemed a little ridiculous."

"So, the only way you could talk to me was to break my arm?"

"Noooo!"

"Just kidding," she said, scooting forward to sit on the edge of her chair. "Where do we go from here?"

"What do you mean?"

"Well, do we just become friends or should we be lovers?"

He shot bolt upright and swung his feet over the edge of her bed as if he were about to escape. "Lovers?"

"No, not like that! I just meant go together—date, that sort of thing."

"Oh."

"Course a little booty couldn't hurt."

"How's that?" he asked, leaning so far forward that he nearly flipped head over heels onto the floor.

"Cool it, Sam. I'm only pulling your leg," she said, and reaching out she tugged on the toe of his sneaker.

"Right. I knew that," he answered, trying to laugh, but it came out more like a burp.

"Get off my bed," she said, slapping his the toe of his shoe again, "and come over here and give me a kiss. Then go tell my mom that I'm hungry."

Her request for a kiss surprised Sam, but he only hesitated for a second before he jumped off her bed, then took one large step and leaned dutifully over her chair. Jennifer reached up with her good arm and grabbed his shirtfront, pulling him closer so that she could take her kiss. When her lips first brushed his their touch was so light and tentative that it tickled, then she gave a quick tug on his collar and brought her lips hard against his. Next, her lips curled back and the edge of her teeth gently captured his lower lip. When she pulled away he felt a sharp pinch and let out a yelp of surprise. The kiss had lasted only a moment, not long enough to raise any real passion, but her action and his reaction shook him.

"Mmmm!" he murmured, testing the spot where she'd nibbled on his lip with his finger.

"Now go," she said, pushing against his hip to get him moving.

His first step tripped him up and he stumbled on the way to the door. "Oops," he said, then he went downstairs to tell Mrs. Hollypepper that her daughter wanted lunch. That resulted in an invitation to join them and he willingly accepted.

Before he had a chance to go and tell Jennifer, he saw her through the doorway coming down the hall toward the kitchen, and noticed that along the way she had picked up an old printed robe. Somehow she had gotten it over her good arm and let the other sleeve hang free while she gathered the rest around her, clutching the collar together in a gesture of modesty that surprised him; especially considering that she hadn't seen a need for that extra covering while they were alone together in her room.

She had jammed her feet into a pair of old slippers. Her hair was a mess, and when she turned to greet her mother he saw that it was matted where she had flattened it into the back of her chair. Standing across from him, leaning against the kitchen counter, looking frumpy and unfashionable, he couldn't imagine how she could be any more unattractive. But he really didn't care.

They ate and talked, and laughed.

As they sat facing each other, Jennifer reached across the table and pushed the stray locks of hair away from his eyes. The gesture suggested nothing more than kindness; his hair, thick and unkempt, always needed attention, but when her fingers raked his scalp the roots tingled and a shiver went down his spine. Later, when the sleeve of her robe brushed the back of his hand as she picked up the ketchup next to his elbow, he felt the same shivery excitement. At the end of the meal he pushed his empty plate away, and seeking some relief for his full stomach he slid down in his chair and banged his knees against hers. One knee jostled her bandage, which made Jennifer wince. He could see that it was still painful, but she didn't utter any complaint.

The stroke of her fingers in his hair surely wasn't meant to entice, and the brush of her sleeve across his hand, and the touch of knee to knee under the table were certainly accidental, yet he couldn't help thinking that these things were important. It seemed like this was some special sort of game, only he didn't understand all the rules.

He stayed until the light in the kitchen grew soft in the late afternoon sun and finally left about five-thirty. The walk home covered old and familiar ground, and one foot followed another, as they always had, but his feet didn't quite seem to reach the pavement.

He came upon an empty soda can and kicked it absentmindedly while he recalled the day's experience. The kiss that Jennifer had demanded from him in her room and the one that she gave him a moment ago, as he was getting ready to leave, hadn't been particularly passionate, but together they had given him a wonderful sense of well-being.

It was hard to accept the notion that this girl was interested in him. They were such an unlikely pair. The idea that she liked him and that he liked her excited him, but he hardly believed that anything as complicated as falling in love could be as simple as liking and being liked. He expected the experience to be dreamy and surreal, and right now, though his head felt light and fuzzy, he knew he wasn't dreaming.

Chapter 23

Working together was awkward now, but Sarah did her best to keep things as they were before, afraid that others might gossip if they thought that an office romance was in the works. Actually her actions were probably more suspect than she believed. If she had done nothing it would have been okay; instead she tried too hard for normalcy and that created all kinds of speculation. Mary was the first to notice the change especially with Martin, but instead of spreading the news, she came to Sarah for verification. Mary had shown an interest in Sarah from the first day, but she had known Martin for much longer and therefore her loyalty went to him.

"So, what's up?" Mary asked one afternoon, stopping by Sarah's workstation on the pretext of giving her the latest memo from the home office.

"What do you mean?"

"Martin is acting strange and you're definitely not your usual self so I figure there has to be a connection."

"Not necessarily," Sarah hedged.

"Give me a break. You know I'll find out anyway, so why make me work for it?"

"Ohhhh, alright, we've been out a couple of times, but that's it."

"Not so. I may have misread you, but I know Martin and he's definitely been smitten."

"Do you think so?" she asked, turning away from her keyboard to read Mary's face.

"Definitely!" Mary winked, then went back to her desk.

The idea that Martin had been *smitten* was an agreeable one, but she still had a hard time believing that she was the cause.

Sarah had been out with Martin several times since that night at the movies. They had gone to dinner at Georgio's and then dancing (which after years of neglect she did badly). Martin did much better—maybe because he knew where he was going and she could only try to follow his lead. They spent a Saturday afternoon bowling, then bought some fried chicken and brought it back to Sarah's house. The following Friday they went to a local play (some high school seniors taking an awkward stab at *Rome & Juliet*) and just yesterday they had managed to sneak out of the bank for a quick lunch at Sally's.

In between there had been evenings in her living room or his, where they had supposedly come together to watch TV or a video, but mostly they talked. Nothing very deep or intimate was discussed, nevertheless these conversations were remarkably revealing. In everything they did together she found a commonality of spirit, which helped to pull her deeper and deeper into Martin's web. And as he wound her into a cottony cocoon, instead of the fear of being trapped, she felt sheltered and safe.

Sarah uncovered a mutual interest in classical music and jazz and she already knew that he liked old movies, which had led them to rent "Notorious" and "North by Northwest"—and last night they had watched "Father Goose." Martin had chosen these titles because Sarah had told him of her fondness for Cary Grant. It was nice to know that he was listening. She had even exposed a couple of Martin's bad habits, which proved she wasn't so enamored that she couldn't recognize his faults. He often draped his coat over the back of the chair, and she caught him once with his feet on the coffee table (no shoes, thank goodness). And he always left the hand towels on the bathroom sink instead of hanging them up on the towel bar—but then Sam did the same thing.

The most disturbing part of their relationship was the subtle passion that was growing between them. Her eager desire, for something physical, was foreign to her; she'd never felt that way before. But as strong as those feelings were she hadn't acted upon them. She hadn't invited him to share her bed or suggested a morning-after breakfast together, though she might have done it all, if Martin had nudged her in that direction. Instead he seemed to know instinctively how destructive that would be. Her life with Robert had been so sordid and debilitating that even the thought of anything more than a kiss or a hug frightened her. She didn't know how much Martin understood about her fears, but he treated her with such tenderness, showed her such respect and restraint that he had to know something.

Had he heard rumors? Should she tell him? Gossip always got so distorted. How could she explain why she spent so many years with a man who had abused her? Still, what she told him would be more accurate than the things he'd heard from God knows where. She was confused and conflicted, but all that conflict seemed to dissolve as soon as she was in his presence and the need to explain seemed to disappear as well.

It was very hard to be near him and not reach out and touch him, and that was especially difficult while they were at work. Before, Martin had been the one to make excuses to see her or to be nearby, and he still did, but now those efforts were doubled as Sarah looked for similar excuses. She even stole a kiss once when they were alone in the copy room. And while she passed secret signals to him, hoping that no one would notice, she could tell by the nervous smiles of her coworkers that she wasn't fooling anyone. It had to be evident to them that she and Martin were no longer just boss and employee.

Chapter 24

Halloween was only two days away and Martin was looking for Sarah to invite her to a costume party. Something his neighbor Laura had thrown together. He hadn't worn make-up or donned a mask or any kind of disguise since he was twelve, and the idea of wearing such an outfit now made him feel foolish. But if it meant a chance to be with Sarah he'd wear any costume, no matter how silly.

He found her in the lunchroom fighting with the soda machine. It had taken her money but refused to give up the Coke that she had selected. Pushing the button repeatedly and pounding ineffectively against the heavy cabinet, she didn't hear Martin approach. When his hand came around her waist she screamed and he swung her around and kissed her.

The scream didn't last long, but it <u>was</u> high and shrill, and Ms. Saunders, the loan officer, came rushing in to investigate. Caught in the act Martin stepped away and stood next to the soda machine, arms folded trying hard to look nonchalant. He started tapping his fingers nervously on his elbows which put a sudden picture in his mind of Ed Sullivan (host of the long-running TV variety show) and he wondered if Ms. Saunders saw the similarity.

When he discovered Sarah alone, he thought that a silent ambush would be harmless. He expected Sarah to squirm and slip out of his grasp, but he never imagined that she would scream.

Sarah must have seen the expression of guilt on Martin's face as he looked first at the floor and then up at the ceiling, because she began to laugh, and he started to laugh with her. A rich deep belly laugh that caused him to hold on to his sides, and when he turned to look at Ms. Saunders he saw her hugging the opposite wall as if she had stepped into a madhouse.

Sarah's laughing had become almost hysterical and Ms. Saunders glanced from one to the other and then backed out of the room. Martin suspected that she would stop the first person she met and tell them that he and Sarah had gone nuts.

Sarah sat down in one of the plastic chairs that surrounded the lunch table and used the back of her hand to wipe the gleeful tears from her eyes. Martin took the seat next to her. He reached across to take hold of her hand, but she pulled it away suddenly to remove several tissues from her pocket and he missed. While she carefully blew her nose, he found his hand suspended in midair and he sheepishly let it drop to his side.

"I'm sorry I frightened you. Who did you think was putting his arms around you anyway, the Boston Strangler?" he asked.

"No, I would have reacted the same way no matter who it was. I was so angry with that stupid machine that I was about to scream anyway."

"Well, our secret is out now. That is, supposing we hadn't already given it away."

"Do you really care?" she asked.

"No. I'm actually relieved. I don't know what I thought would happen or why I thought it should be hidden. I guess I was worried about appearances, especially considering that I'm your boss."

"It's hard to imagine what she must be telling them. I hope she doesn't think badly of me: you know, girl chases boss until boss catches girl—then girl screams," she added with an impish grin.

"Badly? Are you serious? They might come after me, but not you. They all adore you!"

"Honestly?" she asked in surprise. "I never thought of myself as having any enemies, but I hardly believed that people cared that much either."

"You really don't see it, do you? Hasn't anyone ever told you how beautiful you are?"

"Not that I can remember. Am I so unusual?" she asked.

Martin thought that she seemed uncomfortable with the idea that she was anything other than ordinary. Perhaps it was easier for her to believe she was plain and uninteresting. "Yes," he said, "but somehow I have the feeling that you're not happy about that."

She didn't answer. She just brought a tissue to her nose, but stopped short and crumpled it in her hand instead.

"Sarah, there's nothing wrong with being attractive."

"I know—I know. It's just that I've gotten used to the idea of blending into the wall. I guess I feel safer that way."

"You hardly blend into the wall."

When she looked away, Martin realized that he was embarrassing her. It was disheartening to think that she was embarrassed by the idea that she was attractive and that people admired her. How awful, he thought, if she had lived her whole life and never had anyone tell her that she was worthy of such admiration.

He suspected that her relationship with her dead husband had something to do with her tendency toward self-deprecation. He didn't know how much damage had been done, but he'd heard stories and knew what alcoholism could do. Which is why he tried so hard to move slowly and not cue up old emotions or rub against painful memories.

"I love you, Sarah, and that's not something I ever expected to say again. Well, at least not in that way—that is, in the way of a man and a woman." To his ear the words sounded hackneyed and trite, and he felt like an idiot for saying them. Her eyes fluttered and her mouth dropped and he knew he'd spoken too soon. "Sorry, I shouldn't have said that."

"No, you shouldn't," she answered. She pulled her hands off the table and buried them in her lap, pressing them into her gut as if she had a sudden stomachache.

"Don't you see the influence you have over me?" Martin said, trying to save the situation. "The power you have to rob me of my senses and destroy my good judgement?"

"I can see that you're clumsy when you're around me. But that's not love. Is it?"

"Not all by itself," he said.

"Then what is?"

"I know what I feel," he answered.

"Yes, but feelings can be deceptive."

"How's that?" he asked.

"They're too whimsical and impractical. My whole life has been a dark comedy full of mistakes and failure. I'm not going to allow something as unreliable as my feelings to lead me into another disaster," she said, bringing her hands up and gripping the edge of the table, as if that solid object would somehow help ground her in reality.

"Everyone makes mistakes, some of them deadly. That's life. The question is: was it worth the risk?"

"And what makes it worth the risk?" she said, staring down at her blanched fingers.

"Love—happiness."

"For some reason happiness has always eluded me. And love?" Sarah stopped, threw her head back, and groaned.

"Yes?"

"Well," she said, bringing her head down, eyes narrow, lips straight, "that's something that always seems to be just beyond my reach."

"But you must feel something?" he said, wondering if his instincts had deceived him.

"Oh, I do. But I can't—I won't let myself. . ."

"Promise me one thing," he interjected.

"It depends."

"Promise me that you won't let your fears get the better of you." He covered her wrist with his hand and made her let go of the table. "And one day when you can learn to trust your feelings—then we can take the next logical step and—"

"And sleep together," Sarah cut in.

"No—nooo," he said, tightening his hold on her wrist. "Sarah, you can't think that. I know that's the general perception nowadays, but not for me. What I started to say is that we ought to get married."

"Martin!" she said. "Martin," she repeated in a whisper, and nothing else. She pulled her wrist free and wrapped her arms around herself as if she were suddenly cold.

◆ ◆ ◆

Why is he doing this? Why is he pushing? I've only known him for a few weeks and he's already talking about marriage. He's still a stranger. No, that's not true.

She knew it didn't make any sense, but she couldn't call him a stranger. From the beginning she had had an intrinsic understanding that they were connected—not a familial connection, but something deeper, something more esoteric. The first palpable stirrings had come while she shared her ice cream with him at Sally's and again with more urgency during their first kiss. Still, she wasn't ready for the kind of commitment that he suggested. "I can't—Martin—I can't marry you. I'm not ready."

His face clouded over and he looked disappointed—defeated. "You misunderstood," he said, shaking his head. "Things being the way they are these days, after my wife died, I might have had lots of affairs. I was lonely and I can't say I wasn't tempted, but whatever excuse I might have found it would have felt like cheating. "I—I only meant that if we loved each other, the next step ought to be marriage."

"Martin, I'm sorry. I won't say maybe and I won't say never, but . . ." she hesitated, and Martin waited.

"In the short time that we've been together I've been happy and I want to hold onto that, but I can't shake the idea that I don't deserve to be happy. And please don't tell me that's illogical. I know that doesn't make any sense, but it doesn't have to. If that's confusing to you, think what it's doing to me. I've never known the kind of love you're talking about, so you'll have to forgive me if I seem a little disoriented."

She couldn't tell him how desperately she wanted that kind of love. How much she wished she could return his proposal and accept his offer of marriage. But to do that she would have to be a very different person than she was right now.

◆ ◆ ◆

How could she have been with her husband all those years and not loved or been loved in return? There was nothing in Martin's experience that might help him understand what that meant, or what it might be like. He couldn't put the blame on her, so he had to assume that her husband had been a fool. It saddened him to imagine that kind of deprivation, but he knew she wouldn't want his pity, so he remained silent.

For a moment he was afraid to look at her. He wanted to reach out to her, but the distance across the table seemed infinite. Finally he lifted his eyes slowly to meet hers and saw her smile. It came cautiously at first and then grew until it was broad, and curved, and brave, but it couldn't hide the sadness in her eyes.

Touched by this plucky display of courage, he started to speak, but the clock on the wall behind her caught his attention. When he saw the lateness of the hour he panicked. "Look at the time. We've got to get back."

Without a word, Sarah scraped her chair noisily and rose to leave. As she passed the vending machine, Martin heard the clatter of her delinquent soda dropping down the chute. He followed her out of the lunchroom, then veered off to his office. Neither one of them stopped to retrieve the cold soda waiting in the tray at the bottom of the machine.

A quick line of people formed in front of Sarah's window and she wasn't able to consider anything except meeting their demands.

Martin wasn't so lucky. Oh, he had work to do, piles of it, but alone in his office he couldn't bring himself to concentrate on the papers in front of him. Why had he spoken so precipitously? To reveal so much of his feelings now was stupid, And why in the lunchroom? Cluttered and dirty, and smelling of yesterday's garbage, what could possibly be more unromantic? At least she hadn't said no, or told him that she never wanted to see him again. Then suddenly he realized that his original intent had been to ask her to a Halloween party.

He supposed there was no hope for him. He should have known that he wasn't up to dating again. Then he corrected himself. *That's silly. I was never any good at dating.* Even with Maria he'd often made a fool of himself. She was just smart enough to know what she wanted and when she saw that he was out of his element she just worked around it. She guided him through a two-year passage from clueless adolescent to young adult and then drew a proposal out of him word by word, by simply saying—*Yes*—over and over every time he got stuck. Now he was dealing with someone who didn't know what she wanted and he was the one who would have to lead the way.

Chapter 25

When Sarah returned home from work she took a long hot shower. Then, wrapped in a thick terry robe, she lay down on top of her bed to think. Martin's proposal of marriage had been a shocking one, but it had not been entirely unwelcome. She liked Martin well enough, in fact more than well enough, but right now she was not ready to make that kind of commitment. It was flattering that he felt that way, even if in the end he had half taken it back.

If she stripped away all the garbage that was cluttering her mind and was totally honest with herself, she might admit that she was in love with Martin. In fact if she were willing to abolish all the objections that she continually threw in the way of that idea, she might recognize the unfamiliar fire burning inside as passion. Why, then, was she so reluctant? Digging deeper, she discovered that the real answer to that conundrum was buried in her past. Long past.

She thought back to when she was a teenager, back to the time when she had first met Robert. He wasn't very handsome, but he was outgoing and gregarious and that was terribly important to her. She was too withdrawn and she needed someone aggressive enough to draw her out. And Robert did that, though it probably wasn't by design. He would keep talking until she felt compelled to answer. At first it was just a word and that meekly given; eventually she managed to speak whole sentences. In time she began to enjoy a meager degree of confidence. It wasn't astounding, but it was a milestone for her, considering she was normally taciturn and reserved even around her family.

She didn't have any real boyfriend and so when Robert asked her out on a date she was delighted. She said yes; only yes, but it was sufficient.

They were together off and on for a year. He left her more than once to date other girls, but usually only went out with them once or twice before returning to Sarah and begging her to take him back.

In Robert's senior year he invited her to his prom. Sarah felt like she was living in a dream. She hadn't entertained any hope of going to the prom, especially with someone older, and Robert was nineteen. Looking back, he may have been a couple of years ahead of his classmates, but he wasn't any more mature.

For Sarah, it was the Cinderella story, except that when she thought about it, Robert wasn't exactly a prince and she tended to feel more like one of the ugly stepsisters. Still, she was young and naive and the evening seemed full of promise.

When they arrived in the parking lot outside of Dreamworld everyone had a bottle and offers came from all sides. Sarah took some with the others, though she wasn't comfortable doing it. She had never had alcohol before, but she wanted to belong, wanted to be daring and rebellious. And she told herself that she would only have a taste, just a sip. But there were so many who kept shoving something in her hand that even a sip became too much. And on top of that, Robert had his own bottle, and he kept encouraging her to take another swallow. Her stomach rebelled and she excused herself. She never made it to the little girl's room; instead she threw up on the grass in front of one of the cars. When she came back to the dance there were more offers to drink, and sick or not, she was afraid to say no. It was the beginning of a disastrous evening.

The day after the prom all that she could recall were scattered images and tactile sensations that made her skin crawl. Between hugging the toilet and trying to deal with a head that seemed poised to explode like a giant zit, she was only able to pull back bits and pieces of the her wild escapade. Some of those blurry flashbacks were lewd and disgraceful, and because she couldn't get all the pieces to come together she began to panic. By Sunday afternoon those images began to fall into place and when the grainy pictures started to flicker garishly in the wasted recesses of her memory, she saw Robert's twisted face, smelled his foul breath, and felt the touch of his rough hands as they searched the soft mounds and hollows of her midsection. Something hard and blunt poked at her belly then came lower and lower until it invaded the soft folds of the pudendum. Suddenly she felt a sharp pain and knew that she had been penetrated—after that a blessed darkness enveloped her. But now, two days later, the memory of that cruel invasion seemed more real than the act itself and she whimpered as if it she could feel the pain all over again. Once that vicious spasm faded, there was the terrible realization that she had become the victim of her own stupid folly, and for a week she buried herself in an agony of guilt and despair.

Out of that awful beginning came an equally awful marriage that she clung to obsessively for seventeen years. Not out of love, but because of the perverted idea that she had to restore her virtue. Instead she destroyed that virtue by entering into a dishonorable union without any respect or understanding of its sacredness. All this time she had clung to the idea that she was a dutiful wife trying to save her husband from the demon of alcoholism and protect her only child from a fatherless upbringing, when in reality she had been too paralyzed by fear to end it.

Now she saw that no one else would have been so stupid, they would have seen the absurdity of all this from the start and rejected it. Only she was weak enough to believe that marrying Robert and sticking it out could bring her some kind of salvation. Now, lying here on her bed, she felt angry—angry with herself, angry at the world she lived in and the dullness of the life she had created for herself. It was all such a waste! This long introspection that had been exhausting, and she suddenly felt drained and defeated. She lifted her head and slid cautiously off the periwinkle bedspread and planted her feet on the cool hardwood floor. Concentrating on the knot at her waist she undid the cloth belt and let the terry robe fall in a bunch on the floor near her feet. Without dressing for bed she pulled back the covers and scooted between the sheets. Drawing her knees upward and tucking one hand beneath her pillow, she soon carried this awful turmoil into the dark melancholy of her dreams.

Chapter 26

When Sam got home and found the house in darkness he went from room to room in search of his mother. Mounting the stairs, he heard the third step creak under his weight and thought of his dad trying to sneak in after a binge. He tapped on his mother's door and when there was no answer he opened it a crack and peeked in. He could see her frail form huddled beneath the covers, heard her shallow breathing and knew that she had fallen asleep.

He brought the door slowly back until he heard the click of the latch, then crept down the stairs and made his way to the kitchen. Opening and closing cabinets and poking at items in the refrigerator he tried to determine what he wanted to eat. With his limited skills in cooking he decided that scrambled eggs would do. He chopped up half an onion, added salt and pepper and tossed in some oregano for good measure, then toasted some bread and lathered it with peanut butter. In a few minutes time, he was sitting in front of the TV with the volume turned low, eating his half-burned half-runny eggs and sucking on a can of warm soda. Not the best meal he'd ever had, but it filled the hole in his stomach. Rummaging in the freezer he dug out the last of the vanilla ice cream. Eating straight out of the container, he finished it off. And in spite of the egg-encrusted frying pan, a pile of dirty dishes and the mess on the stove and the counter, he'd managed to do all this without waking his mother.

When a string of ads came on and he had the time to think about it, he wondered what in the world had possessed her to rush off to bed so early in the evening. But then she'd been acting oddly ever since she started dating her boss. For one thing he and his mother weren't taking their meals together: sometimes breakfast, but never supper. Still she always had something ready for him to heat in the microwave. *Maybe it's just a woman thing,* he thought as he scrunched up in the chair and watched a rerun of "All in the Family." He had an inkling that there might be something here to worry about, but right now he couldn't bring himself to concentrate on anything that complicated.

Chapter 27

Since their unfortunate accident—or perhaps fateful would be a better description—Sam and Jennifer had become fast friends and nearly constant companions. She was back in school, but he still spent his afternoons and Saturdays at her place. In the beginning, he brought her homework from school, then stayed to help her. They continued to study together, but he didn't have to do her written assignments anymore. Now with the paper turned almost upside down so that her hand didn't cover the words, she began to master a jiggly sideways print that looked almost readable. Because she tended to be the only one who could decipher it whenever she had a composition or a lengthy paper due he would take her dictation. The teachers knew that he was helping her, so they didn't get suspicious when they saw that her new scribble had been replaced by his part print, part cursive handwriting.

She was smart; especially in English and history, and they were on equal ground in science, but he always lost her in math. She did all right with geometry because it was visual, but formulas and equations left her completely in the dark. Her body mended swiftly and she adjusted well enough to her handicaps. So much so that after the first two weeks he really didn't have a reason to be there any more, but since she didn't send him away, he kept on coming. Twice her mother had asked him to stay for supper, and after a brief call home he had accepted. Now it was another Friday evening and again he had been asked to join the family for supper.

After the meal, he and Jennifer left the table and went to sit on the couch in the living room. She snatched up the remote and switched on the TV then leaned back into the softness of the sofa and rubbed her good shoulder against his. Except for the light flickering from the screen the room was dark, which made it feel close and warm. They were alone. Her parents were busy with chores in the kitchen on the other side of the house. The sound of their voices and the clatter of dishes and pans drifted into the room. Sam had noticed that whenever he came to visit, even if her mother and father were at home, they were seldom visible, and he was curious to know if that was just accidental. Not that he suspected Jennifer of any conspiracy, but they did have long periods of privacy, especially when they were in her room, where they might become intimate and no one would have been there to stop her—him—them.

Tonight Sam was in a particularly serious mood and though he watched the picture on the screen in front of him he wasn't concentrating much on the plot. Instead he worried about his mother and Martin; they spent more and more of their evenings together, which left him to come home to an empty house. True that gave him more time to pursue Jennifer, but he didn't see that as a fair trade. He wanted to spread his affection to more than one flower, but he didn't think that his mother ought to be allowed to do the same. It was selfish and irrational to think that his mother should sit at home alone while he went out to have a good time, but he couldn't be rational when it came to sharing her with anyone else. And the idea of her having a boyfriend affected him in the same way as someone running their fingernails down a chalkboard.

He had been so engrossed that he wasn't aware Jennifer had been creeping up on him. Now, he caught a peripheral glimpse of her and realized that she had been steadily closing the gap between. Inch by inch she had sidled across the cushion until she had him firmly pressed into the pillow at his side. Now she reminded him of a cat who has cornered it's prey but has decided to play with it before jumping in for the kill.

Jennifer wore a loose billowy top with large armholes that gave her the same waif-like appearance that had been her fashion since the accident and which still made her look vulnerable. Except in this case he was the one who seemed to be at risk.

Discreetly he removed the pillow at his side and let it fall softly to the floor. That gave him three inches and he took it all in a quick hop to his right. Jennifer followed after him and trapped him solidly against the bulky armrest. Then she leaned in to whisper in his ear and her breath dusted the soft lobe with wicked little puffs that made him scrunch his shoulder and twist his head, in order to save himself from the tickles.

Her didn't exactly want her to stop this playful assault, but each time she blew in his ear the level of sensitivity increased and when he felt the touch of her wet tongue he couldn't stand it any longer. In an effort to get away he straightened his legs and the slippery taffeta upholstery let him slide down out of her reach. But he pushed too hard, and his body slithered completely off the couch. Now he found himself sitting on the floor with his head tipped back on the cushion, staring up into Jennifer's pretty face.

She pinched her mouth together in a tight little 'O' trying to suppress a laugh, which came out anyway mostly through her nose. It escaped in an elongated honk, which sent him into a spasm of laughter that rocked the couch. Then she dove in sideways and slid her wet lips across his. Without disconnecting she adjusted her position until she had perfectly captured his lips under her own, and when she pulled away, she made a kind of suckling sound like a baby leaving its mother's breast. Caught off guard, he could hardly breathe, and as soon as he was free he took in a great gulp of air. "Holy—" he swallowed hard, "moly what brought that on?"

There was no answer. Instead she glided off the couch and plopped down beside him and without hesitation she kissed him again, this time sweeping the line of his chin with the silky edge of her lips then licking him with her tongue.

"You're getting me all wet!" he grimaced.

"So?"

"So stop." She did, but began to probe his waist instead.

"Is this better?" she asked.

"Yes—no! I mean, it tickles," he answered in sweet confusion.

"It's supposed to tickle," she said trying again.

"Cut it out!" he complained, grabbing her wrist. But she twisted loose and he had to tuck in his stomach to stay out of reach of her long fingers. This time he fell over on his side and rolling onto his back he looked up at her and asked: "What's gotten into you tonight?"

"Nothing. I'm just trying to have some fun."

"Yeah, well this kind of fun can get us into trouble."

"I won't break you know." She tried to poke him in the ribs, but she wasn't very accurate as a lefty and hit him solidly in the solar plexus, which put him in some distress.

"No, but I will," he groaned. "And besides you're a girl and—"

"Yeah, I know—me girl, you boy—sooo?"

"So, no horseplay," he said, slapping her hand as she started to walk her fingers up the buttons of his shirt.

"Ouch!" she said, shaking her hand to take away the sting. "Why not?"

"Because—"

"It isn't proper," she said, ending his sentence.

"Well, it isn't."

"Don't be such a prude! It's the eighties, for cryin' out loud."

He would have loved to stroke her hair, stretch out one of her long curls, test the softness of her breast, and if he'd had the license of a child he could do those things with impunity. But at fifteen he couldn't claim that kind of innocence.

"I'm not a prude, and the fact that it's the eighties doesn't change the rules," he answered. "If we were children it would all be in good fun. But we're not children—"

"And that makes it wrong," she finished. "Are you afraid I might touch your Willie or you might touch one of my boobies? Would that be so unforgivable?"

"No it's not unforgivable," he said, "but why should either of us suffer the embarrassment, even if it's unintentional?"

"Why should we be embarrassed?"

Her question took him by surprise and he stared at her in disbelief.
"Are you still afraid of me?" she asked, when he didn't answer
her.

"Sometimes."

"I thought you were past that."

"I am—mostly—except when you get like this. . ."

"Is it so wrong to show a little affection?"

"No," he said, feeling slight abashed. "It's more than that."

"Like what?"

"You jump into everything feet first," he said sitting up, "as if
nothing ever bothers you—as if there's never any consequence. Maybe
you know what you're doing, but I don't. This is all new to me. I mean,
when it comes to the physical stuff, I'm pretty much of a zero."

"Are you serious?" she asked pushing his shoulder roughly and
making him fall on his back again. He felt helpless looking up at her while
she waved her broken arm as if she might hit him with it.

"What's so surprising about that? I don't know how to—"

"No, no, no—I can't buy that," she objected. "For one thing
when I kissed you, you definitely kissed back. And for someone who
doesn't know how, you've certainly been pushing all the right buttons."

"Really?"

"Really," she said, smiling down on him.

"I thought I was kinda clumsy," Sam said, as he pushed himself
up off the floor and shifted his butt so that he could lean his back against
the edge of the couch.

"You are; but that's what makes it such a turn on."

"I don't get it."

"Think about it. If you were that good, I'd have to worry about
who you've been practicing with."

"So being bad is good?"

"Exactly," she said, tweaking the lobe of his ear as if it were the
pull chain on a light. "Tell me, do you ever wonder what if?"

"What'diya mean?"

"What if you didn't have to pretend—if you didn't always have to
get it right, if you could really be yourself and not worry about making
mistakes. Wouldn't it be a lot easier if we could live life as it comes and
not wonder all the time if other people will approve?"

"I don't know, that's a lot of ifs," he postulated.

"Sooooo!"

"So, I like to worry."

"You're hopeless."

"I hope not," he said, with a goofy smile that was too toothy to be
believed. Jennifer kicked his ankle with her big toe

"Ow!" He pulled up his leg and rubbed the spot.

"Serves you right."

"You're mean," he said.

"Loosen up."

"You'll have to show me how."

"Ha—ha," she said, mocking.

"Can't we just go back to the part where we kiss?"

"Yes," she said, and used her fingers to comb her hair back from her face so that he would have a clear path to her lips. His first attempt seemed too light, and a little off target. But when he came back to try again she responded with such urgency that she nearly knocked him over. And when they were finished, and his pucker had become unpuckered, he felt lightheaded and shaky and wondered if Jennifer felt the same way. Since she'd encouraged him to be honest, he decided to ask.

"When we kiss like that, does it do anything to you?"

"What?" she asked, looking straight into his eyes.

He thought she knew what he was asking, but the bewildered expression on her face made him wish he could take it back. "I mean does it do anything to you here," he said, touching his stomach. "Or here?" he said, putting a finger to his forehead.

Jennifer's answer came in a single word, "BOING!

"What do you mean?"

"It's sort of like stretching a rubber band until it snaps—boing! It keeps building and building. While it's happening, it's incredible, but when it's over, it's over."

She spoke as if she understood something he didn't. Yet for all her enthusiasm, his instincts told him that she didn't have any more experience with kissing than he did.

"I liked it too," he said—a gross understatement. The experience was a hell of a lot more complicated than that, but he couldn't find the words to describe it. While they were mouth-to-mouth, he felt a gentle quiver at the base of his spine in that little curved bone that looks like a rudimentary tail. And that quiver affected a nervous current which crossed over to that other boneless tail in front, moving eagerly from root to tip. In the beginning this movement didn't seem particularly alarming, but the longer they were engaged, the more insistent it became and the more it threatened to erupt. And when their lips finally parted he suffered a terrible anxiety as if some needful thing had gone unfinished. He considered sharing these feelings with Jennifer, but he couldn't do it. He decided that he would only get the words all wrong and she'd end up thinking he was crazy.

Chapter 28

$\mathcal{S}$arah awoke early the next morning with the foggy dawn peeking under the partially drawn shades. It must have been a rough night, because her blanket had fallen to the floor and the bottom sheet had pulled loose from the corners of the mattress. The top sheet, crumpled up around her hips and upper legs, left her body uncovered above the waist and her thick auburn hair lay across her face filtering the muted light from her eyes. Turning her head and brushing away her hair, she looked up at the fan that seemed to be falling toward her as it turned slowly round and round in the center of the gray-white ceiling. Shaking loose from the remnants of her last dream, she felt groggy and disoriented. Unconscious of her condition, she turned and lifted her head off the downy pillow to squint at the digital clock. It was five-fifty. But seen through her blurry eyes, it might just as well have been forty-eleven. Coming to a half-recumbent position she shook her head to clear the cottony webs that were still clouding her brain and realized that she had to work today.

It was terribly early, but she knew she wouldn't be able to sleep again, so she untwisted the sheet that trapped her midsection and slipped off the bed. Eyes half-closed, she brushed her foot against her discarded robe, and padded barefoot across the hall to the bathroom. Only then, as she stood facing the mirror above the sink, did she open her sleepy eyes and realize that she was completely naked. What if she had run into Sam? Thankfully, at this hour, he was sleeping soundly in his own bed.

Looking at her reflection, she could see lines across her face where she had pressed it into the folds of her pillowcase, and there were similar creases on her shoulder, above her breasts, and across her stomach from the crumpled sheet that had been wrapped around her middle. Little pieces of last night came trickling back, breaking into her thoughts with painful sharpness. Each brought a reminder of her wasted life, but she refused to dwell upon them. Turning away from the mirror, she opened the shower curtain and reached in to start the water.

An hour later, clean and dressed, her wet hair combed and slicked back away from her face, she sat alone at the kitchen table poking her spoon distractedly at her cereal. She kept trying to sink the little O's, but they persisted in rising to the top, escaping with a circle of bubbles as they popped up around the edge of her spoon. She wasn't really hungry, but she felt that she ought to eat something to sustain her through the workday ahead. Martin would be there when she arrived, and after his proposal yesterday she knew it would be troublesome to face him again.

Last night she had come to a decision. She finally accepted the fact that she had lost all those years pretending to be a victim when in fact she had been a damn fool. But that discovery was not as devastating as she had supposed. Her self-deprecating journey into the past had reopened a lot of old wounds, but now that she had scraped them clean she was surprised to find that there was enough substance left inside that pink slippery mess to make her life worth living. All she had to do was forgive herself and move on. Put aside her old mistakes, and make new ones— well, not necessarily mistakes, this time she hoped to get things right.

She had already decided that she needed to change her habits. Although going to bed at six o'clock and sleeping for almost twelve hours wasn't intended to be one of those new habits.

But there were other changes she could make. Like learning to accept a compliment without checking first to see if they were talking to her or somebody else. And she needed to accept the fact that Martin loved her, and allow herself to love him in return.

Chapter 29

Martin was not himself. He felt terrible; he hadn't slept. And when he passed Mary's desk on the way to his office, he knew by her expression of concern that she could clearly see his distress. When he saw Sarah come through the front doors, he turned quickly and sneaked back into his office. He wasn't ready to face her, especially after yesterday. In fact he wondered if he should say anything at all. Nothing had changed about the way he felt about her; but he wasn't sure if she hadn't changed the way that she felt about him. Assuming that is that she'd ever had any feelings for him—romantic feelings.

Getting through the night had been exhausting. He stayed awake till nearly 3 am rehashing his mistakes and beating himself up for his own stupidity: the timing, the location—the misbegotten logic of his approach. Even if he had entertained some thoughts on the subject of marriage, it had never been his intention to say anything to her so soon. He knew she wasn't ready and frankly he wasn't ready either. "God," he prayed, "let me find a way to fix this—give me another chance."

They had a date for dinner tonight and he still wanted to ask her to the Halloween party on Friday. What should he do? What should he say? Would she even talk to him after yesterday? Should he be casual or serious, funny or direct?

Sarah took the matter out of his hands by knocking on his door and calling for permission to come in.

"It's Sarah, will you talk to me?" she asked, and he looked up to see her shadow moving beyond the beaded glass

"Yes," he answered; surprised that Mary hadn't warned him of her presence.

When Sarah bounced into the office, he recognized a new self-confidence that made him hopeful. And unlike him, she looked bright and well-rested.

"Martin—you look terrible!"

"Gee thanks." He rubbed his tired eyes and put his glasses back on. "You look great!" he said, giving her a smile that might just as easily been painted on.

"I'm sorry about yesterday. You caught me by surprise and I reacted badly."

"I can't blame you, I caught myself by surprise," he said, rolling back his chair and rising. They met at the end of his desk and embraced—nothing too eager or passionate, but wonderfully sweet and reassuring.

"Let's forget the whole thing," Martin said, apologizing for a proposal that he still believed in.

"No, I don't want to forget it."

"Now I'm confused."

"Don't be—it's not a bad idea. In fact, I'm flattered," she said, sounding buoyant. Then unexpectedly she lifted herself on tiptoe and gave him an affectionate peck on the nose. "Last night I did a lot of thinking," she said, switching to a confidential tone. "Some of it was pretty depressing, but in the end I came out feeling a lot better about myself, which considering the magnitude of my past mistakes really surprised me."

"I did too—that is, I did a lot of thinking—only I ended up feeling worse," Martin confessed.

"Why? You didn't do anything wrong. Unless of course you've changed your mind?"

"No, not at all!"

"Good. It'll all work out sooner or later," she said, "but for right now let's hang back a little, okay?"

"Okay."

"By the way, are we still on for dinner tonight at Kimball's?"

"Yes," he said, pleased that she remembered and that she still wanted to go. "When should I pick you up?"

"Sevenish, that will give me time to get some supper for Sam. Lately all he gets is the kind of food that you can heat in the microwave," she said, then swung around and swirled out the door with such suddenness that it sent a breeze back to reshuffle the papers on his desk.

He had arrived this morning with a bad case of what his mother called the mulligrubs, convinced that he had ruined the only thing that'd had any real meaning to him in years. Oh, he knew he hadn't won any great victory here, but he would live to fight again and he would have that second chance he had prayed for. He'd just have to stay clear of the marriage thing, at least for the time being.

Oh damn, he thought, *I let her get away again without bringing up Halloween. Maybe tonight, during dinner. . .*

Chapter 30

When Sam left Jennifer's, after sharing another supper with her and her parents, he decided not to go back home but instead went to his Aunt Em's. Since his mother had started seeing Martin she wasn't around very much, and he wanted desperately to explore his reckless new attraction for Jennifer with someone; and he'd always found it easier to talk to his aunt about these things. Anyway, he couldn't go home and bounce his troubles off the empty walls.

When he didn't get an answer to ringing her bell, he opened the door and came in anyway. Em had the TV going, but as he made his way into the living room, he could see that she wasn't watching it. She had a book in front of her. He figured between the noise from the TV and her involvement in her story she hadn't heard him, but she must have heard his footfall on the hardwood floor as he stepped over the threshold, because without the slightest show of alarm she peeked over the pages of her book and asked, "What's up?"

"Em, if you're reading, why keep the TV on?" he asked as he took the chair opposite her.

"Too quiet without it; makes the house seem spooky. But I doubt that you came over here to ask me about the TV or my book—so, what's up?"

"Jennifer," he said, then fell silent.

After a moment, Em picked up the remote and shut off the TV. She was right. The sudden silence that followed did seem spooky. In the summertime with the windows open you could hear the fetch and curl of the waves, but this time of year unless the surf was particularly fierce, nothing penetrated the walls. He still didn't know where to begin, so the silence continued while Em quietly stared back at him, waiting. After a couple of long minutes had passed, he noticed the tiny creaking sounds of the house as it settled on its foundation. Then was startled by the bang and hiss of steam rushing from the boiler to the radiator behind his chair.

"And?" his aunt prodded.

"Do you remember during the summer?" He began at what he supposed was the beginning. "You know, when we had that talk about Jennifer."

"Since you don't talk much about girls, I'm not likely to forget," she said, laying her book spine-side-up over her knee. "Why do you ask?"

"I told you I was afraid of her," he said, letting his hands hang loosely over the arms of the chair, "and you said she might not be as scary as she seemed."

"Yes."

"At the time that wasn't much help. Then you said I'd figure it out, and I didn't believe that either. But—I just left Jennifer and I have to tell you, you were right. I guess that's not news to you, but it surprises the hell out of me."

"So enlighten me," Em said. She smiled and leaned forward as if she wanted to hear every word. "Tell me what convinced you of my awesome powers of perspicacity."

"Well, when I smashed into her bike and broke her arm, that changed everything. I had to talk to her—I mean, I had to at least tell her I was sorry, and once I did that. . . she turned out to be ordinary, well, not ordinary, but regular—you know? And you were right about the guy thing too. I thought she had it made, but it turns out that being pretty is kind of a curse—well to her anyway. What's so hard to believe about all this is that she likes me—and not just as a friend."

"Why is that so surprising?" Em said, scooting to the edge of her chair as if to challenge him. Her hand accidentally swept the book from her knee onto the red oriental carpet and they both watched the dust rise. Leaving the book, she looked up and said, "Why shouldn't she like you?"

"First of all, she's beautiful, and besides that she has the kind of intelligence and confidence that'll drop an elephant at fifty yards."

"That means she's happy with who she is and knows what she wants. That's not a reason for her not to like you."

"No. But I'm not happy with who I am. Honestly Em, I'm about as exciting to a girl as a worn-out pair of sneakers, and physically I'm a total misfit."

"Don't be such a goose. There's lots to like about you, and if you're not exactly handsome, you're certainly better looking than Clark Gable."

"Who?"

"He was a big heartthrob back in the 30's and 40's. All the women went crazy over him—including me. He had a receding hairline and his ears stuck out so far he looked like a windmill, but there was something about him that made all the women swoon."

"Really?"

"Yeah, really."

"Well anyway, she kissed me. I mean, we've kissed before and—and it was pretty neat. But no other girl has done that—that is, I haven't done that—not that way.

"So, I thought that's what you wanted."

"I thought so too. God, I don't know what I want!"

"And you think I do," Em said, putting her hands down on the arms of her chair as if she was about to get up.

"Maybe."

"And what am I supposed to tell you?"

"What do I do next?"

"Nothing. You kissed Jennifer because she's wonderful, and intelligent, and confidant. And she kissed you back, because she likes you; she likes who you are. So, go on being the same lovable schmuck that you've always been and let things take their course."

"That sounds too simple. There's got to be more to it than that. Besides, how can I be the same, when I'm not the same?"

"Don't nit-pick. Things like this help you to grow up, but they don't change who you are, at least not fundamentally. Believe me, Sam, it's no more complicated than just being yourself. That is, after all, what Jennifer found attractive. The reason she's rejected other boys is because they were too self-involved. They were only interested in being churlish and lewd. . .in meeting their own needs."

"What?"

"They only wanted to plow her field, and plant their seed," she said, guiding her hand in front of her the way a plowshare divides the dirt into rows.

"Oh," he said, and even though the picture she created was clear, the metaphor she'd used reminded him of something from a Dick and Jane primer and made him want to giggle.

"You, on the other hand, wanted to cultivate her friendship. There is nothing sexier to a girl than a young man who's seriously interested in her. Not just because she's pretty, but because she's real—someone with substance and depth. Which is not to say that she doesn't want you to think of her as pretty. . .but. . . Do you understand what I'm saying?"

"Yes, I understand the plowing and the planting and the cultivating," he said, pleased that he'd tied in all her clever metaphors, "but I can't believe that love is as simple as just caring."

"It isn't, but it ought to be, especially at your age. Besides, being unselfish and caring isn't all that simple. Still, if you can master that one principle, you'll attract more girls than you can handle.

"But Jennifer, all by herself, is more girl that I can handle." He had cared about other girls, but it had never led to anything else—nothing so emotional, and certainly nothing physical.

"Don't get the wrong idea, though. A kiss, no matter how passionate, doesn't mean that two people are in love."

"Ahhh," he sighed as if he understood, which he didn't.

"Now go home, Sam," she said with a dismissive wave of her hand, "and let me finish my book." Then she picked her novel up off the rug and started flipping through the pages to find the place where she'd left off.

He let himself out and headed down Beachwood Road. A cool yellow moon, lit up the night and as he walked the fall breeze scuffed the dry leaves across the pavement in front of him.

He supposed Em had been some help, but he still wasn't satisfied. He understood the kissing thing; it was what came after that confused him. Yeah, he knew what two people did when they did it (well, not exactly), but he couldn't see *himself* doing it—especially with Jennifer. Which is what he had hoped that Em would try to explain. But honestly it wasn't an explanation that he needed so much as he did her permission. Not grownup to child permission, but the kind of sanction that is given from one adult to another and that carries with it all the deep and meaningful consequences of life and happiness.

Chapter 31

Sarah was spending a lot of time with Martin, and Sam could see that things were heating up and getting kind of serious. Up to now he'd only met Martin for a minute or two at the front door. Even those evenings that Martin came by to sit with his mother in front of the TV hadn't helped, since his mother always conspired to get rid of him before Martin arrived. Either she talked him into going over to his Aunt Em's or he agreed to spend the time at Jennifer's. He liked being with Jennifer, but he didn't like being edged out of his own house so that his mother could be with some strange man.

One morning at breakfast, the subject shifted to Martin, and his mother suggested that the two of them ought to get to know each other better.

"Do you really like this guy?" Sam asked. He wanted to substitute the word *love* for *like,* but didn't feel comfortable with the idea that she might now or ever be in love with Martin. Aunt Em had warned him about this—had warned him that he'd better not interfere. But didn't he have some responsibility here? Shouldn't he protect his mother from the meatheads—the wolves and mashers who might try to take advantage of her? After all, she had married his father and look what a bust that had turned out to be.

"Yes, I like him."

"How much?" he asked, searching her eyes to see if she would be honest.

"Well, I'm still working on that. Let's say for now that I like him a lot. Why—does that bother you?" She curled her upper lip and raised her eyebrows, seeking his approval.

"No, not as long as you're happy. Maybe when I get to know him I'll like him all right," he said speculatively, though he doubted it.

Martin seemed nice enough. But then a lot of people had liked his dad, especially the losers he hung out with when he went barhopping. Martin could be putting on an act to win his mother's favor. But what would he have to gain? Certainly not her money; there was none. They were barely making it. Maybe his mother just wanted financial security.

No, Martin didn't appear to be terribly self-sufficient. Besides, after being with his dad he didn't think that she would want to be dependent on anyone, especially another man.

His mother reached across and tapped the end of his nose. "Hey, are you in there?" she asked.

"Yeah, I'm here, he said, wrapping his fingers around hers and trapping it in midair. She laughed and pulled her finger free.

"If this is going to work, the three of us need to find something we can do together."

"Don't you think it might be easier if it was just Martin and me?" Otherwise he's going to feel self-conscious. If you're there, then we'll both be trying to make points."

"You may be right, I hadn't thought of it that way," she said, bracing her chin against her folded hands and gazing across the breakfast table at him. "What?" he asked, when she continued to stare at him.

"Nothing. It's just hard for me to think of you as grown-up and having grown-up ideas."

"Mommm," he howled, thinking that this conversation had suddenly gone gooey.

♦ ♦ ♦

The next day when Sarah sat down for a break with Martin, she told him about Sam's suggestion and he was duly impressed.

After tossing a few ideas back and forth, Martin suggested that a morning at the Rice Creek Hunt Club would be the thing to do. "Afterwards we can have lunch together—go to McD's or whatever. That'll give us a chance to talk," Martin said.

"This doesn't involve guns, does it?"

"It's a Sporting Clays competition."

"That doesn't tell me anything," she insisted.

"Are you familiar with skeet or trap?"

"No. Well, a little," she answered, and the crease above the bridge of her nose deepened and divided her brow.

"Well it's like those two combined, only more."

"Martin, you're not going to give him a gun?"

"Not this time. I thought he would enjoy watching."

"But this still involves shooting."

"Rice Creek has a great range," he said, laying his hand over her forearm and rubbing it gently to try and reassure her. "It's sort of like a golf course, but instead of a driver you use a shotgun. Each station offers a different challenge. At one the shooter tries to hit a target that's bouncing along the ground. At the next the clay is rising up in front of him or flying straight overhead."

The gun idea frightened Sarah, and for good reason. When she was fourteen her dad had shot himself in the leg. He'd gone out to hunt rabbits and slipped and fell trying to climb over a stone wall. It was a rifle, not a shotgun—a 22 caliber. The bullet went straight through, making a small clean hole in the muscle. But afterwards it bled like crazy and her father had a hell of a time getting back to his car and going for help.

Martin went on and on about how safe it was, but she wasn't buying it.

"Do you really think Sam will enjoy this?" she asked, still hoping to dissuade him. "He's never been near a gun before and you're proposing to start him out with something that goes off like a cannon."

"Well, you know him better than I do, but I've never met a boy who wasn't excited by the smell of gunpowder."

"And the smell of blood," she added.

"Oh come on, now you're getting morbid."

"You're right," she admitted.

"He'll be safe enough with me. And if you're worried about the noise, he'll wear headgear to protect his ears. They all do."

"Okay, okay, he can go." But she wasn't convinced, not at all. If Sam really liked this sport he would want to try it out for himself, and Martin would likely show him how. She didn't get the connection between boys and guns and she couldn't see the sport in killing small animals. Thankfully these clay things were not alive. Should she tell Martin about her father? She decided not. Instead, she suggested an alternative, "Why not go to a football game? Isn't that violent enough?"

"More so. That's a sport where heads get cracked and bones get broken and there's real blood."

"Yeah, but at least it won't be your blood or my son's."

Glancing around to see if they were alone, she leaned across the table and gave him a kiss. "Be careful," she said.

Of what?" he asked. "Being around you is far more dangerous than any gun."

She laughed at the idea that he considered her dangerous. "True, but I can't kill you."

"Haven't you ever heard of a broken heart?"

"Oh, go away," she said. And he did; he got up and left the room.

◆ ◆ ◆

When their schedule allowed for it, Martin picked Sarah up for work and drove her back home at the end of the day. It saved her gas and even with the high MPG rating of the Escort, her budget was that tight. And it gave them one more excuse to spend time together. Their romance was progressing pretty much as she had hoped it would, and Martin had kept his promise to move slowly—he left the pace solely up to her. She decided what to do, and she suggested how to do it. And this commuting situation was her idea. Today was one of those days that they had shared a ride and now they were leaving the parking lot, heading out of South-bridge, back to her home in Green Harbor.

It was after four-thirty and the sun had already faded behind the horizon. In the dull light Martin glanced at her quickly and then back at the road. That brief movement caught Sarah's attention, but she didn't look his way. Then she saw it again, only this time he studied her profile for a bit longer. He didn't say anything, just looked, and then finally turned back to the road. It occurred to her that he ought to be more mindful of the road and his driving, but she didn't want to tell him that. She had known him long enough to realize that he thought she was pretty. Why, she couldn't fathom, but whether she thought she deserved it or not, Martin obviously believed it.

There it is again—that look. His constant sideway glances were starting to make her nervous. *If he has something to say, I wish he'd say it and get it over with.*

Whatever he had on his mind he wasn't watching the road and she worried about the possibility that they might end up in the ditch. In fact, right now they were headed straight for a road sign with a big curvy arrow on it.

"Watch out!" she warned, as she reached instinctively for the wheel and pressed her foot hard against the floor where the brake would be if she'd been on the driver's side of the car. His eyes shot back to the roadway and quick panic blanched his face as he pulled the car back into the lane.

"Sorry," he said sheepishly. "I'm a little preoccupied."

"So I noticed. Have I got my wig on straight?" she asked facetiously.

"What?"

"Nothing. You keep staring at me, and I wondered if there was something wrong."

"No, not at all. Everything's perfect." And the word *perfect* came out with the slightest inflection, which seemed to imply some special meaning.

All this seemed so strange. Sarah had spent most of her life convincing herself that she was uninteresting, and Martin's sweet adoration seemed so completely contrary to that idea. Not that his love was extravagant or flashy, just the opposite. The ways in which he honored her were simple and touching. In fact it was their simplicity that made them so powerful. A single fat chrysanthemum left at her workstation, the bright green stem sticking out of an old jelly jar; the discovery of a giant chocolate-chip cookie tucked into her lunch bag; and yesterday, part of a poem written on a Post-it and stuck inside the folder that he had handed her as he passed her workstation:

> *Sing and the hills will answer*
> *Sigh (and) it is lost on the air.*

Two weeks ago he'd secretly dropped a Snickers bar into the pocket of her button down cardigan as he brushed past her in the doorway. The following afternoon when the long workday had ended, she reached into her handbag to get her car keys and perched on top of all the clutter she found a delicate sand dollar—something he had obviously picked up off the beach. Attached to it with an elastic band was a tightly rolled piece of paper. And when she flattened it out she had part of another poem:

> *There is rapture on the lonely shore,*
> *There is society where none intrudes*
> *By deep sea and music in its roar.*
> *I love not man less, but nature more.*

As sweet as this was, she couldn't help wondering if he'd done this exclusively for her, or if it had all happened before with Maria. That was the most difficult part of their relationship; it was hard not to bring Maria or Robert into the mix. Sarah and Martin both had a history, a past that for different reasons was too compelling to be ignored. Still, if all this effort was designed to tear down the walls she had put up to defend herself from the pain of her past failures, he was succeeding. In fact, like Jericho, the walls had already begun to crumble. All that he needed was a final blast of the trumpet and the walls would come tumbling down.

Breaking the long silence, Martin spoke to her about the arrangements he had made for Saturday. "I called Rice Creek this afternoon and the tournament starts at eight-thirty in the morning, so I should pick up Sam by seven."

Sarah wanted to tell him no, but she just looked at him and said, "Fine."

"You're still uneasy about this shooting thing, aren't you," he said, as he adjusted his position behind the wheel.

"Yes, but don't let it bother you. Maybe it's just me or maybe it's because I'm a mother, but I don't like guns." It was more than that; she'd seen her dad's wound and had pressed her finger into the deep scars on both sides of his calf. She knew that guns were always dangerous.

"That's understandable," he said, "I promise there won't be any holes in Sam when I bring him back."

"There better not be any holes in you either," she said, giving him a clip on the shoulder with the edge of her hand. "You probably think I'm a nag, but I worry."

"No, not at all. I think it would be strange if you didn't. One day I'd like to teach him to shoot and—"

"Don't even think about it," she snapped.

"Calm down, you know I'd never do anything like that without your blessing."

"I suppose," she said, hedging.

"Loosen up, this is just guy stuff," he explained. Lifting his hands from the wheel, he gave a shrug and then quickly reclaimed control of the car.

"The two of you can do all the guy stuff you want as long as it's not dangerous."

"That's silly. All guy stuff is dangerous."

Martin pulled the car into her drive and she leaned in for a kiss. She felt the edge of his lips touch hers lightly and then pull away. "What was that?" she complained.

"I thought you were mad at me."

"I am, but I'm not that mad." She jogged closer to the dividing console, clamped her hands over Martin's ears and planted a proper kiss on his mouth. Then she reached behind to pop the door and stepped out into the drive, leaving him with his eyes closed and a smile on his face.

Chapter 32

Sam didn't want to go on this outing with Martin. Not that Martin didn't seem nice enough, but 'Hey Sam' at the door whenever he came by to pick up his mom or a few uncomfortable minutes sitting together in front of the TV if his mother hadn't finished getting ready, hardly made them good friends. All Sam knew when he left that morning was that Martin was capable of being polite. After the usual greetings and a perfunctory handshake, they got in the car and headed down Route 3 toward the Sagamore Bridge. The Rice Creek Hunt Club was at the southeast corner of Otis Air Base. They took the Sandwich exit onto 130 and followed it south through Forrestdale, to Wakeby Pond. Passing a sign with the Indian name Mashpee, they turned west off the main road and bumped onto a sandy track lined with stunted pines. Sam glanced back to see the morning fog close in behind and felt the wheels wobble and struggle against the soft sand. At the end they pulled into a clearing and parked the car in front of a newly built cinderblock clubhouse.

There were already a number of people milling around dressed in sporting gear; some carried gun cases, others held empty shotguns, with the breach open—the barrels hanging jauntily over the crook of their arm. Sam was properly impressed by all this firepower.

Behind the clubhouse an open-framed tower rose well above the roofline. Martin told him that the tower was used to launch the overhead targets at station three. When they approached the first shooting station Sam was surprised to see that it was only a four foot high barricade with thick posts rising up on either side. Martin explained that the posts were there to limit the swing of the gun barrel so that the shooter wouldn't track the target too far and accidentally shoot someone.

Sam had some misgivings about this outing when he first heard about it, especially since they were only shooting at clay targets. He wanted to go after something real like ducks or pheasant or better yet something that with horns or claws that might be able to fight back. But once he saw the clays explode in midair, and the small black shards were carried off by the wind, he was hooked.

He couldn't ever remember going anywhere like this with his dad, not even somewhere as harmless as fishing. No, that wasn't exactly true; he had gone to a sports bar with him several times to watch football and hockey on TV, until his mother found out and put the kibosh on it. And his father had tried fishing once. They rented a boat at the pier, but when his father tried to step aboard, the boat drifted away from the side of the dock and he fell in. If Mr. Dwyer, the harbormaster, hadn't been there to pull him out he probably would have drowned.

As Sam followed Martin from station to station, watching the shooters deal with the problems of bouncing targets at the "Hare Affair" or testing their merit at the "Dove Roost", with shots that were almost straight overhead, Martin instructed him in technique. Such things as positioning, gun hold point and gun mount. How to read the target, and how to determine where the target should break. He expressed the need to point, and not aim, then demonstrated the difference. Sam soon realized that Martin was not at all like his father and he began to warm to the idea of being with him.

"I didn't think it would be so loud," Sam complained, as another blast shattered the damp morning air. "Especially with these on." He said touching the orange headset that covered his ears.

"They muffle the higher decibel levels, but you have to be able to hear the Targetmaster," Martin told him. As they followed the shooters up the trail to the next station Sam began to understand what had attracted his mother to this man, and he found it harder and harder to dislike him.

At the end of the tournament as they meandered through a stand of trees on the way back to the parking lot, Sam felt elated. The noise of the competition, the rattle of #9 pellets ripping apart a target, the smoke and the smell of gunpowder, the feel of the empty casings that filled his coat pocket gave him a marvelous rush. He had come here determined to endure this experience for his mother's sake and now he was obsessed with the idea of learning how to do this amazing thing himself.

"Will you teach me how to shoot?" he asked, turning and staring into Martin's ruddy face.

"I have to warn you, I'm not as good as these guys."

"I don't care, so long as you can teach me enough to hit something."

"Well, not just *something*. You need to hit the target."

"Yeah, like, duh!" Sam said, and then they both laughed.

◆ ◆ ◆

By twelve-thirty they were heading down the long drive, back to the road. Martin suggested several fast-food places where they could eat, but Sam thought he had a better idea. He told Martin about a family restaurant in Marston Mills and convinced him to take Route 130 southeast to Mashpee, then directed him to go east on Long Lake Road. Following this curvy country lane they rolled into the middle of Marston Mills twenty minutes later, and parked in front of an old storefront.   Sam opened the cross-buck door and they stepped into a room filled with the steamy smells of clam chowder and Yankee pot roast.   Wending their way through linen clothed tables and bentwood chairs they sat down and picked up a couple of laminated menus.   Soon a young girl in blue jeans and a tight fitting T-shirt came over to take their orders.   She pulled a pad from behind the strings of her folded apron, held a pen poised to write and asked them what they wanted.   When she finished and turned to leave, Martin asked Sam what he thought.

"About what?"

"About her?" Martin said, nodding his head at the back of the girl who had just left them.

Sam admired her lithesome figure as she bumped her hip against a wayward chair and stopped to bus a table before heading to the kitchen.

"Well?" Martin prodded.

"I already have a girl, so why would I be scoping out someone else?"

"It's no sin to admire a pretty girl."

"True," Sam conceded, "as long as you only look."

"So—what do you think?" Martin insisted.

"Oooooh, she's alright."

"That's it?"

"What do you want?   She only stopped here for two minutes to take our order."

"You mean you didn't notice that she was giving you the eye?"

"Was not!" Sam protested, wondering if Martin meant to tease him.

"Well, she certainly wasn't looking at me," Martin exclaimed, pointing a finger at himself and smiling.

"Can't we talk about something else?"

"Pick a subject."

Sam stopped to unfold his napkin and take out the flatware that was trapped inside.   "You.   Let's talk about you."

"Okay, what do you want to know?"

"Do you intend to marry my mother?"

"Whoa," Martin roared.   "There's nothing like going straight for the throat."

"Why not." Sam said, picking up his knife and trying to rub off a water spot.

"A few preliminaries might help to soften the blow.   Besides it's not polite."

"Polite is good but it doesn't get results.   And that's not an unfair question."

"No—you're right, it is a fair question."

"So, have you asked her?" Sam slid the bowl of his spoon between the tines of his fork and balanced the two on the end of his finger, while he waited for an answer that didn't come right away.

"I've asked—but she hasn't said yes."

"Well, she certainly didn't say no, or we wouldn't be here." The spoon dropped and Sam slammed his hand down hard to catch it before it bounced off the table.

Martin laid his hand over Sam's wrist. "Please," he said, nodding toward the scattered flatware.

"Your mother said that she needed time."

"Is that all? Didn't she say that she loved you?"

"Boy—the next thing you'll want to know is if I kissed her and how hard," Martin said, flopping back in the bentwood chair and nearly tipping it over.

"Did you?"

"Yes and she kissed back."

"Did she tell you about my father?" Sam asked, challenging him with his finger.

"I know he died a little over a year ago, and that being alone has been hard on her."

"That's BS! If anything, she's better off. We both are." He watched Martin's sit straight up in his chair.

"Shocked?" Sam asked. He pushed back his sleeves, one at a time, then leaned into the edge of the table and waited for Martin's answer.

"Yes."

"You wouldn't be, if you knew my father," Sam said with youthful perspicacity. "Everything he did seemed designed to bring us misery. And generally Mom got the worst of it."

"It's hard to believe that you were constantly—"

"Not constantly, we had our moments. Mom and I were happy enough whenever he wasn't there."

"He must have loved your mother once."

"Haaah!" Sam erupted. He didn't really understand that kind of love—love between a man and a woman—but he knew from what he'd witnessed that his father and mother didn't have it.

"Well, she had you." Martin observed.

"I can't imagine how," Sam said, literally shuddering from the sudden image of his parents having sex.

◆ ◆ ◆

Martin was stunned by his sagacity. Whatever happened between Sam's mother and father—whatever happened between Sam and his father—had hurt him deeply and robbed him too soon of his childhood innocence. It took Martin a moment to gather his thoughts and he could

see that Sam was disarmed by his prolonged silence. "Forgive me, but—
I—I never expected. . ."

"It's okay—you didn't—you couldn't possibly know."

"No, I had no idea."

"Mom took the worst of it. Whenever my father got drunk, he got
angry, and sometimes he hit her. Dad'd come home slurring his words and
shove Mom around. He'd take his finger and drive it into her chest until he
had her backed against the wall, then he'd cuss her out." He paused
remembering it all over again. "I can see his spit hitting her in the face."

"Arrgh!" Martin croaked, and Sam ignored him.

"When I was little I hid under the table or behind the sofa, or
looked through the balusters at the top of the stairs. He called her a whore
and a bitch—dummy, dingbat, asshole. . .

"I get the idea," he said, his anger increasing with each new
epithet.

"Then he slapped her, or he'd put his hands in hers and bend her
wrist back until she screamed from the pain".

"Once he grabbed the knife she was using to slice potatoes and
drove it through the back of her hand—missed the bone and went straight
through to the cutting board. If you look you can still see the scar. When I
saw that it scared me so bad I pee my pants. But if I'd made a sound he
would've come after me. And if he'd discovered that I had soiled myself
he'd've tossed me across the room."

"Did he do that?"

"—broke this arm here," he said, pointing to his right wrist, "and
left black marks on my neck where his fingers squeezed hard enough to
break the blood vessels—cracked three ribs here," he said counting them
out in a line at a spot below his left arm.

"My God!" The muscles in Martin's jaw tightened as he ground
his teeth, trying to hold back his emotion.

"Why did she let him do it?" Sam asked, though he didn't seem
to be talking to anyone in particular. "Why didn't she just run away and
take me with her?"

"I don't know."

"Maybe that's why she's afraid to marry again."

God, he sounds so old. Sam looked man-sized, and his eyes
reflected the kind of intensity that came from hard experience, but his thick
tousled hair and the zits that dotted his chin gave away his real age. *After
what he's been through, how can I ever win his trust?*

"If my efforts succeed and I actually convince your mother to
marry me, how will you deal with that?"

"To be honest, Mom—that is, *we*—got along fine before you
showed up. And if you go away we'll be fine again. But I can't ignore the
fact that you make her happy. I won't get in your way."

This kid scares the hell out of me, Martin concluded. *I'm an intruder, a threat, someone vying for his mother's affection—someone who can hurt her, at least emotionally, and yet he's willing to give me a chance if it will make his mother happy.* "Sam, I'm impressed."

"By what?

"By your honesty, for one thing."

"More like foot in mouth disease. I always talk too much—say too much. I mean, I throw this crap at Winnie all the time, but she's used to it."

By this time the food had arrived and Martin welcomed the respite. For a few minutes he concentrated on eating, and looking up occasionally he saw that Sam did the same. Then he heard the rattle of Sam's fork as he set it down hard on the edge of his plate.

"I've told you about me, now it's your turn," Sam said with something like a sigh.

"All—right, I guess it's time for me to spill the beans. Is this for the record or just between the two of us?"

"Just between us." Sam promised. "I won't tell Mom. I'll leave that up to you."

"Oooh, so I'm off the hook for now as long as I tell your mother later. Is that it?"

"That's it."

"How will you know?"

"I'll know." And somehow Martin felt sure that he would.

"Okay quit stalling. Let's get on with it."

"Well—I was born in Kingston," Martin began.

"No, no, no," Sam interrupted, "I don't want your life story, just give me the good stuff."

"There isn't any *good stuff.*"

"Oh come on, everybody's got at least one juicy secret to tell."

"Well, I've been married before,"

"Yeah," he said with the sound of satisfaction, "tell me about your wife."

"Okay. I met her in high school. She was my first and only love—well, until now that is."

"What happened to her? Are you divorced?"

"No—not divorced. She died." Saying that hurt, not just the usual mental anguish, but a sharp stitch in Martin's side as if someone had slipped a knife between his ribs, and that surprised him.

"How?" Sam asked.

Martin knew that this would be Sam's next question and he knew he would have to answer it. He pushed his plate of food to the middle of the table, folded his arms, and laid them across the white linen tablecloth then leaned in to reveal all the ghoulish details. "Ten years ago, they found a lump in her breast. She had surgery and radiation treatment, but it came too late. She was gone before I had a chance to understand what was happening. The doctors kept throwing these strange terms at me: radical mastectomy, biopsy, chemotherapy, metastasis. I'd heard of some of them—but didn't know what they meant—not in real terms anyhow. They took the right breast first—cut it away until there was nothing left but an ugly scar. And under her arm, more cutting to remove her lymph nodes." He let his head fall forward as if it were too heavy and with his chin cutting into the zipper on his jacket he continued.

"One evening," Martin said, his voice cracking from the memory, "after she had come home from the first surgery, she showed me what they'd done. It was only that one time, but she seemed driven to make me understand her anguish. She came out of the shower wearing a robe and she pulled it back to reveal the scar. Taking my hand, she brought my fingers to the flat ugly mutilation, and then she cried. Within three months, they had decided to take the second breast." He coughed and cleared his throat. "She was devastated. They had cut her up; taken away something that defined her as a woman. It wasn't a matter of vanity—it made her feel ugly and undesirable. But worse than that, she knew or at least suspected that it was hopeless, that all that cutting wasn't going to keep her alive.

"The doctors never discussed reconstruction. She was too advanced, too weak. Her surgeon explained her condition to her. There were lots of cold medical terms, but never any mention that she was dying. When he had finished he took me aside and asked me what I wanted to do. It was idiotic, all I wanted was to save her." Martin unfolded his arms and picked up his paper napkin. He tried to make it look like he was wiping his mouth, but when he blew his nose, he had to believe that Sam had found him out.

"What was her name?"   Sam asked, after waiting for him to recover.

"Maria."

"Do you miss her?"

"God, yes. I found a keeper and then I lost her. I figure that kind of love only comes once in a lifetime."

"What made you change your mind?"

"Your mother," he said, poking at the wilted parsley that had been used to garnish his fish.

"What about her?"

"Well, that's another story," Martin said, sitting back in his chair.

"Come on, you can't tell me all about your wife and then leave me hanging when it comes to my mother."

Martin pulled in a deep breath, then let it out slowly. "A couple of months ago when your mother came for an interview, I looked up to see a shy delicate creature sitting in the chair on the far side of my office. She was clearly out of her element and my heart went out to her. There wasn't any conscious decision to throw away my comfortable orderly life. My simply folded up and all sense of reason melted away. It was like coming to a crystal clear stream and seeing a bright pebble on the bottom. I had to reach down and pick it up. I had to find out what made it different from all the others."

"Wow! That's deep."

"Yes, it is *kind of deep,* isn't it." He hadn't meant to reveal so much of himself, particularly the pain of losing Maria. But Sam probably hadn't meant to reveal so much of himself either. Now there was a rawness between them that needed time to heal and they each sought refuge in their food. Turning back to his plate, Martin broke through the crusty coating on his fried cod and Sam took another bite out of his half-eaten hamburger.

Although the smell of fresh pastry tempted him, Martin refused dessert and Sam said he wasn't interested either. So while Sam left for the bathroom, Martin dropped some bills on the table and stepped over to the cashier to pay for their meal.

In the car on the way home the conversation came in spits and spats and dealt only with the events at Rice Creek. When they finally pulled into the drive behind Sam's house and turned off the engine, there was a moment of nervous silence when neither one seemed ready to leave the car. Sam sat fidgeting, snapping and unsnapping his jacket and Martin pulled out his keys and poked around under his seat as if he'd lost something, which he knew he hadn't. "We'll have to do this again," Martin promised, looking for a way to break this strange impasse. "If not to Rice Creek, then maybe hunting. Would you like to spend a week in New Hampshire deer hunting?" Sam didn't say anything; he just looked at Martin in disbelief.

"Course, we'll have to ask your mother and she's not too hot on guns. But maybe between the two of us we can wear her down."

That clear look of disbelief didn't surprise Martin. He couldn't blame Sam. There was no reason for him to believe that Martin was serious about a trip to the white mountains to hunt deer. His father probably made lots of promises that he never kept.

Sam opened his door and climbed out of the car. Martin got out on his side and came round to join him and the two let themselves in through the back door.

◆ ◆ ◆

When Sarah heard them call out she came immediately into the kitchen to greet them. Martin continued around the Formica table and when he touched his mother's shoulder and leaned in to give her a kiss it appeared that her whole body came to receive it. Sam wasn't used to such a display of affection; he'd never seen a kiss given by his father that hadn't been forced upon his mother. But even his untrained eye could hardly mistake the symptoms of surrender or her look of embarrassment when she realized that he had been watching. Here he was a young hormonally challenged adolescent struggling to understand his own emotions, while his mother was embroiled in a relationship in which she seemed more confused than he was. It made him wonder if the whole idea of romance wasn't much more complicated than he had imagined.

Chapter 33

Tonight was finally the night. After lots of false starts Sam had at last screwed up enough nerve to ask Jennifer on a date—nothing spectacular, just bowling and a pizza later at D'Angelo's. It really shouldn't be such a big deal: they had been seeing each other regularly for weeks, but somehow it hadn't been official. Maybe that was because all those visits had been in her house where no one could see. Nothing had been done together in public—nothing in front of his friends—or enemies. If this were successful. If? He hadn't considered the possibility of failure. "Pshaw!" he snorted, sounding almost like a sneeze. *The quickest way to kill this thing is to start imagining what might go wrong. God, it isn't as if we're starting from scratch; I know Jennifer and she knows me. Just because the bowling alley will be filled with the guys from school doesn't mean I have to fall apart. I mean, get a grip.*

He spent a long time in the shower, and longer still with his hair and shaving. Yes, shaving—there wasn't much there, but it made him feel grown-up to scrape it off. The tricky part was not slicing open a zit and bleeding all over his undershirt. Then he had to decide what to wear? He didn't want to look like a dufus. His mother insisted on buying his clothes, which meant he could never get the sort of stuff that was 'in' (unfortunately, the cost of being 'in' was more than his mother could afford). As he rummaged through his drawers and snapped the hangers from side to side in his closet, the word *nerd* crossed his mind. The kids had hung that title on him as soon as he left grade school and started junior high. No one had called him that lately, but they didn't have to. He could see it whenever he looked in the mirror.

He found some loose-fitting Dockers and an apple-green sweatshirt with a humpback whale painted on the front, and decided that that was the best he could do. Clunking down the stairs with sneakers untied, tongues flapping, he threw his full weight into every step, and his long-armed gangly movement reminded him of an orangutan. Sitting at the kitchen table, he pulled up his socks, but decided it would be cool to leave his sneakers untied. Instead, he tucked in the ends so he wouldn't trip over them.

His mother couldn't get him to eat. Eventually she drove him over to his Aunt Em's and waited in the car while he went next door to get Jennifer. Her parents let him in and he stood hands in pockets rocking on his heels while he waited for Jennifer to come down. When she stepped into view at the head of the stairs he stopped rocking. Still on his heels, he let the soles of his sneakers slowly reconnect with the floor as she started to descend one careful step at a time. She wore a grape-colored top with vertical ribbing like the old-fashioned sleeveless undershirts his father used to wear. It had a wide crew neck, full-length sleeves, and extended well below her waist, so nothing showed—no skin, at least. But those little ribs followed her figure perfectly, and the white spandex pants below emphasized the long sweep of her legs. He heard a low, appreciative whistle and was shocked when he realized it was blowing past his own lips.

She smiled and said, "Thank you," as she came off the bottom step.

"No. Thank you," he said, wishing he could say more. He didn't know how to express the kind of joy that tickled his insides and made him want to giggle so badly that holding it in actually hurt. When she extended her hand he took it gracefully and led her toward the door.

"Take your jacket," her mothered hollered from somewhere upstairs. Made of brown suede with four inch rawhide fringe along the bottom, she lifted it off the coat tree and draped it over her shoulders. Then he took her hand again and they rushed down the walk to his mother's car.

♦ ♦ ♦

The bowling went all right. Sam lost, not intentionally and not too elegantly. The more he complained about the unfairness of her victory, the more she seemed to enjoy it. And in spite of his forgiveness and the blatant excuses he made about his performance, he secretly blamed her. After all, he couldn't be expected to concentrate on the game when she kept bending over in those perfectly fitted spandex pants. He watched the way she cocked her head to scrutinize the pins before stepping up to the line. Advancing in short quick hops, she would stop so suddenly he could hear the squeak of her shoes as she skidded, then she stood on her toes like a ballet dancer just before letting go of the ball. Once the ball was arching slowly toward the pins, her body would straighten and her hands pushed against the air, a little to the right or the left as needed to guide the ball along the alleyway. If it hit the target she danced excitedly back to the table and shouted out her score. If not—if it went badly—she clapped her hands once lightly and dropped her shoulders, then tramped over to the bench, and slid down on the seat. In this part slouch, part sprawl position she threw her head back, and groaned like a sick walrus. If this performance was designed to further unnerve him, it worked.

When it was over they went to D'Angelo's and ordered a large deep-dish pizza with everything—except anchovies—which made Sam wonder: does anyone ever order pizza with anchovies? They bought a pitcher of root beer and huddled over their hot food. Diddling between slices, their conversation was full of splendid nonsense and they had great fun spreading tomato sauce from mouth to mouth by sharing sloppy kisses.

His mom pulled up at nine forty-five and drove them back to Jennifer's. She left them both in front of the house with the understanding that Sam would walk home later, after he had said goodnight to Jennifer.

When Jennifer unlocked the door and they entered the house, everything was in darkness, and Jennifer had to slide her hand along the striped wallpaper to find the switch. When the hall brightened with incandescent light, she took his hand and dragged him up the stairs to her room. Opening her bedroom door, they saw the moonlight stretched out in long rectangles across the rug, and the mirror above her bureau reflected a bluish glow. Jennifer left the small lamp on her nightstand turned off, but she did click on the stereo. Adjusting the knob, she stopped briefly at a golden-oldies station, then gave a funny grimace when the words from a Forties favorite wafted into the room. "Bewitched, Bothered and Bewildered," Jennifer repeated. "Are they serious?

Continuing her search of the FM band, she pointed to the wicker chair that she had occupied for so many days while her arm was still in a cast and Sam sat down. She gave up on finding the kind of music she wanted and shut off the radio After Sam had settled in the chair he looked up to see Jennifer climbing onto her bed. As she positioned herself on her stomach and propped her hands under her chin, her wide crewneck exposed the soft roundness of her breasts and the moonlight highlighted the frizzy ends of her hair creating a bright nimbus that looked like one of those halos you see in medieval paintings.

Suddenly aware of the absolute stillness, Sam asked, "Are we alone?"

"Totally. My parents won't be back until eleven."

"Should we be—I mean—alone, here in your room?"

"Why not, you've been here before."

"Yeah—but not like this."

"Like what?"

"You know—alone."

"Good grief, you sound like my grandmother."

He hated the sound of that, it made him feel like an old-fashioned chaperone. "You're right. So, what do we do now?" *Silly question.*

"If you have to ask," she said, dropping her head and burying her face in the bedspread, "then all my effort to lure you up here has been wasted."

The idea that this had been her intention—that it was part of a clever plan to seduce him, made him uneasy. If this were a movie, he would say the right words—or no words—give her a passionate kiss and the two of them would be ripping each other's clothes off. Then the room would blur and they would wake up the next morning in bed together. But all that was hardly instructive—and it wasn't real. Whatever was going on out there it had nothing to do with the world he lived in. Besides there were lots of reason why he couldn't do stuff like that: including inexperience and fear, but mostly it had to do with a little voice that kept whispering in his ear. A voice that sounded an awful lot like his Aunt Em.

Coming up again, Jennifer pressed her chin into the hard edge of the mattress, and murmured: "All I want is a kiss. Is that so bad?"

"No. I can do that," he said wondering how he'd gotten the idea that she wanted more.

"Honestly, I'm not going to jump your bones."

"How's a guy suppose to know?" he said, and she laughed.

"Watch the signals."

"You're sending signals?"

"All the time," she assured him

"I don't see why you put up with me."

"Because I know you won't jump to the wrong conclusions."

"Still, it can't be much fun going with a guy who's totally clueless."

"Not totally."

"Thanks."

"And who says we can't have fun?" she said, swinging her legs around and dropping them over the side of the bed. "Come up here." She ordered, tapping the spread to indicate where she wanted him to sit. Sam rose from his chair, and with a short jump launched himself onto the bed beside her. Then combing back his bushy hair, she kissed him playfully letting her wet lips slid into his.

She wiggled her bottom across the bed until her hip scrunched up next to his. A peculiar mixture of fear and delight made him shiver and he wondered what would come next. Then he felt her twist under his arm and she lifted the edge of his sweatshirt. Her cold fingers rubbed his bare stomach and the muscle tightened into a hard knot. He wanted to ask what she was doing, but just held his breath and waited. She pressed against the tightness of his stomach then pulled at the little hairs growing around his navel until he complained.

"Owww!"

"Sorry," she said, and rubbed her fingers in a circle as if that would cure the problem.

"Aren't you afraid?" he asked.

"No," she whispered without asking him what he meant.

"No?"

"Don't get so nervous. All I want you to do is hold me for awhile. You don't have to do anything or say anything. Just hold me."

"I can do that," he sighed and shook off the high charge of tension that had stiffened his body. When she crushed her hair into his shoulder and neck, he folded her into him the way he wrapped himself around his pillow when he couldn't sleep at night. And he breathed in her fragrance, sucking it down deep inside as if it were the essence of her being.

For a long time they sat quietly in the blue glow of the moonlight, listening to the creaking house and the sonorous howl of the fall wind under the eaves.

Jennifer twisted a little closer, and with a puff of warm air, whispered into his neck, "I've waited so long for this."

"For what?"

"For someone I could be this close to and not be afraid."

He thought that was a strange thing to say, and he wasn't sure if he shouldn't take it as an insult. He wasn't a predatory sort of person, but it would be nice if she had at least left him with the illusion of being dangerous.

A flash of headlights and the thrum of a car engine alerted them. "Oh God, it's my parents!" she said, her voice shaking.

"What should we do?"

"Don't panic!" she yelled. She stood, grabbed his upper arm and hauled him off her bed. "Quick!" Digging her fingers into his muscle, she hustled him toward the door and swung it wide. His shoulder slammed hard against hers when they both tried to squeeze through at the same time. Breaking loose, she shot wildly toward the stairs, dragging him after her. Sam missed half the steps and stumbled over the ones he hit. Before he had time to think, Jennifer jumped over the back of the couch in the family room, and he went flying after her. His right foot came over last and when he tried to swing it around he slid headfirst onto the floor. By the time he was upright again, Jennifer had found the remote and switched on the TV. As she turned up the volume Sam heard the rattle of the front door.

When her mother and father entered the room Sam and Jennifer tried to act innocent—and they were, but the fact that they might have been otherwise made Sam feel guilty anyway. Besides, as calm as Jennifer appeared, she was obviously out of breath, and if that didn't look suspicious, then Sam's bumbling effort to say goodnight, while he squeezed past her parents and ran toward the back door, had to give them away.

Walking home he suddenly felt very wise, and bolstered by this new wisdom he decided that this must have been the sort of thing God had in mind when He created Adam and Eve. He wondered if Martin felt the same way about his mother as he did about Jennifer, which on deeper reflection proved to be an eerie thought.

Chapter 34

It was Monday morning and Sarah had come in early. Paul Hargrove, the assistant manager, was just unlocking the front door. He was pleasant and friendly, but since he and Sarah were seldom thrown together at work she knew very little about him.

Paul switched the keys to the inside lock as she walked up, and instructed Sarah to watch for the other employees as they arrived. Getting ready for a new day of business required clear concentration and she hated the constant interruptions. Every five or ten minutes between eight and eight-thirty someone came to pound on the glass to be let in. That meant leaving her station, crossing the lobby to unlock the door and then punching a coded keypad to get back into her workstation. Janice Lu, a dark oriental girl, arrived last.

Janice had started at the bank only three weeks ago and this morning Sarah worked beside Janice to help finish her training. She caught on quickly, but she tended to chatter incessantly when encouraged and whenever she was around Sarah she seemed encouraged. Perky and garrulous she started by asking work-related questions, then switched to the subject of men and sex, something that apparently she knew a lot about, which at eighteen years seemed incredible to Sarah. She said things that were far too intimate and asked personal questions that tested Sarah's patience. Sarah wanted desperately to tell this girl to shut up, but it was against her nature to be so rude.

"Men are liars and cheats," Janice said vociferously. "They never tell the truth."

"Not all men are like that," Sarah said, thinking of her father—and Martin.

"Oh right, like your Mr. McAulliffe is so perfect." Janice parried, with a fiery glint in her eyes.

"First of all, Mr. McAullifee is not mine—I don't own him; but he's never lied to me. Besides, what do you know about it?" Sarah asked.

"I know you've got the hots for each other."

"Crudely put, but. . ."

"I suppose he's told you about Laura."

"Who?" Sarah asked in consternation. A sudden coldness swept over her and she cursed herself for allowing this girl to so easily shake her confidence in Martin.

"Never mind," Janice said. Looking slightly trapped she backed into the corner of their crowded cubicle. "Forget it; I'm in a bitchy mood today. The guy I dated last night thought that a fancy dinner would get him some free booty; and I told him that if he didn't back off, I'd cut him with my knife."

Her graphic description made Sarah grimace. "You wouldn't really do that?"

"You bet I would," Janice said. And pulling on the silver chain around her neck she drew a small pocketknife up from behind the collar of her jersey top. "That's what this is for," she said, opening the blade, which was only two inches long, but sharp enough to do some damage.

"You're dangerous," Sarah observed, and wondered why Janice thought she needed a weapon.

"Don't I know it," Janice said, and the proud expression on her face frightened Sarah. Both went back to work, but Sarah couldn't forget Janice's earlier comment.

"Who is Laura?" she insisted.

At first Janice didn't answer. Clearly ill at ease, she turned away and started opening and closing drawers, pulling out paperwork and deposit slips. But Sarah crowded in behind her and waited. The long silence was ominous and Sarah wondered what kind of Pandora's box she might be opening. Then, with a backward glance that seemed conspiratorial, Janice gave her reply.

"I should have kept my mouth shut. All I can say is that I overheard a few things from the other girls. Gossip, probably an exaggeration, but apparently there is or was something between Mr. McAulliffe and this Laura," she said, using her fingernail to tear the paper band from a stack of bills. "If you really want to know who she is, you'd better ask him yourself."

"What a cop-out."

"I know. But it's the only way to get at the truth."

Damn, what do I do now? Should I ask, or should I leave it alone? There was no reason to believe that Martin had deliberately kept this from her. But Robert had pretty much destroyed her ability to trust anyone, especially a man—and now this Laura thing. How could she ask Martin without revealing her insecurity?

During the long day that followed there were no opportunities for her to speak to Martin confidentially. And even if there had been, she wasn't anxious to question him here at work. She decided she needed a private setting. A quiet comfortable location where Martin might be more open to inquiry and where she might coax him into a confession, if indeed there was anything to confess. An invitation to dinner at her home would be ideal, and it would give her an edge, since she would be negotiating from her own territory. It occurred to her that she was approaching this problem as if she were planning some sort of secret military campaign, and she wondered aloud, "Why am I doing this?" Why couldn't she put down the idea that Martin might be hiding something from her? The fact that he hadn't mentioned Laura before could mean—well, it could mean anything. She assumed that Laura was an old girlfriend, someone from his past— hopefully long past. But. . .

As the day progressed Sarah became increasingly uneasy and whenever their paths crossed she gave Martin long penetrating looks. He returned those looks with a troubled expression that clearly announced his bewilderment. There was nothing hostile in her actions, but she knew that some of her usual good humor was missing. And she knew Martin was sensitive enough to appreciate the difference. Finally, when they left the bank at lunchtime, she pounced upon him with an invitation.

"What about dinner at my house?" she asked, before they had ordered their usual corned-beef sandwiches at Sally's.

"When?"

"Tonight."

"Will Sam be there?"

"No."

"Dinner at your place, alone," he said carefully. "Sounds intriguing."

"It's not what you think," she said, "so don't get your hopes up."

"What is it, then?" he asked.

"Nothing scandalous, just come early."

Chapter 35

Sarah's impulsive invitation worried Martin. They saw each other often, but all their dates were planned and followed a predictable routine; and except for a couple of evenings at her house watching videos, all their previous dates had been public. Who could tell: this evening might hold the promise of some playful shenanigans, or—he could be in trouble.

Sarah had insisted he come early, so he appeared at her doorstep at ten minutes of six. As soon as he stepped through the door she handed him an apron, herded him toward the kitchen and sat him down on a tall stool next to the counter. In front of him was a pile of freshly washed potatoes and a dark blue porcelain pot. Without a word she tucked a peeler in his hand and then went back to the oven to baste a small roast.

Perhaps this was some kind of a test to see if he had any domestic skills. After raising his two boys he was no stranger in the kitchen, but what he'd learned was by happenstance, and she might not approve of some of his methods. When a recipe called for a cup he used an old chipped mug that he filled to the rim. It probably wasn't accurate, but it didn't seem to upset the blend. And when he drained spaghetti he had appropriated a well-worn badminton racket from his boys, which he balanced carefully over the kitchen sink. Still, he wasn't the type to live out of a can or to heat frozen entrees in the microwave. He had a well-worn cookbook and he actually gathered ingredients and mixed them together, and the vegetables he prepared were usually purchased fresh from Costello's produce stand.

By the time the meal was ready and on the table, he could detect a crusty delight in the comments Sarah made about his unconventional cooking methods. Greedy for her approval, he gave up some of his secrets, including the mixture of spices he had concocted for an experimental casserole, which turned out so well he started using that mix on almost everything. And though the preparation had been pretty equally divided between them, Martin had a hand in altering or adjusting every dish Sarah brought to the table. It all looked and smelled delicious, but since Sarah didn't say anything critical or complimentary he wondered if she approved of his efforts.

They sat down at a fifties style Formica table. He leaned over to light the stubby votive candle that she had stuck in the bottom of a custard cup, and when he looked up to blow out the match, he saw a smile so broad it would have made Lewis Carroll's Cheshire cat turn green with envy.

"What are you so happy about?" he asked.

"Nothing," she squeaked, as she popped in her first bite. "Ummm!" she said, jabbing her fork at the roast to indicate that she liked the new taste.

During the meal there was little conversation, and though the room was dark and the candlelight enchanting, Sarah didn't send any romantic signals. There was a brief mention of the weather, and Sarah talked about work. Martin asked questions about Sam. Then he caught her in a vacant stare, which suggested that he had been left behind. Again he suspected that something might be wrong, but he had no idea what.

Once the dishes had been rinsed and put in the dishwasher, they retired to the living room for dessert. Nothing fancy, just a store-bought cream pie. Sarah had taken a particularly large piece, which didn't fit her habit of skimping on desserts. Martin settled on the couch, but felt a sudden stab of disappointment when she didn't join him. Instead, she plopped herself down on the rug, crossed her legs and lifted one foot over her knee. As she cut off the pointed end of her pie with her fork, she glanced up.

"I know—it's awfully big," she said, "but I don't care, I feel like indulging."

"Don't look at me, I didn't say anything. It's good to see that you have such a healthy appetite."

"You mean greedy."

"If you say so," he offered, smiling.

"Ohhh, leave me alone," she said, dropping her fork and giving him a friendly slap on the knee. Then she picked up the remote and switched on the TV. She surfed the channels until she came to a documentary and stopped. It was a National Geographic special, something about alligators. Martin watched as the carcass of some wayward animal was torn apart. It wasn't something he would have expected Sarah to watch, and it certainly didn't go very well with her chocolate-cream pie. The room was dark except for the diffuse light emanating from the TV. And that warm glow dancing across Sarah's face was enticing, but the fierceness of the gators twisting in the mud spoiled the mood.

Sarah dropped the remote in her lap and balancing her plate on the edge of the coffee table, she cut the rest of the pie into even pieces—but she didn't eat any. Instead she pushed her fork under the nearest square and left it. Martin watched the way she gazed at the screen and realized that he had lost her again. They were together, in fact close enough for her shoulder to rub against his knee—yet he felt as isolated as the porcelain bric-a-brac that cluttered the bookcase on the far side of the room. He tried to be patient and wait for her to come back, but his patience deserted him and he reached out and pressed his hand down hard on her shoulder. She looked up, but showed no sign of recognition.

"Where are you tonight?" he asked.

"I'm sorry," she said, blinking once, then shaking her head.

"I thought we were sharing this evening together, at least it seemed that way when we sat down to dinner, but somewhere between the salad and dessert I lost you."

"Don't think badly of me. Janice put a bug in my ear today and I've been trying to get up the courage to ask you about it."

"And?"

"Who's Laura?" she said without further preamble.

Martin felt a prickly sensation between his shoulder blades and it made him stiffen his back. He didn't feel guilty, but he understood or at least thought he understood how this might hurt Sarah. "What have you heard?" he asked, squinting his eyes and giving a curious turn to his head.

"Nothing. Janice just told me to ask you about her."

"I can't imagine anyone making an issue out of Laura. We were good friends—are good friends. Actually, she was more Maria's friend than mine." He scooted to the edge of the couch and leaned out so that he could look down at Sarah's upturned face. "I ought to be angry."

"Why angry?"

"Not with you, but with anyone who would suggest that I had some sort of romantic attachment to Laura. People are always so— suspicious, so anxious to look for scandal."

"If there's nothing to it, why haven't you mentioned her before?"

"There never seemed to be any reason."

"So?" she asked, pivoting at her waist to confront him.

"So—" He cleared his throat, then brought his hand down to brush a loose strand of hair out of her eyes. "Laura and Maria grew up together. Laura married first, and a year later acted as Maria's maid of honor when she married me.

"I knew Laura's husband, Oscar, before. He hated that name and Sesame Street made him hate it even more. His friends called him Opy, which since his last name was Petersen, came from his initials. That worked pretty neatly until the Andy Griffith show came along, and the guys started hassling him again.

"The four of us were inseparable. They spent time at our house, we spent time at theirs—we went out together, we even shared vacations. Then came the draft and almost as soon as Opy finished boot they shipped him off to Vietnam. As for me—it was all a matter of numbers and mine happened to be way down the list.

"In January of '73 Nixon announced the signing of a cease-fire agreement in Paris, but before the official ending of hostilities on January 28th, Opy was reported missing. Two weeks later the Army sent an officer and an enlisted man to her house to tell her he had been killed in action. He stepped on a makeshift mine while humping in the boonies on his last search-and-destroy mission. Laura—well, she had some warning, but she'd worked so hard to convince herself that he was going to be all right that when the news finally came, she completely fell apart. She sat on her front steps, rocking. When Maria dropped down beside Laura hoping to comfort her she let go. There was this god-awful wailing; the kind of high-pitched sound that makes your teeth vibrate. Maria held her and rock her and I took her kids and ours for a long ride."

"That's horrible."

"It was, for awhile. The twins saved her. They needed her. And they didn't allow her much time to feel sorrow for herself."

"Didn't she have any family? I mean other than the kids."

"No. A mother who lived three states away. We were her family. Maria and I and our two boys shared everything, did everything with Laura and her kids. She often complained that she was imposing, but we ignored her.

"After my wife died, a lot of people just assumed that Laura would be Maria's replacement. And we did occasionally go out to a restaurant or a movie, but only as an escape from the kids. I do love Laura, but not that way."

"And I spent all day imagining every sort of affair. . ."

He pressed his fingers over her lips to silence her. "There are no affairs—except for the one I'm having with you."

"Is this an affair?" she asked with a frown.

"A romance then."

"It's so hard for me to believe."

"To believe what?"

"That you're in love with me," she said, rubbing the veins on the back of his hand.

"Why?" he pleaded.

"If I knew why we wouldn't be having this conversation. Sometimes I feel like a cipher, a zero. I know that's foolish—but I can't shake it. For years I walked around like one of those novelties where they take a spring-loaded snake and press it down inside a tin can and wait to scare the person who opens it. All that tension locked away in the dark—all that potential. The idea that you care—that—that you love me. . ."

Martin looked into her eyes and saw that they were bright and glassy and when he brought his hand up under her chin she closed them tight. The tears squeezed out and rolled along her cheeks—each finding its own path until they converged at the corners of her mouth. After a moment she slid her tongue between her lips and licked them away.

"Don't cry," he told her quietly, which had the opposite effect. "Awwww," he moaned, as she pulled her chin free from his hand and let it drop onto her bosom. "Don't," he said, stroking her head. "I'll be okay," she mumbled, wiping her face with her sleeve. Then as he leaned into her, she glanced up and gave him a hopeful half-smile to prove it.

****

The concern in Martin's eyes was priceless, and Sarah couldn't help but broaden her smile. That morphed into a husky laugh, which threw her heavily into his legs as he sat precariously on the edge of the sofa. Tossing her head back over his knees, Martin bent over her, to kiss her, but the angle was al wrong and he touched down on the feathery outline of her right eyebrow.

Holding onto her shoulders so that she wouldn't fall, Martin dropped off the edge of the sofa and came down behind her. She twisted back awkwardly to try and find his mouth and when Martin realized her intention he tried to meet her halfway. But they were still at too great an angle and instead bumped noses hard enough to be painful.

"Ow!" Martin said and laughed.

Gulping in air, Sarah started a fitful spasm of laughter that gave her the hiccups. Then holding her breath, she let go in a whisper. "I feel so—hic—silly."

"Me too," he said.

He unwrapped his legs and came around to face her. Now she could smell the bite of chocolate-cream pie he'd just swallowed. Impulsively she tilted her chin and rose upward. Her kiss landed a little sideways, but this time she didn't miss. She covered his mouth and felt his stubby beard scrape her face as he pushed back.

"MMmmm!" Martin murmured as they uncoupled. "I wasn't expecting that."

"Neither was I," she said, with incredible affection. A moment ago she felt jealous and insecure and now she was apologizing for kissing him. "Are you as confused as I am?" she asked.

"More."

"We're both too old for this," she said.

"Never!" he protested.

"No, I suppose not," she said.

Sarah twisted about, bringing her legs across Martin's lap and while using one hand to rub the back of his neck she used the other to tug on the front of his shirt and then started to undo the buttons. Martin signaled his approval by pulling gently at the edge of her blouse and freeing it inch by inch from the waist of her jeans. Suddenly she felt like a child opening a present—all full of tickles and bubbles—and she had an impatient urge to tear the wrapping away. But before she could slide her long fingers inside his shirt she heard the rattle of the kitchen window as Sam pulled open the back door and all her sweet excitement turned to panic. In her rush to free herself she nearly knocked Martin over. Once she was on her feet she offered Martin her hand, but he had made it on his own and she watched him button and tuck in his shirt while she tried to straighten out her own. Then Sam stepped into the darkened doorway to say goodnight, and Sarah, with her hair sticking up and her top still undone, searched his face to see if he suspected what they'd been up to. But all she saw was a goofy smile.

"Goodnight," he said. The word came in two parts with last a note higher than the first and the crystal sound made it clear that they had been caught.

"Goodnight," she answered struggling to keep her voice level. Sam turned and headed toward the stairs. And once Sarah heard his familiar footfall on the steps, she let herself go. She dropped back down on the floor and lay with her arms stretched out above her head as if she were surrendering to some secret muse. Martin stood over her hands behind his back looking like a kid who'd just been caught stealing from the cookie jar. His befuddled expression brought back her hiccups and she covered her mouth to suppress them. Martin heard them and started to laugh.

"That was embarrassing."

"No kidding," she said.

"What were we thinking?" he said, plopping down on the couch.

"We weren't—thinking," she said. And the two of them laughed until Martin complained that his sides ached.

Chapter 36

The morning after his late-night romp with Jennifer, Sam decided to leave his house and head straight for his aunt's cottage. He wanted to believe that being alone—alone in Jennifer's room—was safe; that just holding each other didn't put them in danger of. . . But being there together on her bed, they'd been terribly close to the edge. And yet truthfully *getting some* would likely have been disappointing. There were lots of reason why they shouldn't have sex, but especially because he felt so conflicted about his body. He hated what he saw and he expected that Jennifer would hate it too. Nevertheless all that animosity and conflict did nothing to remove the desperate need he felt to go as far as nature and circumstances would allow. So he went for the third time to the only person who might help him sort out all these contrary emotions.

◆ ◆ ◆

"What brings you here so early on a Saturday morning?" Em asked, as she came into the living room to join him. When he showed up on her doorstep she had offered him breakfast and he had declined. But she did talk him into a hot chocolate, and now with cup in hand she moved cautiously toward him as she spoke.

"Well—it's—it's about s-s-sex," Sam stuttered.

"Ohhhh," she said, her mouth round, eyebrows raised, "and what makes you think I can help?"

"Maybe you can't, but I don't know who else to ask,"

"So, ask."

"I'm not sure how."

"Is this just about people getting naked, or are we talking about the real thing?"

"What do you mean?"

"Do you want to talk about sex or love?"

"Don't they go together."

"They do when you get it right but they're two very different things."

"I guess I know about the nitty-gritty—it's the emotional stuff that gets me all in a bunch."

"Look, bunch or not, we've talked about this before. You know the rules."

"Yeah. I've always known the rules, but I never had to put them to the test before."

"Sam, this is not a game you win or lose and then go home. It can change your life—it affects you and the girl, her parents and your mom and a whole lot more."

"I know that too!" he insisted.

"What have you and Jennifer been up to?"

"Nothing."

Em just gave him the look. He didn't know how to describe it, but Em and his mother seemed to have a look that said don't fool with me on this.

"Well, nothing that I have to confess."

"Go on." Again that look that said give it to me straight.

"We've spent a lot of time together since the accident and we've kissed; I told you about that. I like her; no, it's more than just like. Last night we went on a date. . ." He stopped, unsure how to describe what happened after.

"And?"

"When I brought her home—that is, when mom dropped us off at her house, Jennifer invited me inside. Her parents hadn't come back yet and the house was dark. Jennifer took me up to her room."

"And."

"And, I've been in her room before, but never when her parents weren't home."

"Why not just turn around and leave?"

"Whenever I'm with Jennifer it's as though I'm on the edge of some big event—something mysterious. It's the strangest feeling. It's like being in a boat in a downpour: the sky and water run together and the land in the distance gets blurry. I want to get to the shore, but I can't find it, and the boat is sinking. Am I crazy or is this what it's like to be in love?" He paused.

"When it happens, Sam, you won't have to ask. People get confused between love and passion. Love is not about *getting some,* as you kids put it, it's about caring and self-sacrifice. It's giving something of yourself everyday without any hope of getting it back."

Em made it sound monumentally complicated, and the idea of sacrifice made him think of throwing a young virgin into a burning volcano.

"So, the two of you were alone. What happened?"

"Nothing?"

"Was it sexual?"

"NOOOO! No." He repeated, lowering his voice. "But I did think that—Jennifer wanted to—and, and I kinda wanted to—or at least part of me did."

"Right, and it's not hard to imagine which part," Em said, then immediately apologized. "Sorry. That wasn't called for."

What Em said embarrassed him, but he couldn't deny that it was true and he couldn't help smiling at her shrewd perception.

"While we were sitting on her bed in the dark listening to the wind outside, she kissed me. Not a real kiss, not the kind that can get you in trouble. But I thought there would be more. Instead she asked me to hold her."

"That's all?"

"She just wanted me to hold her. And at first that seemed to be enough. The sound of the wind outside, and her breathing, and the warmth of her next to me, gave me this humongous high; does that make any sense?"

"It makes wonderful sense, she said."

"Still, there's this niggling itch—this fierce drive to tinker with the forbidden. And that worries me."

Scooting her chair forward to get a little closer, she reached out, put her dry hand over his and rubbed it anxiously. "Sam, you're a good boy—man—whatever. If you weren't, you wouldn't be here now talking to me. Trying to figure out what's right and wrong."

"The kind of affection Jennifer and I shared last night seems incredible and I want to remember it and enjoy it, without feeling guilty. But it gets so complicated and I'm afraid I'll screw things up, say the wrong thing. I'm afraid that one day I'll go too far and we'll both end up angry and hurt."

"The highs and the lows of any relationship can be complicated. And you're right, getting intimate with a girl can lead to a lot of grief. But you're young. You don't have to try everything just because the opportunity presents itself. Don't be in such a god-awful hurry to fall in love."

"I'll try not to be." He looked up and her expression made him think that she wasn't telling him everything, and he wondered why?

"Besides, right now you have other fish to fry," she said.

"How's that?"

"Have you forgotten that Martin is coming to pick you up this morning?"

"No—yes—I guess I'd better go," he said, looking at his watch. Then he checked the bottom of his cup and swallowed down the last of his hot chocolate, knowing that she would be upset if he didn't.

Chapter 37

Martin was late. Sam had been disappointed before, but this time he felt a sharpness in his gut that was new to him. He had this innate desire to test Martin. Whatever he did, whatever he promised had to be proven against Sam's experience with his father. In a way he set Martin up for failure, so that when he didn't live up to his expectations Sam could feel justified. It wasn't fair, but he couldn't help it.

This morning Martin had made plans to take him bowling. He didn't want to go, but Martin had suggested it with his mother standing beside him, and Sam didn't dare say no. If Jennifer had asked, fine, but two guys going bowling seemed kind of dumb. *I mean, how uncool can you get?*

Martin had reserved a ten o'clock slot for them at the Stardust Lanes. Saturdays were always crowded and it was well past ten now. They wouldn't hold their lane open for more than fifteen minutes before they gave it to a walk-in.

Martin burst through the front door at eleven, spouting excuses.

"My car broke down and I couldn't get to a phone," he said, his face flushed, and his voice full of anguish.

"It's alright," Sam told him, but there was no conviction in it. Sam had heard such excuses before—in fact, better ones. Stories with much more detail and drama. "It's no big deal." And in a way it wasn't.

"Finally a driver stopped." Martin continued. "Someone who knew about cars. I don't know what he did—jiggled something under the hood—told me to turn the key and it started. It must have been a bad wire . . ." Martin stopped.

Sam sat on the bench in the vestibule next to the front door and played nervously with the umbrella beside him until the cold stillness made him look up. The furrowed expression on Martin's face convinced him that he wasn't just making this up. At that moment his mother walked into the hallway and when her eyes connected with Martin's Sam saw a strange transition. In that brief exchange he witnessed a kind of quickening. He couldn't tell exactly what it meant, but it reminded him of the sudden brightness that fills a room when heat lightning flashes across the horizon on a muggy summer's night. The rush of the wind tossed a few dry leaves over the threshold of the open door, and when Sarah rushed forward to close it the spell was broken.

"Sam," Martin addressed him, "we still have the rest of the day, what would you like to do with it?"

"What?" Since the bowling thing had fallen through, he fully expected Martin to beg off and go out somewhere with his mom, but instead he was offering him another chance.

"I said, where should we go?"

"We don't have to go anywhere," Sam said, giving him an out.

"No, we don't. But I'd still like to spend some time with you."

"Yeah," he said, still unconvinced.

Martin suggested a sit-down restaurant, take-out Chinese, a movie, the video arcade, watching the game on TV, but nothing appealed to Sam until Martin mentioned "The Glades." This craggy salient that jutted out into the sea at the far end of Horse Neck Beach, just south of the Powder Point Bridge, had always seemed mysterious and unavailable. Built in the early thirties, it had been a private summer retreat for Captain Henry W. Litchfield who fought in the 'Great War' at places like Belleau Wood and Verdun, and came home missing the fingers from his right hand. Later he became a local scholar and historian. He died in the mid-fifties and the property went to a distant relative in Arizona. Sam had gleaned all this from local gossip and the stories that his aunt had told to his mother.

Sarah stepped into the vestibule, pressed aside the gauzy curtain and looked out one of the sidelights. "The weather looks awfully threatening," she warned.

Then as she turned to face Sam and Martin, who were standing in the hallway, Sam noticed that the diffused light coming through the crescent of glass at the top of the door set the fuzzy edge of her auburn hair aglow. Her fiery halo dissolved when she came back into the darkened hallway, but for a moment he had the impression that his mother was beautiful.

"Isn't that private property?" Sarah asked fretfully.

"Yes, but I know the caretaker and a quick call should get us through the gate," Martin answered.

Growing up, Sam had always had a secret desire to explore this forbidden point. It was posted and fenced. And though it was a fence that could easily be scaled, the No Trespassing signs had kept him away. Others had ignored them, only to be caught by the watchful caretaker and brought home by the police.

While Martin went into the kitchen to make his call, Sam turned to his mother restively and pleaded with her not to put the kibosh on this. "Mom, you've got to let me go."

"But Sam, it's the middle of November, it's cold, and it looks like rain."

"All the better!" he said, feeling in a rebellious mood.

"How can you say that?"

He couldn't explain it, but the threat of bad weather made the whole adventure seem even more appealing. "Oh mom," he begged. "Don't make me explain, just let me go!"

She looked over his shoulder and the telltale gleam in her eye told him Martin was coming back down the hall.

"We're all set," Martin said. He seemed to address Sam, but when he turned Martin's focus was on his mother. *God,* he thought, *these two have got it bad!*

"Not so fast," Sarah interrupted. "I don't like this idea, but if you two are determined I can't let you go the way you are," she said, waving her hand at Martin's light-gray sweatshirt.

"What do you mean?" they asked in unison.

"I mean that you'll have to take a raincoat or an umbrella or something."

"You're not serious!" Sam groaned.

"Look, humor me. If you won't wear this stuff," she said holding out a plastic poncho and a windbreaker that she had taken off the coat-tree, "at least take them with you. You can put them in a rucksack," she added, as she went to the vestibule and reached into the boot box to haul out an old canvas bag with leather straps. She advanced toward Sam and shoved it in his hand.

"Yuck!" he said, holding it gingerly by one strap and hanging his arms out in an apish gesture. "Mommm, it's got holes in it!"

"Only little ones," she noted, then turned on Martin. "You're too big for me to boss around, but you ought to have something besides that sweatshirt. Wait—there's an old Mackinaw in the back hall," she said as she rushed off to find it.

As his mother disappeared through the kitchen doorway, Sam gave Martin a disgruntled look that said: *Are you going to let her get away with this?*

"She's your mother. Besides, she said we had to bring this stuff, she didn't say we had to wear it," he reasoned, then gave Sam a conspicuous wink.

But that wasn't the end of it; next she wanted to make them sandwiches and then insisted they take something warm to drink. An hour later, with the rucksack and a gym bag and a plastic shopping bag full of sandwiches, they finally made it out the door to Martin's car.

Considering that it was the middle of the day, the sky looked unusually dark. Its steel-gray color reflected off the cold blackness of the sea. And as they followed Beachwood Road, Sam caught glimpses of the waves between the houses. Further out, the wind stirred up the chop and beat the water into angry whitecaps.

After crossing the Powder Point Bridge, they came to a stop at the corner of Seaside Drive, and on the other side of the intersection Sam saw a signpost, which read: Warning, Private Way, NO THROUGH TRAFFIC. Martin ignored the sign and followed the paved roadway a hundred feet or so where the blacktop disappeared and they continued on a gravel drive. From here, Sam heard the crunch of the tires until they went through an iron gate, which had obviously been left open for them. Martin steered the car into a wide turnaround and switched off the engine.

"I don't want to lug all this gear out to the point, but it would be nice to have something to eat when we get there," Martin said, looking at the bags lined up on his back seat.

Sam reached behind him and grabbed the canvas rucksack. He dumped out all the contents and then opened the shopping bag, extracted a couple of sandwiches and the thermos and tucked them nattily into the rucksack. It was old and carried a musty smell that might infect the food, but he didn't care: it was smaller than the other two bags and the straps made it easier to carry.

"Hey!" Martin shouted in protest when he looked at the mess. "Oh, to hell. . .with it."

Walking deeper into the estate, Martin pointed to the west. "Look," he said. Sam turned to follow his hand and saw the roof and upper floors of a large house swelling up from behind the stubby pine like the carcass of a beached whale. The slate shingles gave it an Old World look and even with half the house buried in the undergrowth he could tell that this place had been built on a grand scale.

"What would you think about living in that?" Martin asked

The straight line of the roof, broken in several places by tiny dormers and beefy gables, and obscured by wisps of wet fog, reminded Sam of the sort of manor house that appeared in old black-and-white horror movies. There was an extravagance of chimneys thrusting skyward, some tall and skinny had iron bracing for support, and others broad and substantial had a line of clay pots capping each flue. Having dreamed up all kinds of fantasies about this place, he was not disappointed. It proved to be just as barren and foreboding as he had imagined it. And the house had the same sense of mystery and decadence that he'd read about in Poe's, "The Fall of the House of Usher," one of three scary tales which he had studied last year in Mrs. Pomeroy's English class.

"Not me," he answered. "It's too big, too cold looking to be a real home."

"It may be big, but if you were to see it on a sunny day I think you'd find it a lot more enchanting. I should bring you back sometime to meet the owner so that you can get a look at the inside."

"I'd like that," Sam agreed. But it wasn't the house he was interested in. "How do we get out there?" he said, raising his hand and waving it toward the sea.

"It depends."

In front of them the weather-beaten terrain stretched out in an implacable tangle of rocks and dry coarse grass. A mixture of grays and browns and other earthy colors, which were subdued in the dreary afternoon light, gave the scene the same sluggish charm that Sam remembered seeing in a painting of the Maine coast by Andrew Wyeth. At the edge of the sea huge ledges of rock rose up to the north and south like two great arms extending out on either side to form a cozy inlet. Under warmer and calmer conditions this would have been a lovely place to swim—private and isolated—cut off from the rest of the shoreline. But today it was cold and uninviting.

"Do you want this to be easy or hard?" Martin asked.

"Hard, of course."

"Truly said—whenever there are two ways to do something, real men always choose the hard way."

Sam ignored this kooky bit of philosophy and scrambled to the top of a tilted slab of rock. From his new vantagepoint he could see a well-worn path, which led more or less directly to the beach, but he knew there was nothing to conquer if he went that way. He wanted danger—and even injury, not the kind worthy of a Purple Heart, but something deep enough to form a scab and maybe leave a scar.

He clambered over the scabrous terrain, climbing up craggy rocks and dropping into the narrow spaces between until he came to one that rose higher than the others. On one side he found a crevice that angled upward and wedging his sneaker into the opening he hauled himself up and edged his way along using whatever handholds he could find until he reached the top. Standing, he surveyed the scene, scanning ahead to the angry sea; then turning back to observe how far they had come. For all his effort to reach the shore the mansion had not diminished that much in size. Past the house a grassy slope rose gently upward to a row of elms whose webby branches were silhouetted against the scudding clouds. From so high up he was wholly exposed to the wind and it pulled at his light clothing and snapped the hair back from his scalp. Gathering up the collar of his jacket, he began to appreciate his mother's warning to dress warmly. He buttoned the extra tab around his neck and stuffed his hands deep into his pockets. For a moment he felt like an explorer discovering a new country, but as the skin on his cheeks began to sting, he decided to come down. Sitting, then dropping his legs over the edge, he took Martin's extended hand and jumped to the ground. The stony surface penetrated the soles of his shoes, sending quick shock waves up his calves as he tensed his muscles and fought to hold his balance.

Now to avoid the cold they stayed in the channels between the rocks, weaving back and forth, pressing deep into the maze until they finally broke out onto the stony shingle facing the sea. A wide ribbon of rocks, round and smooth from the constant friction of the waves, created a treacherous barrier that was hard to negotiate. Beyond, he saw a narrow strip of fine wet sand that seemed far less hostile. So pulling at Martin's sleeve they crossed directly to the sand, and staying close to the edge of the shingle, which was only a few feet away from the shallow wash of the waves, they walked along heading toward the rocky ledge that closed off one end of the beach.

Sam's shoes were soon dowsed by a rogue wave that rushed up to surround him, rising above his soles and coming in through his laces to soak his socks. After that he was more watchful. When he and Martin had traveled a hundred yards or so the sand disappeared in front of a steep stone wall and they were forced to slog back up the sloping shingle before they found a spot where they could climb out onto the granite salient that blocked their way.

They scrambled along a scaly path, stepping over cracks and fissures that divided the ledge into a series of broken blocks. Some openings were three or four feet wide and at least as many deep; others only inches apart. Each section seemed to rise a little higher than the last until they came to the end. Here they dropped down a foot or so onto a low promontory where the waves beat savagely against every side.

A briny mixture shot upwards, shattering into thousands of tiny particles. Driven by the wind this wet cloud swept over them, and the cold spray pelted Sam's face with a sharpness that was strangely exhilarating. Whether he was being brave or foolhardy didn't matter, he was enjoying himself. Nevertheless, after a few minutes his light jacket soaked through and he had to withdraw. Martin retreated with him and they fell back several feet and descended into the shelter of a wide crevasse. Slipping on the mossy sides they climbed down and put their backs to the sea.

Sam hauled the thermos out of the bag and tried to pour some of the hot drink into the cup, but the stiff wind sucked it away. "Damn," he shouted, tasting the salt air. Sam clamped the metal cup between his knees and took a pull directly from the thermos, then passed it to Martin. Handing it back and forth, the hot herbal tea felt good going down.

He couldn't say why—but as far back as he could remember he had always associated the Glades with a kind of somber mythology. Probably that image had been exaggerated, but today it didn't seem so farfetched. And in spite of the numbing cold, inside he was on fire. He suspected that being here with Martin had something to do with that feeling, but he tried to pass that off as nonsense, or as Scrooge might say: "Humbug!" But it wasn't humbug: he knew that Martin had done something his father couldn't—maybe because his father didn't want to, or because he didn't care, or maybe because he didn't know how.

He heard Martin complaining as he rubbed his thick hands together. "Now I wish I'd taken that old mackinaw. We could both use the jackets we left on the back seat of the car."

"I guess," Sam said.

Sam cared for this man in a way that had never been possible with his father, and for some reason that ticked him off. Martin had a fundamental goodness that was so contrary to his experience with his father that it frightened him and he wondered if that was normal—could any man really be that decent or was it just a cruel trick to win his confidence?

"Haven't you had enough of this?" Martin asked, with a tinge of desperation in his voice.

"No, not yet," Sam shouted into the wind. "Couldn't we eat those sandwiches first?"

"My fingers are too numb. I'm not sure I could hold onto a sandwich. Besides, I don't want to take my hands out of my pockets to find out," Martin answered.

"Couldn't we just sit here then? I don't want to go—not yet."

Martin turned to him and Sam could see the concern in his eyes. He couldn't tell whether that concern was generated by the cold or if it held some deeper meaning.

Without saying a word Martin put his arm around him. Huddled together on this gloomy point, wedged between these moss-covered rocks, bracing against the cold, Sam suddenly understood why he was afraid. He liked this man—trusted him—but a long history of betrayal warned him how dangerous that could be.

Unexpectedly, Martin's burly fingers came up and plowed deep into the tangled mop on top of Sam's head. A tingle of excitement disturbed the roots and a thick bubble rose in Sam's throat, making it hard to breathe. With a gasp he filled his lungs with cold air; and when he let go, he spit out his fear in a low growl and let it blow away on the wind. Martin pressed Sam's face tightly into his shoulder, and when he inhaled the pungent mix of dampness and sweat from Martin's sweatshirt he suddenly felt warm and safe.

Chapter 38

Not yet five o'clock and it was already dark. The lights from Martin's car sent back a blurry glare from the wet pavement and the windshield wipers whumped back and forth in a sleepy cadence. The rain had come in earnest shortly after they pulled out onto the road. Returning to the car hadn't been nearly as much fun as the trip out to the point, and now in the afterglow, Sam's perspective had changed. He wondered, why did this little adventure seem like such a big deal? And what exactly had been going on during those few minutes while the two of them were squished together between the rocks?

He should have been exhausted, and he was; but in a contradictory sort of way he also felt invigorated. That too confused him. None of this seemed real, and his reaction to it was fractured and irrational. When Martin stopped the car in front of the house, neither one got out. They both said, "Well," and since they said it at the same time they both laughed.

Sam reached back and started to gather up the mess on the back seat.

"Leave it," Martin instructed. "I'll get that later. Let's not tell your mother we didn't use this stuff. Okay?"

"Sure."

"She went to a lot of trouble. I don't want her to think we didn't appreciate it. If they're not too soggy, I'll eat the sandwiches on the way home," Martin added, flexing his fingers nervously on the steering wheel.

"Well, was it worth it?" Martin asked as Sam grasped the door handle.

"Ya. I mean, it was pretty raw, but it was awesome too."

Martin pulled back his sleeve to check his watch. "Damn," he said, seemingly to himself. "I've got to get going!"

"You're not coming in?" Sam knew Martin had plans to go out with his mother that evening—as a matter of fact, he had made similar plans with Jennifer. But that was hours away and Martin never missed an opportunity to be with his mother, even if it was only for ten minutes.

"No, I loved to, but I'm already due at the doctor's."

The word doctor set off some bells, but Sam didn't ask. Instead he stepped out onto the wet drive and shielding his face from the rain, ran across the soggy lawn to the front door. He could tell that his mother had been waiting because she had the door open before he got there. He must have looked a mess, but she didn't say anything.

"Hi mom," he muttered, and he kissed her on the cheek. He popped off his muddy shoes in the vestibule and rushed past her to bound up the stairs to his room. As he stripped off his dirty clothes he could see that he was soaked through and his skin felt damp and clammy. A hot shower seemed the sensible way to restore his body temperature and peeking into the hallway he streaked bare-assed into the bathroom.

Once he was standing under the steamy spray he wondered about tonight—in public he would be fine, but what if they ended up alone again? Em's words were still fresh in his mind, but not wholly digested. He knew that what she said made sense, and by himself in his room he could treat her advice sensibly; but in Jennifer's presence, where he could touch her and smell her, and get lost in the sparkle of her eyes, things always got a little crazy. How could he expect to control himself when just the thought of her caused him problems? In fact, he could look down right now and see the rapid onset of one of those problems and Jennifer wasn't even there.

After all these weeks, did he even know Jennifer that well? Maybe some of the little things. Her smile, for example—incredible—but it often showed on her lips and not in her eyes, and that could be bad. Sometimes that sweet smile came before a laugh, and sometimes before her tears. And he couldn't always tell which would lead to which.

And when it came to the big stuff like kissing he had no idea what she wanted. One moment she'd ask for a quick peck on the cheek and that felt fine, but if the kiss were mouth to mouth and lasted longer than thirty seconds, or if she decided to swap spit then that really put his boxers in a bunch. And he wondered if she had any idea how easily she could take him through all these conflicting changes. He supposed that if he didn't hold her in so much awe, he might have had more control. But he did hold her in awe and that clearly affected his judgement.

Now that he was out of the bathroom and trying to decide what to wear, his mind shifted back to Martin. Here was another conundrum. He could certainly understand why his mother found him so agreeable. Martin was caring and genuine and his father had been such a fraud.

"Sam," his mother called up the stairs, "do you want something to eat before you go?"

"No."

"You really should have something—otherwise you'll just fill up on junk," she said, with a solicitous squeak as she tried to get her voice to carry up the stairwell.

"So, what's wrong with junk as long as I don't eat it every day?"

"Nothing, I suppose," she said. And when he heard her walk away without winning her argument, he thought that she had given in too easily.

Chapter 39

𝒜n hour later, Sam stood outside Jennifer's door. When she welcomed him in, he didn't say a word, not even *Wha'sup*.

She turned to get her coat off the hook, and when she faced him again she said: "You look choked—what's got you down?"

"What makes you think I'm down?"

"Because I've seen that mug often enough to know when you're bummed out. Is it me?"

"NO—well, in a way yes," he said. How could Jennifer be so much more sensitive to his moods than he was to hers?

"Don't get funny—which is it?"

"Well, you didn't do anything, but it's still your fault," he said.

"What?"

"I can't explain it," he answered, peevishly. "It's too crazy."

"Coward!"

"Am not," he argued, as he tried to straighten out the collar on his jacket.

"Then tell me about it."

"Maybe later."

"Okay, you're off the hook for now, but. . ."

"Can we go?" he asked, taking her hand.

"Absolutely!" she said, and walking just behind she gave him a friendly whack on the bum.

"Hey," he yelped, taking a double step.

"Hey yourself," she said, closing the door.

Sarah and Martin were waiting in the car and had already honked twice to show their impatience. Hand in hand they rushed across Jennifer's sandy yard and Sam helped Jennifer into the back before scooting over onto the seat beside her.

As the car pulled away Jennifer sat quietly watching the couple in the front. She'd met Sam's mother a couple of times and he had told her something about Martin. Jennifer pumped Sam continually for information, acting as if she were following her favorite soap opera. Generally she wanted details he couldn't provide, but with all her interest she had never seen the two together before and Sam guessed that she was anxious to witness some tantalizing display of affection. She wasn't entirely disappointed. There was a special tremor—a sparkling intent—in Sarah's voice whenever she spoke to Martin, and Sam could tell by the smile on Jennifer's face that she heard it too.

Sam tried to distract Jennifer by laying his hand over hers, but she slapped it away.

"Hey!" he said.

"Not now," she answered without taking her eyes off of his mother.

This was embarrassing. It simply wasn't cool to be on a date with your own mother, especially when she was sitting in the front seat with her boyfriend. Boyfriend? God, that sounded weird. If he had a car of his own, maybe next year when he turned sixteen,but right now he could only dream of the kind of independence that would bring. As he stared straight ahead the lights from an oncoming car flashed in his eyes and he squinted against the brightness.

He had learned something from Martin: all relationships were not built around anger and betrayal. He could see that Martin loved his mother and he supposed that that was good, but it also made him jealous. Once his father died Sam didn't have to share his mother's love with anyone and now Martin threatened to spoil all that. He knew he was being selfish, but he didn't care. And besides, he envied Martin. The little things he did: a glance, a smile, a word of approval, seemed to come so easily as if he were reading his mother's mind. Yet every effort Sam made with Jennifer always seemed somehow off the mark, like hitting the keys on a piano that's constantly out of tune.

"Sam—Sam!" Jennifer called, tugging on the sleeve of his jacket.

"What?" He asked, as she began to shove him toward the car door.

"Boy, you were really lunchin'! I mean totally tuned out."

"Sorry," he said, feeling a little disoriented.

"Sorry for what? We're here—you have to get out."

Leaving the car, they both ran across the crowded plaza to get to the front of the theater. It was Friday night and a long line waited to buy tickets. The kids in front kept changing places. One friend would recognize another and they would jump ahead to join them. This continual reorganization put Sam and Jennifer near some friends of their own.

"Sam! Jennifer!" Richard Gordon flapped his hands in the air to get their attention.

At sixteen, Richie had a license and wheels, which made him a man of the world, and his girlfriend, Amy, hugged him in her arms like a momma bear protecting her cub. "Join the posse!" he invited.

When they moved up, there were a few catcalls, and Sam cowered as they pressed forward. But Jennifer was incensed and drove back their curses with an intelligent prattle that cut their four-letter words to pieces. Once they were in line again Richie introduced them to another couple, Walker and Lauren. Walker was part of the Gibson family, not Sam's Gibsons, but the ones who ran the hardware store in Southbridge. Suddenly the ticket booth opened and the line began to surge forward. After they got their tickets and stepped into the lobby, they pooled their funds and used the money to buy a super-size barrel of popcorn, a large box of Milk Duds, and a tray of soft drinks. During the time it had taken to meet and get through the doors leading down the aisle, they had evolved from separate couples into a group. Schmoozing and joking, this dewy-eyed six-some elbowed their way between the rows of seats and settled in somewhere near the middle of the theater. They managed to get through the movie more or less peacefully. But frequent whisperings and giggles did provoke some reprimands from an elderly couple who sat nearby. *Jeeze,* Sam thought, *what do they expect? It's a Saturday night date movie and most of the seats are filled with teenagers.*

The movie they'd chosen was "Crocodile Dundee" and Sam often studied Jennifer's face in the glow from the screen. Her intense reactions to Paul Hogan amused him. "Do you think he's hot?" Sam asked, as he leaned in surreptitiously and sprayed his envy into her ear. She brought her fingers up to wipe away a tiny bit of spittle and started to laugh. Nothing sissified, but a hearty guffaw that made other people look and wonder.

"And like you don't think Linda Kozlowski is hot?"

"Hoo ya," he said, a little too enthusiastically.

"Well, then?" She waited, but he had no defense.

"Yeah, I think Hogan is stud material, and that Aussie accent is definitely sexy. Does that bother you?"

"Some, but I'm not wrapped up in it. Besides, he's up there on the screen and I'm the one down here sitting next to you."

She giggled deliciously at this, and pulled his hand from the armrest down onto her knee. Then in a surprisingly swift maneuver she trapped his hand beneath her own and dragged it slowly down so that his fingers rested on the softness of her thigh. He didn't want to believe that she had anything indecent in mind, but analyzing her motives did nothing at all to relieve his anxiety. From that point on he was never really sure what was happening on the screen, and when the movie ended and the credits rolled down, his hand was still caught beneath hers.

Before they stood to leave Richie whispered something in Jennifer's ear. And when she rose from her seat, she turned and bent over Sam, letting her hair fall forward. Sam's upturned face was suddenly hidden by a curly curtain that gave them an odd kind of privacy. He thought she wanted to kiss him, but it was only to pass on Richie's message.

"Richie has his car and he wants us to join him," she said softly.

"But Martin will be out there waiting for us."

"I know, but can't you talk to him—talk to your mother?" she begged.

Sam knew that Richie's car was too small for six, but with Jennifer hovering over him, her breath smelling of popcorn, her hair tickling his cheeks, he couldn't say no. "I'll try," he promised.

Richie brought his car to the front and Jennifer and the others piled in while Sam crossed the road to talk to his mother. He pleaded and groveled and spread on the honey until he wore his mother down. "Eleven o'clock, no later," she said, caving in.

"Okay—whatever," he agreed hastily, then ran toward the cloud of smoke rising from Richie's exhaust. No way could he be back by eleven, but as long as he got in before midnight things would be cool. It was a kind of code: his mother would name a time and he would add to it, but he understood that if he added anything more than an hour there would be reprisals.

Richie had a small Toyota wagon and the seats were filled, so Sam lifted the tailgate and climbed in. Curled up in a box-like space behind the second seat, he couldn't easily close the gate and Richie had to get out and slam it shut. The car shook so hard when it pulled away from the curb Sam thought that parts of the body might separate from the frame. They took off down the main drag and every bump made it clear that Richie's car had no shocks. Cruising the side streets of Freetown got old quickly, and after some spirited discussion they decided to drive out on Silver Beach Road to the lighthouse.

The Silver Beach Station had been closed for over forty years. The government still owned the property and had posted it against trespassing, but with no fences or gates, everybody, young and old, went there to make out.

Starting on Gannett Road and heading northwest, they turned south onto Kent and then east on Silver Beach Road, continuing cautiously along the rutted path until it ended in a dirt and gravel clearing in front of the lighthouse. If the weather were warmer, everyone would have piled out and scattered to hiding places among the rocks—places where they could do private things and not be seen. But this late in the season the cold kept them all in the car—well, not all. Because there were too many of them and no sensible way for everyone to pair off, Sam and Jennifer volunteered to step outside. Hot and sweaty from the closeness of the car, the sharp ocean breeze cut through Sam's jacket, raising the hair on his arms and shrinking the tiny capillaries under his skin.

Sam took Jennifer's hand and they hustled off into the dark, hoping to find some shelter on the leeward side of the lighthouse. They worked their way over the uneven piles of loose stones until they reached the base of the red-and-white banded tower. A walkway made of canted granite slabs led around to the other side and they followed it till they came to a shingled wall that connected the keeper's cottage to the tower. They felt their way along the rough cedar, stopping under an open portico. Here they pressed into a corner next to an old doorway and found some protection from the constant wind. Nearby, they could hear the slapping of the waves against the rocks. It was too dark for them to see anything beyond the slatted fence that ran in a wavy line from the cottage to the end of the point. The two crouched together for warmth, but Jennifer still complained of the cold. In an effort to give her some relief Sam opened his jacket, stretched it around her and zipped her inside.

"This is crazy," she said.

"No kidding."

He could barely see her face reflected in the dim light from the last quarter of the old moon and even that came and went as the dark clouds scudded across the sky. When a thread of light emerged from behind a cloud, it painted her forehead and nose and a spot on her right cheek in a blue softness, and left the rest of her features to blend with the inky blackness of the sheltering portico. The effect was tantalizing and he shuddered with anticipation. He felt on edge. Keenly aware of her presence and filled by a desire to protect her. Not just by wrapping his coat around her, but somehow he wanted to draw her in and pull her down inside in the same way that he drew in the cold night air. Jennifer's warm breath rose like smoke in front of his face. He watched his own misty breath mingle with hers and wished that it were as easy for them to blend soul to soul.

"Kiss me," she whispered in the stillness, and Sam froze. He heard the blood rushing in his ears, shutting out the gentle wash of the waves. He wanted this. He wanted to kiss her to taste her, to swallow her sweetness as if it were some kind of magic elixir, but Em's warnings were out there floating on the breeze, bumping and scratching at the threshold of his conscience, and the conflict was electrifying.

His height matched hers and when he shifted his feet they rubbed noses. Squished inside Sam's jacket Jennifer slipped her cold fingers up under the loose edge of his shirt, which had already come undone in the car. She slid her hands along either side of his spine and pressed her fingers into his hot skin. A moment before her firm breasts barely touched him, now they were crushed hard against his own. He dropped his mouth anxiously over hers and when he felt the flutter of her tongue seeking entry he thought he could hear the ends of his nerves snap. He parted his lips, and when that eager serpent dove in and scraped against the roof of his mouth it set off a warm explosion deep in his gut and his penis quickly began to grow. Cramped for space he squirmed to make some accommodation. Then, just as the beast uncurled, Jennifer withdrew and the tension quickly fell away. Now that he could breathe, he drew heavily from the damp night air and when he let it out a kind of velvet trill escaped from his throat—a primal sound of exaltation so strange that he wouldn't have believed it came from inside him if he hadn't felt it vibrate in his own throat.

Body to body inside his jacket, he felt her softness trapped against the solid frame of his ribs, and he wondered how far this might have gone and what she might have expected of him if they weren't standing outside in the cold.

He couldn't say anything—he had no words. And he imagined from Jennifer's long silence that she felt the same. After an eternity, which probably lasted little more than a minute, she began to giggle—a kind of jittery explosion—girlish and childlike.

"Have you ever done that before?" she asked, burying her chin in the furry collar of his jacket.

"Kiss, yes—that way, never," he said. Nor had a single kiss ever brought such an immediate reaction. For the first time that freakish part of him had served for something other than an embarrassment. It actually made him feel normal; but he didn't dare tell her that.

"Me either," she mumbled into his soft collar. She lifted her hands from his back, walked them around and pressed them into the muscle just below his ribs. The ticklish movement made him scrunch and pull away, which opened a space between them and his nerves began to unfold and relax.

"Really?" he asked.

"Really."

The idea that he had been the first, that she had saved herself for him when he knew at least a dozen guys who would have sold their soul for . . . well, that was an exaggeration, but it was an exaggeration that pleased him.

Breathing deeply, he drew her in. "Do I smell roses?" he asked.

"It's my soap," she confirmed.

"And . . ." he hesitated, trying to identify a dry sweetness that mingled with the soap, "and baby powder?"

"Yes," she approved. "I sprinkled a little on after my shower."

He didn't say anything about the conspicuous taste of the lemon drop that she had eaten on the way out to the lighthouse. Instead he started to equivocate. "I like this. I mean you and I—here," he said, giving her a quick squeeze, "but—"

"How can there be a but?" she asked.

"Well . . .I," he said stopping to sort out his thoughts. "I mean, this is the stuff that our parents warn us about—you know?"

"Yep," she said popping the 'p' at the end.

"Doesn't this scare you?"

"Yes," she said. "I get a little conked."

"What's it like? I mean for a girl what's it feel like?"

"I don't know," she said, shaking her head. "It's hard to explain. Deep down there's this tiny pull as if I were shrinking—getting tighter. And I'm all anxious as if my nerves are getting ready to explode."

"And that's good?"

"Yes, absolutely. It's a little strange—but—I like it. And—then there's this smell. Maybe it's in your hair or on your clothes, but—"

"Are you trying to tell me that I stink?"

"No. No, it's not like that. It's more basic. Something that identifies you and only you. Whatever it is, it's incredible, and if I could find the source I swear I'd cover my whole body with it."

"That sounds kinda groady," he said, thankful that she couldn't find the source."

"IS NOT! You're terrible," she said, moving the fingers of one hand up to his breast and digging her nails into him.

"Owww!"

"Well, you asked for it," she said, rubbing the muscle to repair the damage. Moving in a circle she bumped against his hard nipple repeatedly, which set his nerves on edge and got him excited all over again.

"That's not helping," he said squirming and rolling his shoulder into hers to get her to stop. She withdrew her hand and giggled as if she suddenly guessed what she'd been doing to him. For several minutes neither one spoke. Then Jennifer took a different tack.

"The guys," she said, "the ones who come scatchin' around, looking for—well, you know. Always seem so full of themselves. They can't wait to tell me how great they are. But you're different."

"You mean I'm a nerd," he said, putting his hands in his jacket pockets, which effectively pulled the two of them together again.

"No. Well, yeah. But when these guys start their scammin', warning lights go off and my first instinct is to find a way to puncture their crusty little egos, and that—that gets me a reputation for being a bitch."

"Not!" he insisted.

"But I am," she said, then banged her forehead against his hard enough to make it hurt. "Sometimes I get a little crazy."

"Don't let em get to you. These are the same jocks who brag about nailing every girl they meet. They strut around in the locker room talking about T&A, and acting like they're some kind of expert. It's B S."

"What do they say about me?" she asked.

He hadn't expected her to ask that and he didn't want to tell her. "Nothing," he lied, then changed the subject. "They think I'm a dork," he continued. "Too brainy—wouldn't know what to do with a girl if she tore her clothes off and begged for it."

"You don't buy that crap, do you?"

"I try to tell myself it doesn't matter, but the fact is they're right. Still—I can't change who I am. They act like girls are only good for one thing. If you can't get into their pants. . . Jeeze, I can't believe I'm telling you this!"

"Don't worry, the girls aren't any better, it's all about the size of a guy's—well. Cathy even complains that her boyfriend's—you know," she shrugged, "is crooked. She says that it sticks out sideways when he's excited. Is that possible?"

"What?" he gulped, not knowing what else to say. He didn't think girls talked about this stuff. And her question indicated that Cathy hadn't just seen this guy naked, which meant that she was doing more than just looking.

"Forget it," she said. "This is getting way weird." Her quick dismissal made Sam suspect that Jennifer knew what he was thinking.

"It's cool," he said, trying not to show his horror.

"Cool?"

"Well, maybe not cool. But a coupla months ago I couldn't even say hello to you, and now it's like nothing's off limits."

"I suppose," she said, "but maybe some things should be—off limits, that is."

Shifting nervously, he could feel a trickle of cold sweat run down his back, and he shivered.

Jennifer felt the shiver and asked if he was okay.

"Fine." His hands still in his jacket pockets he gave her a squeeze to reassure her.

"All summer long, I worried and watched," he said. Afraid to get too close and now you're here tucked inside my jacket. Em told me to take a chance—do something—say something—"

"What're you talking about?"

"I don't know," he answered, pressing his cheek against the cool softness of her hair.

"I don't know either, Sam. "Sometimes I think you're too analytical."

"You're right. It's just that whenever I'm really happy, I have to pull it apart and find out why."

Another cloud switched off the moonlight and he searched in the blackness for her mouth and kissed her.

"Mmmm, that's more like it," she said. "Give me another, a nice greasy one and then let's get out of here, my legs are getting numb."

Once he had freed her from his jacket, he zippered the front and pushed up the collar. Pulling his head down, he leaned into the wind and led her around the tower. The polished round stones were treacherous, crunching and popping under foot they constantly lost their balance and had to prop each other up.

Jennifer clutched at his waist for support, and with an unexpected lurch Sam remembered that he hadn't answered her question. "Why did you want to know about that guy being crooked?"

"What?" she squawked, as if she were a crow and he had just pulled out one of her tail feathers.

"You know—crooked. Like your girlfriend's boyfriend?" he explained, then wished he hadn't brought this up again.

"Ooooh," she said with sudden realization. "Curiosity. Once I get a picture like that in my head it keeps popping up, and it's hard to shake." He nearly gagged on her choice of words.

"Do you think I'm terrible for having such thoughts?"

"No way! I wouldn't dare tell you about the kooky things that come into my head," he revealed.

"Why not?"

"Because they'd be too gross," he said, tripping and falling into her again. They stood there holding onto each other and she looked into his eyes. What if she could read his thoughts right now or worse, if she could have gotten into his mind while they were on the other side of the lighthouse?

"Are you okay?" she asked

"Ya, yeah," he said, thinking that a second ago he was a wreck but oddly, right now, at this moment he couldn't possibly feel any more okay.

Coming up to the rusty gray wagon they could see that the others had not been idle. Warm bodies and heavy breathing had fogged the glass and even with the dome light on they couldn't see inside. Sam had to tap on the driver's window to get Richie's attention. Richie opened his door and stepped out with keys in hand, so he could open the rear hatch. Stopping for a moment, he tucked in his shirt and pushed his unruly hair back from his face. Even in the dull light from the open door Sam noticed the dark smudges on his face. It wasn't hard to tell where they came from and he wanted to laugh, but didn't dare. As he curled up in back, Jennifer scrunched in beside Walker and Lauren. The couple rushed to straighten their rumpled clothing, and Sam silently pictured the sort of touchie-feelie thingies that had gotten them into this condition.

While they all passed around a towel and tried to clear the windows, Richie started the engine, and spinning the wheels, they turned around and headed back toward Green Harbor.

When Sam brought Jennifer to her back door it was well past his curfew, and before they had a chance to kiss goodnight her father switched on the porch light. Then when Sam didn't take the hint he swung the door wide and stood menacingly in the entryway. He said nothing, just took his daughter by the arm, pulled her inside, then closed the door. It was kind of a letdown, but Sam was glad he had escaped her father's acrimony. He supposed that if he had a daughter who was that gorgeous; he would be protective too.

♦ ♦ ♦

Sarah and Martin were waiting when he got in. Mom just told him to go up to bed, saying they could talk in the morning. He wondered what she meant by that, as he stripped down to his boxer shorts and T-shirt; then went into the bathroom to brush his teeth. Would she just ask him about his date with Jennifer or would he get one of those "I'm the parent, you're the child" lectures.

Chapter 40

Sam did have that talk the next morning, but it didn't amount to much—just the usual parent child thing. His mother worried that he and Jennifer were getting too serious and she cautioned him to be careful. He told her he was being careful, but he knew he was only treading water and that the smallest wave might drown him. Right or wrong, when Jennifer had him in her embrace, he doubted he had the resolve to walk away especially if it meant putting his relationship with her in jeopardy.

♦ ♦ ♦

Thanksgiving came, and compared to past Thanksgivings it was uneventful—that is, nothing bad happened. Sam's mother invited Martin and he didn't come just to eat, he also came to cook. Two days before, Sarah pulled out the cookbooks and sprinkled and rolled and baked, filling the house with the smell of cookies and pies; but Martin took over the dinner. He showed up at seven in the morning with a wrinkled brown paper bag filled with secret ingredients and went to work.

After years of living with a father who sometimes didn't even show up, watching Martin stuff the bird and cut up vegetables was a benchmark and gave Sam new respect for this gentle man. He sat with his elbows on the table, hands under his chin, his eyes wide open, following the action, as Martin hustled determinedly around the kitchen, only asking for his mother's help when he needed to find a bowl or pan that eluded him in this strange setting. And when the bird went into the oven and everything began to boil on top of the stove, Martin wiped his hands on the pinstriped apron Sarah had tied around his waist, and went into the living room to sit down and wait.

When the meal was finally on the table, arranged in heaping bowls, and the sweet smell of rosemary and sage rose up from the stuffing, Martin gave a short prayer (another oddity in a day filled with oddities), then plunged the knife into the turkey. When they were done, a bony carcass stood in the center of the table, surrounded by dirty dishes and half-empty water glasses. Sarah scraped the leavings into an empty bowl that had held the mashed potatoes and stacked the empty dishes for transport to the kitchen sink.

Sam and Martin retired to the living room to watch the game, and between plays they caught glimpses of Sarah in the dining room as she shuttled back and forth. Later they heard a crash of pans and the tinkle of dishes as she attacked the mess in the kitchen, but neither made a move to help. It wasn't fair, but Sarah didn't complain.

◆ ◆ ◆

Sam couldn't remember a Thanksgiving like this. The last one that he had spent with his father was full of tension and fear—the kind that tied his stomach in knots. After dinner he'd sat on the couch waiting for his father to do something stupid. His father had been drinking all morning and now crashed through the house like a raging bull. An hour later he passed out—sprawled across the living room floor. Sam and his mother took advantage of the peaceful stillness and stepping over him they retired to the small TV in the kitchen to enjoy what remained of the day. When bedtime came Robert still lay unconscious and they hoped that he'd stay that way through the night and not come up to terrorize them in their sleep. Sometime in the early morning hours Sam awoke to hear his father stumbling through the kitchen, slamming cabinet doors, looking for a hidden bottle. Swearing, he smashed objects against the walls and banged into furniture, frustrated because he couldn't find what he wanted. Frightened, Sam dragged the blankets off the bed and curled up with the smell of mothballs in the blackness of his closet.

Finally his father slammed the back door and he heard his pickup groan as he cranked it over in the cold. The engine rattled to life and Robert ground the gears as he beat the mangled truck into submission and took off down the road. Only then did Sam ease his ragged breathing and release his aching muscles from the effort to remain perfectly still.

◆ ◆ ◆

Sitting beside Martin, slouched down on the couch belt unbuckled to relieve the pressure on his full stomach, Sam wondered: *Is this the way it's supposed to be—is this normal?*

When his mother came into the room wiping her hands on a dishtowel he looked up and saw her smiling, but that narrow curve pinching the corners of her mouth seemed wider than usual, the glint in her eyes brighter, as she squinted at them in the late afternoon sun.

"Well, don't you two look comfortable," she said, as if she intended to reprimand them for their slothfulness, but there wasn't any reproach in her words.

"You're welcome to join us," Martin invited, drawing a circle on the cushion at his side.

She dropped the dishtowel on the coffee table, then plopped down on the couch hard enough to make it shudder. Martin's arm fell easily around her shoulder and he gave her a quick buss on the cheek, which brought a throaty chuckle so full of delight that Sam leaned out to look at her.

"What?" she said, looking back at Sam with her eyebrows raised.

"Nothing," he answered, and he fell back into the thick cushions to watch the game on TV. This was a kind of happiness that he had rarely experienced. Not the get-up-and-dance kind of happiness, but something more like the feeling he got when he stood on the bridge at Beaver Creek, especially when it was running clear and he could see the ochre hues of the muddy bottom as the clean water slid over it.

◆ ◆ ◆

This Thanksgiving had brought a kind of epiphany. For years a horny seed had huddled fearfully in his heart, and now hope had forced it to take root and sprout. It grew on hardened ground and might easily wither if exposed to too much sun, but it was a beginning.

Sam and his mother plunged into the holiday bustle with an unusual lightness of spirit. They went shopping together, then came home to wrap. They talked about having a real tree instead of the battle-scarred one that was jammed into a box in the attic. And they discussed the idea of putting some lights on the front of the house; something his dad had always refused to allow.

On the 21st (the first official day of winter) it snowed—only a couple of inches, but it was sufficient. Wet and sticky, the thick flakes clung to the low hanging branches of the evergreens that lined the edge of the road, and created a cold, arching wonderland. Even though this would probably melt in a day or two, snow at this time of the year was always appreciated.

In the evening just before the sun went down Sam dragged the sled out of the garage and he and his mother pulled it up Lindenhurst Road, to the top of the hill. It was an ancient sleigh, one of those bulky contraptions made out of wooden slats and steel, with narrow runners that needed to be polished and waxed to get the best performance. They each managed to make one trip down the hill before the setting sun turned the clouds into a string of fiery plumes then dropped quickly behind the black pines. Afterwards they walked home watching their smoky breath condense in the cold air. And when they stamped their feet and removed their wet boots, his mother promised him a cup of hot chocolate with miniature marshmallows melting on top. All of this seemed so predictable, so Norman Rockwellish, that Sam could hardly stand it, but at the same time he couldn't get enough of it. There had been laughter on the hill and a word or two spoken reverently while the teapot heated on the stove, and in between a cheerful silence that was sometimes scary. Scary because it gave him time to worry that all this was too good to be believed.

♦ ♦ ♦

On Christmas Eve there was a pageant at the Episcopal Church in Southbridge and they all went, including Aunt Em. The ho-hum program was full of tradition: the same old carols and the same story from the gospel of Luke. He'd heard all this before, felt its dull impact pricking at the edge of his consciousness, had observed the smiles that lit up the faces of the congregation and wondered why he couldn't feel that way too. But tonight something got through—not perfectly, but enough so that he could feel a smile on his face that wouldn't go away.

The next morning Martin came over early and the three of them ate a special Christmas breakfast: blueberry pancakes with real blueberries and real maple syrup. Then they opened presents. Late in the afternoon Sam went to his aunt Em's, and then on to Jennifer's, where he gave her a small white box with a green bow taped on top. Jewelry. A shiny brass casting of an elephant with a baby hanging onto its mother's tail. Nothing expensive, only a small piece of costume jewelry, but he'd never given a gift like this to a girl, especially a girl that he thought he was falling in love with.

Jennifer's reaction—the slant of her smile and the lavish hug that smelled like a whole field of wildflowers—filled him with such an outrageous sense of bliss that he didn't know what to do with himself. He started humming; discordant at first, it evolved into a jubilant "Deck the Halls" and he had to clamp his hands over his mouth to stop himself. Jennifer seemed to interpret this as some sort of joke and smiled approvingly.

When the day ended and he had gone home to huddle under the puffy covers of his bed, he had only one concern: what could he do to make these good feelings last? The next morning the high was gone, but it had left a warm afterglow that stayed with him and sustained him through the week. New Year's Eve came and he saw a second chance to fire up his emotions.

His mother and Martin went to a nightclub in Boston, while he and Jennifer were left behind. Home alone, they sat in front of the TV, stuffed themselves with snacks and surfed the channels until it was almost midnight. Switching to the coverage of the crowd in Times Square, they watched the ball slide slowly down the pole and kissed. Then kissed again, and when Jennifer started to unbutton his shirt Sam felt his pulse quicken.

"What are you doing?" he asked.

"Relax, I'm undoing a button, I'm not taking off your clothes."

But when she slipped her hand inside, she sounded disappointed. "What's this?" she asked, rubbing the thick flannel of his undershirt.

"Long-johns," he answered reluctantly.

"Not those things with the flap in the back?"

"No they're two pieces. I don't think they make the flap kind any more."

She undid another button and spread his shirt apart. "Well, at least they're not red."

"What did you expect? It's wintertime; it's cold out."

"Out there yes, but not in here." Whatever Jennifer had in mind, this discovery seemed to knock the wind out of her sails. She scooted to the far side of the couch and picked up a bag of chips, which she munched on with a frightening fierceness.

The coolness of the space between them made him shiver in spite of his long johns, but he knew he couldn't leave this alone. In tiny movements he slowly closed in on Jennifer, then extended his hand in a gesture of peace. She took it, gave it a yank and he fell into her. The embrace that she gave him and the kiss, and another kiss and another, made him hot, and he had no desire to cool things down. At the lighthouse the wind and the cold had made any real intimacy impossible, but here on the couch anything might happen. And Jennifer's agreeable whispers, the yielding arch of her back, the pressure of her fingers pulling at his ears, showed her willingness, but in the end his conscience overtook his desire and he quit.

When Jennifer realized that he wasn't kissing back, she opened her eyes, then turned away quickly to straighten her blouse and pull down her skirt.

"I'm sorry," he said, choking.

"It's okay," she said. But when she swiped the back of her hand across her eyes, he knew it wasn't okay. How could he tell her that he was afraid? Not of her—well, yes, of her too. But the cruelty of being called a freak had taken its toll. All right, he knew that Karl and his friends had grossly exaggerated his condition, but he <u>was</u> imperfect—an unsightly aberration. And aside from any moral considerations, he could never let Jennifer see that imperfection. He was also afraid that his mother and Martin might walk in and catch them, which besides being life-threatening would have been incredibly embarrassing.

Chapter 41

On Friday January 15th, Sam was shaken out of his sleep by the shrill ringing of the phone. Sitting upright in bed, eyes half open, his mind still cobwebby from his last dream, he listened. Another shrill ring pierced the stillness and he wondered if his mother heard it too. But when it rang a third time he knew he would have to answer it. Untangling the bedclothes that were wrapped around his legs, he slid off the edge and was stunned by the cold that had leaked through the windows and penetrated the walls. Crossing the icy wooden floor, he stepped into the hallway and immediately appreciated that it was carpeted. Groping for the phone, he banged his fingers hard against the rim of the hall table, and swore. "Damn!" On the fifth ring his hand closed over the receiver and he brought it to his ear.

"Hello," he said, shivering and wondering how early it was. Only the grayest hint of dawn drifted toward him from the small window at the far end of the hall.

An unfamiliar voice came from the other end of the phone. "Who's this?" a woman asked.

"It's Sam. Who's this?"

"Laura, Martin's neighbor. Is your mother there?" she asked.

"She's in bed," he answered, irritated by having to state the obvious.

"Well, get her up," she ordered. "Now!" she insisted, when he started to mumble in protest.

"Why?" he asked, his mind suddenly alert to the tinge of excitement in Laura's voice.

"Just get her, please," she pleaded, saying the words carefully.

His irritation gave way to fear, and he left the receiver swinging from the edge of the table while he took three quick strides to his mother's door. Pounding, he called out to her.

"Mom—MOM," he repeated.

"Wha—what is it?" she called back in a dry whisper.

"Someone named Laura is on the phone."

When he opened the door he could see that she had turned on the lamp next to her bed. The small bulb barely lit the corner of her room, but enough crept up the wall behind to silhouette her tangled hair.

"What's this about?" She sounded groggy. She rose and shuffled toward him, her forehead knotted with concern. Her nightgown was cockeyed, one thin strap hung loosely off her shoulder, and a pointed corner of her bodice had fallen away, leaving her right breast nearly exposed. Without waiting for an answer she pushed Sam aside, and finding the phone on the table she followed the cord until she got hold of the other end.

"Hello? Laura? Yes."

From that point on Sam listened carefully, trying to pick up clues from this end of the conversation, but it wasn't much use. He could tell it was about Martin and the hospital and he heard the word *angina*, which he knew had something to do with the heart. Even with the light coming through his mother's door the hall was dark and Sarah's face was hidden in shadow and partially covered by her hand as she held the receiver to her ear, so he couldn't tell much about his mother's reaction. The few words she spoke were full of apprehension, and he understood this was serious.

"Yes," she continued, "I see. Ohhhh, could you do that Laura? I don't think there's any way I could drive. . ." She shifted the phone. "Okay, I'll throw something on and wait for you." His mother let the phone drop from her ear and absently jiggled it onto the cradle, then stood silently staring into the dark.

"So, what's up?"

"Martin's in the hospital," she said unequivocally.

"Why?"

"Heart attack—apparently he has a history of angina." No emotion.

"He's not going to die, is he?"

"Nooo! What is this, twenty questions? I don't have time to explain." She pulled up her loose strap. "Now go back to bed!" Lots of emotion.

"NO WAY!"

"Look—Laura's on her way over to drive me to the hospital and I can't go like this," she said, sweeping her hand dramatically down the front of her nightgown. "If you don't want to go back to bed, get dressed and go to your aunt's until it's time for school."

"MOM, you don't think I'm going to school, I want to go with you."

"I'm not in the mood to argue with you. . ." she stopped.

"But mommm!"

"Oh damn it, do whatever you want. Come; just stay out of the way, and no more questions."

He popped into his room and without turning on the lights grabbed his pants, which were hanging on the bedpost. Kicking around the floor with his bare feet, he located one sock and then another, then removed yesterday's shirt from the laundry bag that was strung over the doorknob. Because he was willing to put on whatever he could grab, he finished dressing long before his mother. The fact that his socks were mismatched and every color he had on clashed with the one next to it didn't faze him. All the important parts were covered and his knit sweater, though full of pulls and tears, would keep him warm. He couldn't find his shoes. Then he remembered that he had an extra pair of sneakers by the back door, so he went down to the kitchen. When his mother heard him on the stairs, she hollered out to him.

"Go watch for Laura, will you?"

Sneakers in hand, he padded down the hall into the living room. At the front window he parted the brocade drapes and looked out. His eyes swept the dark street, then he turned back into the room and shouted toward the stairs: "What kind of a car does she drive?"

"I don't know. I've never seen it, but who else would be pulling up in front of our house at this hour?"

After several long minutes Laura stopped at the curb and flashed her headlights. "HEY MOM! She's here." His voice shook the little crystals hanging on the hall light and his mother rushed down the stairs to join him. Snatching her ski jacket off the clothes tree, she pushed Sam through the doorway and closed it behind her without turning the lock.

The trip to the hospital was a silent one, which frustrated Sam. He had expected his mother to pump Laura for information, so that he could conveniently listen in. He desperately wanted to know about Martin's condition, but considering his mother's present mood he didn't dare ask.

◆ ◆ ◆

The main hospital, built in the thirties, had a weathered brick front that needed repair and repointing. Following the signs to emergency, they drove around back and came to a modern new wing. Laura let them off at the door and went to the lot nearby to park.

Coming through the sliding doors, Sam and his mother were accosted by bright lights and harsh barren walls. After checking with a security guard they headed for the reception desk, but no one was there. Searching the waiting room, they saw several people who needed help. One cradled a kidney-shaped dish in her hand, which held some brown viscous liquid that she had apparently coughed up. A mother who sat with her little boy on her lap, spoke to him in a foreign tongue, and pressed a bloody gauze pad over one eye. A couple sat in the corner holding hands, looking more like they were on a date than visiting the ER. A gray-haired gentleman in a topcoat, with a worn-out magazine stretched across his lap, nodded on the edge of sleep. Hair uncombed, eyes wide, a man in greasy work-clothes paced. A young girl, her belly distended, gripped the arms of her wheelchair, and cried out in pain. A boy (possibly the father?) stood behind, poised to push her into delivery. The room smelled of unwashed bodies and vomit.

Finally a nurse wearing a cranberry-colored jumpsuit came through the doors behind the reception desk and Sarah pounced on her.

"Excuse me," she waved, "excuse me, can you tell me where I can find Martin McAulliffe?"

"Just a moment," the nurse said as she stepped past Sarah into the waiting area. Announcing a foreign-sounding name, she hovered, searching the faces staring back at her. No one answered and the nurse returned to the desk. "What was that name again?" she asked, as she sat in front of a monitor and started punching keys.

"McAulliffe, Martin McAulliffe," his mother repeated.

"He's in unit five, but you can't go back there unless you're family."

"But I am family—well, almost," she said. Hands below the counter, she worked off Robert's wedding band, but left the engagement ring.

"How's that?" the nurse asked.

"I'm his fiancée," Sarah said matter-of-factly, and lifted her hand to show her the ring.

Laura, who had just come in to join them, looked at Sam questioningly and he shrugged his shoulders. If Martin and his mother were engaged, he didn't know anything about it. The nurse looked doubtful, but didn't argue.

"Follow me then," she directed, and when the nurse turned her back, his mother brought her finger to her mouth to warn Sam not to say anything. After the nurse and his mother had disappeared into the trauma center, he went to sit beside Laura, who had already started digging through a pile of battered magazines looking for something to read.

Chapter 42

Listening to the squeak of the nurse's shoes, Sarah thought, *Why is this happening to me?* Martin had plucked at her dull heart, stripping away the protective layers like the tightfisted petals of a budding flower. The first pull at the thick green sheath brought its own special pain, but once the softer florets came away and the warm wet core lay exposed, Sarah felt as free and happy as a child. Martin had given her his love and promised the kind of security that she had wished for all her life and now he was in trouble.

Why hadn't he told her about his heart? Laura must have known. *If he could confide in her, why not me?*

The beaded chain in the track rattled as the nurse pushed the curtain aside to reveal Martin lying on a gurney with wires stuck to his chest and a red clamp coming off the end of his finger. Her reaction wasn't what she expected. Instead of worrying about all those wires and the beeping of the heart monitor beside him, she only saw the furry coat of hair that covered him from his neck to his navel, and then disappeared beneath the waist of his boxer shorts, which showed above the edge of his unbuttoned trousers. Furry, that is, except where they'd cut holes in it to get the EKG patches to stick. This was the first time she'd seen Martin without his shirt. She'd never dreamed that he was such a Teddy-bear. And now, instead of feeling worried and full of pain, all she wanted to do was laugh. The image of some nurse having to shave those spots filled her with irrepressible glee and she had to rub her hand across her mouth to cancel a smile.

Once she moved inside the circle she heard the nurse rattle the curtain closed behind her. Martin's forehead wrinkled in dismay. "Sarah, how'd you get here?"

"Laura drove me."

"I told her not to worry you."

"I'm glad she didn't listen."

"It's not as serious as it looks. Besides, I've had these attacks before."

"Really! And how long did you expect to keep this from me?" she asked, gripping the rail at his side hard enough to blanche the skin over her knuckles.

"Just until I got out of here," he said.

"And these attacks," she said, twisting her hands on the bar. "How often do they happen?"

"Not often and never this bad. But if I push too hard I get these pains across here," he said, raking his fingers through the mat of hair on his chest.

"What does the doctor say?" she asked, shifting from contention to concern.

"The one I saw tonight had a lot to say. He told me he thought I had a narrowing in one of the coronary arteries and when I'm under stress or overdo I don't get enough oxygen to the heart muscle."

"And?"

"And, he told me to see my doctor. I've already done that. He wants me to have surgery."

"SURGERY!"

"Yeah, he's been after me to have a single by-pass—says that would take care of the problem—but he won't give me any guarantees."

Her eyes squinted as she stared down at him, but she didn't speak.

"Don't look at me like that. I hate hospitals—people die in hospitals. And this guy wants to cut me open. . ." His voice trailed off and she reached out, searching for a spot that didn't have tubes and bandages, and ended up covering his hospital wristband. "There's just no way," he said. "No way I'm going to let some hotshot cut me up."

"Sooo," she said, pursing her lips, "how did this happen? What were you doing that landed you in the emergency room?"

"Walking the dog," he said in an embarrassed whisper.

"You don't have a dog—do you?"

"I sometimes take care of Laura's dog. She worked late last night and I called and offered to come walk her dog."

"But that shouldn't. . ."

"I know. It wasn't the dog; it was the cold. It was only five degrees, and the fact that I had to take him out at four in the morning—"

"Four?"

"Chester is old, and he has a bladder problem," he explained. "Anyway, by the time I made it as far as Laura's back door, my chest felt like it was in a vise and I couldn't breathe. The doctor said extreme cold can trigger this sort of thing. There's no damage done and I'll be able to leave in a little while."

"If that's true, then I'll wait."

"Fine, you can sit over there," he said, wagging his finger at a circular examination stool.

Martin looked like he'd gone too long without sleep, and when he closed his eyes she waited, and listened, first to his breathing, and then to the noises beyond the curtain: the cacking of the man in the next cubicle as he threw up, the wobble of a cart with a bad wheel, the footfalls of people racing to the call of a code blue. Sarah felt relieved that Martin's emergency had past, that in an hour or so he could dress and they could all leave. She would have to convince him somehow to have that surgery. She knew many people lived well enough with angina, especially if the episodes were mild, but this had been a bad one, and besides she didn't want to have to rush to the ER every time his heart kicked out, wondering if this trip would be his last.

Chapter 43

On the way home Sarah had to share the back seat with Sam. Martin needed the extra legroom up front. Laura drove. That gave Sarah a chance to study the two of them together. She didn't feel jealous or suspicious anymore, but she was curious to see how these two interacted.

Laura seemed to be Martin's age, very attractive and judging by her makeup—or the lack of it—she didn't have to work very hard to look that good. Worse still, she didn't seem to be aware of her looks. There was none of the haughty superiority that some good-looking women project, which made it hard not to like her.

The two talked about the weather, the crappy job the city did plowing their street after the last snowstorm, the age and deteriorating health of their neighbor across the street. Nothing was said about Martin's heart or the seriousness of this last episode, and Sarah wondered how much more Laura knew about Martin's condition than she did. Well, that was easy: until a few minutes ago, she had been completely in the dark. Facial expression and body language made it clear that these two liked each other, with the emphasis on *like* not love—at least not romantic love.

When the car pulled up in front of their house she and Sam got out and Martin rolled down his window. He promised to call her later, and then he and Laura drove off.

Sam said nothing—asked nothing on the way home, but now that they were in the house, he swamped Sarah with questions, which she dispatched in due course while she tried to get them both a late breakfast. But Sam refused breakfast. Instead he told her he was going over to Aunt Em's, and shot out the front door before she could object.

Looking at her watch, she saw that there was still time to make it to work and decided that she would be happier if she had something to do rather than just banging around in an empty house.

To her surprise Martin had arrived ahead of her, which irritated the hell out of her because she'd overheard the doctor tell him to go home and rest. Sitting behind his desk wasn't very physical, but there were other kinds of stress.

Instead of going to set up at her station she went directly to his office and talked Mary into letting her in. She spent twenty minutes trying gently to persuade Martin to go home, then gave up and left without changing his mind. She had never thought of Martin being afraid of anything, which wasn't realistic, but up to now nothing had come up to demonstrate otherwise. He had a right to be afraid: people did die in hospitals and bypass surgery, even single bypass surgery, could be risky. But if it would take care of the problem she would feel safer, and for selfish reasons she wanted this problem to go away. Damn it, she had fallen in love with this man, and even if she couldn't tell him that just yet, she still thought she had the right to express her opinion. Martin had explained that he wouldn't likely die, not any time soon anyway. But she knew that if this condition went untreated it could easily turn into a double or triple by-pass and then the chances of his dying would increase exponentially.

At the end of the day he came by her workstation and insisted on driving her home.

"But my car's here," she pointed out.

"So, leave it, you can drive it back tomorrow."

"And what do I do if I need to go somewhere tonight?"

"Don't give me a hard time—I have a bad heart," he said, clutching his chest, and she laughed in spite of herself.

She got into his car. He pulled out slowly into traffic and they drove all the way home in strained silence. Once he had shut off the engine he came around and opened her door, a simple old-fashioned courtesy that she secretly loved. When she unlocked her front door Martin didn't wait for an invitation, but actually stepped in ahead of her. She followed him into the foyer and before she knew what was happening he had taken her into his arms and kissed her. Then, noses touching, he said matter-of-factly. "Did I frighten you?"

"Yes."

"I mean with my heart—not the kiss."

"I know."

"It's not so bad. I can go for months without a problem, then it starts like a bad case of heartburn, only the pain is sharper. This morning it hit hard—went all the way across here," he said, dragging his fingers from armpit to armpit, "and knocked me straight to my knees."

"Weren't you afraid?" she said, pressing her forehead against his and giving him an eye-to-eye look that made his face blur.

"A little."

"Only a little?"

"Okay, more than a little."

"Then why wait?" she asked, pulling away and squeezing her hands around his throat as if she intended to strangle him.

"Because the surgery scares me a lot more." And she heard a gurgle in his throat that was obviously faked for her benefit. She smiled, then frowned.

"But it'll only get worse, and then what?"

"Then I guess I'll have to do something."

"And how bad will it have to be?"

"Pretty bad," he said, putting his hands over hers, which were still around his neck.

She knew she was pushing, but the idea that he could die and that this could save him made her persist. "What if *pretty bad* kills you?"

"Why are you so anxious for someone to cut me up?"

"Oh damn you," she moaned. "Don't say it like that, it sounds macabre."

"It is macabre. The methods may have changed, but surgeons are still a bunch of butchers."

"You don't believe that?"

"Maybe that's an exaggeration, but it's true."

She slid her hands out from under his and brought them down to wrap around his waist. "I love you," she said.

He looked stunned. "This is the first I've heard about it."

"Awright, I know I haven't said it, but you can't say you hadn't already guessed."

"That's not the same as hearing you say it."

"Love you, love you, love you," she said, each time emphasizing the word love with a quick buss on the end of his nose.

"Okay, okay, I'll call Dr. MacIntyre."

"When?"

"Is tomorrow good enough?"

"Yes. Now give me a proper kiss and go home."

He bent down and kissed her hard and when his arms came around her back he lifted her off her feet. The energy of that connection swept all the way to her toes and the sharp skip of her heart made her wonder why being this happy was also painful.

Chapter 44

Martin kept his word and went in for the surgery on February 9th. Sarah made arrangements to go in with him and wait through the operation and recovery, so that she would be there when he came out of the anesthesia. Alone—no Sam, no Aunt Em and no Laura, she had brought a novel along to help fill the hours that lay ahead, though she didn't know if she could concentrate on it.

The fact that he was 'going under the knife,' as Martin put it, was worrisome, but she had come to terms with it. Martin's doctor had taken a few minutes to explain the surgery and the likelihood of success. It was only a single bypass and Martin was in good health with an otherwise normal functioning heart. Statistically he had less than a five-percent chance of heart attack while they had him cut open, less than a one percent chance of dying. It would have been a lot more comforting if the doctor hadn't mentioned the word dying—and with all his explanations he had never said anything about stroke. So when word came back that Martin had still not regained consciousness and that they suspected a stroke, she took it badly. First mute shock—then, babbling, then a whirling dizziness that made her sit down and bend over in an effort to keep from blacking out. When she came back up the nurse had left and Martin's doctor was standing in front of her. Her eyes were dry and itchy as if she had made herself stay awake all night. She wanted to rub them, but thought that the doctor would misinterpret her action. He stepped to the right, pulled a heavy chair across the carpet and sat down to face her. Placing one hand over hers in a well-practiced bedside manner, he tried to explain Martin's condition.

"It's hard to say exactly what happened, but apparently the surgery dislodged a small clot, which temporarily cut off the flow of blood to the left side of his brain. It's disconcerting, but he will recover. How much damage has been done or how long it will take is impossible to assess right now. The most important thing is to watch him and hope that he comes out of this coma quickly."

Sarah looked at him numbly and said nothing. After a moment he stood, patted her hair as if she were a sick puppy, then headed back to the recovery room.

An hour later they moved Martin into ICU and the nurse came to tell her she might sit with him if she wanted, but that he was still unresponsive. As the elevator doors slowly closed and it began the short journey from four to five, Sarah thought, *This wouldn't be happening if I hadn't talked him into it.* The fact that he wasn't dying wasn't particularly comforting: she knew that she should be thankful he was alive, but she also knew that stroke could mean paralysis and a long, painful recovery.

The elevator opened to a softly lit hallway, with a colorful sailing print on the wall, and immediately in front a freestanding blue sign directed her to the intensive-care unit. Pushing open one of two heavy oak doors, she moved into a semi-darkened reception area, where two attendants in lavender scrubs scurried past. The atmosphere seemed charged with a somber intensity and in the shadowy corners she could detect the odor of formalin, alcohol and detergents, and the light smell of urine. A long circular counter separated her from the ICU nurses and the glass-enclosed rooms gave off the soft glow of night-time routine. Flickering monitors, mounted on an island in the center, announced the condition of the various patients and the rhythmic beeping sounds gave assurance that for the moment all was well. Walking up to the counter, Sarah tried to get someone's attention.

"Excuse me," she said, feeling like an intruder. "Please, could you help me?" This came out louder than she intended and an attendant working in the medical supply room leaned her head back to look in her direction. "I'm here for Martin McAulliffe," she explained to whoever was listening, and a nurse in a pastel pink uniform came round and led her to one of the cubicles. Outside the door the nurse tucked Sarah's hair under a poofy cap and helped her slip on a yellow gown that had the crinkly sound of paper, then handed her plastic covers to put over her shoes.

Whispering, the nurse explained Martin's condition in terms that were much too clinical for Sarah to understand. Through the glass wall she could already see Martin lying on a mechanical hospital bed connected to a profusion of devices that made him look like he was being made ready for a launched into space. It was the sort of image she had seen many times in movies and on TV, but this was real, and the danger implied by all this equipment was unnerving. Stepping inside, she searched Martin's face for some assurance that he was all right, but she only saw a cold stillness and a chalky-gray pallor that made her think of death.

When Robert had died the police had brought her to the morgue. That was another scene that she had seen portrayed before in make-believe. But Hollywood couldn't reproduce the feeling of the hard cement floor under her feet, or the chill, or the pungent odor of formaldehyde. Standing there, facing a wall of stainless-steel doors, a man in a white lab coat had rolled a metal slab from a narrow cubbyhole and pulled back a plastic sheet to uncover Robert's face, which had been ruined from three days in the water. Then after a nod of recognition the attendant had whisked his body back into the cool darkness and she heard the loud snap of the latch as the door closed and sealed him in. She didn't ever want to go through that again.

A fluorescent fixture on the wall behind Martin's head illuminated the bed, and the light seemed harsh against the bedding and his white hospital gown. Tubes had been fed into every orifice, or at least that was her impression. She gasped as she sucked in the sterile air, and a quick blackness closed in around her, then just as quickly opened again. An awful coldness filled her veins as if the blood had stopped moving—even her heart felt cold. Once that had passed, and the blood began to move again, her mind shut down, her emotions went on hold and she came to Martin's side with an unflappable presence that was totally unlike her. Somehow her brain tricked her; closed off and left her with the dry courage she needed to face this ordeal. Reaching out, she took hold of Martin's hand and bent to speak softly into his ear. The hand she picked up was warm and that warmth was reassuring.

"Martin, I'm here." Turning to the nurse, she asked, "Can he hear me?"

"Probably, but he won't understand—and he won't remember."

"Martin." She leaned over and touched his cheek, then immediately pulled back when she discovered that it was wet with drool. A small white towel lay on the pillow and she used it to wipe her fingers. Afterwards she used it to collect the spittle from around his mouth. "Martin," she whispered, "I love you." She hadn't expected to say that. It seemed meaningless under the circumstances. Would she have had the guts to tell him that—to tell him how fiercely she loved, how much it hurt to see him like this—if she thought he could understand her?

"How bad is he? I mean what do they expect?" she asked, turning back to the nurse.

The nurse shook her head. "There's no way to know for sure until he wakes up."

"May I stay?"

"Yes, if you'd like. Here, let me get you a chair," the nurse offered, as she pulled a straight chair from the corner and placed it by the bed. Sarah sat down and deliberately took Martin's hand again. There was a swishing sound behind her and a click as the door closed automatically. She was alone, though the glass wall didn't give her very much privacy.

Sitting in the chair brought her face nearly level with his. His nose seemed puffy and under his eyes the skin was bruised as if he had been in a fight and someone had punched him out. She watched his lids flutter and waited for them to open, but they didn't. He might have been asleep, but this wasn't sleep; some part of him had gone away and she wanted desperately to bring that part back. Whispering at first, as if her normal voice might startle him, she began a ridiculous one-sided conversation. She scolded and cajoled and complained for an hour. Nothing rational, just a jumble of nonsense that couldn't possibly help Martin, but all that venting helped her to depressurize.

Empty and exhausted she suddenly needed to find a phone. They let her call out from the nurse's station and she tried to explain to Sam and Em that Martin was all right, but of course he wasn't. Then she called Laura and tried to tell her the same thing.

Returning to Martin's bedside, Sarah sat down quietly. He had one arm across his abdomen, his hand and fingers taped to a board with a plastic tube rising up from somewhere under the bandages to an IV bottle, which was dripping a clear fluid. The other hand lay next to her with a flesh colored Band-Aid on the back of his wrist. She touched the Band-Aid, then came down to trace the tendons and veins, which stood out roughly under Martin's leathery skin. After a moment she took both her hands and sandwiched his bulky fingers in between. All this time she listened carefully to his slow even breathing.

"Damn you," she whispered. "My life's been a screw-up, but at least it was my life until you came along. . .and forced me to change it." She shifted her sore bum on the hard seat, which had the effect of putting her face closer to his.

"I married Robert at seventeen because I thought that no one else would have me. I never loved him, but I was afraid—afraid of being alone. Then he died, and I was alone. Well, not entirely. I had Sam. When Robert drank, he bitched and swore and hit, and sometimes knocked Sam around, but he worked hard and he paid the bills. For the first few months I actually missed him. One morning I woke up and realized I had no money. I needed a job. So I took a night course at Massasoit Community College. The idea was to study something useful; instead I ended up with world history, which didn't qualify me for anything.

"Qualified or not, I went looking for work. The interviews were awful. I'd get nervous and clumsy—give all the wrong answers. We'll be in touch—we'll call you, they said, but they never did. In one place I dropped my pen and when I got up to retrieve it, I stepped on it, and left a black stain on the gray berber carpet. Then I walked into your office and. . ." She stopped to rub her itchy nose. "And now my boss has the hots for me and he keeps telling me I'm beautiful. Go figure. Don't get me wrong, I like it, but after spending years conditioning myself to expect the worst, I'm having a hard time convincing myself that this is real." She fell silent while she dug the fingers of her free hand into her gut, trying to root out the pain that twisted her innards into a tight little knot. "I don't know. Maybe after so long the hurt has gone too deep. Maybe there's nothing that can ever make it go away.

"Now that I've met Laura I like her, and I can see that she likes you," she said, forcing a crooked grin. "But I can't help wondering why there isn't something more. I mean, she's attractive, intelligent, capable. Yet, you've chosen me. Someone who's clumsy and plain, an emotional cripple," She stopped for a moment to consider how illogical that choice seemed to be.

"Sam's not dealing with this very well; he's not equipped for it. I can see that he has some deep feelings for you, but he won't admit it." Staring at the heart monitor, her thoughts drifted. If she actually married this man, how would Sam react?

"Em's been great. She doesn't miss a thing. She's only met you twice and she's sure that you and I were made for each other. 'That man's a keeper,' she says, 'don't let him get away.' And I—well, it's silly really." Rubbing her nose again, she sucked back a sniffle. She couldn't let herself cry—not now.

"I wish it were that simple," she said, lifting his warm hand and pressing it against her cool cheek.

"Mary called from work while you were in surgery. She's worried about you. She doesn't know about this, of course," she said, scanning the machinery that surrounded him.

"You didn't want this—the surgery, that is. But no, I had to push and beg until I got my way. And now here I am sitting here jawing away to a man who can't understand a word I'm saying."

This long wandering monologue had made her tired. She put her head down on the edge of the bed and closed her eyes. She hadn't intended to fall asleep and when she awoke hours later from a troubled dream, she didn't lift her head, but simply peeked out at Martin. One arm, which she had flung across his waist felt thick and heavy, the other rested on the edge of the bed with her fingertips lightly creeping over his. Her throat, plugged with mucus, brought up an involuntary cough, and the movement banged her head into his hip. He moaned. She lifted her head and brushed her hair away from her face. Letting go, her hair fell back feather-like along the length of his forearm, and his fingers rippled under hers. Still half-awake, she froze—had she actually felt movement or was it just an involuntary spasm. Lifting her hand slightly she wrapped it around Martin's and began to squeeze. Lightly at first, and then harder and harder until it must have been painful. Martin's muscles contracted as he resisted the pressure.

"Martin, can you hear me?" she asked. She loosened her grip and looked for a sign. There was a weak response as he moved one finger then another, and another, in a soft cascade that looked almost like playing the scales on a piano.

"Can you open your eyes?" she asked with a burst of hope. His eyelids fluttered as he made an effort to open them. He couldn't seem to get control, and then the movement stopped. A moment later his lids suddenly shot back as if they were spring-loaded and she saw him staring up at the fluorescent light above his bed. She stood and leaned in, deliberately putting her face in front of his. His eyes flickered, but she didn't see any recognition in them.

"Can you speak?" Sarah asked. His lips moved dryly, but nothing came out but a raspy breath. She grabbed the call button at his side and waited for someone to come.

Several attendants sprang through the door and the nurse Sarah had spoken to earlier stepped up beside her. Sarah looked up at the monitors and saw that they were alive with new activity as Martin reacted to the hands that were poking and probing, checking for reflex and vitals. A man dressed in a long white lab coat flashed a penlight across his field of vision and called out instructions.

Sarah was asked to leave. Glancing back as she stepped through the doorway, she saw that Martin's eyes following her. They were dark and full of fear.

◆ ◆ ◆

At long last someone remembered where she was and came out to speak to her. "Obviously this is good," the doctor told her. "I mean, considering his time in recovery before he went into ICU and before you came up and the time since you arrived, he's been out about sixteen hours. But it could just as easily have been days."

"What happens now?"

"Now, I think you should go home, take a shower, get something to eat, get some real sleep, in a real bed, and then come back here later this afternoon. I assume you're going to want to become his primary caregiver."

"Yes," she said, without thinking what that meant.

"Well then, you'll have to meet with his surgeon and with Dr. Ballard our neurologist, and of course you'll have to spend time with the recovery team—the rehabilitation nurses, the speech therapist and the physical therapist. You're going to have to learn a lot if you expect to be of any help to him."

"God, I had no idea!" she moaned.

"You'll be alright; you'll figure it out. Now go home." The doctor put his thick, hairy arms around her, but the hug, light and tenuous, didn't seem genuine.

The long night, the looming specter of meetings with doctors and therapists and the promise of months and months of recovery ate up the last of her reserve, and she wondered how she would ever be able to drive home in such an exhausted state

Chapter 45

His chances for a complete recovery were excellent, but it might take months, or a year—maybe more. The rehabilitation team did as much as they could to prepare Sarah. The stroke had injured the left side of Martin's brain, causing some right-side paralysis and loss of speech. He knew what he wanted to say, but because of something called dysarhria he didn't have any fine-motor control and his speech sounded mushy and slurred, and sometimes the words were pure invention. He had general right-side paralysis at first, but by the time they let him go home only his right arm and right foot were in trouble. The arm hung uselessly by his side and had to be constantly repositioned, and the foot was floppy and unresponsive when he tried to walk.

Sarah came to pick him up on March 8th. His stay in the hospital had lasted for more than a month. The nurse pushed him out in his own wheelchair (a rental), and once the two of them had positioned Martin in the front seat, Sarah collapsed it and put it through the rear hatch of her Escort. The rental company provided a fold-up walker for the house, but the wheel chair would be needed if he went out.

Driving over the cold black country roads to Martin's house, she didn't try to make him talk. During the last week his speech had improved, but she knew he was uncomfortable and easily frustrated. In the hospital everything had been done for him; now the responsibility fell on her and she was filled with apprehension.

She had a list of names and phone numbers, a written schedule for therapy, and times for medications. But because Martin's insurance didn't provide for a home healthcare worker, Sarah intended to do it all, and now that no one would be there to step in if she made a mistake, she felt hopelessly unprepared.

In the last couple of days there had been some high points, but in the beginning Martin seemed like a stranger. Sometimes during the therapy he would begin to sob, then suddenly shift into a rage. She couldn't tell if he was in pain or suffering from depression and his emotional reactions didn't always fit the circumstances. His highs and lows confused her and she wondered how she would cope with Martin's changing personality now that she had him all to herself.

When she wasn't with Martin at the hospital—when she had a moment at home alone—she thought a lot about herself, about Martin, and about the two of them together. All through her teens she had suffered. Happiness was a tenuous fleeting idea that she seldom got hold of. Her dad was the only one who provided any real stability. And her marriage to Robert had been particularly destructive. If it hadn't been for Sam she might have gone mad. Now she was with someone who was the complete antithesis of Robert. Reflecting back to that first day, the day of her interview, she could see how Martin had affected her from the beginning. He showed a genuine interest in her, looked straight at her and listened to what she said as if every word had some great importance. Once they started to date, his incredible devotion had boosted her self-image and made her feel that she was desirable. At first his attention was so novel it frightened her. Yet it hadn't taken long for her to gobble up that special attention. Like a starving child she never seemed to get enough to fill her needs. Now because a little bolus of blood had cut off the flow of oxygen to his brain, everything had changed. Martin struggled with a sloppy ungraceful body that wouldn't do what he told it to, and his sudden dependence on her frightened her. Somehow fate had cheated her again—had cheated both of them.

Sarah turned down Bailey Road and pulled up in the driveway at the back of Martin's house. It was a charming Cape Cod, yellow with black shutters, surrounded by old-growth trees and well-established landscaping. The house looked ancient, probably built in the seventeen hundreds, and she knew that Martin had lived there for almost a generation. It was the home he had shared with his wife and where he had raised his two sons. One of the unique things about living in such an old New England community was that so many of these homes had a history. On a cold afternoon in January (before his surgery and the stroke) Martin had told her about the first owners and how many generations had lived there before it had passed to the Connollys and then finally to him and his family.

Getting out, Sarah went back to retrieve the wheelchair and came round to open Martin's door. Helping him into it was harder this time without the assistance of the discharge nurse.

"Pull your right leg out and then use your good arm to grab the door-post," she instructed, as she swung his dead arm around her shoulder and tried to shift his weight toward the canvas seat. He didn't answer; he just grunted and tried to do what she asked.

Dragging the chair up over the low step and backing him through the doorway, she gave an extra tug to get the wheels to jump over the threshold. The chair twisted and jammed her fingers against the doorjamb. "Ouch!" she complained as she heard a crunch and felt the pain of bone and flesh being pinched between wood and steel—Martin weighed a good fifty pounds more than she did, and it was hard to jockey him around. Suddenly she knew what handicapped-accessible meant. Everything seemed to be in the way.

"Damn," she said, catching the front wheel on the corner of the island, and swinging his extended foot hard against it. The sudden stop sent the handle into her gut.

"Aww—youu—awwright?" He struggled to get the words past his sagging lips.

"Yeah," she breathed. It wasn't true, but she wasn't about to tell him so. "I just have to learn how to drive this contraption."

She wheeled him through the dining room and living room and into a small den, which had been reorganized so that it could accommodate a borrowed hospital bed. Here she got him to lean forward and lift himself enough so that she could scoot the tail of his car-coat out from under him, and when he sat back down she wriggled it off of him one arm at a time, then made him lean forward again while she dragged it out from behind. Hanging it on a hook on the inside of the door, she wondered if everything would be this much work.

He motioned for her to get him a pad of paper; he still didn't want to talk. Writing wasn't easy either because he was right-handed. But he had mastered a readable scrawl in rehab: *No bed—psh to liv room*—he wrote in a kind of shorthand.

Once in the living room he waved his good hand at the TV, then kept pointing while she changed the channels until he was satisfied, then put his hand out like a traffic cop to tell her to stop.

She stayed with him for the moment, and in a few minutes he indicated that he wanted out of the wheelchair. Even though he gave her all the help he could she had a hard time getting him up, and the few steps to the easy chair made her groan under the weight of his arm, which was pinching the nerve in her shoulder. Then he shifted his weight the wrong way and nearly took her down. If that happened she had no idea how she would ever get him off the floor. Once she had him in front of the chair she let go of his hand and he slid away from her and fell back. Next she bent to position his weak arm, then knelt on the floor and adjusted his foot, which hung crookedly from his ankle as if something inside were broken or disconnected. Every time she moved him she would have to reposition these two limbs. She had never realized how the body could shift out of shape when left to its own devices.

The hospital had given her a loose-leaf binder full of Xerox copies with sketchy black-and-white drawings, which weren't much help. The rehab team had walked her through Martin's routine and made her repeat the exercises over and over until she understood what was expected. Then the doctor had reviewed his medications and when he was done she clearly saw what a hard responsibility she had agreed to take on, and wondered how she would survive.

Fortunately Martin could do some simple things for himself and she didn't have to watch him every minute. Em brought Sam over often and they stayed on to help. Occasionally one of his boys would come by, though they did little more than visit, and twice a week an OT or PT worker would show up to work on Martin. These therapists would adjust his treatment as he progressed, and he did progress, but sometimes it seemed so slow as to be insignificant.

Sarah slept in one of the extra bedrooms upstairs. Martin had written a note indicating that she should take his bed, but she didn't like that idea. It wasn't a matter of propriety; the age of civility was long gone, but the bed had a history. It was the bed he had shared with his wife, where they had made love and conceived two children. Not that she believed in ghosts, but she already felt like an intruder.

Now, early in the morning, too early to start her daily routine, she lay awake, her pillow across her breast, her head back on the mattress while she stared at the old cowboy-print wallpaper above the headboard. What in the world made her think that she could do this? Wishful thinking? Stupidity? She loved Martin, but he was so changed by the stroke: irritable, depressed, impatient with her and with himself. And yesterday, when he realized that he couldn't perform the most basic computation, he lost it. He wanted to make out a check and he did, but when it came time to subtract the amount from the balance he was lost. She watched him sitting there, squeezing his eyes open and shut until a clear drop escaped, then another. The tears were silent but his frustration was obvious.

She knew she was being selfish, but hadn't she gone through enough dealing with Robert for all those years? When she fell in love with Martin, and she was definitely in love, the future looked so bright. Then the surgery and the damaging effects of the coma turned it all upside-down.

Oh, the doctor said he was doing admirably and that he would make a full recovery, but now six weeks into this thing she was simply worn out. *Well,* she thought, *I got myself into this mess and I'm not about to walk out. Instead of lying here feeling sorry for myself, what I really need is a good kick in the ass.* Disgusted by her own weakness, she threw the pillow across the room and knocked a picture off the wall. The frame splintered when it hit the hard floor.

"Damn!" she said, tossing back the covers. She plunked her feet down onto the bare floor and went to retrieve the pieces of the picture. Fortunately there was no glass in it. Then, grabbing her robe, she plunged her arms into the sleeves, and leaving the front open trudged down the stairs to the kitchen. Slamming cabinet doors, at first she thought of cooking, then losing her ambition decided to have cold cereal instead.

Chapter 46

Tearing the top off the cereal box, Sarah heard the clatter of Martin's walker and the scuff of his slippers as he crossed the dining room floor. His muscle control had recovered slowly, from the limp and floppy stage to quick spastic movements, which he couldn't control, then to hyperactive reflexes. Now he was approaching a kind of normalcy where he had increased voluntary control over his muscles.

She knew he would need help with the swinging door, but she didn't make any move to open it. As he made slow progress and had more and more successes Martin's temperament had improved, but there were rules: she wasn't to offer any assistance unless he signaled for it. And later, when his language skills improved, he would tell her what he wanted. In the beginning his words were fragmented and some of them proved to be pure invention. One afternoon he kept coming up sporadically with the word *bug-a-boost,* until she finally figured out he wanted the newspaper.

She soon realized that he had his cane as she heard its hard contact with the door and watched it swing slowly into the kitchen. With his good arm he held it there and jostled the walker a few inches forward until it was half across the threshold, then dragged his bad foot and took a step. He repeated this until he was past the edge of the door, which he released with a swish and a thwack, then lost his grip on the cane and it clattered across the linoleum floor.

Sarah started automatically to reach for it, then looked up for his approval. There was a definite hurt in his eyes, but he nodded in the direction of the cane and said, "Yes."

She stepped forward and scooped it up, then started to hand it back. "No—the table," he said, with his now common hesitancy.

"Cereal?" she asked.

"Yes."

"Orange juice?"

"Yes," he said.

Five minutes later she asked: "Is the food alright?"

"It's—good," he said, the last word sounding like *dud.* She didn't dare make the conversation anymore complicated. Sometimes he would try to say more, but he became frustrated when the words got tangled up, and his writing wasn't much better. It had improved considerably since he had gotten home, but some of the words ended in a squiggly line as if he couldn't remember how to form the last letter.

When breakfast was done, he struggled to his feet. "I have—something—to show youuu," he said. Whereupon he pushed the walker aside and started carefully moving toward the door on his own. Whenever he made any headway, she tried to be enthusiastic, but not overly so. He was terribly offended if he thought she was being patronizing, but this was real progress and she couldn't help her excitement.

"MARTIN!" she said. Jumping forward to embrace him, she nearly knocked him over.

Between deep breaths Martin gasped, "That was—good—wasn't it? Let me—go—back," he said. And he did go back, this time more smoothly, and when he reached the table Sarah came to him and rewarded him with a kiss. He wouldn't allow that in the beginning. Part of his faced sagged from the stroke, and he had managed to convey to her that he felt ugly. But now he smiled, and the curve looked nearly as perfect as it used to.

Somehow this little stroll across the kitchen floor was a turning point, and during the next few weeks his progress was phenomenal. Before, every gain had been hard-won and sometimes took days to achieve. Now every day brought a new milestone, and Sarah was more and more hopeful for his full recovery.

Chapter 47

It was April 1st, April Fool's Day. And when Martin awoke he could smell breakfast cooking in the kitchen. This morning he caught the aroma of frying bacon. But the bacon didn't interest him. It was the sudden realization that he had an erection. Before his stroke that hadn't been an uncommon experience, especially when he first woke up. But until this morning that natural phenomenon had been missing, or perhaps it had risen and fallen during those dreamy moments before he awoke. He knew this wasn't a sexual thing, but it did prove that the damn thing still worked.

He kicked his legs over the side of the bed and reached for his robe, which hung conveniently over the chair in front of him. Putting on a bathrobe with only one arm was difficult, but he had learned a few tricks and soon had the whole thing wrapped around him. Somewhere in the middle of that effort his erection collapsed—another sign of his return to normalcy. Wriggling forward, he let his feet touch the floor, and righting himself, moved toward the bathroom. Step, slide, step, slide, he progressed until he made it to the sink. Brushing his teeth was nearly impossible. He knew where his mouth was but he couldn't always get his toothbrush to find it. He might have used his left hand, but he needed it to hold on to the edge of the sink for support.

Sarah had been a saint. He wondered how she had managed it all. For weeks she had attended to his needs and put up with his constant temper. He had never been so impatient and unforgiving with himself, and he had taken it all out on her. When his wife died he had been the caregiver. And whereas she'd been an excellent patient he felt certain that he was being a horrible one. In the beginning he was completely dependent upon Sarah and he hated it. Even now that he was making real strides and gradually taking over his own care, he felt far too dependent.

He looked at his robe in the mirror. With all his struggles to get it on, it still hung lopsided off one shoulder. With a twist and a shrug, he shifted it to a more orderly position. He hesitated; then took in a deep breath before switching his weight onto his bad foot. He shuffled through the house and into the kitchen, and said a crisp "Hello" as he eased himself onto the plastic-covered chair. He glanced up at Sarah when she returned his greeting. She was wearing one of his old nappy cardigans, and lost in its ample folds he was suddenly conscious of how fragile she looked. He saw the wide hem of her nightgown and below he followed her pale skinny legs down to her bare feet. The whole get-up was flatly unattractive. When she leaned over to set his plate on the table, the front of her gown fell away enough to expose the sweet roundness of her beasts. She held that position while she cut up his food, and the sawing action of the knife set them both in motion, which in turn set him in motion. His arousal came quick and sure, pushing against the fabric of his pajama bottoms like a furry mouse looking for a way to escape. And though nothing showed he had a sudden desire to cover himself. When she straighten up, and went to the stove for her own food, he dropped almost as quickly as he had risen, but unlike this morning's bedtime incident, which was purely involuntary, this time Sarah had brought the little bugger to life.

"What's the matter?" she asked.

"Nothing," he said, his voice sounding a little too high-pitched.

"Then what's that funny look on your face?"

"If I tell—you'll—think—I'm crazy," he said, consciously pulling his words down to a normal level.

"No I won't," she insisted.

"It's—too personal."

"Hey, a month ago I was helping you in and out of the shower. How personal can it be?"

"I think—you're—ss–sexy," he said.

"You're right, you are crazy. Either that or you're very, very sick," she said and she reached out and covered his brow with her cool hand to check his temperature.

True—she wasn't exactly beautiful at the moment. He couldn't express it, but he knew that the beauty he saw, and the excitement he felt, had a lot more to do with kinship, with a heartfelt affinity toward her sweetness and innate goodness, than it did with her physical appearance.

"Fred—thinks—you're ss-sexy," he said, glad that she was behind him and that he didn't have to look her in the eye. Fred was the nickname they had invented when she'd had to bathe him in the tub, and later when she helped him in and out of the shower.

At first there was no reaction. She went to the fridge to get out the orange juice. Then turning, carton in hand, she looked at him and said, "Oh? Ooooh." And he was amazed at the transformation as her face flushed from pale to russet. Even her forearms colored and he wondered how, under the circumstances, she could be so easily embarrassed.

"You're terrible."

"It wasn't—my—fault."

"Well, I didn't do anything. I mean if this turns you on," she said, dragging her fingernails across the crooked weave of his old sweater, "what would happen if I put my hair up in rollers?"

"Ugh," he said, and they both laughed.

He picked up his fork and tried the eggs, then soon got lost in his own thoughts.

For weeks he hadn't paid much attention to the sacrifices that Sarah was making for him. He was too wounded, too wrapped up in his own pain. Now he wanted to give her a hug. He needed so much to hold her and have her hold him in return, but he was afraid to act.

"Is the food all right?"

"Yes," he said, coming back to recognize that she was sitting across from him.

"You're not eating," she said, circling her finger over his plate. "Would you like some ketchup to give it a little color?"

"Yes," he said.

When she came back and set the bottle down in front of him, she took her place at the table again and he continued to stare at her.

"Are you happy?" she asked.

"Why—do—you ask?"

"I don't know, you seem a little brighter, a little more with it today."

"I am better," he said confidently. "I want you—to stay."

"I am staying,"

True, but he wanted her to stay forever. He couldn't say that. Instead he told her: "I like—the—company."

Sarah smiled and that made him smile.

When they had finished eating he made his way to the living room to watch TV. Within twenty minutes he had fallen asleep.

◆ ◆ ◆

At eleven Sarah came in to wake him and remind him of his PT–OT (physical therapy/occupational therapy). Considering the progress he had made, his therapy now consisted of a full range of motion exercises. And as soon as he had discarded his walker for a quad cane, Sarah encouraged him to get out of the house and walk. Appearing in public bothered him. He knew so many people in the neighborhood and he didn't want them to see him limping around. But he discovered that if he went out in the middle of the day while people were away at work, no one noticed his slow, mechanical meanderings.

Sarah finished putting him through his paces and then told him to make the trip down the drive to the mailbox. Next came lunch, and more walking, this time around the block, and then more sleep. Around five, his two sons showed up together for a brief visit.

"Hi Dad. How ya doin'? You look better today." They always spoke loudly, carefully forming their words as if the stroke had affected his hearing. They didn't really seem to notice his progress and made exaggerated efforts to help when he was trying so hard to do things on his own. They treated him as if he were now the child and they the parents. It made him angry, but he kept his mouth shut and fortunately they left quickly—they didn't seem comfortable around him any more.

"Bye, Dad!" they shouted in unison as they escaped out the front door.

"Brrrrr!" he breathed aloud as he shivered with relief. The TV was off and the room was quiet again. He could hear Sarah in the kitchen, starting supper. Strange how his days had come to be defined by meals, with a constantly boring routine in between.

That's another thing, he thought, they always ignore Sarah when they come. They never went back to greet her and if she had been in the room they wouldn't have made any real effort to include her—why was that? He picked up the evening paper and tried to read: it was part of his therapy and he was getting much better at it. Except that most of what he read was depressing: Government corruption, another shooting in Boston, an increase in the local property taxes. To flush all that garbage out he always finished with the comics.

When he was done he set the paper aside, leaned back in the chair and listened to the sound of Sarah working on supper.

Chapter 48

Sarah noticed the stillness in the house and glancing out the window above the sink realized that darkness had overtaken her. She peeked through the kitchen door to check on Martin. Only the yellow halo of the reading lamp behind Martin's chair illuminated the living room; in between were broad black shapes that showed in the soft glow of twilight. Satisfied that he was all right, she let the spring-loaded door swish closed, and went back to cutting carrots.

Sarah knew from talking to the doctor, and the things she'd read that Martin's recovery had bordered on the miraculous. Miraculous or not there had been problems. Depression and anger and occasional crying jags—nothing on the scale she had been given to expect, but in the midst of his melancholy scale didn't seem to matter: it was still almost overwhelming to watch him suffer. Now, looking back, she could be thankful that the worst had passed and that during the last several days he had accelerated to the point where the doctor was considering letting him return to work—at least for half-days—and the bank had agreed. He desperately needed to get back to his old routine and she needed the relief that those three or four hours would bring.

◆ ◆ ◆

When Martin first came home he was so changed and being with him 24 hours a day left her empty and used up. For the first three weeks he made no significant change and he constantly chafed at the deadness of his body. One evening Sarah came into his room with a tray and set it on the edge of his bed, which had been cranked up at a sharp angle so that he could eat. She shifted the tray onto a wicker breakfast table that straddled his legs and asked: "Do you want my help?"

He shook his head no, but didn't make any effort to pick up the adaptive spoon. It had a special built-up handle to make it easier for him to grasp. She had to admit the food wasn't very appetizing. The doctor insisted on fat-free and suggested applesauce, cream soups and purees prepared in the blender. She waited.

"You need to eat something," she prodded. He reached out with his left hand. He drove the spoon into the sloppy mix and lifted it mechanically, but when he tried to find his mouth the dollop of food slipped and fell onto the front of his pajama top (he wouldn't have a bib, it was too humiliating). Making guttural sounds, he exploded. He dropped the spoon, swept his left hand up under the bed-table and sent it flying. Some of the food hit her in the face; the rest spread across the floor.

"Dammmmn," he said, as if his mouth were sewn shut.

She bent to pick up the tray and gather up the broken pieces of expensive china—plastic would have made so much more sense.

"Nooooo," he shouted.

"But I have to."

"Noooo!" he shouted again and used his good hand to wave her away. "Get—out," he howled.

She stood to look at him and saw that his face was twisted and ugly, and she wanted to cry but couldn't.

"L-l-leave—it," he said, and used his good hand to scoop some puree off the blanket and fling it at her.

She let the broken pieces of glass fall from her fingers and walked out with the tray still in hand. When she closed the door behind her, her whole body started to shake. Where had Martin gone; and who was this monster who had come to take his place?

She returned an hour later and peeked in the door. He was sleeping and she went in quietly to clean up. Moving carefully, she tried to keep the noise down, but soon had the feeling she was being watched. When she turned to check on Martin she saw a painful sadness in his eyes and his lopsided expression made him look like he'd been in a terrible fight.

"S-s-ssorry," he said with a lisp, and immediately rolled over to face the wall.

Once he got past the ground-up mush and she found ways to spice up the flat taste of non-fat food, his disposition improved. But there were other crises and other explosions of anger and tears—his and hers—and however destructive or abusive, she tolerated them until gradually he improved. He always apologized, sometimes in words, more often with notes written in his new back-slanted handwriting. She knew he couldn't help himself and could only imagine the fits of despair that plunged him into these ugly moods.

Bit by bit, day by day, with tiny—almost immeasurable triumphs, he came back. Martin's eyes, now bright and alert, shone even brighter when he smiled, and his speech, though still slow and broken, sounded clearer and rolled off his tongue with a familiar intonation. And the last couple of days had been his best yet. Sarah had come through the refiners fire—hard and sure—confident in her feelings for Martin, and more than ever committed to his care and to his full recovery.

◆ ◆ ◆

Tonight Sarah was in an adventurous mood, and decided that it might be fun to get a little fancy with dinner. She took down two fluted plates, gathered some silverware from the bottom drawer of the china cabinet and brought them to the dining room table. A vase of dried flowers and two candlesticks decorated the middle of the shiny maple-wood top. There were no candles in the holders and she started to search the center drawer of the sideboard to find some. Rummaging through the shallow drawer in the semi-darkness, she felt Martin's hands come round her waist and his warm breath disturbed the wispy hairs at the back of her neck. She had been listening to the faint scrape of his slippers as he padded into the dining room behind her. So his sudden touch hadn't frightened her, but when he pressed his fingers deeply into her soft abdomen it made her jump.

"Did I—I—scare—you?" Martin asked.

"No, not really. Are you okay? I mean, should you be up?"

"I'm fine. I couldn't—just sit there—had to get the kinks out," he said, shifting his weight. "What are you up to?"

"Ooh, lots of exciting stuff. I'm looking for some candles for the table. Can you tell me where they are?"

"Not here. The kitchen—second drawer—to the, to the right of the stove." That was a long sentence and she noted that he had gotten the sequence perfect.

"Okay," she said, as she turned to move away. But he kept his hands on her waist and half turning she got to see the outline of his face in the rosy light from the dining room windows. When he first came out of the hospital he had lost weight and his cheeks looked sharp and gaunt; now they were full again, and the color had changed from parchment to well-scrubbed sandalwood. During all these weeks there hadn't been anything even vaguely romantic between them, not even holding hands—so this embrace seemed downright frisky.

"What are you up to?" she said with a grin. She brought her hands down to grab his wrist, to get him to release her, but he was surprisingly strong. Besides, she wasn't that anxious to get away.

"Do, do I have to say . . . tell you? " he corrected himself.

"No," she answered, as she let him lean in and steal a kiss—nothing demanding or eager, just easy and sweet. And she realized suddenly that she needed a kiss. She enjoyed the touch of his cheek, the stale smell of his after-shave. Even the scratchy stubble of his beard felt good—reassuring.

"Are, we—we getting fancy," he said, nodding at the dishes and linen napkins on the table.

"Maybe," she answered, as she pulled away and went to find the candles in the kitchen. When she came back, he stood with his hands pressing down hard on the back of one of the dining room chairs for support. She put the candles in the holders and lit them with the matches she'd put in her apron pocket.

"Romantic," Martin observed.

"A little atmosphere," she answered. "Besides, the food will taste better if we can't see where I burned it."

"Really!"

"Really," she confirmed. "You know my cooking is no good. I never had a good reason to work at it. Robert wasn't there; and when he was, he didn't much care. He was more apt to throw it than eat it.

"Ouch!"

"Yes. Sometimes it was an ouch. Especially when it hit me instead of the wall."

It wasn't funny, but Martin started to laugh, then said he was sorry. But it was infectious and Sarah started laughing too. The chair Martin used to hold himself up tipped and gave way and he nearly fell over, but instead of rushing to help him she laughed even harder. To keep his balance, Martin had to get all four legs back on the floor.

"Stop!" she cried, worried that he would hurt himself.

"I can't," he giggled.

"You'll get hurt."

"I don't care."

"You have to get hold of yourself!" she shouted.

"I already have," he answered, tightening the grip he had round his ribs.

She looked at him, bent forward, the chair wobbling under his weight, and she struggled to keep from laughing. In a moment, when they had both settled down, he asked her: "What's for dinner?"

"Fish," she said plainly. "Oh jeeze!" she exploded, and rushed pell-mell into the kitchen in time to see little wisps of smoke coming out from around the edge of the oven door.

"I told you it would be burnt," she shouted as she pulled the tray out with the folded dishtowel that was next to the sink, "and now it is."

♦ ♦ ♦

Twenty minutes later they sat down to dinner. The soft flutter of the candles did hide some of the damage. Sarah had tried to scrape away the blackened edges of the fish, but it was beginning to look awfully beat-up, so she had to leave some behind. Martin tried to reassure her. "It's fine." But he drank lots water every time he took a bite of his charcoal fillet of sole. Still it was *fine* and certainly a lot better than the food she had tried to serve when he first came home from the hospital.

The meal continued quietly with a smattering of dull conversation tucked in here and there, which came mostly from Sarah. And when they were finished she gathered up the dirty dishes and returned with dessert.

"Thank you," Martin said.

"For what? The pie? It's just store-bought—all I did was take it out of the box."

"No, not—not the pie. For everything. For the—work, and—long—hours."

"Whatever," she said, turning her hands up and swinging them in a short dismissive arc, to indicate that no thanks were necessary.

"No. It—it must have been—hard," he said, pushing out the last word.

"Welll," she said waving her fork at him, "when the doctor told me that you'd had a stroke and were in a coma , I heard it, and I saw you lying there, but I didn't want to believe it. Then when you woke up, you weren't the same. And it looked like you might never be the same again," she added, shaking her head.

Martin reached out with his left hand and took the fork away, then brought his right hand forward and wrapped his fingers around hers. "I'm sorry," he said.

"I'm alright. I went into denial, got mad, had a good cry, and then I got over it. Besides, I volunteered for this. Although, if I hadn't told the nurse at the hospital I was your fiancé—

"You what?" Martin said, pulling back his hand as if it had been in the mouth of a shark.

"They, they wouldn't let me see you. Only relatives—and once I'd said it, I didn't know how to take it back," she said. "What was I supposed to do?" she asked with a shrug of her shoulders. "Besides, you did propose to me."

"A long time—ago."

"Have your changed your mind?"

"No, nooo," he said with a frown. "Have you?"

"What do you mean?"

"You—said no."

"So?" she said as if that mattered. She hadn't actually said no, she told him that she needed time. "June would be good," she continued, fingering the wax at the base of one of the candles. "Traditional—"

"What—what?" he repeated, cupping his hand to his ear as if there was something wrong with his hearing.

"Well, we are going to get married, aren't we?" she said with an impish grin. "You're not going to make a liar out of me."

"But, but you. . ."

"I know, I couldn't make up my mind. I guess I thought I had all the time in the world, and then. . ."

"I'm sorry."

"Stop saying that, it's not your fault. You didn't do this; I didn't do this, although for a while I thought I did. You're getting better. At least the worst is behind us," she said, pointing at the folded wheelchair in the corner of the room.

"Yes," he said with a smile.

"When?" she asked.

"When what?"

"When do we get married?"

"I—don't want—to wait a long time," he said carefully.

"July?"

"I—I guess," he said, with a note of disappointment.

"We could get married right now, if all we did was say the words. But I want more than that. With Robert it was a judge in a dingy courtroom. This time I want it all: the church, the gown, the bridesmaids—the whole shebang."

"If that's. . .you want, then—you should—have it."

She understood his urgency; she felt it too. She didn't think that sex would ever interest her, and her lack of romantic experience had left her without hope. But Martin had touched a secret place deep down in her soul and made it burn. She would be lying if she told him that she didn't want to get physical. "You know this is the eighties," she said, testing. "Nowadays sex before marriage is perfectly acceptable."

"I—I know it is, but I'm not comfortable—I don't—like that idea, do you?"

"No."

"Then—then, let's leave it that way," he said.

She stood and came round to sit in his lap. He complained, but not too loudly. "Have you—gained weight?"

"Oh you!" she answered with a sharp rap on the shoulder. Then they kissed and she felt that spot deep in her gut grow hot and expand until it seemed that her whole body was on fire.

Chapter 49

His mother called Sam the next morning with the news. His loud hurrah shot through the line and pierced his mother's ear. "You don't have to break my ear," she said, but the squeak in her voice let him know that she was happy that he was happy. There hadn't been a formal proposal and no ring, so Sarah cautioned Sam to keep it a secret. Over the next few days those particulars were taken care of and on April 28th the announcement appeared in the "The Quincy Patriot Ledger". Now the engagement was official

His mother seemed transformed. Sam had never seen her so happy. And he had some feelings for this man as well. That didn't mean he didn't have any misgivings. How was he supposed to relate to Martin? He could hardly think of him as his father and the proverbial *uncle* made him shudder. Could he share his mother with another man? Yes, he had already done that, but giving her up for a few hours while she and Martin spent an evening together wasn't the same as having them all living in the same house. Which presented another problem. Where would they live? In his mother's home, or with Martin? That second idea roared in his stomach like an undigested piece of raw hamburger. Moving into a strange house, a strange room, and with his mother sleeping in the same bed as Martin, doing God knows what. Well, he knew what, which made him want to gag. Mothers didn't do that sort of stuff! Well, they did—but. . .

How would he handle a new school, and being separated from his aunt, who had been his mainstay and who'd always been only walking distance from his home? And even worse, what would he do about Jennifer? Suddenly he realized that his mother's happiness could bring him a lot of grief.

Now that the "Ledger" had announced it to the world, he was allowed to share the news with his friends, and he headed out immediately to tell Jennifer. But before he got to her house, he met up with Winnie. He hadn't thought a lot about her lately, though he'd caught sight of her briefly at the drugstore, and he passed her in the halls everyday at school.

Winnie saw him first, and began running to catch up as she called out his name.

"Hey, wait up!" she said, with her usual eagerness, as she closed the distance between them, then adjusted her pace to match his. "Howzit goin'?"

"It's goin'," he said, with a shrug. "I haven't seen much of you lately," he added off-handedly.

"I've been there," she reminded him. "Maybe if you weren't lunchin'—walking around with your head in the clouds you'd've noticed."

"How's that?" he asked, feeling a little taken aback.

"Honestly, you haven't said more than two words to me for weeks. We always used to talk about everything, and now you hardly say hello. And not even that, unless I get in your way. What happened?" Then after a pause, she answered her own question—"Never mind, I know what happened—Jennifer happened." She whipped the palm of her hand hard against his shoulder and he fell back a step.

"Hey!" he said, rubbing the spot where she'd hit him. "Okay, I admit it. I've become a little preoccupied."

"Preoccupied? More like obsessed."

"Obsessed then. That doesn't mean that I don't care about you." Then he thought: *Is that really true? Have I given any honest thought to Winnie since Jennifer came along?* "Does it bother you that I'm spending so much time with her—Jennifer, that is?"

"That's not fair. First of all Jennifer is my friend and I'm never jealous of my friends. Secondly, I'm not some kind of bitch with a branding iron; I don't own you."

He hadn't expected such a caustic answer. But she was right; it wasn't a fair question. They'd known each other forever and the beauty of their relationship was the fact that there were no strings; neither had ever made demands upon the other. "I didn't mean it that way."

"Maybe not, but it sure sounded like it."

◆ ◆ ◆

Their friendship had started when they were both three. And all that time, whenever he was in trouble and needed someone to talk to—someone his own age—she was there. Thinking back, he realized that he had shared some very personal things with Winnie, some of which seemed silly now and some embarrassing. Like the summer before they started first grade: old enough to be curious, but not old enough to understand why.

They were sitting in the grassy dunes at the top of the beach, playing with plastic shovels and digging holes in the sand. He couldn't remember anymore how the subject came up. But he mentioned his Willie (the name he used to describe his penis) and she told him she didn't have one. He didn't believe her. How could she go to the bathroom without one? So they settled their childish argument by peeling off their swimsuits. He could still remember his shock when he saw that there was nothing there but a soft mound with a deep gash in it. Had it fallen off or somehow been swallowed up inside her?

"You're such a monkey," she giggled. "My brother has a pickle like that too," she said, pointing. "But girls don't. Girls are different."

"Can I touch it?" he asked.

"If I can touch yours," she answered and gave it a quick poke.

But before his little fingers could test the pale softness of her pubis his mother stepped up behind him and laid a hard slap across his bare butt that left a stinging imprint. She picked up his red trunks, and then grabbing him under his armpits, she carried him down the beach. His mother's reaction scared him, and what he saw worried him, but since such mysteries were beyond his understanding, he had to let it go. He probably wouldn't have remembered it so clearly if it hadn't been for his mother's anger and the second spanking he got before she finished pulling up his trunks.

As he grew older he had often sought comfort from Winnie. When his dad was abusive, he went to her. She couldn't actually do anything, but she listened and sometimes she held him the way a mother does a child, and that was enough. They had never failed to share secrets and they both talked about the things they were afraid of. One day he admitted that spiders gave him nightmares. Snakes affected him the same way until he got up the courage to touch one and found out that they weren't slimy but dry and scaly. After that he sought them out and turned them into pets. Winnie was the only one who knew. She told him of her fear of the water and of drowning. "You never show it," he said.

"No, I'm more afraid that someone will find out." But she kept his secrets and he kept hers.

Later, when they were ten, they discussed being grown-up and having kids. They compared numbers—she wanted three, in any order: all girls, all boys, or mixed. He wanted two: one of each. Their speculation ended when he proposed. "You and I ought to get married."

"No way," she said.

"Why not?" he asked, feeling hurt.

"Well, maybe," she said, kicking a soda can into the gutter. "All I can promise is that I won't marry anyone else."

That seemed fair and he dropped the subject.

Somewhere along the line he had forgotten that promise, and he wondered if she had forgotten it too.

◆ ◆ ◆

"I'm sorry," he said. But he didn't explain what it was he was sorry for. He didn't have to. She knew, just the way she knew everything else about him. If he believed in such things he would say she was psychic or that she had some magic power. Whatever possessed her, her understanding of his changing thoughts and moods seemed uncanny.

"You're forgiven." And then she did something unexpected; she took hold of his hand. She slipped her fingers between so that they were interlocked—snapping into place like two pieces of a puzzle; not the flat cardboard kind, but one of those wooden blocks that have to fit together in just the right order. And it felt just as natural, just as comfortable as it had that evening when they went to the fair together. That feeling of belonging had surprised him then and it surprised him now.

As they walked along the edge of the sandy road he glanced down the length of his arm to confirm the connection between them and wondered if the feelings he had for Winnie ran deeper than just friendship.

"Winnie, I've got great news," he said, tossing his head and squeezing her hand.

"Your mother's getting married," she said, before he could ask her to guess.

"How'd you know?"

"Well, it's not exactly a secret."

"No, I suppose not, but mom made me promise not to say anything until it went into the papers." He turned in front of her and continued, walking backwards so that he could confront her. "You're the first—the first to know, officially," he said.

"Don't do me any favors."

"What do you mean?"

"Good Grief, Sam, I'm not stupid, I know where you're headed. If I hadn't happened along, I'd hardly have been the first."

Bang zoom, he felt an explosion in his chest as if she had just punched him. "Please don't be mad."

"Don't sweat it. Just don't go all queer on me. Okay?"

"Okay."

Then she stopped in the middle of the road, and he stopped his backward waddle. She looked at him then away then looked at him again and said something that was obviously difficult for her. "Sam, you don't you don't have a clue—do you?"

"About what?"

"About how much it hurts when you leave me out—ignore me"

He dropped his chin, staring at his feet as if his shoes were suddenly soaked in shame. When he brought his head up to address her she was gone. He could only see the flash of her red jacket as she disappeared behind the corner of the nearest cottage.

He hadn't considered that his cavalier attitude over recent weeks might have hurt Winnie. He'd never excluded her before from even the most private details of his life—it had never been necessary. He turned up the road and started again, heading toward Jennifer's, but the brightness of spirit that had possessed him when he set out had deserted him. In a few minutes he walked up to Jennifer's door and rang her bell.

Chapter 50

Sam had come to Jennifer's full of blissful intent, sure of himself and anxious to tell her about the wedding. At least that had been his purpose when he left home, but after meeting Winnie those good intentions had turned sour.

He was pleased about his mother's engagement, and the happiness that had come into her life. Pleased that Martin had included him, by asking him to be part of the ceremony, and more surprisingly by asking for his permission. Not that he could have refused him and made it stick, but at least Martin had thought it necessary to ask for his approval. Then Winnie had reminded him of something that he had forgotten. No, not forgotten: more accurately she had made him aware of feelings that he had not known or understood until a few minutes ago. Even the thought that he might care for Winnie in a way that was more complicated than just friendship was discomforting. And his ignorance of her feelings combined with his recent action or inaction made him feel like a putz.

Altogether he wasn't ready to present his best self, and when Jennifer opened the door to greet him she seemed to recognize that he was in trouble.

"You look beat, what's up?"

"Nothing," he said, trying to smile. "I came to bring you some good news."

"Your mother's getting married," she said, wrapping her arm around his waist and drawing him into the hallway.

"Get out—how— ?"

"Oh, come on, this is a small town—everybody knows."

"Yeah," he said, with a disappointed groan

"You don't sound too happy about it," she said, taking his hand and leading him up the stairs.

"Well, no, it's great for mom, but it's not—that is, there's lots of prickly problems that go along with it."

"Like what?" They were in her room now. She took the wicker chair and he leaned against the edge of her bed.

"Like having to move to a strange house, and going to a strange school—away from my friends, away from my aunt—and miles away from you."

"Ahhh, well, that's not good," she said with an understanding frown.

"It sucks," he said.

"No, no, no," she said, going tap, tap, tap with her fingernail on the arm of her chair. "We're being selfish. This isn't about you and me, it's about your mother—and Martin."

"You're right," he said. "Besides, what am I worried about? No one's made any decisions yet." He bent his legs and slid down onto the floor, arms folded across his knees, back to the bed-frame.

"And if you move, you move. No biggy!"

Jennifer's last comment made him uneasy. Was she trying to be funny? For several days now Jennifer had been dropping subtle hints, but he couldn't figure out what they meant. If something was bugging her, why couldn't she just tell him?

Earlier, on the bus coming home from school, Jennifer had asked him to stop by and study with her. Sam hadn't brought any books, he figured that he could use hers, but folded into his back pocket was a notebook full of scribblings from his biology class and a sheet with tomorrow's math assignment on it. He had scoffed a couple of pens from the kitchen drawer on the way out and now reaching back to pull the notebook free, he tossed it and the pens onto the rug in front of him.

"Let's start with math," he suggested.

"I hate math!"

"I know, that's why I want to get to it first."

Jennifer dropped down from the chair and stretched out on the rug in front of him. The Algebra book sat unopened beside her. Instead, she used her arms to push herself up and leaned in to steal a kiss. Sam enjoyed this pleasant diversion and returned her kiss, but he knew that they had to make an effort to study if they wanted to pass the test on Friday. "Come on open the book," he said, flipping the pages of the textbook in front of Jennifer.

Soon they gave up the gritty business of solving for X and Y, and while Sam shuffled the papers that they had been working on, Jennifer picked up Shakespeare's *Hamlet*. They read portions of the play aloud, and tried to uncover their hidden meaning, but the language bemused them, and when Jennifer started to giggle, Sam joined in her silliness. So instead of scholarly effort they huddled over the book and played ticklish games, which wrecked their concentration. When Sam tried to read again, Jennifer blew warm air into the horn of his ear. He lifted his fingers to rub it away and she did it again. Sam flinched, but continued to read the passage from Act IV: "*Good sir, whose powers are these?*"

Laying side by side, Jennifer deliberately bumped her hip against his and Sam thought about the words he'd just read—not about Shakespeare's meaning, but their meaning right now, at this moment. Jennifer's closeness certainly had a powerful influence over his mind and body. The smallest movement, the lightest touch, a puff of air, a hint of perfume, the brush of her fingers across his wrist caused the blood to rush through his veins and made his hands feel sweaty. Worse than that he felt hot and cold at the same time.

"What is man, if his chief good and market of his time be but to sleep and feel?" Sam persisted. He slipped his free hand behind her neck putting her in a chokehold, then gave her a quick pull, which brought the softness of her cheek in contact with the roughness of his own. That friction excited him, and when she pushed him away they started to wrestle. He needed to make her stop, but he didn't want her to stop.

He rolled away then picked up the book and read again: *"So full of artless jealously is guilt, it spills itself in fearing to be spilt,".* At the word *guilt* he had a sudden image of Winnies face when she accused him of being clueless. Jennifer gave him a funny look and asked: "What?" but he didn't answer. Then the mood changed, and she grabbed the book and she took her turn at reading.

As the light dissolved, and the softness of evening filtered into every corner, Jennifer got up to turn on the lamp. Which made Sam check his watch.

"It's getting late," he observed.

When he stood to leave, Jennifer rose up beside him. Sam looked toward the mirror over her dresser and saw her soft-lit beauty reflecting back from the dark mahogany frame. He was in that frame too, but somehow his plainness spoiled the picture, and he thought how odd they looked as a couple. Her beauty seemed so extraordinary that it made his heart ache.

"Do you have to go?" she asked, with a clownish smile.

"Kinda."

"But we never got to the biology assignment."

The thought of the biology lesson made him laugh.

"What's so funny?"

"Maybe it's better that we didn't—it's on reproduction,"

"Yeah the reproduction of some stinky pond plants," she said, wrinkling her nose.

"True, but the principle is the same," he said, pulling playfully at a long strand of hair that had fallen in front of her face, then he used the end to tickle her nose. She put her arm around his waist and pulled him in for a gentle kiss and when she was done she said: "Don't worry I won't let your stamen come anywhere near my stigma."

He'd heard those terms before and knew they were parts of a flower, but couldn't say exactly what those parts were for. "See, you already know more than I do," he said. And he suspected that was true of the human side as well. Her clinical statement sounded proper but the picture it painted in his mind wasn't. And even though it was only in his mind, he felt guilty. *Honestly, if being good means I can't even think about sex, where's the fun in life?*

He gave Jennifer a kiss on the cheek, then excused himself. Opening the door, the bright light in the hall spilled into the room and temporarily blinded him.

"Love ya!" she said, as he stepped across the threshold.

"Me too," he called back.

♦ ♦ ♦

Walking home in the dark gave him time to think about the last couple of hours. He couldn't ignore what he'd seen in Jennifer's mirror, or expunge the impact of Winnie's parting words. If he were Aladdin, and had only one wish left, whom would he choose? Jennifer had such perfect beauty, and he knew that beneath that perfect exterior she had a good heart, but when he thought of Winnie, he wondered if he'd missed a more profound beauty, wrapped in a plainer cover. Could she be like the cactus his mother kept on the windowsill in the kitchen? All green and prickly and unimposing until one bright morning he came down to find a tiny red flower blooming at the end of a spindly stalk. Was there something he had missed in Winnie?

What made him think he had to choose between them? He wanted to believe that he loved Jennifer, but if that was love, then what did he feel for Winnie? One he had known for only a few weeks—the other had been his friend for his whole life. But should that make a difference? Did you have to know someone for a lifetime in order to love them?

As he made his way along the shadowy street, passing from lamppost to lamppost, conflicting images of these two girls confronted him, and he began to have doubts about what his relationship with each ought to be.

By the time he unlocked his back door and stepped into the inky blackness of the kitchen, he was more confused than ever. Feeling his way along the wall, he found the switch, and the fluorescent bulbs flickered to life. Both of these girls were important to him and before today it had seemed clear to him how each fit into his life. Couldn't he just separate them neatly and give them each a place and time? But if that were so easy, why had he ignored one completely while he devoted himself wholly to the other? No, this was more than just a matter of choosing and more than a matter of time; that is, more than how he divided his attention between them. What he needed was wisdom. He needed to talk to someone older, but who? It couldn't be Winnie and this time at least he couldn't ask his Aunt Em. He half hoped that the solution would jump up suddenly and hit him in the face. Not literally, of course. That would be painful.

♦ ♦ ♦

The note on the table told him to help himself to the ham in the refrigerator. He took a couple of slices and stuck it on a piece of bread, which he had lathered with mustard and with a can of warm soda in hand he went to watch TV. According to the note, his mother wouldn't be back until after ten. He dribbled mustard on his T-shirt and had to return to the kitchen for paper towels, which only spread the mustard wider. He dug some green olives out of a jar and went back to the television. He laughed at the jokes, but couldn't remember afterwards what he watched. When the news came on he switched the TV off and went upstairs.

He brushed his teeth, then crossed the hall to undress in the dim light filtering through his bedroom window. These habitual tasks didn't require much concentration, and he climbed into bed without any clear idea of how he got there. Drifting up out of his first dream, he realized that he had pulled off his shorts with his pants, which left him with only his T-shirt, but the thought of getting up and digging his boxers out of the pile of dirty clothes in the corner seemed like too much work. So he pulled the sheet and blankets up over his shoulders and turned onto his side. Curling his spine and drawing his legs up, he tried hard to drive away the confusion of the last few hours, but he couldn't sleep. He heard his mother come in, heard her get ready for bed. The last time he looked at the clock it was after two, and when sleep came the images were just as mixed up and confused as the reality he was trying to escape, only worse, because his dreams took him from one embarrassing situation to another. It seemed that wherever he went Jennifer and Winnie were both there to point their finger at him and laugh but he couldn't figure out what they were laughing at.

Chapter 51

For a while Sam had to put this quandary aside. Other things crowded it out: school exams, spring vacation, and the wedding. Though he was only to be an usher and not directly responsible for the preparations, Martin and his mother included him directly in all the details. To him it seemed like a girl-thing and he knew he didn't have any authority when it came to making decisions, but he could see that they honestly wanted his opinion and he honestly tried to give it. And occasionally they actually took his advice—or at least part of it. They let him pick the style of print on the invitations and they let him choose the color of the bridesmaid dresses. He didn't like either one, but thought that pink had to be better than lime green.

Sometimes though, all this attention made him uncomfortable, especially when it came from Martin. He suspected that Martin felt guilty about stealing his mother and taking up all her time, first with the stroke and now the wedding. To make up for it, he worked sometimes timidly and sometimes boldly to convince Sam that having two parents (two loving parents) was better than just having one. Martin planned all sorts of things for them to do together. But he didn't always ask, and his assumptions bothered Sam. He didn't want to appear ungrateful, but some of the things that Martin found for them to do were irritating. He had gotten tickets for the Home Improvement Show at the Centrum in Worcester. Granted it was a man's thing and Sam had no doubt about Martin's interest: he knew Martin had a woodshop and that he built small pieces of furniture when the mood struck him. But Sam had never done much with his hands except to bang his fingers when he tried to fix the broken railing on the porch with his father's rusty hammer. Whether he was genuinely clumsy or just hadn't had the chance to learn, he couldn't say, but the idea of looking at tools all day didn't appeal to him. Especially considering that he didn't know what half of them were for.

Still, his reluctance to go never turned into open rebellion, and he quietly followed Martin from one display to another. After he'd watched a demonstrator cut out a fancy pattern on an expensive jigsaw, stood and talked to a white-haired gentleman who was carving wild birds, then walked through a full-sized modular home that had been set up inside the convention hall, he discovered that he was having a good time.

Martin took him to Symphony Hall to hear the Boston Pops. This was definitely something Sam had no interest in. Rock, maybe some popular country music, but never classical. He left determined not to enjoy this, and yet when he returned several hours later he had to admit it was better than he expected. Maybe some classical music was okay, though he would never say that out loud.

Martin often talked about doing this kind of stuff with his own kids before they went off to college, and Sam had the feeling that he was trying to prove to him that he was just as important. It was clear that Martin wanted to establish a certain equity, to demonstrate that his love was available if Sam had the courage to accept it. He knew that Martin loved him in a way that his real father had not. Maybe his father just wasn't capable of that kind of love. He wondered if his father had ever loved anyone, including himself. Sam was aware that what Martin offered him was the real thing, but this sort of devotion was so unfamiliar and his own experience so limited, he hardly knew what to do, or how to react. When it came to his mother, he understood what he felt: he'd always had her love and it was easy to return it. But his father had been the enemy, and as much as he wanted to, Sam couldn't seem to find a way to express that kind of love toward Martin. Consciously, he understood that there was a world of difference between the two, but on a more primitive level he couldn't get past the fact that men, especially fathers, couldn't be trusted. And different or not, Martin was trying to act like a father.

They went bowling one evening, to make up for the Saturday that they had missed, and like so many of the things they did together Sam was out of his element. Not that he hadn't tried this with some of the kids and recently with Jennifer, but he had never bowled with any regularity, which meant he was doomed to failure. Especially since Martin bowled weekly with a league. His only advantage was that Martin had quit the league once he started to date his mother.

Sam hadn't considered, though, what the stroke had done to Martin. He had most of his movement back, but once he had made a few passes and watched the ball drift into the gutter, it was obvious that he'd lost his touch. Sam felt sorry for him. He didn't know what to do, so after flubbing a couple of balls of his own he begged off, complaining that his rented shoes were cutting into his instep.

"We could get another pair."

"Forget it!"

Sam put aside the offensive shoes and slipped into his own. While he was tying his sneakers, Martin placed a hand on his shoulder to get his attention and asked, "What's wrong?"

"I'm just a lousy bowler, that's all!"

"That's not what I meant."

"What do you want from me?" Sam said, shaking Martin's hand loose from his shoulder.

"Sam, I don't know what to do. I've worked hard to convince you that I'm interested, and you always seem just a razor's edge away from being reached. Why? Why do you keep putting up walls?" Sam could hear the frustration in Martin's voice and knew he needed an answer, but he had no idea what to say. For a long painful moment he sat there in silence. If he could just look at him it might help, but even that was impossible. It would have been too intimidating.

Martin waited. The gentle squeeze of his hand against Sam's shoulder told him that he was growing impatient.

"What do you want from me?" Sam asked again, sounding combative. "All I can say is I'm not used to all this attention."

"Do you want me to stop?"

"No, just don't try so hard," Sam said. "And before you plan something, ask me first."

"It's a deal," Martin said, searching clumsily for Sam's hand as a way to seal the bargain. Then on a softer note: "I didn't mean to put you on the spot, but I couldn't tell if any of this was getting through."

"It's getting through. I just don't know what to do with it."

Chapter 52

Jennifer and Sam continued to date and to spend time together, but something had changed. It was difficult to know just what it was. And after meeting Winnie on Beachwood Road, she had become part of the mix, which only added to his confusion. But Jennifer didn't know about that, so that wouldn't account for the brief moments of cool indifference that sprang up between them. It was like standing next to a hot fire and having a strong wind suddenly sweep the heat away. When the wind died the heat instantly returned, but these little storms seemed to come more and more often.

Now when he met Winnie accidentally in the hallway at school or sat beside her at lunch, he gave her his undivided attention. The school split the lunch break into two periods and it turned out that Jennifer had the first and Winnie the second. Sam also had the second period and he saw no reason why he shouldn't share his meal with Winnie. Soon they had settled into a familiar routine. No, that wasn't exactly true—he couldn't say why, but it wasn't familiar or routine at all. A new kind of intensity had taken over their relationship, but more than that he was listening, really listening; not so much to what she said as to her tone and intent.

Before it had always been about him, about his father or his mother and later Jennifer. As they grew up together Winnie drank up his pain and poured out her concern, and he became addicted to her generous spirit. He sucked up that spirit like a thirsty man at a desert oasis. But he never stopped to consider that maybe Winnie gave more than she could afford to. What about her needs?

Now he kept his mouth shut and listened.

At first there were long periods of silence, but Winnie seemed to feel the need to fill the silence with something and she began to talk. "Mr. Sampson, the biology teacher, gave me a hard time about my assignment. I had it in on time, but he was mad because it didn't have one of those fancy report covers." She took a bite out of her apple. "I made my own from poster-board, but that wasn't good enough." Sam knew she couldn't afford to buy the readymade stuff, but he never thought before how embarrassing it might be, and even now she didn't offer this as an excuse.

"Polly made a nasty comment this morning about my pants."

"What did she say?" he asked.

"She told me I looked like a guy. That my pants were baggy and they bulged in all the wrong places." He watched her toss the apple core back into her lunch-bag. Winnie had on some sort of military garb and the bottoms had extra large pockets down the legs.

She did wear boy's clothes most of the time, and the other girls must've ranked on her mercilessly for it. All of a sudden he began to see Winnie very differently, and he realized that she had problems all her own. Hard stuff that she'd had to deal with by herself while he continually piled on his troubles, never considering whether or not she needed the extra burden. And now that he was spending time with both girls, he seemed more conflicted than ever. Jennifer was wonderful, but he began to question whether he was really in love with her. Did he even know what that meant? That's not to say that he wasn't powerfully affected by his feelings for her. But it became more difficult to figure out the origin of those feelings, and harder still to understand the root of the passion that made pleasant things happen to him down under. Yes, he was a teenager, and nature and biology stirred up those parts every day, but while nature pulled him one way, his conscience pulled him back and that tug of war sometimes drove him crazy.

When it came to Winnie, he saw a distinct contrast. His feelings for her were softer, more controlled, and while she often stirred his heart, she left those other parts undisturbed. He respected the secrets that they had shared—the private communion—and recognized a soulful depth in the kind of intimacy that that implied, but couldn't decide what it all should mean. Nor could he determine if any of those feelings might translate into love.

The problem between Jennifer and Winnie seemed to be his perception of them sexually. He couldn't see himself kissing Winnie. Okay, maybe he could kiss her, but he couldn't see the two of them having sex. Even the thought of it struck him as a kind of betrayal. Of course, even with Jennifer, the idea of having sex wasn't easy to imagine. Well imagine, yes, but it still scared the hell out of him. He didn't have the experience, or the courage to make it happen—assuming, that is, that Jennifer wanted it to happen.

The idea that he was infatuated with Jennifer frustrated him, but it was not an idea that he wrestled with constantly. Sex however, *had* become an obsession. He tried hard to control himself, but it was impossible. Everywhere he turned there were stimulating reminders—advertisements, TV, movies—and there were other provocations: rude jokes told by his peers, pictures clipped from *Playboy* and *Hustler* taped to the inside of Bruce's locker at school, and the full-sized poster of Kathy Ireland in a bikini that he had tacked to his closet door.

Plus the recurring dream that he had at night: He's standing in the middle of a ballroom wearing a black tie and tux and he's dancing with a woman that looks a lot like Jamie Lee Curtis. She's wearing a long white gown, strapless with tons of cleavage. The woman loosens his tie and starts to unbutton his shirt, which excites him. He leans in to kiss her and suddenly his viewpoint changes. Through some piece of wizardry he shrinks from a man six feet tall down to the size of a ten-year-old boy. The woman pats him affectionately on the head and he sits bolt upright in his bed—awakening with a cry of frustration and disappointment.

Added to that frustration were the kind of daydreams, that came out of nowhere, sweet fantasies that were always interrupted by the real world just when they seem most promising. Sam was certain that all those unwanted interruptions tended to short-circuited the underdeveloped synapses in his brain, and helped to drive him crazy.

Whenever he had the courage to reveal some of this conflict to his Aunt Em she would tell him that this craziness was all perfectly normal—but that didn't seem to give him much hope.

Martin tried to keep him busy and that turned out to be a blessing. It meant fewer opportunities to be with Jennifer, but at least while they were engaged in hitting duckpins at a bowling alley, or watching an action film at a matinee, or concentrating on a complex game of chess, his mind was distracted enough to keep him out of trouble.

When spring finally settled in and Sam's youthful hormones started to attack in earnest, Martin took him to a golf course and tried to teach him how to hit a ball. Actually Martin wasn't very good. Sam couldn't tell if he had been bad from the beginning or if he was still uncoordinated because of the stroke. It seemed that little glob of blood crashing into his brain had done a lot of damage. Martin ended up sending Sam to the club-pro for instruction. Sam was an awful hacker and did a terrible job of getting the ball down the fairway, but he was enjoying himself. It wasn't very hard for him to figure out why Martin liked this game even if he wasn't very good at it.

◆ ◆ ◆

"David sat with us at lunch today," Jennifer said to Sam as they cuddled together in her living room.

Lately David had been sneaking into their discussions. Sam didn't know him well, but he seemed a likeable fellow. A loner who didn't fit into the group—he had to wonder why Jennifer was so interested in him.

"Since Karl has shunned him, he doesn't seem to have any place to go," she said.

"Karl's always got a burr up his butt about something," he said, thinking that anyone Karl didn't like automatically deserved his support.

"He's smart, good-looking, easy to talk to, and next fall he wants to go out for basketball."

"Who?"

"David," she said, bumping her shoulder against his, which knocked him into the arm of the sofa. "That's why Karl doesn't like him, he's competition."

After that, Sam introduced David to Bruce and he was included with the nerds on the far end of the football field. They gathered there in the morning before first bell and at midday for a fifteen-minute recess. David wasn't exactly a jock or a nerd, but Sam and his friends were the only ones generous enough to take him in.

Three weeks later the subject of David came up again. They were in Jennifer's room, studying.

"David talked to me at lunch today and then we met under the bleachers during the noon break," she said, brushing the hair away from her eyes and peeking up at him as if she wanted to judge his reaction.

"And?"

"And nothing." She let her hair fall back as she leaned over her book.

If it was nothing, then why bring it up? Whenever she mentioned David she would stop mid-sentence as if she might have said too much, and it made Sam nervous.

"Is there something going on between you two?"

"Naaahhh," she said, shaking her head too hard. "Well, I like him of course—but . . ." She stopped and he waited.

"But what?" he asked pulling the book from her hand to get her attention. She didn't answer. Instead she got hold of the corner of the book and tried to take it back. That started a tug-of-war, and when she let go he lost his balance and went down, and she went down after him. Sprawled between his legs she looked up the length of his body and started to laugh. Whatever worries he'd had about David were blown away while the two wrestled on the floor and then kissed.

The next morning he closed his locker door and turned to see David and Jennifer, hand in hand, heading away from him. When the bell rang Jennifer nuzzled her face into David's neck and they stepped through the doorway into room 202. Mrs. Delmare, the French teacher, followed after them and closed the door.

Sam's rage caused a reflux of hot bile to rise in his throat and he attacked the side of his locker with his fist, hitting it so hard his knuckles started to bleed. Still, when they met in her room after school she said nothing, and his not so subtle hints led to a cold, black silence.

On Friday Jennifer rushed up to him as he started to climb onto the bus. Her arms full of books, she used them to help block his way. Her lilting voice and pleasant smile were disarming and he smiled back at her, thinking that she was finally ready to apologize to him for the other day.

"Sam, we've got to talk," she said. "Can you come over right after you get home?"

"Yeah," he said with some misgiving. It didn't matter whether it came from a friend or an enemy, whenever he had heard those words in the past it usually meant something had to be said that he didn't want to hear.

Surprisingly Jennifer didn't climb on the bus with him, but took off toward the parking lot where she apparently had a ride waiting.

Chapter 53

After a worrisome trip home on the bus, Sam deposited his books on the table inside the front door. Searching the house and finding it empty, he made an immediate determination to leave, and headed straight to Jennifer's. In the interest of speed he took his bike out of the shed and pedaled down the road toward the beach.

The bright afternoon sun, a sharp salty breeze, and the pungent sweetness of Irish moss drying on the shore filled the air with the promise of spring and warmer weather. Under different circumstances he might have taken the time to appreciate this, but a discordant churning in his stomach frustrated his senses, and he directed all his energy toward getting to Jennifer's. A powerful need to discover the meaning of her mysterious summons drove him on, but he was afraid that whatever she had to say was bound to make him unhappy.

When the door opened to the sound of his knock he was surprised to see Mrs. Hollypepper. It was her home, and her front door, but Jennifer usually came to welcome him, especially when she knew he was on his way over.

After ten long minutes of pacing the hallway, she clamored down the stairs. "Hi Sam. Sorry about the wait." Her greeting had the same brightness, her smile the same sweeping curve, but he sensed a certain undercurrent that made him uneasy.

"Let's go up," she said, pinching his arm in her grip and pushing him toward the stairs. Directing him to the wicker chair, she ordered him to sit, then she jumped up on her bed and wriggled back until her feet dangled above the floor. Nervously folding and unfolding her arms, she glanced up at him and said, "God, this is hard!" There was an unfamiliar anguish in her voice, and when she spoke these words she tossed her head back and looked straight up at the ceiling. Holding this position briefly, she brought her head slowly forward, then down, until her face was hidden behind a frizzy curtain of long golden hair. Silent, she kept kicking her feet back and forth like a little child.

Hanging on tenterhooks, strangled by her indecision, Sam waited for her to end the long silence. He thought maybe he should speak, but he didn't know what to say. Jennifer had become such an important part of him. The quality of what he thought the idea of who he was seemed totally dependent upon what she thought and felt. Until recently every day began and ended with her, with only short spaces between for sleep and study. It seemed that nothing could be planned without first considering how it would affect her—or more accurately, how it would affect *them*. She had been the first—first obsession, first love, first real kiss. He had no experience here, but he sensed that all that was about to end. Finally losing his patience, he shouted: "What? What is it?"

"Damn—damn—damn!" she said, bringing her head up a notch at a time until her hair slid back enough to expose part of her face. "This is so hard."

"How awful can it be?" he asked. Seeing the sadness in her eyes filled him with panic. If this was going to hurt him as much as it was obviously hurting her, he needed to find a way to brace himself for it. He rose from his chair initially to go to her, but he changed his mind and went to the window instead.

"Sam, you've been a wonderful friend and I don't want to lose that friendship."

"Why should you lose my friendship?" he asked, still facing the window. "Besides, I thought we were a lot more than just friends."

"We were—we are." she corrected.

"If this is so bad, why do you have to say anything at all?"

"Because, not saying it won't change the way I feel and—and— Damn, I don't know how to do this." He turned and she looked at him through the unkempt strands of her hair. As she lifted her head higher those strands fell away and he could see that her eyes were wet, a clear witness to the struggle that was raging inside.

"I've met this new boy, David. I'm sure you know him."

"Yeah, I know him," he acknowledged. Looking out the window and down the length of the shore he watched a long white comber break over the rocks at Land's End. He liked this guy. They'd talked about him a lot, but he'd never seen him as a rival.

"I've mentioned him before. He's approached me a couple of times in the halls between classes. No biggie—he's new and just a little lost. We sit together during lunch and talk. Everything was fine until he asked me out. I didn't know what to say. I haven't said yes, but I like him. I like him a lot."

"And you want to go out with him, but there's me, and you don't want to hurt my feelings," Sam said, hoping it was true, but wondering if it really mattered.

"If I had gone out with him, you'd have heard about it. One of your friends would have come to you. The story would be twisted—they'd tell you that it was for your own good, then add a little lie, and while you bled all over them, they'd put their arm around you and tell you that it was all my fault. I know, I've been there."

"So this is better?" he asked, feeling a sharp pain in his stomach. The pain that she promised to save him from.

"Maybe."

"Are you asking for my permission?"

"No way! I just wanted this to come from me. At least you're getting the truth."

"Truth? The truth is, I took this seriously and you didn't."

"It wasn't love, if that's what you mean. I'm too young to be in love. But that doesn't mean I wasn't serious."

"Then what's this about David?"

"Being serious doesn't mean being exclusive, Sam. Is it wrong for me to want to see other guys?"

"Guys? You mean there's more than one?" He knew that wasn't what she meant, but he couldn't resist making the accusation.

"No!" she said, spewing the word out angrily.

"So you want to date David and I'm in the way. Out with the old, in with the new," he said. Taking a couple of strides, he dropped heavily back into the chair and sat staring at his outstretched feet.

"Please don't put it that way. If you're trying to be cruel, you're not very good at it." She was right: he wanted to hurt her, but his heart wasn't in it.

"I'm not very good at being dumped either," he challenged.

"I don't remember making any promises," she said. "Did you really think that this would last forever?"

"Yes." His response was certain because until this moment he had believed that his feelings for Jennifer would last forever.

"Don't be foolish, we're too young."

"What does age have to do with it? Is there a rule—is there a special age when you're allowed to fall in love? And before that it's all nonsense." He couldn't help pushing this, even though inwardly he had already begun to see that it was hopeless.

"I'm not going to argue with you. Anything's possible, but it's not true for us. You're the first boy I've dated more than once, the first one who treated me like a person and not some object to be fondled and groped. I've come to have deep feelings for you, but I know it's not love, not the kind of love you're thinking of anyway," she added. "You've been decent, but so has David. You'd really like him, if you gave him a chance."

"I do like him. I just don't like the fact that you have to choose him over me."

"This isn't about choosing, but do you honestly think that you or David would be willing to share the same girl? I wouldn't mind, but I don't think that you two could handle it. Maybe it's territorial, but guys don't share—especially girls. I never intended to hurt you, Sam, but I'm a teenager and I want to enjoy being a teenager. I want to have a good time."

"Didn't we have a good time?"

"Of course we did. It was great. Nothing in my life has been more intense. But it's over."

"Why? Because of David?"

"No, not entirely. It's lots of things. Lots of silly girl things that you wouldn't understand."

She had obviously chewed this over in her mind, whereas he had hardly had time to swallow the bitter taste of it. He had a desperate desire to strike back, to jab at her with some of the anger that was welling up inside of him. But he still loved her, and that emotion strangled his rage.

"I know that you're angry," she said. "But don't be."

"So I'm just supposed to grin and bear it?"

"We've been good friends. I hope we can remain friends, but I don't think you're ready for that. Maybe later, when you've had a chance to think this through, things will be different."

"Maybe," he conceded, but right now he couldn't see how. The difference between being friends and lovers seemed worlds apart and he never thought he would have to trade one for the other.

Chapter 54

Jennifer was right about one thing: he needed a different perspective on this, and so instead of going home he headed across her back yard to find out if Aunt Em was available. He wanted to talk to his aunt, yet he wasn't sure if he could explain to her or anyone else how he felt right now. His only clear emotion was anger. Once he was at Aunt Em's door he changed his mind and instead went back to pick up his bike, which was leaning against the slatted snow fencing between the two houses. Dragging it through the soft sand and up onto the road, he pushed off and started toward home.

Once on the road, he changed his mind again and decided to head for a place he hadn't been to or thought about for a long time. After a twenty-minute ride he dismounted, and leaving his bike at the garden gate he walked into the park past the bench and the reflecting pond and went behind the pagoda to the stone wall at the edge of the harbor. He sat and swung his legs around to let them dangle over the water and watched as the waves climbed up toward his feet, then fell away again.

He couldn't remember ever having come here alone. In the past he'd always shared this place with Winnie.

How had this happened? He tried to remember what he had said to Jennifer, what she had said to him, looking for some clue, but it was all a muddle. For all his effort only one thing seemed certain: he was too young to have a broken heart. Then he thought: *Maybe it's not broken.* Maybe he could win her back. But he couldn't come up with any logical reason why she would take him back, unless—as she suggested—he agreed to share her with David. Eventually he accepted the fact that he had been dumped and went back home.

The next day, coming down the hallway at school, he studied the faces of those who greeted him and wondered how much they knew. Probably nothing, but he assumed that everybody was whispering about him anyway. It never occurred to him that no one really cared.

When he entered the stairwell he saw Jennifer step off the last step and head straight for him. He had no idea what to say to her. At first he closed his eyes, then when he opened them she smiled instantly and said, "Hello, Sam." He heard the same familiar lilt in her voice and he tried to answer, but she sidled past him before the words came out. He started to go after her, but stopped abruptly when he saw her catch up to David and take his arm. Did she have to be so public? Then they shared a kiss. Shouldn't there be some kind of mourning period—time for him to get used to this, before she gave herself so completely to someone else?

Suddenly he heard the second bell and realized that he was standing in the middle of a deserted stairwell. He breathed a cocky reprisal: "I hope she chokes on he own tongue," then rushed off to his English class.

Several days went by before he felt at all comfortable with Jennifer—with himself—or anyone else. The only one that he could talk to was Winnie. Her friendship with Jennifer must have given her privilege to their breakup, but she said nothing. Nor did she try to offer solutions, or utter brainless platitudes. Sam never explained and she never asked; she was just there.

One rainy noon while they sat together in the cafeteria sharing lunch, Sam felt the need to tell her about Jennifer. The mention of Jennifer's name brought a shadow across Winnie's face, which surprised him, but he plunged ahead anyway. "I know it's stupid, but I can't seem to let this go. I guess I want to play the martyr and have people feel sorry for me."

"That's understandable," Winnie said, lifting the top of her sandwich and exposing the innards. Sardines. How could she eat that? It looked like rotten fish and bones with a trail of brown mustard winding across the middle. She looked up at him, then said, "Sorry," and pressed the bread together again.

"I know you're friends with Jennifer and in a way I still want to be her friend too, but I can't."

"No, you can't."

"I thought that she loved me."

"How do you know?" she asked, putting down the carton of milk she'd just taken a swallow from.

"Know what?" He pushed his lunch bag aside. He still hadn't opened it—he didn't want to eat right now.

"Know when it's love?" She scrunched her eyes closed as if she wished she hadn't asked.

"Yeah, like I'm the one to ask," he said, putting his elbows on the table and propping up his chin as if his head were suddenly to heavy to stay up there on its own.

"At least you know when it isn't."

"Yeah, I suppose."

"Besides, you could have spent years loving her and not have her love you back and that would hurt even more." As soon as she said this, Winnie dropped the apple she'd just taken a bite out of and fumbled to retrieve it before it rolled off the table. She seemed flustered as if she'd given away some dark secret, but he couldn't imagine what.

"Are you okay?"

"Fine." The word was clipped and she immediately began to toss her leftovers back into her lunch bag. Suddenly he was worried about her and not himself, and somehow that made him feel better. She stood to leave and he watched her walk through the cafeteria. *It's odd,* he thought, *with everything I know about her I still don't understand her.*

♦ ♦ ♦

In the days that followed, he began to study Winnie. He kept trying to determine why he felt uneasy around her. He noticed that when he addressed her about any subject, simple or profound, she would look directly at him. Her eyes would stare into his and the softness behind them suggested she knew something about him that he <u>didn't</u> know. That made him self-conscious, and that too was reflected in her eyes, which compounded the problem, and if he were talking he would falter in mid-sentence.

"Am I bothering you?" she would ask.

"N-n-no," he insisted, as he fidgeted and stretched out his collar.

"Something has you flustered," she said. "I've never heard you stutter before."

If he looked away for a moment and kept his mouth shut he could get back on track. "Um, I'm okay," he said, before continuing his thought. He'd never realized before how attentive Winnie could be. Her interest sometimes seemed intense and yet that intensity was so tender that she could have reached in and lifted his heart out of his chest and held it up to the sun and only the fact that he suddenly felt warmer and safer would have registered.

His ego was so terribly bruised when Jennifer first dumped him that he imagined the pain he was suffering to be unbearable—that it would never go away. But as always Winnie absorbed that pain and through some sweet magic made it disappear—and that was somehow disappointing. How could he play the role of the spurned lover if he didn't feel it? It took him several days to come to his senses and realize that he was acting like a buffoon.

He avoided Jennifer until he had recovered and when he did finally see her again he was able to approach her as a friend.

♦ ♦ ♦

It had been a month since Jennifer dumped him, and another birthday was just a few days off. Because he was turning sixteen, his mom got the bright idea that this should be *le grande affaire.* So she asked him to consider who he would like to invite to his party. A small party, she cautioned. "How small?" Sam wanted to know, and she told him no more than ten people. So much for *le grande affaire.* Sarah defended herself by explaining that the cost of the wedding was rising daily.

Sam decided to be magnanimous, and the first two people that he put on his list were Jennifer and David. The next person he thought of was Winnie, then Bruce, and of course Richie and Amy; after that, it didn't seem to make much difference who he invited.

Winnie couldn't come. She begged his forgiveness, but she would be in New Hampshire with her aunt and uncle and wouldn't be returning until after school let out for the summer.

The party was a disappointment. Sam thought that turning sixteen was going to be pivotal. Instead, the beginning of the day was not much different from the end. When he was twelve he'd had the idea that sixteen would be grown-up. During the last four years, he was supposed to have acquired some special wisdom. He certainly had tried, and there had been some progress toward that end, but whatever knowledge he'd aquired it couldn't be called wisdom and he certainly didn't feel any more grown-up. Instead things had become infinitely more complicated, and he seemed to understand less and less.

Look at my life, he thought. He'd lost Jennifer and never saw it coming, and Winnie, who had been his longtime friend, steady as a rock, had somehow become something else. Now, here he was at his own party—the only one without a partner.

Depressed, he stole a dance with Amy, Richie's girl, which made him noticeably angry. And in the middle of the dance Sam spotted one of the girls pouring whiskey into the punch bowl. It seemed like such a predictable thing to do that he could hardly believe it was happening. But when he pried the bottle from her hand there was no mistaking the label.

"If my mother ever gets wind of this, she'll have my hide." Richie encouraged him to be cool, but as far as he was concerned the party was over. "Out," he shouted. Everybody out." And he groused and complained until he had hustled all his guests out the front door.

His birthday had been a bust. This great coming of age—at least driving age—hadn't changed anything. His future was just as confusing and he felt more depressed than ever. The next major event in his life would be his mother's wedding, and that only led to other problems. There was still no decision about where they would live and where he would got to school, and if he had to move away from Green Harbor that would pretty much put the kibosh on his social life.

The Summer of 1987

Chapter 55

Winnie didn't return from New Hampshire until June 20th.

This year, an early summer sent the temperatures soaring into the eighties, and Sam spent every waking hour at the beach. After two hot weeks in the sun he had a little burning across the shoulders and the back of his neck, which had already begun to peel. Everywhere else his skin had turned to a toasty brown. He loved the sound and color of the surf, the cooling breeze, and the biting coldness of the water. This summer it occurred to him that he might one day have to leave the water and the beach behind. He was sure to go away to college, maybe Lewiston-Auburn in Maine or New London Connecticut, or possibly somewhere in the Midwest. And once he married and started a career he could end up anywhere, even in another country.

One late afternoon as he stood at the edge of the wash looking out to sea, someone came up behind him and gently put their hands over his eyes. Their softness suggested a girl, but she didn't ask him to guess who she was.

"I supposed I should know who this is, but I haven't got a clue."

He took away her hands, swung her around, and saw Winnie smiling back at him. Only it wasn't Winnie—at least not the Winnie he knew. She wore a sleek two-piece swimsuit that revealed some dramatic changes. During the long winter months while she had been wrapped in a cocoon of coats, baggy sweaters and long pants, a marvelous metamorphosis had taken place. She hadn't suddenly gone from mousy to magnificent, but what he saw in front of him certainly pleased the eye. The tall angular body that he remembered had taken on a softer shape—and she had breasts. Not that they were particularly large, but last summer they had only been two bumps, which showed vaguely under the ruffles of her old bathing suit. Now they were full and pointy, and the top she was wearing pushed them up and in, adding a delightful pinch of cleavage. Her waist, once straight and uninteresting, looked narrow, and her bony hips were no longer sharp, but pushed out in a gradual curve that was only interrupted slightly by the tightness of the bikini bottoms that barely covered. . .well, he didn't want to think about what they covered. He had never seen so much of Winnie before and he supposed that if she had her old boyish figure he wouldn't have wanted to. But today, as his eyes followed her long fluid legs down to a pair of narrow feet, which no longer seemed too big for her, he was suddenly aware that his jaw had dropped and he had to consciously pull it shut. What he observed and especially what he felt seemed almost incestuous. His first impulse was to cover her up, but he knew that would be an insult.

The new bathing suit hadn't been worn much, because her tan-lines didn't match. He could see a pale band of skin above and below her bikini briefs and another line a couple of inches below her top, which left a tawny stripe across her middle. There was also a thin delicate track that went up around her neck. The marks suggested shorts and a halter-top. A few days in the hot sun and this pale outline would blend in with the rest. But for the moment, the cool contrast between white and tan fascinated him.

Generally she kept her hair in a short boyish cut. During the weeks that she had been away she'd let it grow. It wasn't long, but longer than he was used to. She tipped her head down when she saw that he was staring and this coy display of shyness made him chuckle. Head still tipped forward, she shifted her weight to one leg, pushing her right hip out and when she lifted her hand and brought her fingers to rest delicately on her tight stomach her pose looked as sexy as one of those supermodel posters for sale in the department stores.

After a moment she looked up at him through a gash in her thick hair and when her eye met his he caught the hint of a smile. "Aren't you going to say anything?"

He didn't know what to say. Finally he blurted out the truth. "You're <u>different!</u>"

"Is that bad?" she asked guilelessly.

It was hard to believe that she wasn't aware of how hot she looked. Yet when he reached out to push her hair from her face he could see that she didn't fully appreciate the transformation that had taken her from plain to pretty.

"It's good, of course," he said. Words like *awesome, bodacious,* and *boobiferous* (something he'd heard on late night TV), came to mind, but he didn't dare say them. This wasn't Winnie—not his Winnie. He'd never imagined—never dreamed that she could be so beautiful. Not showy or flamboyant, not the same brightness as Jennifer—but then he didn't want to see her that way. In fact, her soft new femininity made her seem more accessible. He couldn't take his eyes off of her, and his fixed gaze clearly made her uncomfortable.

"Don't! Don't look at me like that," she said, folding her arms to hide her breasts. "This wasn't my idea. I wanted something less showy, but my cousin Sandy kept shoving this thing at me and insisting that I try it on—and when I did, well, Sandy said I looked hot and that I had to have it."

"It does—look great, that is." He didn't dare use the word *hot*—not out loud, and it couldn't possibly be less anything and still be wearable. He wondered: *how could I have missed all this? Was I asleep or just too wrapped up in myself to see that Winnie wasn't one of the guys anymore?* He decided that it wasn't his fault. It was the way she dressed. She had worked very hard to keep this a secret—perhaps even from herself.

He wanted to invite her to go for a swim, but he wasn't sure what the water would do to her new suit. It didn't seem to be designed for swimming, and he worried that any kind of strenuous activity might cause her to lose it. While he was thinking about this, Winnie interrupted with her own invitation.

"Let's go for a swim."

He had no idea what to say as she took his hand and dragged him toward the water. She waded in up to her hips, took a quick dip, then decided she'd had enough. Perhaps the frigid water discouraged her. The suit held together, but his fears were not totally unfounded. The cold raised her nipples, and the wet cloth followed their shape, revealing dark circles that were the size of a sand dollar. He'd seen that all before when she was younger and swam in just her T-shirt and shorts, but then the circles were much smaller and she had no breasts to make them leap out at him. Coming up the beach after their swim he suggested that she looked cold and quickly wrapped her in his huge beach-towel.

Once the suit dried, the opaque quality of the material returned, and the problem went away. She kept the towel draped over her shoulders and that made Sam feel a lot more comfortable. He would never see Winnie the same way again. She could no longer be the skinny little girl that he had grown up with. Which didn't mean that her new appearance had destroyed her innocence, but it had destroyed his.

Sitting there on the warm sand, they began to talk as they always had, of ordinary things, of hopes and wishes, irony and contradiction and that old familiarity helped him to relax. Eventually the conversation switched briefly to her trip to New Hampshire and ended with the plans for his mother's upcoming wedding. It was now firmly set for July 10th. He would stay with his Aunt Em until they (Sarah and Martin) came home from their honeymoon. That led to unwanted thoughts about what they would be doing once they reached Bermuda, which made him feel kind of creepy. . .of course he dreamed of the day that he would love and marry and enjoy the sweet intimacy of his own honeymoon, but that was different.

Winnie looked at him and asked, "What are you thinking?"

Oh sure, like he was going to tell her that he was worried about Martin and his mother having sex. But he did tell her. "Well, you know, I was—ah—thinking about Mom and Martin in Bermuda and, what—they'd be doing there."

"Jeeze, what do you think they'll be doing? They'll be on their honeymoon for cryin' out loud," she said, this emphatically as if it were as natural as her dog having puppies.

How did she do that? How did she just say whatever she wanted without even a wrinkle of embarrassment?

"Okay, okay," he said and she laughed at him. He liked her laugh: it was fresh an unaffected. Not that he hadn't heard her laugh before, but today like everything else it seemed brand new. The girlish sound was high and clear and didn't drop off at the end. And she didn't try to adjust the pitch by adding that hoarse little growl of hers.

Winnie interrupted his thoughts. "Shouldn't we be going?"

Turning his wrist, his watch showed ten minutes to five and glancing around he noticed that many of the beach-goers had already left. Winnie gave Sam back his towel and they started to walk, staying near the water's edge.

Leaving the beach through a break in the seawall, they crossed Beachwood Road and continued up Jacob's Lane sticking to the cool grass on the shoulder until they had reached the top of the hill behind her house. Coming through the gate Sam walked Winnie to her door, then stood for a moment holding both her hands in his. Along with all the other changes she had grown a couple of inches taller and he found himself staring straight into her eyes. For the first time since he had come to know her he had a desire to kiss her. Considering their relationship up to now, the idea of kissing her seemed ludicrous. But he thought he saw a certain look—a brightness in her eye—a tiny pucker of her lips that suggested she might want to be kissed. Was he reading that look correctly or just imagining things? *No,* he decided, *it's not my imagination.* But he just didn't know how to make it happen.

"It's—it's been great," he muttered ineffectually. Then he gave a kind of straight-lipped half smile and ran for the gate. Before heading down the road he turned and saw her watching him, and thought that she looked a little disappointed.

For years his life had been discordant, full of deception and desperation. But all during that time Winnie had been there acting like an anchor in the storm. His sense of reality was governed by her presence, and until now he hadn't realized how much she had given and how little she has asked in return.

It wasn't fair. He owed her so much and he had no real way to repay her. Then like a bright flash of lightning that blossoms on the summer horizon he realized it was a gift—something she had freely given. Winnie had never set out to drive him into emotional debt or to make him feel guilty. Being a child herself, she probably didn't appreciate how desperately he needed her understanding, or how much pain he was in because of his father—but she didn't have to. All she had to do was be there.

His thinking shifted suddenly to an idea he had never considered before. Could it be that her interest in him had been something more than childish devotion, something deeper than friendship? Perhaps not in the beginning, but now that she was older and more sensitive to such things—and had he simply been too stupid to see it.

Thinking back, especially over the last few months, he could recall a number of things that might have been interpreted differently if he had only been alert to their subtle meaning.

In history class, she sat at the desk just behind him to his right. And one afternoon looking back over his shoulder, he saw her head rise slowly from her work, and when her eyes caught his she froze. Then he remembered a smile. Not a broad smile—just a quick turn at the corners of her mouth: after that her head fell and she seemed engrossed in her work. But he kept staring at her until her head rose again, and this time, when she saw that he was still watching, her face came alive and her smile spread broadly from ear to ear.

She always listened quietly to his troubled ruminations, but now and then she interrupted with a gentle voice that sounded very different from her usual growl. What she said wasn't profound, but the tone and inflection rubbed up against his injured spirit the same way his cat did when she wanted to feel the long stroke of his hand down her back.

They never walked arm in arm, but she often took his hand, and she often touched him. Though it was only when they were roughhousing: and then it was only a quick poke in the ribs, a slap on the bum—maybe a punch in the arm—and when they were still children he'd actually gotten down on the floor and wrestled with her. Not that it ever got out hand—nothing happened that seemed inappropriate.

Now and again she would wet the edge of her sleeve with her spit and scrub a spot off his face; and if he happened to get cut or bruised she always had a Band-Aid or one of those pre-packaged wet-wipes mixed in with all the junk she carried around in her pockets. Frequently she pulled out her comb to fix his hair, and if she noticed his shirt-tail had come out she would always tuck it back in. Sometimes he thought she did more mothering than his own mother.

One afternoon, sitting together on her front porch, pushing back and forth on her old green glider, she complained of being tired. And before he knew what she was up to, she had folded her legs, pulled them up onto the padded green canvas covering and stretched out in the space between him and the metal arm that bracketed the far end. She laid her head in his lap as if she did that sort of thing everyday and he never questioned it; he just stroked her boyish hair carefully until he could tell by her slow breathing that she had fallen asleep.

Though having her head in his lap might have been full of sexual portent, he never considered that it had any particular meaning, and even now he wondered if he wasn't over-interpreting.

The question was: what should he do? He wanted desperately to make up for his indifference and insensitivity, but how? If he changed too abruptly, she would ask questions that he didn't know how to answer. Here he was again, wavering—full of uncertainty. He wanted to think of himself as grown-up, but he wasn't ready yet to act grown-up. Part of him still wanted to be a child, to be protected and taken care of. Which was why whenever his father drove him away, and his mother was too incapacitated to reach out and comfort him, he had always gone to Winnie. And somehow, even though she was only a child herself, she had managed to fill that roll. And he still wanted her to fill that roll. But he also saw that she could be a lot more than just his comforter. He wanted desperately to do what was right, but he simply didn't know where to begin.

After brooding over this all evening he finally went to bed, but he couldn't put it out of his mind. The room was filled with the sticky heat of the day and he kept tossing and turning, trying to find relief. At last exhaustion took him off to rocky dreams of Winnie—the sort of dreams that are full of energy and that keep jumping from scene to scene until he felt worn out and used up.

Chapter 56

*O*nce asleep, Sam stayed asleep. It was almost seven before he awoke, and then he just lay there staring up at the dirty fan mounted on the ceiling, listening to the muffled whap, whap, whap as it slowly beat the air. His active dreams had worn him down as if the physical effort had been real, and his body refused to move. When he finally reached over and picked up the clock and saw that it was past eight, he decided that he had to get up.

Even at this early hour the air already felt thick and heavy and he knew that any exercise would drain his energy. He expected to spend the day seeking relief in the cold waters of the Atlantic, but first he wanted to scrub away the sweat from a restless night that had left his sheets rumpled and rank. Crossing the room, he grabbed a large towel that hung from the hook on the back of his bedroom door hung it around his neck and padded down the hall to the bathroom.

Adjusting the water, he took a cool shower and worried about what to say to Winnie when he met her today. It occurred to him that he could avoid the problem altogether if he didn't go to the beach as he had promised, but however confused he might be he didn't want to run away. Winnie had never frightened him before, but then he had never considered the possibility that she might be in love with him. Whatever—even if she now made him uncomfortable, he trusted Winnie.

He put on his new swim trunks. His mom had found a sporty style, red with white piping, shorter than his usual boxers that had little overlapping slits on either side. The dark shiny material contrasted nicely with the white polo shirt that he pulled over his head. With his mom at work, he had to fix his own breakfast. When he'd filled his stomach, he locked the house and headed down Lindenhurst Road, to Beachwood, stopping at Aunt Em's cottage.

He didn't have to meet Winnie until two, so he thought he would spend the time in between with Em; if she were at home. No one answered when he rang the rusty bell, so he stepped inside and hollered. Still no answer. Maybe this would be one of those rare times that she wasn't there. Somewhere in the back of his mind he had the idea that he could talk to his aunt about Winnie, but when he couldn't find her he began to feel relieved.

Now he wouldn't have to figure out what to say—or what not to say. Making his way down the darkened hall into the living room, he stepped out onto the empty front porch and went to look out over the railing. That's when he saw his friend Bruce coming through the gate in the seawall. He thought, *I haven't been much of a friend lately.* Since he started dating Jennifer last fall he'd seen Bruce rarely: sometimes at school or in church, and on those occasions they'd hardly had time to talk. He'd even ignored him at his party. Seeing him now made Sam wish he hadn't done that—hadn't shut him out for all those months and he decided to try and catch up to him.

Rushing down the front stairs to the beach, he started jogging toward Bruce, who was headed straight for the water's edge. "Hey, Bruce!" he shouted, as he kicked off his sneakers and dropped his beach-towel onto the sand. "Wait up!"

Bruce turned to see who was calling to him, and put his hand up to shade his eyes. Then he used that same hand to give a short wave before starting off in Sam's direction. Shortly they were at each other's side, and Bruce's greeting was unexpectedly blunt. "Hey, kid howzit goin'?"

"I'm doin' okay."

"Sorry to hear about Jennifer."

"What have you heard?"

"Well, Jennifer's not talking, but lots of others are. Jeeze you two guys were practically attached at the hip and lately that hip seems to be connected to David. What happened?"

"Yeah, I should've been the one to tell you, but lately my life has been on hold. I'm sorry, you should have heard about Jennifer from me. Actually, Jennifer's old news. Right now, it's Winnie that's giving me trouble."

"Jeeze! I should have such problems—I don't even have one girl, and you've got two of them to worry about."

"What happened to Kelly?"

"She's long gone. But a month ago, I found someone who would do more than just talk to me at lunch."

"Great!"

"Not so great. Yesterday, she and I split."

"Why?"

"I don't know, she said something about my never taking her anyplace. Dang, last summer we didn't have a girl between us and we were happy. True, you spent a lot of time mooning over Jennifer, but it's hard to get into trouble when you're only looking. "How 'bout we make a pact to have nothing to do with girls—at least for the summer."

"I'm tempted, but right now I couldn't keep that promise."

"Why not? Didn't Jennifer screw you over enough to make you want to give up girls? At least for awhile?"

"Yeah—in a way. But then there's Winnie."

"I don't get it. Winnie is Winnie; you know—one of the guys."

"Have you seen her lately? She's hardly one of the guys. She's not drop-dead-gorgeous, but she's definitely hot."

"Are we talkin' about the same Winnie?"

"Definitely."

"Really."

"You won't believe it, when you see her." At that moment the proof of his argument stepped into view. She had on the same white bikini, but today she had covered herself with an oversized man's shirt. The cuffs were rolled back and the front unbuttoned; and at first this cover made the whole get-up seem much less provocative. But whenever the wind filled the back of her shirt, lifting it and making it billow like a spinnaker on a quickening sea, the sudden exposure was clearly more exciting than the unencumbered version he had seen yesterday. Before she got close enough to hear, Bruce's mouth fell open and the word "boomin'," fell out.

"Not too shabby, eh? Makes it hard to remember the skinny little kid that used to hang out with us," Sam observed. Then, leaning into Bruce, he whispered: "You gotta help me out. I need to be alone with Winnie, so give some excuse and then disappear. Okay?"

"I'll do it. But it's definitely not okay."

By now Winnie was beside them. "Hi Sam—hi Bruce, what's up?"

"Not much," Bruce answered. "I came down for a quick swim, and Sam caught up to me before I made it to the water." Then he excused himself and turned away in time to run smack into a breaking wave.

"Wait!" Winnie called after him. "We'll join you."

Remembering what the water had done to her suit yesterday, Sam panicked. "Nooo, that's not a good idea. Not now. Let's go in later. Okay?"

"That's rude! Why can't we spend a few minutes swimming before Bruce has to go?"

A perfectly fair question and under any other circumstances he would have been quick to agree. How could he explain to her that he didn't want Bruce to see any more of her than he already had? "He won't mind!" he sighed. Winnie must have seen the exasperated look on his face, because her own expression softened and she took his hand and started along the shore.

"I don't understand, Sam. Are you sure you wouldn't like to go for a swim? You look awfully hot."

"Yeah, I guess," he said. He was hot, and his shirt was already stained with perspiration. Maybe if he asked her to keep her shirt on. Course he'd have to do the same.

"Let's both keep our shirts on. . ."

"Are you serious?" she interrupted.

"Yes," he said, taking matters into his own hands and reaching out to button her top. "When we're done, the wetness will keep us cool."

She slapped his hand and finished the job herself, but she didn't give him any further argument. Bruce was a little surprised to find them both in the frigid water beside him, but he enjoyed their company. And when they were done, and had climbed back up onto the shore, he proved himself a true friend and left them alone as he had promised.

Now, with just the two of them—well, they were in the middle of a crowded beach, but at least these people were strangers, or relatively so. They started walking toward the end of the beach with the idea of putting a little distance between them and the other beach-goers who now surrounded them. As they progressed, a warm steady breeze came in off the water and dried their shirts. The process of evaporation did keep them cooler just as he had predicted, but for the moment the effect was less than desirable because they were still cold from the icy sea. Coming to a low rock sticking out of the sand, they sat down on its flat surface. This was not a very private place, but at least they were out of earshot and could sit close together and confer without being overheard. Since their shirts were dry, they took them off and draped them over the edge of the rock.

At first they talked about the burning sand, the intensity of the bright afternoon sun, the fact that even the wind felt hot and then they both fell silent. Sam shifted on the hard surface to get off a sharp spot that made his butt sore. When he swung round to face Winnie again they bumped foreheads and when they both reached up to rub the spot they banged elbows. "Ouch," she complained, and they both came eye-to-eye. He wanted to turn away, but Winnie's gazed held him captive. Her eyes were brown. He knew that, but the brightness of the sun constricted her pupils and there was so much more color. Darker at the edges, golden in the center: he thought of the expression "the eyes are the windows of the soul," and suddenly knew what that meant. Her soul came in layers; first peace, then joy, then goodness and self-sacrifice, and finally sadness. He couldn't see these layers all at once and it disturbed him when sadness came last and stayed the longest.

"Why do you look so sad?"

His question broke her gaze, and her face flushed crimson. "Are you serious?"

"Yes," he smiled. "Why? Are you afraid to say?"

"Maybe. But if you really want to do this, you go first."

What she suggested was fair enough and a shrewd turnabout. "You're right, I can't expect you to give up any secrets if I'm not willing to give up one of my own." He'd always believed there were no secrets between them, but now he understood that even the best of friends never tell all.

"Well," she said with a quick toss of her head that sent her hair swirling across her face, "let's hear it." When her hair had settled along side of her face she looked straight at him with an expression of sweet satisfaction that said: *Ha, got you this time.*

He knew what was in his mind, but in truth he didn't know how to say it without embarrassing both of them, and his dumb silence made Winnie laugh.

"That's not fair," he complained. "I know what I'm thinking, but I'm not sure if I can say it."

"Don't think about it, just do it."

"Aaaah," he hesitated, "your eyes—are different."

"That's it?"

"No." That's not what he wanted to say; it was just the first thing to come out

"What, then?"

"Damn," he said, throwing his head back and staring up at the puffy clouds as if they could save him from this embarrassment.

"Give it up, Sam. You've seen my eyes practically since the day I was born—they're brown—there's no secret in that."

"Okay, okay," he said, straightening up and swinging his hand in a circle that framed the top of her suit. "It's this. You used to be skinny, and now—"

"And now I've got boobs," she interrupted. Then put her fingers under one side and lifted herself slightly as if to illustrate her assertion.

"You never looked like this—dressed like this. You've never been so, so, uncovered. What happened?" he asked, bringing his hand down to indicate what she had on.

"This? This was all Sally's idea."

"How's that?" he asked.

"All the while I was staying with her at Lake Winnipesaukee, she kept telling me I had to stop looking like a boy."

"She's right. The only girlish thing you've ever worn is that tube thing you call a bathing suit. But how did you change from just Winnie to—to WOW!"

The word *WOW* made her cringe and look away. He meant that as a compliment, but it was obvious that she was embarrassed, and he'd never known anything to embarrass her before. "That's kinda complicated," she said.

"I'm all ears," he said, pinching his lobes between his fingers and stretching them out until he started to look like a caricature of Aunt Em's Clark Gable.

The gesture made her laugh and he laughed with her.

"A few days ago," she said rubbing her eyes, "last Friday to be exact, Sally and I went to Alton Bay to stay with her girlfriend Cassie. Early the next morning she and her friend coaxed me down to the bathhouse at the edge of the lake and convinced me that I should go swimming with them. I didn't have my suit, and they wouldn't let me swim in just my top and shorts. They told me there were several swimsuits in the bathhouse and one would probably fit me. Sure enough, when we got inside, Sally grabbed one off a hook and told me to try it on. That's when I realized there were no changing stalls, just one big room," she said, squirming on the rock and crossing her legs. Then he watched as she rubbed her hands together in front of her, as if she were trying to warm them on a cold day.

"I can't remember when anyone has seen me naked—not even my mother," she said with a rasp. "Gym is the hardest. I always make sure I get to the showers last. And I always take a locker in the corner where I can turn my back and change behind the locker door. It's one of the reasons I don't fit in. The other girls like to parade around and show off their bubbies and brag abour the little brown curlies that are supposed to prove they're a woman—"

"Yuuuk," he said, covering his eyes as if that could somehow hide what she was describing.

"Oh, shut up. You wanted to know."

"I did, but can't we skip the groady stuff?"

"It is what it is, take it or leave it." She sounded impatient, but her quick smile let him know that she wasn't offended.

"The other girls started to undress," she continued, "and I figured I'm stuck. So, I turned my back and took off my clothes, but before I could step into my suit, Cassie pushed Sally, and she bumped into me and knocked me on the floor. There must have been a nail, because I got a gash in my leg and I screamed.

"There I was, sitting bare-assed on the floor, blood gushing out of my leg, with the two of them hanging over me. When Sally saw the blood, she ripped six inches off the end of her towel and tied it around my leg, then told me to stand up and put some weight on it, and I did. It still hurt, but my leg held. When I straightened up, Sally stepped back and started gawking at me.

"Oh my Gawwd, she said. *Why are you hiding a figure like that?* I covered myself with my arms and wished that there were some way for me to squeeze through one of the cracks in the floor and disappear.

"I look awful! I told her.

"You're crazy! Sally said, and pushed me in front of the mirror. One of those long ones, that hangs on a door, only this one had black spots where some of the silver had worn off.

"Look. Look at yourself, she said. I just bent over and tried to hide myself.

"No, stand up, she insisted, and started to tug on my arms.

"NO, I said.

"Well we continued to argue—until finally I gave up. A circle of blood started to show though the towel and I just wanted her to give me back my clothes.

Stand up straight, she said. *Let your hands hang loose.* I was so embarrassed, but when I stopped fussing and put my hands down, what I saw didn't look half-bad."

She looked at Sam to see his reaction, but he just scrunched up his eyes as if the sun was too bright and said nothing.

"After that she bugged me for two days until I agreed to buy some new clothes. She made me try on a lot of stuff, and frankly I didn't like any of it. But she kept saying: *You look great!,* and using words like: *super-licious, and fantabulous!* I bought the stuff to shut her up. Well—actually her mother bought it. Whatever!"

"You do look super—super-"

"-*licious."* Winnie finished.

"Yeah," he said, giving her the thumbs-up.

"This," Winnie said, sliding her thumb under the strap of her bikini top, "was Sally's idea. She made me promise to wear it when I got home, and I did. But I'm not happy about it. And that's the story," she said, uncrossing her legs and slapping her hands down hard on her knees.

"At least!" he said, thinking that he liked Winnies new look. Yes, it disturbed his adolescent sensibilities and put a tremor in his hand whenever he had reason to touch her, but he still liked what he saw.

"I never did get to go swimming," she said absently. "I went to the emergency room instead. It took six stitches. They came out the day I left—see," she said, lifting her leg to show him her new scar.

It wasn't the first time she'd gotten banged up and it probably wouldn't be the last, but he suddenly felt solicitous and overcoming that little tremor he reached out to touch her scar. And when she winced, and pulled her leg away, he apologized. "Sorry."

"It's okay, it didn't hurt."

He wondered what to think of this girl who had shared so much of her life with him, and who now seemed so uncomfortable with who she was. He wondered too if the touch of his finger against her scar had hurt or if she had pulled her leg away for some other reason.

"I've been thinking," he said. "You and I have been friends for a long time, but it seems to me that it's been awful one-sided. You're always giving and I'm always taking"

"At least!" she said, with the same sense of understatement that he had used a moment ago.

"Winnie, have I hurt you—I mean—really hurt you?"

"Sometimes. Jennifer. . ." she said. Nothing else, just her name.

"I thought you'd be happy for me."

"Oh, I listened, the way I always do, all the while wondering how you could be such a bonehead."

"I didn't know," he said.

"No, you didn't."

"That's not fair! We were friends—you never said—there were never any secrets between us, I told you everything."

"Whatever there was between us. . ." she said, stopping again. "For a long time it felt natural like breathing, and then it changed. The feelings I had for you weren't the same as the ones you had for me."

He didn't answer, just kept looking at his feet—pushing them deep into the soft sand then pulling them out.

"I'm not a little kid any more," she said. "I've grown up and—"

"That's for sure," Sam observed, appreciatively. And he wasn't just talking about her new look.

"I know what I feel," she said, but didn't explain.

"Tell me—what you feel."

"I'm not sure I can make you understand," she said, facing away.

"Try," he insisted, pulling her back.

"If I hafta explain, then it's already hopeless."

"Look, you just said I was a bonehead, so throw out all this foolish hype and give it to me straight."

"First of all I don't wanna hold your hand every time you're angry or depressed. You can't dump on me whenever you feel like it just because I'm there. I'm not your buddy or your pal. I mean, I am—and I do—that is you can, but. . . I want a whole lot more than that. I'm not ready to get horizontal. . .not even with a Trojan; but that doesn't mean I haven't thought about it—"

"Say what?" he asked, suddenly grasping the meaning of what she was saying.

"I said, I wouldn't do it—even if we had protection."

"No way!" he said, in disbelief.

"Get real Sam! . . .you're not listening. "

Fanning the air as if to dismiss him, she stood up and started to leave.

Tentatively, he reached out for her, then pulled back. He wanted to take her hand, but realized that Winnie was upset; and she had a right to be. He asked her to be candid and then turned all jiggy when things got too personal.

Winnie took off at a quick clip and he was forced to run after her. He caught up just as she passed through the gate in the seawall. Then she stopped abruptly in her tracks and he nearly collided with her.

"My shirt is back there."

"Mine too."

"Cheese it!" she said. "That's my dad's shirt and I never asked. It's not a new one, but he'll still have a fit if he finds out it's gone!"

"I'll run back—you go home and I'll bring the shirt to you later. Okay?"

"What's later?" she asked.

"After supper."

Chapter 57

Arriving at Winnie's front door, with the dress shirt in hand, Sam was anxious to see her again, hopeful that more discussion might help him sort out his conflicted emotions. The revelations that had spilled forth this afternoon had muddied the waters and Sam wasn't sure what his relationship with Winnie was, or what it ought to be.

When she opened the door he handed her the shirt. "Thanks," she said, as she rolled it into a ball and tossed it in the air. He watched it billow and collapse over the back of the hall chair. Then she stepped outside to join him.

The first two or three minutes were spent trying to decide where to go.

"I don't know," Winnie said. "Why can't we just go back to the beach?'

"I'd rather find someplace that's less public," he argued.

"Well, we could continue out under the cliffs until we reach Land's End."

He agreed, and a few minutes later they were trudging through the deep sand next to the canted seawall. When they ran out of beach they stopped to look ahead at the rocky face of the headland. The late evening sun had already left everything in shadow and Sam could see that if they continued it would be nearly dark by the time they reached the point. Above, the rusty-brown walls seemed warm and inviting, but in a couple of hours the rising tide would cover the damp green moss and rockweed at the base.

"We're not likely to drown, but we might get stuck out there." Sam noted.

"So, we've done crazier things," Winnie said, scrubbing the ends of her fingers into his scalp.

Even though the sun had dropped close to the horizon, the heat of the day hung heavily along the shore and clamoring over the rough terrain made Sam perspire. So he pulled his T-shirt over his head and tucked the sleeves into the waist of his shorts, letting the tail hang down over his backside. They had both worn light clothing, but Winnie had returned to her old wardrobe. She had on denim pants, cut off above the knee, the edges badly frayed. They were two sizes too big, and she had used a man's belt to make them stay up. Punched full of extra holes, the tongue, which was longer than a donkey's dong, dangled in front of her, and slapped against the inside of her legs as she climbed over the rocks. Her shirt, faded and threadbare, hung loosely off the points of her breasts and the left sleeve fell away where the stitching had pulled out. Just above the fold of the hem a long tear left a narrow strip of binding hanging in a loop that extended from hip to hip, and the upper edge of the tear rose high enough to expose her navel. But it wasn't what was exposed that bothered him. Though mostly camouflaged by the sloppy folds of her top, he could see her breasts bouncing freely as she stumbled over the stone shale and slipped on the pebbly surface between. She had no bra. She'd probably gone without a bra lots of times, but he'd never imagined that there was ever anything under her shirt that needed one, and now he couldn't imagine anything else. When she started to climb larger obstacles the movement increased, and he was fascinated by the fact that neither one seemed to head in the same direction at the same time—almost as if they were trying to get away from each other. It took a gigantic effort for him to concentrate on what he was doing, so as not to trip and break his neck.

Finally they came to a breach in the stone shingle where a rivulet of hard-packed sand wandered from a deep gash in the cliff-side to the water's edge. Intrigued, Sam took Winnie's hand and led her up the sandy path to this black hole. Cautiously, they probed deeper into the V-shaped cut, until it opened into a small grotto. The walls, still wet from the last tide, showed a line well above their heads—not the place to be when the coming tide crested.

A few feet deeper the rocks pinched off into a tight passage that Sam couldn't negotiate and he discouraged Winnie from even trying. Though they had not penetrated very far under the cliff, the darkness quickly blurred their features. Turning around, the light from the entrance led them back outside. Once beyond the sharp rim of the cave they took a several paces toward a line of dried seaweed and stopped. Here the hard-packed sand looked warm and inviting and they sat down side-by-side.

The steep rock-fall that they had crossed to get out to the end of the point was already narrowing from the encroaching tide and the watery spindrift that rushed upward between the rocks made the way back look treacherous. Sam knew that shortly the spot they were sitting on would be under water, and the thought that they might be trapped out here worried him.

He felt a little spasm between his shoulders and he pulled up one leg and wrapped his arms around it.

"Are you cold?" Winnie asked.

"No, I'm fine," he lied. "What about you?"

She didn't answer, and he wondered about her fear of drowning.

He reached out impulsively to take her hand and when he brought it to him he accidentally twisted her wrist.

"Hey, take it easy!" she said. "Here, let me come around," and she moved to find a more comfortable angle. Picking up her right foot, she lifted it over his leg, which was stretched out in front of him. Then she set her foot down on the sand under his other leg, which was pulled up. Scooting forward and stretching her left leg out, she dropped it down until she trapped Sam's own leg beneath. Then, pulling the other foot in, she pressed the back of her thigh into his butt. The weight of one leg coming down on top of his and the other hugging his backside made Sam uneasy, and he gave a nervous little cough to announce his discomfort. She put her hand on his shoulder and leaned in to rest her chin against the inside of her forearm. Looking up at him, the wind blew her hair against his face and he leaned down to kiss her. Surprisingly, she came up to meet him. Thick and warm, her lips rubbed his with a shaky uncertainty that agitated his blood and made the image behind his eyes spin as if he had fallen into a whirlwind. If she had come at him eagerly it would have frightened him. Instead, her timidity sucked him in, and when her soft lips surrounded his, that spinning image behind his eyes turned upside down and several times he thought he might tip over. Except for Winnie's hand on his shoulder and the contact with her legs, there was no touching and neither made and effort to change that. Then after a moment she lifted her hand from his shoulder and slid it behind his neck, and when she brought her other one up to join it, his hands began to wander as well. One flattened the back of her shirt against her spine and the other moved clumsily up her arm. Suddenly he could feel the point of her one of her breasts bump gently against his own, and the intense awareness of that movement caused his penis to grow straight out until it was restrained by the tightness of his shorts. He made a cute little hop to pull himself in and relieve the tension.

"Are you all right?" Winnie asked.

He didn't know how to answer that. Nothing in his experience with Jennifer had ever felt like this. Physically his response had been the same, but emotionally the two experiences were worlds apart. His mind, full of chaotic thoughts pulsed with sentient emotions: loneliness, love, pain and guilt, sadness and joy—and his senses exploded: the sweetness of her touch, the taste of her lips, the lusty scent of her body, all combined to drive him to distraction. "I'm fine. Well, not fine," he amended, "I mean this is major."

"Did you plan on doing that?" Winnie interrupted.

"Kissing you? No," he said

"Are you sorry you did?" she returned.

He remained quiet for a moment and that introspection allowed time for the problem in his shorts to collapse. It had only been a kiss; well, not just any kiss, and his reaction had been clearly sexual. Yet he felt so conflicted—he certainly didn't feel sorry, but that didn't mean that part of him wasn't full of disdain. "No I'm not," he whispered, as if he were sharing a guarded secret. "Are you—sorry, that is?"

She hesitated too, and it made him nervous. The sun had fallen and only the dullest light was able to reach them under the steep face of the cliffs. He stared into the dark holes that swallowed up the shape of her eyes and thought he caught a wet glimmer that defied the darkness. "No, I'm not sorry it happened, but I am sorry it took so long."

Took so long? Had she been waiting for this?

While they had been so engaged, the rising tide had snuck up on them, and now he looked behind Winnie and saw some foamy wash sink into the sand.

"Say something. Tell me—what's going on in there?" Winnie asked, tapping her finger just above the bridge of his nose.

"Oh no. We're not going to do that again."

"Why not?" she begged. "You show me yours and I'll show you mine—I mean tell me. . .yours"

"It was a kiss!"

"That's it?"

"No."

Winnie waited for more, but he said nothing. "Is that all?" she asked impatiently.

"No, there's more. Lots more, but I can't possibly put it into words."

"Wellll, I could say a lot, but if you're not talkin'. . ."

"Come on, give me a break!"

"Try!" she said, brushing the back of her hand against his cheek in a tender gesture that disarmed him.

He turned his face away from hers and looked over her shoulder at the dark sea. "I've—I've kissed before, but it never made me feel so confused."

"Why confused?" she asked.

"I haven't figured that out yet," he said. Then, when a puddle of cold water surrounded the heel of his foot: "I'm getting wet."

"How?"

"There," he pointed and she twisted to see the water pulling away. They unknotted themselves and stood up. Moving a few feet closer to the gash in the rocks, they sat again on the cool hard sand. This time they faced each other with their legs pulled up, arms crossed, resting on their knees.

"How did this happen?" he asked. "Is this love? Am I in love with you? Are you in love with me?"

"Am I supposed to answer that?" she asked.

"If you can't answer—I certainly can't." Actually he was afraid to answer. It meant abandoning the idea that he and Winnie were just friends. The fact that she also made him horny was too bewildering to consider.

"Not good enough!" she threatened.

"And you can do better?"

"Yes," she said, but she didn't elaborate.

"Well. . ." he challenged.

In the silence that followed she unfolded her arms, and putting them on the sand behind for support, she scooted in. Almost knee to knee, she pushed his arms aside and pressed down on his knees, forcing his legs to drop until they spread out in a V on either side of her. Lifting one foot at a time, she brought them over his legs and scooted in to straddle his waist. Now, with her knees flanking his ribs, they sat eye to eye, in almost the same position they had assumed before, except now they were exactly face to face.

They sat there alone beneath the brooding presence of the cliff. The new moon had risen, and breaking from behind some scudding clouds dappled them in its light. The dull glow softly defined Winnie's features, highlighting the gentle curve of her cheeks and the puffy fullness of her lips. He could barely see her eyes, but he knew they were focused on his. It was like trying to stare down a ferocious animal, waiting to see who would blink first.

"It's not about who can do this better," she said. "It's about who's willing to tell the truth."

That last word hung in the air, and he wondered what to do with it. "Until you kissed me—until you asked," he said, "I don't think I had any idea what the truth was. And even now I don't know if I dare say it."

"If you don't feel it right here," she said, jabbing him in the heart with her bony finger, "then don't even try."

He put his arms around her waist, then waddling from butt-cheek to butt-cheek he closed the space between. The effort dragged his shorts tightly under his crotch, and gave him a wedgy, and he reached down to tug at the legs to make more room. Winnie must have guessed at his problem because she started to laugh, and he laughed along with her, which broke the tension.

Winnie hadn't said so, but all her effort—all this maneuvering—could only serve one purpose. She wanted him to kiss her again, and because it was easier than finding the words to explain how he felt, he was more than willing to accommodate her

The breeze picked up, and tugged at her hair. Shimmering, some of the loose ends played against his cheek. He puckered, took a shot at her mouth and missed. She laughed, and he tried again. This time she gave him some help, and they connected. The kiss was wet and he slid off.

"This isn't right," he said, before she could reconnect.

"Don't worry, there's plenty of time to get it right," she answered.

"No, I mean we shouldn't be doing this."

"If you don't want to—"

"Oh, I <u>want</u> to. I definitely <u>want</u> to—" and before he could say any more she trapped his lips inside her own. Each pucker and pull fed an impatient surge below as if some magical connection existed between the two, and his penis grew in quick little increments until it came in contact with the soft curve of Winnie's stomach. Sam felt somehow detached from the whole process as if there were a small independent animal trapped inside his shorts stretching to escape and he had a terrible urge to help push for its release. But when Winnie shifted and closed the space between them, and that little animal had no place to go, he was filled with anxiety— did she have any idea what she was doing to him?

Suddenly Winnie came back and kissed him with such an audacious energy that it took his breath away and when she finally disconnected he gasped.

"Are you okay?" she asked. But she didn't wait for his answer: instead she folded her arms over her head, and arched her back. "Whooo-ey!" she called out, then let herself fall back on the sand between his outstretched legs.

"That literally gave me the shivers," she said, lifting her head off the sand and staring down the length of her body. And when he looked where she looked, he could see the telltale tent he'd made out of his shorts and knew that she knew. He leaned forward and folded his hands over his lap to hide his embarrassment. "Don't," she said, propping herself up on her elbows.

At first he didn't understand.

"I'm not offended," she said, and her smile gave him the impression that she was pleased to see what she had done. He groaned. Then she fell back on the sand where a husky laugh bubbled up and rattled in the back of her throat.

"It's not funny," he said.

"No. It's not funny," and her tone said she wasn't really laughing at him.

He unfolded his hands and was surprised to see that the tent hadn't gone away. Winnie came back up on her elbows to admire her handiwork. "Hmmm," she hummed as if she were considering something utterly unfathomable

"Don't look," he insisted, as if she could see much more than just the wrinkled pouch in the front of his shorts.

"Sam," she said. "I understand, I mean—I know what's happening—what that is," she nodded. "It's just the way nature does things. You oughtn't to be ashamed."

"Cut it out," he said, and folded his hands again to hide his problem.

"Oh come on Sam, you're taking this too hard—I mean, too seriously."

"It is serious," he argued.

"Noooo. It's just the way your body works," she said, sitting up and holding him the way she always did—comforting him like a lost child.

"That may be, but you don't understand seeing—"

"But I can't see anything, really." And she reached down to take his wrists and pull his hands away.

She was right the tent had disappeared and nothing had actually been exposed. But she had kissed him and he'd reacted and she had clearly seen his reaction—it was a kind of intimacy that he hadn't intended to share and he supposed that what she couldn't see she could imagine. "No, but it's the idea—"

"Do you honestly think that something like this will make me think less of you? That my opinion of you will change because I've discovered that you're normal?"

He didn't answer. He felt something cold swirling around the heel of his foot and he looked past Winnie to see a thin pool of water swirling around his heel and watched as it slid back toward the sea.

"What's wrong?"

"I'm getting wet again."

"Me too," she confirmed, when the wash of the next wave came high enough to wet the bottom of her shorts.

"We've gotta go back," he said, flatly and they separated and stood up. He could see that the rising tide had nearly cut them off from the mainland. Not that they were in danger of drowning: they could certainly climb high enough to get out of the reach of the water. There were ledges where they could hunker beneath an overhang and find some shelter from the wind and waves.

On the other hand it would be hours before the tide crested and fell, and it would be morning before they could go home. Sam could deal with his mother's wrath and the fact that Winnie's parent's would probably want a piece of his hide, but once the word got out, certain assumptions would be made, and most people wouldn't worry about whether those assumptions were true or not. When the next wave rushed up and rose well above their ankles he made up his mind. "Let's go!" he said, taking her hand.

"Abso-positively!" she affirmed, and took off ahead of him. The pathway between the edge of the water and the base of the cliff narrowed quickly and the course they took now was much more rugged than they one they'd used to get out there. The surf rushed in between the broken rocks, and spume shot up, and slithered back between the cracks, restoring the dry green surface to a slimy trap. The broad strip of sand that meant safety lay at least 400 yards ahead and it took dogged determination to negotiate the greasy barrier that stood in their way.

By the time Sam finally stumbled out onto the beach, he was limping badly. Shortly after they started he had lost his footing, and slammed down onto the sharp corner of the ledge in front of him. His bony shin was bleeding badly, and Winnie had torn away part of her shirt to use as a bandage, which made it even more raggedy.

Once they cleared the rocks they fell onto the cool sand, exhausted. Sam, lying on his back, started banging his head against the mossy wrack: whump, whump, whump, as if he were trying to knock some sense into his bony noggin. It wasn't funny, but when he heard the ticklish rasp of laughter coming from the back of Winnie's throat, he tossed up a deep belly-laugh of his own.

◆ ◆ ◆

Sam hobbled up to Winnie's back door and she turned to thank him. "This is not a night I will soon forget. For a lot of reasons," she added, knowingly. She tried the door to see if her mother had left it unlocked and it popped open in front of her.

"Kudos," Sam whispered loudly, then turned and hopped back to her gate. He stopped, and used the gatepost for support for a moment, and she held up two fingers for victory before he started down the road—step hop, step hop—toward his own home.

Chapter 58

After that night under the cliffs at Land's End, Sam was kept busy thinking about what had happened, and why, and what he was going to do about it. How had he gone from his obsession with Jennifer to this harder, deeper, more powerful experience with Winnie? The things they did together now weren't very different from what they had always done, but they seemed to take on a new and extraordinary importance. They were more physically involved, but even taking Winnie's hand was more physical. Considering that this change might have happened sooner if Sam hadn't been such a numbskull, he couldn't help wondering: *what if?* But it wasn't what he might have done that worried him; it was where to go from here that had him flummoxed. At first he was anxious to prove that he could be as caring and unselfish as she had always been, but that wasn't easy. That put him at odds with himself—it was hard to do things for her without the secret hope of gaining some reward. And since Winnie responded so completely, even to the smallest kindness, there was always some kind of reward, which kept him continually in her debt.

They talked a lot about everything—which was good. But they didn't talk about the sticky stuff—the sexual attraction was too deep and too personal. After their experience at Land's End there seemed to be an implied license to experiment, and they did. But when they kissed it was painfully disturbing and Winnie didn't seem to appreciate the danger they were in. In her hands—that is, literally in her embrace—his body function-ed independently of his mind, and the longer she worked upon him the bigger the chance that he would give in and do something that he would surely regret. There had always been that possibility with Jennifer, but somehow he knew it would never happen. With her it was like jumping in over his head: he could always tread water. But with Winnie he felt the undertow, and knew that it would drag him under and drown him. They had talked about everything else; why couldn't he explain the kind of physical torture that she was putting him through?

One afternoon he sucked up his courage and spit out his frustrations. He had no way of knowing what her understanding had been before, but if his directness now, made her uneasy, she didn't show it. Instead she threw it back at him.

"Excuse me! You don't think that I get turned on?"

"Not exactly."

"Get real! Maybe the parts are put together differently, but I am made out of flesh and blood."

"But it's not the same for a girl," he said, in feeble protest.

"Oh, right! Don't make me gag. Just because I don't put up a flag, doesn't mean that nothing's happening."

"Okay, okay, I get the idea." Her openness impressed him, and though he didn't know exactly what she meant he didn't dare ask for any more detail. Not that she wouldn't have given it—she would. That was the problem.

Unfortunately, this discussion didn't help. Physical contact, afterwards, seemed even more awkward. They both became terribly self-conscious. He was afraid to hold, or touch, or kiss too often, or for too long, and he suspected that Winnie felt the same—well, perhaps not the same, but at least that she suffered from similar anxieties. He soon realized that their efforts to be candid, and adult, had backfired. They were now more anxious and frustrated than ever.

One afternoon while they were lying on an old blanket sunning themselves and sucking up the salty air, Sam decided that he couldn't take it anymore. Winnie was on her stomach and he was lying on his side propped up on one elbow. "This is really a bust!"

"What is?" she asked, looking up at him in dismay.

"Us. Wellll, not exactly us—it's just that this is such a let-down."

"Sam you're freakin' me out. What are you talking about?"

"We've been there for each other—I mean, friends—forever. And now we're supposed to be a couple."

"So?"

"I can't handle it. Before, I could say anything, do anything, and I didn't have to think about it. Now I wonder: what does she want? What does that look mean? Should I take her hand? Does she want me to kiss her? If we keep going, will we end up wompin' each other?"

"What?"

"You know—doing the deed."

"Forget about it, Sam, that's not going to happen."

"No, I guess not, but that doesn't mean it's not hanging out there like a banner waiting to be whipped up by the first good wind."

"Do you want to call it quits?"

"No way! But if we could go back. Well—not really back. But everything was fine until you went away on vacation and came home as a girl."

"What's that supposed to mean? I've always been a girl."

"Yeah, but it was never this obvious."

"Sam, that's mean!"

"I know—I know. That's not what I meant. It's just that you were you—you were Winnie, and I was Sam, and now it's all so complicated."

"So, my being a girl isn't good."

"Kind of—no—not really, see that's the whole thing. Before, everything made sense, and now it's all upside down!"

"So, what do we do about it?"

"I don't know. Jennifer always kept me a little off-balance. But being around you is much worse."

"Gee, thanks!"

"There I go again. Everything I say seems to come out bass-ackwards. You and I used to understand each other. Now there's a gap between us—a sort of no mans-land where we're not supposed to go. We've still got all this history together—that hasn't changed. But now that we've gotten physical, I don't know when to turn it on, or how to turn it off."

"How do we avoid it?" she asked.

"Well, that's pretty much what we've done for the last week. We haven't touched each other, not even to hold hands"

"Maybe we need some rules," she suggested.

"What kind of rules?"

"I don't know," she said. "Let's find something we can agree on, set some boundaries and then stick to them."

"Is it that easy?"

"No, it's not easy at all," she said. "It's hard as hell. But it's a place to start."

"For example?" he said.

"For example I know that kissing can raise problems with that—that—well you know, down under. And I've got problems of my own. Different—not as visible, but righteous stuff all the same. Still, I can't always tell when you're in trouble and you can't tell when I'm in trouble."

"So?"

"So, whenever we feel things are getting out of hand, each of us has to take the initiative and pull the plug."

"But if I stop I'm afraid you'll think I don't care or that I don't like what you're doing—and I do like what you're doing."

"That's the whole point. With a rule like this we don't have to explain to each other what's wrong and we don't have to worry about hurting the other person's feelings."

"And that's good?"

"And that's good," she affirmed.

"What are the other rules?"

"The rest we can make up as we go along."

Chapter 58

Martin and Sarah had gone for a late-night dinner at the Timberlake Lodge on Gannett Road just outside of Freetown. They ate slowly, talking about the wedding—Sarah talked about the wedding and Martin listened. Later the conversation turned to more everyday things: the politics at work, politics in general, the house fire at the top of Lindenhurst Road, the rising cost of milk. Sarah talked about Sam, and Martin talked about his oldest son Peter, who had been promoted to section boss at his new job. Finally they started to reminisce, not about each other or recent events, but the past—the distant past, when they were both children.

"So, where did you grow up?" Sarah asked.

"West Gansett," he said, with a thoughtful frown on his face. "Boy, that seems eons ago! We had a house on Peconic Pond Road. There were two huge maples in the front yard and out back a bunch of open fields—part of an old farm. At the far side of one field there was a rusty wire-fence, and beyond that, something we called the woods. Actually it was a swamp filled with old dead trees." He stopped for a moment to push a slice of mushroom off his steak, then he stabbed it with his fork and popped it into his mouth.

"We used to play war—run up and down with cap pistols— mmmm—and wooden rifles. Charging through the high grass, getting shot. I was very good at getting shot. Then Vietnam came along," he said with a vacant stare, "and it wasn't a game any more."

"But you didn't go—did you?"

"No, I never got called up, and I certainly didn't volunteer, but a lot of my friends went. Some didn't come back, and the ones who did came back broken—if not on the outside, definitely on the inside. You always hear about the young kids who died over there, but no one talks about the people who got left behind. The mothers and fathers, brothers and sisters, grandparents—friends. There's this enormous hole; and then you wonder about all that lost potential."

"I saw the news at night, the black-and-white pictures, the helicopters, but it wasn't real," she said, looking down, embarrassed to admit that she had had no opinion.

"You were a kid. You should have been doing kid things."

"I was. I ran in the fields with the guys wearing a plastic helmet on my head, playing war, just the way you did."

"You were a tomboy?"

"Yeah, I guess; but not by choice. I didn't want the dolls and teacups and fancy clothes, so the other girls kept their distance. Baseball, basketball, cowboys and Indians were a heck of a lot more fun. In a sandlot game, I could hold my own and in a good fistfight I gave as much as I took. At home, in my neighborhood, everything worked out fine; but at school it was different. The same guys who knocked me down at first base or shot hoops in front of my garage would tease me shamefully on the school grounds, particularly if my mother had forced me to wear a dress. And no matter what—home or school, dress or pants, the girls called me *butch* and *lesbo*.

"When I hit my teens the boys started to see girls as girls, and I couldn't convince them I wasn't one of them—a girl, that is. Then the dating thing started, and I got left out again. Over the next couple of years my looks improved a little, but I was still straight as a board. Then in my junior year I began to round out a little. That's when I met Robert."

"Didn't you have any friends?"

"I thought Ditsy was my friend. His real name was *Meredith*; boy, did he take a drubbing over that."

"What happened?"

"I don't know. One day I saw him in the crowd throwing insults along with the rest and that ended it." Staring at the candle in the middle of the table, she could see Ditsy's red face hurling catcalls and mocking her. She knew him well enough to know that they weren't his words. He was only repeating what he heard, but she still couldn't forgive him for it.

"You must have had some dates!" Martin seemed determined to find a bright spot in her depressing story.

"It's not that no one asked," she said, shaking her head. "I dated, but no one came back to ask again. The real kicker came when I found out that these guys had only asked me on a dare.

"Eventually I went from ugly duckling to swan. Well, maybe not a swan—but my hair darkened, and my freckles went away."

"Not all of them," he noted, reaching out to brush his finger across the bridge of her nose.

"No," she smiled and trapped his finger in hers.

"Why are you telling me this?" he asked, pulling free.

"Because you need to know," she said, reaching across the table to recapture his hand. "By the time I was twenty I began to fill out my dresses, but I didn't care any more. My marriage was a disaster and the last thing I wanted was to be attractive. I wore grungy clothes, and stopped using makeup, but it didn't matter. Robert never took any interest in me unless he was drunk, and then he didn't care what I looked like.

"Robert had no long term goals no ambition, but he worked hard on one thing. He constantly reminded me how worthless I was. When he died, there wasn't enough left of me to spit on."

Martin looked drained, as if someone had sucked the spirit out of him with an enormous vacuum.

"It's—it's—how could he." Martin muttered. "Couldn't he see what I see?

"Stop—stop," she said gently. She still had his hand from before and she moved her fingers up to separate the cuff of his shirt and stroked the back of his wrist. "Maybe he couldn't. Maybe the person you know wasn't there—didn't exist."

"I'm not a fool. The person I see in front of me is real."

"I know you mean that Martin, but you've only known me a few months and before that there was no Sarah. At least not the one you see now."

"How did you end up marrying this guy in the first place?"

"Oh God," she sighed. A frown wrinkled her forehead while she dug up the memory of something she had long chosen to forget. "If you must know it was at the prom. Robert invited me to the Senior Prom. For me it seemed like the Cinderella story. I mean, Robert was older than his classmates—nineteen—and he wanted me to go to the biggest event of the year with him. My mother found me a gown. Blue taffeta, strapless with a wide bow across the top that made me look bustier. After weeks of anticipation he was there, in my front hall, trying to pin a corsage on my shoulder and finding nothing to attach it to.

"When we drove into the parking lot at Dreamworld most of the kids already had a buzz on. I'd never touched alcohol in my life, but I figured—one sip wouldn't do me any harm. Everyone had a bottle and they kept pushing me to try theirs. Trouble was Robert had one of his own and he kept shoving it into my hand and telling me to take a swallow."

"Big mistake." Martin said, with a grimace.

"Don't I know it," she said.

"Later, after the dance, a bunch of us went cruising along the Cross River Parkway. We drove west, away from the ocean out to Turtle Lake. The girls were dressed in taffeta and satin, the boys in black tuxes. One of the girls pulled her gown over her head and dropped it on the ground; then peeled off her petticoats and underwear on the way down to the water. That's when they all decided to go skinny-dipping. Not together. The guys separated and took off down the shore. I went in with the other girls, but even drunk, I couldn't take it all off—I kept my underwire bra and panties."

"So far this doesn't sound so terrible," he said, shifting in his chair.

"Be patient, it gets worse," she said, bending her head and scrunching over her plate, afraid of being overheard. "Afterwards, when I got dressed again, I pulled my wet panties out from under my petticoat and tossed them into the back of Robert's Chevy. Looking back, I probably shouldn't have done that.

"The girls finished before the boys and we drove a couple of the cars down to where they were swimming and faced the headlights toward the lake, then switched them on. That way the guys couldn't get to their clothes without exposing themselves. Course most of them were too drunk to care. And the girls made a game of it as they came out of the water—shouting out size."

"What do you mean size?" Martin interrupted.

"Penis size," she said, whispering, hand to mouth, so only he could hear.

"You're kidding?"

"I told you it got worse," she said, then paused. "Besides, you couldn't see much, just some jiggling and a bunch of arms and legs as they ran up and bent over to put on their pants. But when Isaac Taylor sashayed out of the water, he took his time. Isaac wasn't terribly tall, maybe five-five/five-six, but he was solidly built. He had a flat stomach and a decent amount of muscle on his arms and legs. Definitely athletic, and not too bad to look at; but judging by the way he was strutting around he was particularly proud of that jaunty little hose that stuck out in front. The thing looked fat and ugly to me, but he seemed determined to show it off anyway."

The word *hose* made Martin choked and he put his napkin over his mouth as if to catch whatever might come up. She ignored his reaction and kept on going. "The girls screamed, and I laughed so hard I nearly peed my pants—except I wasn't wearing any."

"I can't imagine—well, I can imagine, but I can't see you—"

"Neither can I," she interposed, "but you wanted the story and that's the way it happened.

"After the swim I started drinking again, a little here, a little there, mostly vodka. And as the night got old, things got kind of foggy." Not that foggy—but she couldn't tell him everything. She couldn't tell him that earlier, when she was more aware of what was going on, she'd kissed Robert in the front seat of his car and then let him fondle her breasts. And though they were only half the size they are now, he seemed perfectly happy to get hold of them. Everything she'd been taught, all the dogma that had been drilled into her at home and in church, made such things forbidden. She had sinned; and even now she couldn't shake the notion that through her indiscretion she'd ultimately given Robert permission for what happened to her later.

"At the far end of Turtle Lake there's a little bay and a dock that leads out to an old boathouse, and somehow I ended up inside, laying in the bottom of an open boat with my back pressed against a pile of canvas. I remember the smell of gasoline and oil, and dead fish. It was dark except for a dull light that came through the dirty windows, and I kept blowing against the ruffles on my petticoat, which for some reason covered half my face. Robert was on top of me and I complained that he was too heavy. Then I felt a sharp breach as if someone had shoved a knife inside of me, and the pain made everything turn black.

Later on, when I understood such things, I realized that Robert was unusually large, and according to the gynecologist who examined me a couple of days later I was nearly intact, which led to a bit of bleeding and a lot of pain. The next day, after I'd sobered up, more came back to me—and—then I knew what I'd done."

"Damn," Martin said, looking dumbstruck.

"I felt so incredibly guilty."

"But it wasn't your fault."

"That's what Lindsey said, when I told her. But if I hadn't gotten drunk. . ."

"So you married Robert because you were pregnant?"

"No, I wasn't. But Robert thought I had to be, and at the time I thought so too. He asked me to marry him and I said yes."

"Why?"

"I was afraid. Afraid no one else would ask, afraid of being alone.

"When Robert died I felt empty, dried up. It seemed unnatural, after all the damage he had done, but I missed him."

"How?"

"My grandmother had a cat. She called him Fuzznuts—an old tom that probably had fathered every stray in the county. If you reached out to pat him, he'd scratch your hand. He peed on her rug, shredded her curtains, shed piles of fur wherever he slept. I was glad when he died. But he'd been a part of my grandmother's life for thirteen years and she missed him."

"Are you trying to tell me that you can get used to anything?"

"I'm not sure. Maybe there's more to it than that."

"Sarah, from what I've heard, this guy beat you!"

"True."

"How did you live with that?"

"The bruises and black eyes healed. It was the mind games that did the most damage."

"What do you mean?"

"The way he belittled me in front of my family and friends, until after a while they avoided me. "

"I'm sorry," he said.

"But that's the point, I don't want you to be sorry. I don't want your pity, I want your understanding," she said, tapping the tines of her fork against the white tablecloth for emphasis.

"And I <u>want</u> to understand," he said. "But I don't know the little girl who grew up as a tomboy, or the teenager who couldn't get dates, or the woman who suffered at the hands of an abusive husband. . ."

"I know I've changed. But only recently"

"No one could change that much or that fast."

"Why not?" she said, staring him down.

"Because I can't believe that the neat, sensitive girl who walked into my office last summer came out of nowhere. She had to have been there all along. Hiding—waiting."

"Maybe. But that's too easy."

"Oh, it's not easy, believe me. To press a whole person down into a tiny little shell takes tons of effort."

"I don't understand!"

"People always find ways to protect themselves. Then when the danger is gone and they feel safe, they crawl back out into the sun."

" Okay. Then using your analogy, I've only just come of my shell."

"I suppose."

"How do you know I won't crawl right back in at the first sign of danger?

"I don't."

"And that doesn't scare you?"

"Some of the time."

"You don't know what it's like to want something you can't have."

"You've lost me."

"All those years—wanting to be held—I ached for the warmth of another body next to mine; one that didn't reek of beer and sweat.

"Late at night I would slip out of bed, grope my way through the dark house, scrunch down on one end of the sofa, and wait—listening to the bangs and ticks of the house—until the tears came."

"I'm sorry—I'm sorry!" he said. And she heard his voice catch and half expected him to cry.

"See, there you go again."

"Couldn't you leave?" he asked, as if that were as easy as opening the front door and stepping outside

"Get real!" she said, filled with the paralyzing fear that always came when she considered that question—and she had considered it many times.

"Why did you stay if you were so unhappy?"

"I don't know. We were both Catholic—well, not practicing Catholics, but it's hard to give up the beliefs that you grew up with."

"But it <u>is</u> done."

"Yes, it is, but I was afraid. I married so young. There wasn't time for me to grow up, to be on my own. I had a home; I had Sam; Robert paid the bills; at least some of the time I felt safe."

"And that was enough?"

"No. But I didn't know anything else. I could only guess at what other people had, and many of my friends weren't that happy either."

"I can't imagine!"

"Isn't that what I've been trying to tell you?"

"Yes. You're right. So, try harder—make me see it, be brutally honest."

"Are you sure you want that?"

"Yes."

"After the tears, after the trees outside the front window began to blur, one image would sweep over another until my mind went numb, and then I'd wake up in the cold light of dawn, with Robert's snores scratching the walls.

"I want desperately to love and to be loved. Not the sort of thing I feel for Sam, but the kind of love that ought to exist between a man and a woman. But I'm not sure what that is. I only know I've never had it."

"There must have been something between you and Robert—at least in the beginning?" Martin asked, sounding incredulous.

"No, only the coldness of his hand on my shoulder when he wanted sex. And that was always forced, and painful."

"Don't!" he said, grabbing her hand and dragging it toward the center of the table. She could see that her words cut into him and brought him grief.

"Martin, I love you, and I don't want you to be hurt. But you have to see that my experience with Robert could corrupt what we feel for each other. Do you really want that?"

"No of course not. But it doesn't have to be like that."

"Do you want the truth?"

"Yes."

"The fact is, I want to feel the roughness of your skin against my own; I want your arms around me; I want you to touch every part of me. I want you inside of me, hard and excited, knowing that I made you that way. I want to experience all that, and not feel used and ashamed." Martin tried to object, but she freed her hand from his and reached across the table to silence him by covering his mouth with her fingers.

"My instincts tell me that lovemaking should be something more than just the slamming of flesh against flesh. Or a clumsy ordeal that ends in failure because your partner is too drunk to perform," she said, the tears running slowly down her cheeks.

"God!" Martin groaned.

"Oooooh, if only God had intervened. When Robert pushed himself inside of me it felt like a sharp stick—thick and dry. The pain practically cut me in two and I begged for relief. I tried to close my mind, to block it out. Thank God the pain didn't last long. Robert never had any staying power; he either came quickly, or he gave up. But the stench of his breath, and the taste of stale beer and vomit was suffocating."

Now Martin had both her hands in his. Snatching them free, she pulled them down into her lap, then pushed hard into her gut, trying to staunch the rising nausea.

"Is there any way to make this go away?" Martin asked.

"No," she said, without emotion.

"How could you stand to have me—touch you—after. . ."

"I don't know. Maybe because what I feel for you is so completely opposite," she said. "But I am afraid."

"Of me?"

"No."

"Then what?"

"Most of my life has been a disaster, and now that the golden ring is at my fingertips, I'm afraid to reach out for it. I wonder if I have the right to be happy—if I deserve it."

"Don't be foolish!"

"I know it's not logical, but that's the way I feel."

"Why are you doing this?"

"What do you mean?"

"I mean, we're about to be married and you're scaring the hell out of me."

"When you say 'I do,' I want you to know what you're getting."

"If you mean to tell me you're no saint, I already knew that; but then, neither am I."

"It's not the imperfections I worry about, it's all the garbage that I still haven't unloaded from my first marriage."

"You don't think I'm bringing along a few things of my own?" he asked.

"But your experience was different. You were in love—you were happy"

Sarah had been so caught up in her reminiscence that most of her meal had gone untouched. Now, looking over Martin's shoulder she saw the maitre d' waiting in the shadows. The tables around them, which once had bustled with happy diners, now stood empty. Martin, attending to her glance, turned to see what she was looking at; then, checking his watch: "These people would probably appreciate it if we paid our bill and got the hell out of here."

Obviously they had to leave, but Sarah wasn't ready for the evening to end. "I don't want to go home. Can't we go someplace else and talk?"

"Well, we could go out to Lighthouse Point," he said, smiling.

"Martin, isn't that also known as Make-out Point? What about my reputation?" she said, and the tickle in her stomach leapt up to scrape the pain off her face.

"Aren't we too old to worry about reputations—yours or mine?"

As they passed through the swinging doors and headed for Martin's car, Sarah felt a sweet release. She had a sudden presentiment that her honesty had brought some resolution—that she was finally free from twenty years of guilt that had weighed down upon her like a truckload of cement. She found some truth in the old adage that confession is good for the soul.

Chapter 60

Because they had to stop for gas (no running out, Martin was too sensible for that) they didn't get to the point until after eleven. Oddly enough, especially on such a wonderful warm summer's night, the gravel parking lot was nearly deserted. They saw only a single vehicle: a highly polished sports model that was popular with the kids, with wings on the hood—a Thunderbird—no a Firebird. The paint looked dark, probably red, and as far as they could tell there was no one in it, which meant that the couple had sought out a hiding place in the rocks, or they might have crawled through a broken window in the deserted light-keepers cottage.

"Let's get out and find a spot to sit where we can get a good view of the harbor," Sarah suggested. She removed her high heels and left them on the front seat while Martin pulled a tattered army blanket from the trunk. Then they moved carefully over the stony shingle and into the maze of boulders that had been strewn over a sandy spit to keep the waves from tearing it away.

Sarah was glad that she had removed her shoes. Her bare feet gripped the uneven surface and helped to keep her upright. Martin stopped and held her hand to guide her over the more difficult obstacles. Barefoot was good, but her full-length dress had a tight hem that restricted her legs and she wished that she had on shorts or jeans.

When they had gone as far as they could, they climbed onto a flat chiseled slab of granite and walked to the side overlooking the harbor. Martin left the blanket folded and dropped it on the hard surface to serve as a cushion for Sarah, and they both sat with their feet hanging over the coarse face and gazed inward toward the boats swinging slowly against their moorings. The lights from the expensive yachts shimmered across the water and they could detect shadowy movements and the tinkling voices of the owners as they called to each other. Sam and Sarah sat, watching, as the lights went out, one by one, and the harbor became quiet except for the steady slap of the waves just below their feet.

For the first twenty minutes they said nothing just leaned against each other arm in arm, and after the painful debate at the restaurant that seemed appropriate. Then for the next hour there was simple conversation—a comment on the breeze—a word about the waves—a critique of the novel Sarah was currently reading, and in between long minutes of silence. Now, without any discussion or preamble, they picked themselves up and headed back toward the car. But before they were halfway there they came to a level patch of sand sheltered between two large rocks, which seemed far too inviting to ignore. The sand still felt warm under their bare feet and Sarah turned to Martin and gave him a friendly tap on the shoulder. "This is too nice to pass up," she said. "Can't we lay here for a minute and look at the stars?"

Martin spread out the blanket and they both plopped down, arms raised hands clasped behind their heads, staring up into the blackness at a thousand points of light—again silent. The stars made them feel small and insignificant and time seemed irrelevant.

The slamming of car doors and the cranking of an engine interrupted the stillness, and the crunch of gravel spinning under tires told them that their young friends were leaving. Now they were truly alone.

Sarah heard Martin roll onto his side and knew that he was studying her. With her hands still folded neatly behind the back of her head she remained perfectly still, taking slow measured breaths, waiting for him to move or speak.

"Sarah," he whispered. She felt the evening breeze creep softly between the rocks and tug at the hem of her skirt, but she didn't answer. Martin repeated her name. "Sarah." This time his voice deep and masculine filled her with a tingly excitement that disturbed the tiny hairs on her arms and spread across the back of her shoulders.

"Yes," she answered, so quietly that she wasn't sure he could hear.

"I thought I'd lost you," he said, with the same deep rasp, which now sent that tingle down her spine and made the muscle tighten between her shoulder-blades.

That shivery movement must have been visible, because Martin laid his bulky hand below her breast and asked. "Are you comfortable?"

"Yes." She was more than comfortable, and the warm presence of his hand gave her a special kind of peace. But when his fingers moved up under her breast she felt a sudden contraction in her uterus. Was this what it was like to feel horny? She really didn't like that word, but she couldn't think of a better one to describe her present condition. *If that's not what's happening to me, what is? Am I just ovulating?*

Martin scooted in a little closer, and she pulled one hand from behind her head and stretched it out so that she could cradle him under her arm. Bending her elbow, she circled his neck and gave a little squeeze to signal that she welcomed his embrace. And he dropped his arm down and wrapped it around her waist.

"You're being awfully quiet," he said.

"Does that bother you?" she asked.

"Normally it wouldn't, but right now it's unnerving."

"Why?"

"It's hard to say."

"Does it have anything to do with dinner?"

"No, the dinner was fine."

"I'm not talking about what we ate, or didn't eat," she said, pulling her other hand down and giving him a poke in the ribs.

"Hey!" he said, with a gasp, then returned the gesture with a playful pinch to her waist.

"Cut it out!" she giggled. Then reminded him: "You didn't answer my question."

"I know," he said. He seemed uneasy and Sarah thought that he was reluctant to open that door again. "What you said was frightening."

"Did it make you angry?"

"Angry? No, not at you, anyway."

"At Robert, then?"

"Yes."

"Don't be. I didn't have to marry him."

"Why didn't your parents try to stop you?" Martin asked, swinging his hand through the air and banging his knuckles into the rock behind him.

"They did—but that only made us more determined. Maybe if they'd left us alone we would have come to our senses. Marriage turned out to be a huge mistake, but I couldn't bring myself to leave him." Sarah paused to finger one of the buttons on his shirt. "I don't think there were other women. At least nothing ever got back to me. And there were times when he was sober that he could be really sweet." She paused again and one of Martin's buttons came undone. "He was so helpless. I swear, left to himself he wouldn't have known how put his pants on straight. He'd forget to button something or to zip up."

"Are you trying to tell me you felt sorry for him?"

"Maybe. I guess I felt more like his mother than his wife."

"You realize that if you had gone to a priest; under the circumstances, he probably would have given you an annulment."

"Probably, but that never occurred to me—not until later, and by then I had Sam. I wasn't about to turn him into a bastard."

◆ ◆ ◆

Martin took that as a rebuke and said nothing.

"My experience with Robert has left me wary. It' hard for me to trust men."

"What about me?" he asked, pushing himself up off the blanket and looking down on her.

"From the beginning, being with you has been easy."

"How's that?"

"I don't know," she said, swinging herself up to confront him. "When I met you—when I saw your smile and the sadness in your eyes, you reminded me of my father."

"And that was good?"

"Yes," she said with conviction. "He was a gentle man and I could see that same gentleness in you." She reached out and rubbed the back of her hand across the stubble on his cheek "I love you so much."

"If you feel that way, why are you so reluctant to admit it." He whispered.

"Because I'm afraid I'll hurt you." She let her fingers slide through the opening where she had unbuttoned his shirt

"You probably will, at least some of the time, but that's why we promise to love each other *for better or worse.*"

"I've already had the worst."

"But that wasn't love," he reminded her.

"No, it wasn't."

With her hand still inside his shirt she pushed Martin down onto the blanket and he looked up at her in surprise. "I want to make you happy, but you have to show me how."

Instantly she brought her face down in an awkward search for his lips. When she found them, he could feel their soft wetness sliding over his. Then she kissed him repeatedly—stck, stck stck, and the sound made him laugh. Which was hard to do while her lips kept bumping into his. This wasn't what he expected for an answer.

Sarah pulled away to suck in her breath and Martin felt a lock of her hair sweep his cheek and come to rest on his chin. Opening one eye, he could see part of her face, but it was too close for him to bring into focus, and he was forced to look past her at the black roughness of the rock silhouetted by the moon. But without his glasses even that looked fuzzy. So he closed his eye and enjoyed the tickle of her fingers as she undid another button on his shirt.

"What're you doing?" he asked.

"Nothing," she said. But when she drove her hand through this wider opening and started to explore the ribbing on his undershirt, he had to believe that she was trying to seduce him.

"Do you have any idea what you're doing to me?" he mumbled. She kissed him again and his tongue felt thick.

She cuddled closer, cheek to cheek. "No—not exactly," she breathed and her breath felt moist and warm.

"Would you like me to explain it to you?"

"It might be more interesting if you showed me," she said, sitting up and reaching down to tug at his shirttail.

"Stop," he giggled. She started to pull on his belt and he brought his hand up to restrain her. Her kisses had excited him and now this playful tug of war with his belt filled him up. How had she come to this when just moments ago she seemed to be so embroiled in the painful memories of her past?

"Ooooo," she said, pursing her lips, "don't be shy. Remember I've seen it all."

"Yes, you have." he said, squirming. "But if you keep this up what you see down there may look very different, and that could get us into a lot of trouble."

"Is that bad?" she said, with a wholesome smile that even under the cover of darkness showed a row of healthy white teeth.

"I thought that we agreed to wait for this sort of thing until after the wedding."

"We did, but I've changed my mind," she said, as she pulled herself up. Then she stood on her knees and faced away from him.

This confused him even more. If she wanted to get frisky, why had she turned her back to him? But there could be no question of her intentions when she said: "Damn, Can you get my zipper? I can't reach it."

"Excuse me?" he asked.

"I can't get it undone," she explained.

"Aha," he said, and sat up to ratchet her zipper down to a spot that exposed the top of her panties. That done, he dropped down on the blanket and watched. Still facing away she pulled her sleeves past her elbows and wriggled out of her long dress. Then asked for his help again with the hooks on the back of her bra. When she'd finished undressing, she turned and sat in front of him, naked. Her skin was a warm eggshell brown and when she hunched forward he saw wrinkles form between her breasts and notice a cluster of freckles that he'd never seen before.

Now it was his turn. Sitting up, he loosened the knot of his tie, undid the top button of his dress shirt, (the others were already undone) and pulled that and his undershirt over his head all at the same time. Normally hairy, his chest had a wide swath cut down the middle that made him look like he'd been run over by a lawnmower and the moonlight highlighted the soft downy fuzz where his furry coat struggled to grow back. The long scar from his surgery had changed from crimson to seaweed brown. He hadn't let Sarah see it uncovered in weeks and he when he saw her staring at it now he bunched his shirt in front of him to hide his injury.

He waited until she looked away, then started on his trousers. Laying down he wriggled them past his hips and pulled one leg off at a time. The diet he had been forced to follow after the stroke had trimmed most of the fat off his middle and his new figure pleased him. But when he removed his boxers, he was disappointed to see that *Fred* (the name they had chosen that first day when she'd had to bathe him) just lay there limp and useless. A minute ago he had been full and ready and somewhere in between he had lost it. He sat up again and looked at Sarah who's gaze was now fixed upon his wrinkled penis, and wondered what she would think.

"Poor thing. Is it asleep?" she asked, and his laughter mixed with hers and took away some of the sting. She extended her hand to test its softness and when her finger touched the crest of the soft helmet, Fred began to move, but the moment she pulled her finger away, Fred withdrew and this second failure filled him with dismay. After twelve years with Marie, all this should be old hat. Instead it was like trying to start a race when he couldn't even get his motor running. A knot suddenly twisted in his gut and he had to press down hard with the heel of his hand to relieve the pain.

Sarah scooted in closer and pressed her fingers against his chest. Coaxing him to lean back, she made him lay down on the blanket and then came down beside him.

Laying flat and straight alongside of Sarah, he was still unaroused, and he wondered if the stroke had robbed him of his potency. Not that it wouldn't work at all (he'd had an erection two minutes ago) but that it wouldn't come to life now, when he needed it most. Maybe he was just too nervous about his ability to perform after such a long hiatus. That uneasy thought seemed to shrink him even more.

Sarah shifted to her side, poked her fingertips into the thick fur below his waist and crept slowly downward until the palm of her hand covered him. At first he held his breath, but under her gentle massage he felt a restive movement.

"Aaaaaah!" she sighed, as Fred started to grow. "It seems I have the magic touch," and her laugh, rich and thick as honey, filled him with delight.

He could smell her now—a hint of perfume and something more pungent that he couldn't describe. Not sea salt, or the dried and blackened rockweed—not the smell of Maria, though it was similar—perhaps something more primitive? Whatever it was, it pulled at him like the tendrils of steam rising off his mother's Irish stew, and begged for indulgence. That he had somehow compared Sarah to the tempting aroma of his mother's best stew made him chuckle, and she wanted to know what was so funny.

"I can't tell you."

"No secrets," she warned.

"No, really, there's just no way to put it into words."

Martin reacted cautiously to the lusty cues that she gave him. He understood that her sexual encounters with Robert had been rough and he knew intuitively that he had to alter his approach, mindful that the wrong move, the wrong touch, might trigger painful memories.

Not since his wife had died had he enjoyed the softness of a woman's body, and each time he touched Sarah's silky skin he experienced a heady intensity that left him weak. He let her determine the progress of their lovemaking, and in the end, when he thought she was ready, he encouraged her to get on top. Again he sensed her need to be in charge, which he felt certain hadn't been the case when she had been with Robert.

Even in the dimness of the moonlight he could see her expression, which was full of happiness and surprise. As she hovered over him, working herself into position, he caught a glancing reflection of wetness in her eyes and suspected that she was close to tears. A single drop escaped and splashed unexpectedly upon his breast. It landed on his scar and he felt for a moment that his heart would break. He knew somehow that her tears had nothing to do with sadness, yet he wanted to be sure that she was all right with this. So just before she brought herself down to capture his erection, he whispered: "Are you sure?" And she whispered an eager: "Yes!"

It was not passionate, not wild or full of frenzy, but soft and measured. She seemed determined to make the moment last and he ground his teeth in a stubborn effort to contain himself. It didn't work; he simply didn't know her well enough. That is, he didn't know this part of her, and couldn't adequately read the signals that would tell him that she was ready—that she was about to come. She might have been direct and simply told him, but she remained silent. The only clues came from her rapid breathing and the gushy little noises that crawled up from deep inside, spilling into the night air as if she were uttering some primeval spell.

Too soon he exploded, and she gave a disappointed cry and then collapsed. For a moment he felt her full weight pressing against him. Then slowly she slid off, and when he turned and tried to stay with her, they came apart. His rapidly diminishing size unlocked the connection that briefly made them one and Martin felt suddenly alone. Exhausted he closed his eyes and found solace in the swirling blackness behind his lids. Taking in deep breaths, he tried to bring his fast beating heart to rest.

Opening his eyes, he looked into hers, but with the low-hanging moon behind, he only caught a glimmer before she closed them. And since he couldn't see her eyes, he could only hope that they were full of satisfaction. If not with him, at least with herself—and if he was lucky, maybe both.

He lay naked beside her on the crumpled blanket while the summer breeze wandered through the steep sides of the rocks and disturbed the thick curly hair that covered most of his body. She turned on her side and pressing closer crushed one breast into his upper arm. Soft and hot, it warmed his skin and he imagined a strange transference, as if her blood were suddenly seeping into his.

The lateness of the hour, the seclusion of the rocks, the heat still radiating from the sand beneath, worked together to wipe away the larger world. And even though in his present condition he was vulnerable and unprotected, he felt safe and secure as if these rocks were like the walls of an ancient citadel, solid and impenetrable. In fact, there were wide spaces at either end, which in daylight would have left them both exposed to anyone passing by.

Whether it was circumstance or reality, the stars seemed brighter than usual, and when he noted that brightness—she said the same. Then, waxing philosophical, he spoke to her of wisdom and excellence, love and passion. And while she responded Martin watched, fascinated by the quick sweep of her hand as it punctuated her words. Lifting her right arm, she waved her fingers aimlessly in the air, then brought them down delicately against her bare breast (to demonstrate that what she was saying came from her heart). From there her hand flew upward to sweep a few wayward curls over the back of her ear. Now shifting on the blanket and propping herself on one elbow, that same active hand came to rest on his shoulder. First it landed with just the pads of her fingers—so delicately that it tickled. Then she became more coltish and pushed harder against his shoulder to give emphasis to her argument. He heard what she was saying and more or less gave the right answers, but he wasn't really concentrating on the words. The meaning and emotion came through clearly, but these wrestled more with his heart than his mind.

Laughing, she moved her hand from his shoulder to his cheek in a meaningful caress; then urged her fingers lovingly upward raking them through the thickness of his hair as if she were carding wool. When she finished her body shook with laughter.

"What's so funny?" he asked.

"Your hair. It's standing straight on end."

Coming up off her elbow, she straightened her arm for support, then from her half-recumbent position she leaned over him. First she patted the top of his head to flatten his hair; then, losing her balance, she reached for his shoulder and missed. The inside of her wrist bounced off the clavicle near the joint and her hand landed awkwardly in the folds of the blanket. That caused her breasts to fall loosely against his own, and the pointy ends shifted lightly when Sarah laughed. Inches away from Martin's face their weighty fullness rose and fell and the light touch of her nipples against his skin drove him to distraction.

Then, mouth open, her wet lips inviting, she descended and gave him a sloppy kiss. Sloppy or not, it sent electric signals to all the right places. And when she kissed him again, this time on the nose, then the ear and the neck, those electric signals all went out to the same place and he was surprised to feel a new erection rise from the shrunken remnants of the old one. "Are you ready to do this again?" he asked.

"Are you?" she asked, pulling away and sitting up.

"It kind of looks that way," he said, lifting his head off the blanket and glancing down over the crest of his stomach.

"How did that happen?" she cried, observing that he was indeed *ready*.

"Does it matter?" he said, then they watched it move, as if it were an independent creature that had taken on a life of its own. "All I know is that if we don't do something quickly the little bugger will turn to mush again."

"Oh?" she said, then: "Ohhh!" as she came excitedly to her knees, and with her hands and arms tucked in, she looked like a rabbit ready to hop. She shifted her weight forward, reached out tentatively and withdrew, then asked: "Do you want me on top again?"

"Why not?" he answered, putting his hands on her waist, and guiding her as she moved over him and straddled his hips.

Once they had joined, it took him much longer to come, but it felt infinitely more satisfying when he did. When they had finished and he and Sarah had rested, he noticed the stars were beginning to fade as the dull mist of dawn began to rise off the water in the east. "If we don't leave soon we'll be watching the sunrise."

"Would that be so bad?"

"No, but it might cause some tongues to wag."

"Are you serious? This is the eighties, nobody cares."

"Tell that to the tabloids!" he said, giving her an affectionate slap on her bottom.

His clothes were in a pile next to hers. He dressed without a word, and she did the same. Then he stepped up behind her to finish closing her zipper.

"Isn't this where we started?" she asked.

"Doesn't it make you wonder who designed these dresses? If you could do the zipper alone, maybe there'd be a lot less sex."

"Are you suggesting some kind of conspiracy?" she asked, looking back over her shoulder.

"Well, if you believe in that sort of stuff, you could certainly make a good case for it here," he said, bending and scooping up the blanket.

He took Sarah's hand and led her out over the stony surface. The car sat by itself in the center of the empty lot. After helping her in, he leaned in for a quick kiss, then came around with keys in hand to start the engine.

Chapter 61

In the car on their way back, Sarah asked to see Martin's watch. "You don't really want to know," he said. "Besides, does it really matter?"

"No," she said, pleasantly recalling the wonderful coupling of mind and body, and even more the incredible thread of peace that wound itself around her heart afterward. She had started this miraculous affair as a sexual cripple never having made love—sweet gentle love—to any man before. And she supposed that after his stroke Martin had developed a few problems of his own, which means he probably had to tackle as many uncertainties as she had. Yet when the deed was done she felt immensely satisfied and twice as satisfied later on, when she saw that he was ready to do it all over again.

◆ ◆ ◆

When they rolled quietly into her drive, with the engine already shut down, Sarah had nodded off and Martin had to wake her before he came round to open her door.

As she poked her key at the lock she wondered if she was making too much noise. Inside, standing next to Martin, she considered whether or not to ask him to stay. There were only a couple more hours before they both had to get up and go to work and he looked beat. The evening had been full of contradictions, and though some were deliciously wicked, the effort to sort them out was ultimately exhausting. *What if he fell asleep at the wheel?*

"Would you like to sleep here?" she asked. "On the couch?"

She heard a single cacking sound as if he were clearing his throat, but nothing followed. "There are fresh sheets and a pillow in that cedar chest by the front window," she explained, as she led him into the living room, holding onto his index finger.

◆ ◆ ◆

Later, lying alone on the bare sheets, while the white ceiling fan dusted her body with sticky air, Sarah thought the separation a bit silly.

After what had happened, allowing Martin to share the comfort of her bed (as opposed to the lumpy couch) seemed relatively harmless. In a few days they would be married, and everything would be legal. But legal or not, she couldn't find anything evil about what had transpired between them an hour ago on the point. A public ceremony in a church might make the whole affair more sacred, but it couldn't make her love for Martin any more real. And inviting him upstairs now wouldn't add or detract from that, she reasoned, but it would certainly send the wrong message if Sam discovered the two of them together in the morning.

She tried to think this through rationally. She had been so depressingly candid with Martin about Robert, almost to the point of driving him away. And she was half convinced that somehow she was trying to drive him away. If she could be dark enough—gross enough—then. . . But he hadn't tried to run. Instead she had flip-flopped and talked him into getting naked. Well, not exactly, but unloading all that junk on him and seeing that he wasn't turned off had turned her on. In fact she'd never wanted any man that way before. She'd always been a good Catholic girl—that wasn't true either—she hadn't been active in the church since marrying Robert. But she'd never been promiscuous. What had happened tonight was an aberration. Still, if Martin were here right now, could she trust herself not to take advantage of him? Yes, she probably could, but only because she was so bone-crushingly tired, she couldn't see straight. Grabbing the binding on the edge of the sheet she hauled it up from the foot of the bed, and rolling onto her side she tried to wish herself to sleep. But it didn't work.

She thought of Martin: saw him naked while they lay together between the rocks. She'd had little to do with Robert physically, except when he wanted sex, and then he'd just dropped his trousers and presented himself ready for action. Which gave her the impression that men were ready more or less instantaneously. He was a big man, painfully well en-dowed, and he was never gentle, he used his erection like a weapon to tear her apart. Occasionally Robert couldn't maintain his arousal and it shriveled and fell flat; that always made him foul and furious and she had to take the blame. But Martin was different; he didn't rush at her like a monster bent on destruction. When he came unwrapped he needed her help; and the idea that she had to make it happen, pleased her immensely. It meant that for once in her life she was in control. Just as he had through the whole relationship, Martin let her determine the pace—gave her the freedom to choose what the next step would be.

Chapter 62

Martin wasn't any different from Sarah: kicking at the arm of the sofa, which was too short for him, he wished for sleep too, but couldn't get his mind to shut down. This had been a strange evening. The way it had begun seemed almost cruel—the way it ended confused the hell out of him. But he decided that analyzing this sort of thing could only spoil it. Instead, hands behind his head, he watched the lights from passing cars flicker across the walls and ceiling. In between, when it was dark, he dragged up pictures of Sarah's pale form lying lazily beside him on his old khaki army blanket. Why had she done it? And she did it—there was no doubt about that. Getting naked was her idea, and her eagerness during intercourse proved that she wasn't just giving in to his fundamental craving for sex (assuming that she knew that he had such cravings).

Another flash of light swept across the room and when the blackness returned a clear and palpable image leapt to his mind that was almost surreal. Her spent body lay heavily upon him, shaking, and he was holding onto her, stroking her back. Her breathing slowed; she gasped "sweet Jesus"(which sounded like a supplication); then sobbed quietly into his shoulder until he felt he could taste her salty tears. Only it wasn't her tears he was tasting, but his own, which had rolled so gently down the crevices of his face that he hadn't detected them until he turned to press his cheek against hers and they spilled onto the tip of his tongue. Once he had invited her to cover him—once he was surrounded by her warm, wet softness—he became sensitive to every refinement, to every tremor, till the smallest ripple was enough to make him come. That intense concentration took away some of his edge, and when it was over he wondered if he had gotten it right. In retrospect those withering doubts seemed silly, but he loved Sarah so much that he would do anything to satisfy her. None of this would have entered his mind if it wasn't for her history with Robert. He knew that that experience had been cruel and debilitating, which is why, from the beginning, he tried to subdue his own needs in favor of hers.

Still, he couldn't help wonder if he should have let it happen. He'd shaken the dew off his lily, done the horizontal bop, gotten a little nookie—*why can't you describe intercourse in a way that doesn't sound like some kind of farce from Monty Python's Flying Circus?* Had they made a mistake? Would there be regrets? Perhaps if she had invited him to her bed instead of making him take the couch, he wouldn't be having these thoughts. Finally, he forced his mind to shut down and just when sleep reached out to grab him, the memory of Maria made him feel suddenly unfaithful. Would he have to go through this craziness every time he and Sarah made love?

Chapter 63

Although Sarah did mention the events of that evening in whispered confidences whenever there was a private or semi-private moment with Martin, she never mentioned any regrets.

In the ensuing confusion of the bachelor party (which Martin attended reluctantly because Maria's brother was in charge and was likely to promote something obnoxious) and the wedding rehearsal, and the dinner following, and last-minute problems with the honeymoon reservations, along with additional meetings with the priest and the caterer, he discovered there were few opportunities for such confidential exchanges.

Alone or not, however, Sarah found snippets of time for a quick aside, and what she said was blasphemous. Her irreverent references to their moonlit tryst shocked him. And when Sarah saw by his reaction that her comments left him flustered and unbalanced, she nearly collapsed in laughter. Somehow her teasing indicated a new confidence in their relationship; but while her confidence grew, his diminished. Why couldn't he give her back some of the same? And if he did, would she act insulted or contrite or would she just laugh at him again? Did he still have doubts about his performance at the lighthouse? Considering his dysfunctional beginnings and the need for her help, such doubts might be justified. But in the end everything turned out right—the one-eyed wonder worked—and her present good spirits indicated that she was well-pleased with him. So why couldn't he accept that and move on?

When the night of the wedding rehearsal came he couldn't remember what to do, where he was supposed to stand, whether to say "I do" or "I will". Later, at the dinner, everyone seemed to want Sarah's attention and he had no chance to speak to her, even to ask her a simple question. Afterwards, sitting with her at the dinner table, the empty chairs in disarray, the guests gone, he wanted to say something, but couldn't find a place to start. Instead he reached out to smooth the wrinkles in her dress. She used both her hands to cover his, and once she had his fingers trapped she asked, "What's the matter, Martin? Is it the wedding—is all this pomp and circumstance making you nervous?"

"No. Well, yes, in a way, but I'm fine."

"What, then?"

"Nothing."

"Is it the other evening, then?"

He didn't answer, just wondered how she had come so quickly to that conclusion.

"At first," she said, "I had some misgivings, but once we started— I don't have any regrets."

"Really?"

"There were times when I wasn't sure what to do—whether to start or stop. I wanted you to be pleased, but then . . . then . . ."

"Then what?" he asked, wanting her to finish.

"I was frightened."

"Why?"

"I'd never done that before."

"How can that be?"

"Oh, I've had sex—well, the sort of aimless prodding and poking that Robert called sex. But I've never made love."

Martin, sitting on the edge of his chair, came up ramrod straight and looked into her eyes expecting to see sadness, but instead her eyes were bright and she was smiling at him.

"Then when I saw there was nothing there, that you weren't ready, I thought it was me—that it was my fault, my inexperience."

"That's—that's—" he couldn't describe his sense of relief. "All that stuff you said at the restaurant. By the time we got to the lighthouse, I felt like I was walking on broken glass. . ."

"I know," she said. "I had this depressing need to tell all."

"That's okay," he said. "It's just that the sudden switch confused me and I've worried ever since that somehow I'd gotten it all wrong."

"No, no, you got it all right—perfectly, wonderfully right," she said, putting her hands on his shoulders and shaking him once to emphasize the intensity of her feelings.

Well, *perfectly* seemed an exaggeration; but he understood, or thought he understood. Now that he could put aside his anxiety, all his foolish misgivings, he was free to look back on that singular experience as the most intimate, the most profound, of his life. Okay, that was an exaggeration too; and yes, he'd had these feelings before with his wife, but never with the same intensity. Perhaps age and adversity had taught him that these moments don't last—and that life passes too quickly to gather them all in. But mostly he thought it was because Sarah needed that kind of intimacy more. Needed it the way someone hanging from a ledge needs a lifeline.

Suddenly she tugged at his shoulders, and when he leaned in she closed the space between and kissed him.

Chapter 64

Sam was aware that in the Gibson family (those were the people on his mother's side) there were two big events in life that brought everyone together: weddings and funerals. Everything else seemed to exclude somebody, either by accident or design. Of course there was more of a tendency for the children to show up at a wedding than at a funeral. "After all, who knew what damage might be done to an impressionable young mind if the child were exposed too soon to the Grim Reaper?"—one of a long list of Grandma Gibson's pronouncements (Great-grandma Gibson to Sam). At 96, she was more than just an ancient matriarch; she was a kind of soothsayer or prophet. The problem was she never said anything that didn't forecast some sort of doom, which was why his mother felt reluctant to invite her to the wedding. Sarah was not generally disposed to superstition, *but under the circumstances,* she told Sam, *she could believe in anything, including her grandmother's black prophecies.*

Today was the big day. As the living room filled with the soft light of dawn, Sam lay on his side, awake, staring at the glasses and plates from last nights snacks including an empty popcorn bag that he'd nuked in the microwave. He hadn't slept, not because he didn't want to, but because the house was bulging with company and he had to occupy the couch. The cracks between the cushions never seemed to hit him in the right place; and lots of tossing and turning had made his muscles ache and left him exhausted.

Uncle Jack ("Fat Jack") had taken over his room, and even from down here Sam could hear his bed complain every time his uncle shifted his three hundred pounds against the puny bedsprings. His mother's older brother from Towanda, Pennsylvania (ten years her senior), had always been short and round, even as a kid. Sam had never seen a picture of him when he wasn't overweight, and he knew all the stories of the cruel things Jack's classmates did to him at school. The stories weren't funny and Sam suspected that his mother told him these things hoping that he would learn to be more sensitive to the kinds of kids who didn't fit in. She never guessed that he was one of them.

From the creak and groan of the floorboards he could tell that his uncle had moved across the hall and into the bathroom. Sam had decided it was time to get up and now stood in front of the bathroom door, waiting for Uncle Jack to come out. In one hand Sam had a towel and a new tube of toothpaste taken from the hall cabinet. He used his other hand to hold up his pajama bottoms. The string had disappeared during the night, so he needed to haul them up every time they threatened to slide past his hips. Twice during the night he'd found them down around his knees and he was glad to be awake and covered when Grandma Gibson came through the living room early in the morning to get the newspaper off the front step.

Sam could hear Uncle Jack in the shower: the water running and the throaty sound of his singing penetrated the flimsy walls. When Sam hollered through the door, his uncle's operatic aria ended with a croak, and Sam tried to muffle his laughter by crushing the folded towel over his mouth.

At that moment his mother poked her head out of her bedroom door, saw Sam with one hand cinching his waist and the other holding a towel over his mouth, and was nonplused. Then she noticed that his hair was sticking up.

"Sam, fix your hair; it looks like you just took your fingers out of the light socket," she said, holding her hand to her throat as if she were about to laugh. But of course he couldn't fix his hair without letting go of his towel or dropping his bottoms.

"Mom," he moaned. "It'll be fine after I wash it."

"I'll wait till everyone's had their shower," she said, as if she hadn't heard him. "I don't want to be sticky when I try to squeeze into that fitted gown." Then she closed her door again.

His mother was right: it was going to be a hot day. Sam could already feel the stickiness in the tepid breeze that came in fits and starts through the screened window at the end of the hall. Considering the heavily starched shirt, cummerbund and jacket that he had to wear today, he was glad that the church would be air-conditioned.

Aunt Em had come over earlierto handle breakfast, and was already rattling around in the kitchen. Apparently Grandma Gibson was trying to help, because he could hear Em complaining, "Turn off that burner, I'm not ready for that yet! No, I don't want that pan—it's too small! Will you please leave that tray alone!" A tinny crash echoed through the hall and up the stairs.

◆ ◆ ◆

Sarah heard the argument and the clatter of the falling tray coming through the crack under her door and thought. *I can't deal with this, not today. It'll take all my energy and concentration just to get through the ceremony.*

The public ceremony, which would bind her and Martin together, was a necessary one. She knew that standing before a roomful of people and declaring her love and commitment to Martin was a valuable and sensible ritual: a sacrament that every civilization had adopted in one form or another. But its complexities left the process fraught with possibilities for disaster, and that worried her. Even the most confident and collected person could find ways to make a fool of themselves under these circumstances, and she knew she was neither of those.

She was not without moral support; she didn't have to do this alone. Her sister-in-law Em was her maid of honor, and her mother would come later to help her dress, to pin her veil in place and put the finishing touches to her hair.

One person, however, wouldn't be there: her father. More than three years had passed and she still wasn't used to his absence. Parents are supposed to get old and die, but he hadn't been old enough, and she wasn't ready yet to let him go. She still needed him, probably more than she was willing to admit. The suddenness of his death had been hard. If he had suffered a long illness and there had been time to see what was coming, maybe it would have been a little easier. Of course, she wouldn't have wanted that either. If he were bedridden, full of pain unable to care for himself, that would have been awful too. He was too active, too independent, to be confined like that. But having died in a matter of minutes right in front of her, while they were coming out of the theater, was almost more than she could handle. In fact, she'd handled it well enough at the time; it was later, when the ambulance had taken him away, that she finally broke down.

Her dad had been a perceptive man. He knew exactly what Robert was doing to her, which is why they were at the theater when he died. In the beginning her father had tried to talk her into leaving Robert, but when she refused, he took a different approach. Over all those years, as often as he could, he looked for excuses to take her out—out to a restaurant, a ball game, the park, a walk in the woods, shopping at the mall, any place where at least for a little while she could be free from Robert's tyranny. The fact that he manufactured those adventures just to help her escape made his loss even more traumatic. Afterwards, there was no respite from her husband's unpredictable moods, which left her in a constant state of anxiety.

She felt certain, especially when there was physical evidence of abuse, that her father would liked to have hit Robert, to pounce upon him, strangle him, beat him the way he had beaten her. She could see her father's rage, and it frightened her, because he was not a violent man. He was gentle and forgiving, sometimes to a fault. It dawned on her now that those were the same qualities that she saw in Martin.

Her mother had insisted that someone had to give Sarah away, and they discussed substitutes, but no one was really suitable, and there was no one who could be asked without hurting someone else's feelings. So her mother finally dropped the matter, and Sarah was relieved. When the time came, she would remember her father, and that would be enough.

♦ ♦ ♦

Em had made plans for a fancy wedding breakfast and had packed in the ingredients for it the night before. There were marvelous fixings scattered over the countertops and the room was filled with the aroma of onions and flour and spices. The chopping board was in front of Em and she was furiously slicing mushrooms when Sarah walked into the kitchen in just her terrycloth robe with her hair under a plastic cap to protect the beautician's handiwork from the ravages of the steamy shower. "Em, I know I said I wasn't eating any breakfast, but where's the food? The tablecloth and napkins, the plates and the good silverware are all laid out in the dining room, but I don't see anything to eat."

"You weren't the only one who wasn't interested in eating. Uncle Jack said toast and coffee was enough, Sam helped himself to a bowl of cereal and your mother and Grandma Gibson both had herbal tea."

"Oh God, I hope this isn't a bad omen."

"I hardly think that there's any evil portent."

"If no one's eating, what's all this?" Sarah asked, waving her fingers over the food on the chopping board and spread out over the counters.

I intended to quit, but the work was already half done, so I decided to cook it anyway. I'll put the whole lot in the freezer, and when you and Martin return you can nuke it in the microwave. There ought to be enough here to last the two of you for a week. Sorry: the three of you."

"Blech!"

"Gee thanks!"

"No, I appreciate all your effort, really I do. It's just not pleasant to think of eating the same thing everyday for a week."

"There's coffee made, would you like some?" Em offered.

"No, somehow caffeine doesn't seem like a good idea right now. Is there any orange juice?" Sarah asked, as she took half a step toward the refrigerator.

"Hold on," Em answered with her hand in the air. "I'll pour you a glass. Just sit down and relax."

"Relax? Are you kidding?" Sarah protested, but she did drag the stool over to the counter and wriggled her tush up onto it. "I can't remember being this nervous the first time. But looking back, I wasn't terribly anxious to go through with that one either. I think I was half hoping that Robert wouldn't show up."

"Do you have any doubts?" Em asked as she pulled a clear carafe of orange juice from the refrigerator.

"Don't be silly, Em; I'm nervous, not frightened. When I think about it, except for a few childhood years, my life has been crap. Now, for whatever reason, God has decided to give me a second chance. Maybe it's some kind of dispensation, a special act of mercy. I'm not sure, but I don't want to screw it up; this time I want to get it right."

"You will," Em said, taking down a juice glass and filling it to the brim.

"Just because Martin loves me doesn't guarantee that I'll be happy, but I'm certain to be miserable without him. That sounds terribly corny, doesn't it."

"Yes, terribly, but so what," Em said, holding the glass in front of her. "Martin's a saint, or at least as close as you can get to sainthood in this world. And you? You're not the same person."

"No I'm not, am I," Sarah said, suddenly aware of the new spirit that had recently come to possess her. "Now and then I still see the shadow of my old self, but the moment Martin walks in, it runs away to hide."

"No, it's more than that. The last couple of days you've been positively glowing. It shows in your eyes. Something's changed, but I swear I can't imagine what." Em said, first pointing a finger at Sarah and then using it to push her glasses up where they belonged.

"Have I really been that obvious?" Sarah said, trying to take a sip of her orange juice without spilling it.

"Yes, and it's got me buffaloed." Em used the back of her hand to brush a drop of sweat from the end of her nose. She started to wipe it on her apron, then thought better of it and went to the sink to wash her hands. "I'll tell you one thing, Martin is the cause."

"What makes you say that?"

"Because whenever you see him you go from sensible to addlepated.

"What?"

"Oh, it's one of Grandma Gibson's words. It means loopy, or bonkers."

"Gee thanks."

"Okay, so it loses something in the translation."

"Yeah, I guess," Sarah said.

"So, why is that?"

"What?'

"That look on your face?"

"I'm in love."

"No, that's not it. Well, it is, but there's something more. OOO, ooo, ooo. No, it couldn't be. You wouldn't—would you?"

"Never mind," Sarah said.

"You son of a gun. You did it, didn't you."

"NEVER MIND," Sarah repeated, lifting her glass to try and hide her face. At that moment Sam came through the doorway.

"Aunt Em, can you help me put these on?" he said, extending his hand and showing her the shiny black studs that fastened to the front of his pleated shirt. "Mom, don't you need to shower?" he asked when he saw her sitting with the shower cap on her head.

"Oh good Lord!" she answered, looking up at the kitchen clock. She took another swallow from her glass, which was still more than half full, and set it down on the countertop. Then, pulling the ends of her robe together, she slid off the stool, and dodging Sam, who stood in her path, rushed out of the kitchen.

Chapter 65

Martin was pacing back and forth in the anteroom next to the chapel. He was upset because there was only fifteen minutes left before the ceremony and his best man had rushed off on some errand and hadn't come back yet. Sam sat watching Martin, aware of his agitated movements as he paced from the narrow window to the chair in the far corner, to the door and then back to the center of the room. His lips were moving and Sam thought he could make out the words, but he tried to push them aside feeling that he was intruding. He had seen Martin in this condition before: when he was so engrossed in thought that the words in his head came out in a low whisper. Then Sam had thought it was terribly funny, but it wasn't funny today.

Sam shouldn't have been there at all. He was supposed to be seating guests, and he had been, until the best man came rushing out of the anteroom and told him not to leave Martin alone. He didn't explain why, he just hurried out the door to his car and left Sam standing there in the foyer. Half-walking, half-running down the aisle, he tried to maintain a certain decorum as he made his way anxiously to the front of the church. He took a quick turn at the last pew and coming around the communion rail stepped up to the door. It was set deeply in a gothic stone archway and the heavy brass hardware caught the glint of light coming from the tall candle-stand behind him. He wondered if he should knock or just open it. He decided to try the knob first to see if it was locked. It wasn't, so he turned it slowly, and stepped inside.

Martin was so preoccupied he didn't see Sam enter. Not knowing what else to do, he took a chair beside an odd piece of furniture with narrow drawers in it. It was dark mahogany and looked like a cross between a bureau and a desk.

Martin still hadn't recognized his presence, and not wanting to break his concentration, Sam just sat staring at the antique handles that hung neatly, one above the other, at the center of each drawer. As Martin paced he interrupted the sunlight that was coming in the window, and after crossing the room several times he suddenly stopped and looked at Sam.

"Where did you come from? Shouldn't you be out there?" he said, pointing toward the door.
"Frank asked me to come in here with you. He was in an awful hurry. He didn't say why he was in a hurry, or why I should come in here, but it seemed important to him."
"The idiot forgot to bring the rings."
"Oh," Sam said. He knew that was serious, but he couldn't think of anything more to say about it.
"I'm alright; you should be in the foyer greeting people."
"Not really."
"Why not?"
"Because it was my job to seat Mom's side of the family and there aren't that many. Besides, most of those who were coming are already here. We sent invitations to everyone because Lillian said we had to. I know I shouldn't call her that, but she hates to think of herself as a grandmother. She also wanted to invite some of my father's relatives and that didn't go over. Mom got really mad."
"Are they really that bad?"
"Worse. They don't approve of this; they see it as a betrayal to my father's memory. I think it's a bunch of crap. Why are people like that?"
"Well, they probably loved your father," Martin observed.
"No they didn't. But now that he's dead they seemed to have forgotten all the rotten things he did."
"People do that. When someone dies they're reluctant to pass judgment. Maybe they hope to cover some of their own sins by making less of other's."
"Maybe."
"I know you didn't like your father—"
"No, I hated him," Sam spat back.
"I'm sorry."
"Don't be. I don't need your pity." He hadn't meant to be so harsh, but Martin had touched a nerve.
Martin looked hurt. "Have I ever offered you pity?"
"No," Sam said, dropping his chin, which brought it against his sharp collar again.
Frank burst through the door. "All set," he said, opening his hand to show Martin that he had both rings. "Sarah's here with your mother. The minister is looking for you—and me," he added, as he brushed some imaginary lint from Martin's shoulder and stepped in to adjust Martin's tie. His efforts failed; the tie looked worse now than when he started.
"Frank, will you leave me alone? I'm the one getting married here," Martin reminded him, slapping Frank's hands away from his collar. "And you're the one with the jitters."

There wasn't any reason now for Sam to stay and he headed for the door. As he turned the handle he looked over his shoulder, and when he saw Martin looking back, he said: "I want you to know that I'm glad you're marrying my mother." Once the words were out, he hurried to close the door behind him. Focusing on the entrance to the chapel, he stood at attention, then moved deliberately forward, pacing himself until he reached the back of the room. Then he did an about-face and waited with his hands locked together in front of him, as if he were protecting his old bicycle injury. Searching the crowd, he could see the backs of heads, some with curly hairdos and some neatly trimmed. The guests whispered, and fidgeted, and turned frequently to see if the bride was ready yet. About midway, he found Winnie and Bruce sitting next to each other and thought that if he could have such good friends as these, his life wasn't a total mess.

Looking upward, at the vaulted ceiling, he studied a procession of painted angels and cherubs chasing each other through the clouds. He came here to this church every Sunday and knew every detail, but today it seemed different. Of course the added flowers and candles and the crimson runner that proceeded unevenly along the center of the aisle didn't belong, but it was something more than that. It wasn't so much what he saw around him, it wasn't the people or the decorations: it was a feeling—a bright, buoyant feeling that made him smile self-consciously when he saw that Winnie had turned and was staring at him.

The sunlight filtering through the tall side windows struck the heavy cross that hung on wires above the altar and a deep shadow behind made it appear to float precariously over the spot where the bride and groom would stand.

How strange it seemed to be here, serving as an usher at his own mother's wedding. After all, weren't the children supposed to come after the ceremony? Though he guessed that wasn't nearly as true as it used to be.

The organist who had been playing soft prelude music stopped suddenly in the middle of Handel's, *Largo* to begin the robust strains of the *Bridal Chorus* from Wagner's, *Lohengrin*. Pounding energetically on the keys, the familiar strains bounced extravagantly through the vaulted chamber and brought the congregation thundering to its feet. Sam turned with the others to view his mother as she marched through the entrance at the back of the chapel.

He knew all brides were supposed to be beautiful, but he had never seen his mother like this before, and the swelling that rose up from deep in his stomach almost popped the studs out of his shirtfront as he realized how pretty she looked. The dress from the waist downward was full and puffy, held out by some mysterious device hidden underneath. But it was not the traditional floor-length, instead it stopped just below her knees, and from there he could see opaque white stockings and low-heeled white satin pumps. From the waist upward it was tightly fitted, hugging her so closely that he wondered how she could breathe. The bodice pushed up against an embroidered panel that lifted her breasts and gave them a fullness that he had never seen before. It was cut in a wide V from shoulder to shoulder that was just low enough to reveal a tiny shadow of cleavage. The sleeves were made of a stiff crinoline that stood out boldly from her shoulders. From there to her wrists, her arms were bare, and on her hands were short lace gloves with the ends of the fingers missing.

She stepped forward, hesitated, took a second step, and hesitated again, then another step. Aunt Em and Laura were well ahead of his mother, and had almost reached the point where they would break off to the left and leave the way open for the bride to approach the rail. Suddenly Sam woke up to the fact that he wasn't supposed to be here at the back of the church. His job was to bring Lillian to the front and seat her as the final cue to begin the ceremony. Afterwards, he was supposed to take his place at the outside end of the first pew. At first he panicked, then he looked to the front of the church and saw that someone else had done his job for him. *But what about me,* he thought. *Where do I go now?* His first impulse was to rush down the aisle ahead of his mother and find his seat. Fortunately he didn't act on that reckless idea. Instead he decided to stay put.

◆ ◆ ◆

Sarah, now about halfway along, with her maid of honor watching her approach, thought: *This didn't seem like such a long walk last night at rehearsal. Doesn't Martin look handsome in that black tux? And look at his face—his grin is so wide it makes him look goofy. What was that word Em used this morning? Addlepated?* When Martin saw her he straightened up and pushed out his chest, and except for his receding hairline, she thought he looked like the handsome maitre d' at Christo's Greek restaurant.

I know I'm supposed to be this wonderful vision of beauty, but do I look that good? I mean, it's not as if I'm a fresh young bride: this old model has been around the block. Maybe that doesn't count. Maybe for this one day God clouds the groom's vision and all the imperfections—large and small—disappear in a blur. Come to think of it, Martin doesn't have his glasses on, so maybe I am a blur.

Boy, am I hungry! Other than a couple of sips of orange juice I haven't had anything, not even water, since last night. . Besides being nervous, she'd been afraid to eat—afraid that it might interfere with her getting into her gown, and right now she was beginning to think that was a mistake.

I thought this place was supposed to be air-conditioned. It certainly doesn't feel like it. Is it me? she wondered. *No, a lot of these people are fanning themselves, so they must be hot too.*

Finally she reached the end, and shuffled up beside Martin. His best man stepped back, and the priest came forward, opening a small book with gilt edges. Sarah tried to pay attention, but there was a kind of buzzing sound in her ears, like a horde of green-bottle flies whirring around a pile of poop. She squinted at the priest trying to improve her vision, but it was no good. *He's looking at me as if he expects me to say something. Why is he weaving like that? Oh my God, this isn't happening,* she thought, as everything turned blurry. Then the darkness folded in, and she fell forward into the priest's arms.

♦ ♦ ♦

When the priest saw her coming, he let his prayer book fly and reached out to grab her. By then Martin had his hands on her too, and they both lowered her slowly to the floor. Turning her over, they laid her face up.

Pandemonium followed as several others rushed forward and everyone began talking and shouting at once. Someone ran down the aisle with a first-aid kit. There were all kinds of bandages and tape and creams, but nothing that could help in this situation. Ellen Gooding, the local postmistress, had the good sense to go to the custodian's closet and come back with a bottle of ammonia and a clean rag. Soaking one corner, she elbowed through the crowd and suggested that Martin wave it in front of Sarah's nose. By then the priest had propped up her feet and she was starting to come around on her own. Martin caught the offensive odor and brought it toward her face. He saw an awful expression as the smell from the cloth jolted her senses and she tossed her head to one side.

♦ ♦ ♦

Opening her eyes, she saw a dozen faces leaning over her. When she realized that she was on the floor, looking up at this mass of contorted faces, she thought, *This has to be a dream! All I have to do is close my eyes and I'll wake up!* Scrunching her lids tightly together, she held them shut for a moment, presenting an unsightly grimace to the few guests who were close enough to see. When the room fell suddenly silent she thought that maybe it was a time to test her theory, and her right eye opened slowly, hoping to see the dirty fan that hung from her bedroom ceiling. But instead she saw the same faces, staring down at her. They hadn't gone away—this wasn't a dream!

She decided that she wanted to sit up, but when she tried, the dizziness returned. After a moment the dizziness cleared, and with Martin on one side and Frank on the other, she made it from the floor to a sitting position in the first pew. Her mother sat down beside her and offered her a glass of water with ice in it. She drank greedily while her mother kept telling her to slow down, but it tasted so good. When she was this thirsty, nothing seemed to satisfy her more than ice-cold water. With the glass empty, she pushed her fingers to the bottom and slid out what was left of one of the ice cubes, then ran it quickly across her forehead and did the same to her cheeks. She even held it under her chin and ran it down to the hollow of her throat, holding it there long enough to let a trickle of melted ice run down into the cleft between her breasts. Finally she popped what was left into her mouth and let it melt on her tongue. It tasted a little like the Revlon foundation she had used to color her skin, but it was still cool and refreshing.

Reflecting on her performance she decided that it probably wasn't appropriate and she wasn't sure what she looked like with a wet face and neck, but while she was doing it every step had brought her splendid relief. It took away the awful buzzing that had sent her crashing to the floor. Well—thanks to Father Sullivan—at least there hadn't been any crashing.

The priest squatted down in front of her and asked if she wanted to continue.

"Continue!" she shouted. Then, hearing the loudness of her own voice, she dropped it to a whisper and said: "Of course I want to continue. I came here to get married and one way or another I intend to get through it." That hadn't come out the way she meant it to. It sounded more like she was struggling through some terrible ordeal, instead of marrying the man that she loved. *Loved—oh God! I just get to the* 'I do's' *and then I faint dead away.*

"I'm sorry, Martin," she said, staring up into his wounded eyes.

"You didn't do this on purpose—did you?"

"NO."

"Then what are you sorry for?"

"For scaring the hell out of everyone. Excuse me, Father."

"Are you ready to start again?" Martin asked the priest.

"Yes."

"Do we have to start over?" Sarah asked. "Can't we begin where we left off?"

"We can if Father Sullivan can remember where that was."

At that point apparently the priest remembered something, and started searching around the base of the altar. "What's wrong?" Martin asked.

"I can't find my book," he said, "I flipped it out of my hand so that I could catch Sarah, and now I don't know where it went."

Martin and one of the guests started to look with him, but it was Frank who finally located it behind the communion rail to the left of the altar.

Everyone returned to his or her seat, and a nervous silence fell over the congregation. Moving into position in front of the priest, Sarah turned to take Martin's hand and stepped on his foot. "Sorry," she said again.

Father Sullivan ran his finger down the page until he found his place and he started to read. "Do you take this man—"

"Yes—I do,' Sarah said before he finished.

"Slow down," he whispered. "I know you're anxious, but you don't want to confuse me, do you?"

"Sorry," she whispered back. Then scolded herself for using that word so much.

The priest continued, and during the next few minutes Sarah and Martin made solemn promises to "Love and honor—For better or worse— Until death do us part", and though she couldn't determine how it might affect Robert or Maria, Sarah silently hoped that God might keep them together long after death. She removed her glove and when she felt the coolness of the ring slide easily onto her finger, she thought she would cry. Then she slid Martin's ring on his finger she did cry. It was nothing elaborate, just the sniffles. But when the priest told Martin: "You may kiss the bride," all those sweet emotions boiled over.

Before he had time to react, Sarah pounced upon him and her eagerness surprised Martin—and the guests—and the priest, and herself. Afterwards, she hoped that her eager kiss would remove any doubt about her desire to be sealed to this man.

When they turned to go back down the aisle Sarah made a slight detour, stopping to hug her mother and then Grandma Gibson. And her grandmother whispered, "Good Lord, girl, couldn't you have saved that for the honeymoon?"

But she was unabashed. "No Grandma, I couldn't." And she really couldn't. Love, happiness, and especially passion had eluded her for too long. Now that they were within her grasp, she was in a gosh-awful hurry enjoy them. In fact, turning away from her grandmother, she threw her arms defiantly around Martin and kissed him again. He stumbled under her unexpected attack, but when he recovered he swept her up in his arms and lifted her swiftly off her feet. She made a little squeal before she kissed him for a third time, then they hurried hand-in-hand down the aisle and pushed through the doors into the foyer.

Chapter 66

Clowns—just like a parade of clowns at the circus. The comic confusion, the strident shouts and good wishes of the guests mixed with minor pratfalls and silly misdeeds. Martin and Sarah tripping down the steps under a shower of confetti and birdseed (better for the pigeons than rice). A spray of hard seeds stung Sam's face when the breeze stiffened and tossed them back in his direction. The photographer had a terrible time trying to get the other guests away from the bride and groom long enough for him to get some candid shots of them in front of their limousine.

People kept stumbling over themselves and each other trying to take their own pictures. Some had little pocket cameras: others had big expensive ones with fancy attachments and bulky lenses that their owners constantly adjusted, as if they couldn't ever quite get their subject in focus.

Two men in coveralls rushed back and forth, removing the flowers from the church and loading them into the back of a white van. They were to be taken to the reception, where they would be used to decorate the head table and to help complete the bower where the bride and groom stood for the receiving line.

People left in dribs and drabs, until only the wedding party remained. There were actually two limousines scheduled to come and pick them up. One for the best man, the maid of honor and the bridesmaids, and the other for Lillian and Grandma Gibson and Aunt Em and Uncle Jack, but neither had arrived yet.

Lillian kept pulling on Em's sleeve, asking if she could see the limos. "They're long and white, and hard to miss," Em said. "If I could see them, you'd certainly see them too."

Sam and Frank were talking at the back of the church while the others drifted about in the foyer.

"Well, this certainly wasn't any cakewalk, but the deed is done: they're married." Frank said, randomly pinching the creases in his trousers trying to get them to hang straight.

"Is that normal?" Sam asked. "I mean the fainting."

"Who knows? I've only been to two of these things," Frank answered.

"It's my first. Just imagine what it's like for people who do this stuff all the time."

"What do you mean?" Frank asked.

"You know—like priests and photographers and caterers."

"Oh, yeah," Frank said, knowingly. "And there's more to come. There's still the reception."

"Does that mean more fainting?"

"Who knows?" Frank answered. "You can't plan stuff like this and not have something go wrong. Of course whatever happens, you hope that no one will notice."

At that moment a sudden stir in the foyer announced the arrival of the limos. Sam stuck his head through the doorway just in time to see Em rustling toward the chapel to tell the others to hurry.

The girls, with their full dresses and high heels, had a little trouble getting in, but soon they were all tucked and folded and surrounded by the velvet luxury of thick carpeting and rich leather upholstery. The limos left the yellow curbing slowly rounding the church drive and stretching out onto the main street.

◆ ◆ ◆

The Women's Club—or Women's Auxiliary—had a suitable hall, which Sarah and Martin had rented for a small fee. Martin had a friend who did some catering, and what this guy didn't supply, friends and relatives brought themselves. Nearly everything was volunteered, borrowed or bought at a discount. The dishes were from the church kitchen and the silverware too. Actually it wasn't silver at all, but common stainless-steel flatware. All the tablecloths were white and newly starched and pressed. Some were plain and others had lacy patterns stitched into them—all were donated. The band included an old college friend of Martin's, three church members who oddly enough called themselves a quartet, and the organist from the church came to play the piano. It wasn't the sort of reception that would be written up in some fashion magazine or the tabloids, but everyone did their part and everything looked perfectly lovely. Well, that's what Aunt Em thought anyway.

The guests were milling about in homey little groups or had located their tables by reading the stiffly folded nametags in the center of each dinner plate.

Sarah didn't drink and neither did Martin, so there wasn't any liquor, just small glasses of white wine at each table to be used to toast the bride and groom when the time came. Lillian had had a fit. They had to have an open bar. How could they impose their standards on everyone else? But they both stuck to their guns and Lillian's grumbling was ignored.

When Sarah and Martin, Sam and Frank, and Em and Laura finally came through the doors and into the reception hall, a brief cheer went up from the crowd, and then the photographer whisked them off again for more pictures. Eventually the wedding party made its way back to the main hall, and amid cheers and applause they formed a receiving line and began the process of endless smiles and handshakes and kisses especially for the bride. The kisses, mostly lopsided or misplaced, were quick and innocent, except for the one guy who always lingers too long— the guy who's always half-crocked and who secretly thinks that the bride is in love with him and needs a real kiss from a real man before she faces the disappointment of the honeymoon.

◆ ◆ ◆

As part of the wedding party Sam had certain obligations, but as soon as he could break away, he went in search of Winnie. He found her at a corner table near the wedding cake, finishing off a second dessert—a slice of green and pink ice cream with a thick swirl of red claret sauce at the center.

"Hi," he said nonchalantly as he sat down in the vacant chair beside her.

"Hi," she threw back, with just as much detachment.

"Are you enjoying yourself?" he asked, nodding at the dish in her hand.

"I might have enjoyed myself more if I hadn't been alone. Is it okay for you to be here?"

"Yes, it's pretty much over, except for the dancing. Are you going to try and catch the bouquet?"

"No way!"

"Why not?" he asked. "Don't you believe in tradition?"

"That's like totally lame!" she said, with a spoonful of claret sauce halfway to her mouth.

"Yeah, I guess," he said, wondering if he should try and get the garter.

"Besides, there's a lot of years ahead, before I even think about getting married," she said. "God! I'm just getting used to boys, and then there's this dating thing."

"Boys?" he said. The worried crease above the bridge of his nose grew longer and deeper.

"Well, boy, then," she said, scraping up the last spoonful of claret and offering it to him.

Sam opened his mouth to accept; then, licking a drop from his upper lip, he smiled as if she had just given him a secret love potion.

"What?" she asked.

"Nothing."

"Then why the goofy look?"

"It's not goofy."

"Lovesick, then?"

"That's bogus," he said.

"Why? You could never hide your feelings. Your face is absolutely beaming."

"And what about you?" he asked

"Why? Haven't I made my feelings clear?"

"Lately—yes," he said.

"So, what more do you want?"

"I want to stop feeling like a dufus," he said. "I want to know how I can make you happy."

"Well, for starters you can give me a kiss."

He dragged his chair closer and leaned in to comply.

"Not here, silly."

"Where, then? I know," he said, before she could answer. He took her hand, pulled her up from her seat, and directed her around several tables and through a doorway at the back of the room. Walking along a dimly lit passageway, he took her to the end—to a door that opened into the alleyway. Hedged in by high walls, it was closed off by an equally high stockade fence. A row of rubbish barrels stood along the fence. Beaten and scarred from long abuse, some had ill-fitting covers and some had no covers at all. Next to the wall a heavy machine hummed loudly and dripped water. The heat of the day made the odor of garbage thick and pungent, but this was a place they could be alone if they wanted to take advantage of it.

"Will this work?" Sam asked.

"Yes, if we can get past the smell."

They took two steps down and moved along the alleyway to the noisy machine that served as the building's central air-conditioner. There they sidled into a shady space between the louvered frame and the cool brick wall behind. It was narrow and close, but the cooling fan helped to push the odor of rotting fruit away from them.

Before leaving the hall Sam had removed his jacket, popped out the cuff links and rolled up his sleeves. The stringy ends of his bow tie fell across the pleated front of his shirt and he wore a wide cummerbund and red suspenders. It was the suspenders that caught Winnie's eye.

"I like these," she said as she slid her fingers beneath the wide ribbon of elastic that held his trousers. Suddenly she plucked one away, then let it snap back with a thunk against his heavily starched shirt.

"Ouch!" he complained.

"Did that hurt?" she said, circling her fingers over the spot where she had just stung him.

"Hey!" he said, covering her hand with his. The movement of her fingers caused the stiff material to scrape against his bruised nipple.

"What's the matter?" she asked, hearing him whimper.

"I'm sore, that's all."

"Here," she said, pressing down, "let me rub it and make it better."

"Nooo!" he panicked, "you don't want to do that." Grabbing both her wrists, he pulled them down then stretched her arms straight out, which had the added effect of bringing the two of them closer together. Winnie lost her balance and fell into him. With their noses touching he looked into her eyes and his vision blurred. Cocking his head back, he tried to bring her into focus and saw that her pupils were big and dark. Then she closed her eyes and he watched her wet lips pucker, and she held that pose waiting for a kiss. He felt suddenly silly, but he didn't disappoint her, and when his mouth slid over hers, she pushed back greedily. The softness of her upper lip scrubbed against the unshaven fuzz that he hoped someday would grow into a moustache. Without releasing her he tried to catch his breath and drew in the staleness of the alleyway. But he also brought in something stronger: the sweet aroma of claret and talc, and the sticky odor of sweat—both his and hers. First he wrinkled his nose; then decided that this peculiar mix was strangely exotic. She mumbled something and he started to laugh. But with his lips pressed to hers it came out as a quick snort.

"This isn't supposed to be funny," she said, breaking away.

"It's not. I don't know how to explain it. I feel like the fizz in a soda bottle—one that's so full of bubbles it's about to explode."

"All that from a kiss?"

"It's not the kiss: it's having you so close—it gives me the tingles."

"What in God's name are the tingles?"

"Never mind."

She dropped her chin on his shoulder and asked, "Is it something catching?"

"Yes—in a way. You may have already been infected."

"Whatever," she said. Then she lifted her head from his shoulder and kissed him again. It lasted only for a moment before she pushed him away. Flattening him against the wall, she slipped from his arms and escaped. Before he knew what had happened she was running toward the back door, though running doesn't accurately describe her condition. The heels and fitted party dress that she wore, constricted her movement and made her waddle like a duck. As she rushed to climb the steps, she got into trouble and started to fall. Sam, immediately behind, caught her. Though once he had her in his arms he didn't know what to do with her. Winnie didn't have that problem: she shook herself loose, then opened the door and rushed headlong down the shadowy passageway.

Winnie didn't seem angry, but her actions left Sam bewildered. Why did she kiss him and then make him chase after her? As he entered the reception hall he saw her standing on the other side near the dance floor. She didn't seem to be paying attention to whether or not he was

326 ~ Safe Harbor ~

following her, and Sam decided that if she wanted to be pursued, he would stalk her with all the subtle skill he could muster. Starting along the far wall, he went from table to table, sometimes sitting quickly behind an unsuspecting guest whenever Winnie glanced his way. He couldn't tell if she had spotted him, but she never made any effort to increase the distance between them. Finally he made a quick move between the tables and tapped her on the shoulder.

Turning to face him, she asked: "Wanna dance?" The invitation sounded off-handed, as if she had been waiting for him to show up just so she could get him on the dance floor.

"That's it? That's all you have to say?"

"Well, if you don't want to dance, I can find someone else." And she started to look around the room.

"Okay, okay, I'll dance." He took her hand to bring her onto the floor and she stopped him. "This is exciting," she said. He wanted to ask her what she meant. Was she talking about them, their kiss and then the chase, or was it about his mother and Martin and the wedding? But when she rested her chin on his shoulder and began to sway with the music, he felt as though they were the only two dancers on the floor.

While they danced, he whispered sweet posy (inane little verses made up on the spot), and she gave him a hug for each one. The reception continued around them, but they had ceased to be a part of it. Finally Sarah and Martin cut the cake and fed each other. She nibbled on her piece then took Martin's portion and lathered his face with the frosting. Sam and Winnie watched from a distant corner, while they tasted the wine from a couple of half-empty glasses. It was a cheap house-variety tasteless and flat, and they decided to quit after the first swallow. The bride's bouquet landed in Laura's arms, and the garter sailed through the air, to be caught by one of the ushers. Sam's best friend Bruce danced with a cute little blond girl, a niece from Martin's side of the family. Jennifer hung on David's arm and paid little attention to anyone else. Sam and Winnie heard the constant clink of glasses demanding that the groom kiss the bride or vice versa, but they mostly ignored the events that were going on around them.

Happy and self-absorbed, Sam and Winnie had escaped into their own secret whimsy, and when the announcement came that Sarah and Martin were leaving Sam felt suddenly guilty that he hadn't been paying more attention. After all, this day belonged to his mother, and he and Winnie had stolen it for themselves. Still, if he had any regrets, there wasn't time to belabor them. Sam looked at Winnie, but didn't say anything. Then he started immediately across the dance floor, trying to work his way through the guests that had crowded around the head table. But no one gave way, and when he saw his mother grab Martin's arm and begin to hustle him toward the side door to make their escape, he shouted, "Mom, wait!"

He saw her turn to find him, then tugged Martin's arm to stop his progress. Sam skirted the guests and rushed into his mother's arms.

"Mom, I didn't want you to go without saying goodbye."

"I looked for you earlier, but couldn't find you," she said, as she hugged him.

Then Martin did something Sam hadn't expected. He gently separated him from his mother and wrapped his arms around him. At first Sam didn't know how to respond, then he brought up his arms and returned Martin's hug. The strength of his embrace knocked Martin off balance and he had to take a step back.

Sam couldn't say why, but suddenly he felt terribly alone. "Take care of her," he whispered.

"Hey, we're only going for a week. After that, you'll be there to make sure I treat her right."

Martin reached out for Sarah's shoulder and pulled her in for a group hug, and the photographer, who had hounded their every action, snapped a picture. As soon as the brightness of the flash burned away, Martin and Sarah loosened their hold on Sam and turned to leave. Sam stood watching until they had disappeared through the doorway, then went back to rejoin Winnie.

◆ ◆ ◆

An hour later most of the guests and relatives had gone too. The band packed up their instruments and the people who worked for the caterer hustled about, scraping plates, rolling up the linens and folding tables and chairs.

Winnie and Sam sat alone on a couple of folding chairs that hadn't been packed away yet. Someone turned out the lights in the hall, leaving them in the soft incandescent glow from the backlighting on the stage. Winnie deliberately separated the pleats on Sam's shirtfront, bending them out of shape and ruining its form, then calmly asked him what was thinking.

"I'm thinking that after today nothing will be the same."

"What do you think will be different?"

"For one thing, my mother won't be the same."

"Sam, your mother will always be your mother, so what are you worried about?"

"Yes, but now she has Martin."

"And you have me. Does that mean you love your mother less?"

"No." He pushed his damp hair back as if somehow that would sweep the cobwebs from his mind.

"Do I have you?" he asked, looking up at a darkened light-fixture on the ceiling that was wrapped in a wire cage.

"You always have—always will," she promised.

"I just don't want things to change."

"Everything has to change. That's why one day is different from another. All you have to ask yourself is: Am I better off today than I was yesterday?"

"That sounds lame," he said.

"Why because it's not profoundly intellectual?"

"No, because I'm always suspicious when someone gives a simple answer to a complicated problem."

"Life isn't complicated, people just like to make it that way because it gives them a sense of importance."

They sat face-to-face and he took her hand in his. "So according to your philosophy this is where the happy ending comes in?"

"That's only in books and movies. The only real ending is death."

"Gruesome," he noted, bending forward.

She leaned in and touched her forehead to his. "Not if you believe in a hereafter."

A series of clicking noises from the stage took out the last of the lights, and they heard the sound of a door closing. It was as black as a moonless night in the middle of a forest, but they continued to sit there quietly, basking in the peaceful coolness that surrounded them.

Chapter 67

Sam sat in a lone tree at the edge of a field. The morning sun had not yet boiled up out of the ocean, and it already felt too hot. Hauling his T-shirt up over his head, he used it to wipe the perspiration from his face and under arms, then draped it across his lap. In a moment a line of trucks swept by one by one, and spread out onto the thick green grass. Each stopped in its pre-prescribed place and the men descended from their cabs to begin to set up for St. Bartholomew's Annual Fair. Sam had come here every year to pay homage to this singular event. It marked the end of summer—or at least the end of *his* summer—and the beginning of a new school year. Giving up the freedom of the beach and the water for the restrictions of the classroom and the drudgery of homework always depressed him.

This year he was not alone. Winnie was sitting above and behind him, one hand holding onto the branch beside her and the other locked around the trunk of the tree.

The two were hardly visible through the leafy branches and no one on the ground even glanced their way. The roustabouts were hauling tents and heavy gear off their trucks, and the noise and shouting reverberated in the thickness of the morning air. Winnie leaned forward and dug her fingers into Sam's shoulder.

"Thanks," Winnie said.

"For what?"

"For sharing this with me."

Two summers ago he had sat in this same spot, wondering what had become of his father, knowing that he had gone out on a toot, but never suspecting that he lay somewhere beside the highway, facedown in a ditch, drowned.

"Are you okay?" Winnie asked.

"I guess."

"I mean are you happy?"

"About what?" he asked.

"About your mom and . . ."

"Mom's happy," he interrupted.

"And you?"

"Eh," he said, shrugging his shoulders. "Happiness is overrated."

"What do you mean?"

"It never lasts."

"That's true. It comes and goes, but that's what makes it worth having.

The renewed pressure of her hand on his shoulder made him glance back. She put her bare feet on the branch to either side of his legs and let her weight fall against him. The roughness of her ribbed cotton top rubbed his sweaty skin and he could feel the softness of her breasts flatten across his back. Letting both arms fall loosely around his neck Winnie pressed her chin into his shoulder and left her hands dangling just a few inches in front of his stomach.

"You know I'm just as hot and sticky as you are only I don't get to take my shirt off and go around bare-chested."

"You can if you want," he challenged.

"Maybe when I was five, but not any more, and you know it."

"Yes, I do," he said, sounding altogether too gleeful.

"But you'd like me to take it off anyway. Right?"

"Yes—and no." he waffled, and she pinched a couple of the new hairs that were growing out of the middle of his chest. "Take it easy!"

"Then stop giving me a hard time, or I'll rip these little buggers out by the roots."

"Okay, okay, let go," he begged and she did.

"When do you move?" The closeness of Winnie's mouth to his ear made the words tickle and he brought his fingers up to scratch the tickle away.

"We don't," he said, lightly gripping her forearm just above the wrist.

"No?"

"Well, mom's selling our house—but so is Martin. They're going to build something new out on Silver Beach Road.

"Wow! That sounds expensive."

"Not really. Martin's grandfather owns a piece of land on the point and he's willing to give it to them for next to nothing. With the money from the sale of both houses there should be enough to build a new place of their own and some leftover to invest in their future."

"Will it be big?"

"I guess. The plans show lots of windows," Sam said, absently, and they both fell silent.

The clatter of chains brought their attention back to a crane that had just dropped one of two ticket booths onto the ground and a bulky little man with thick arms scrambled to get out of its way.

"Have you heard about Jennifer? She broke up with David."

"I know," he said, snapping a green leaf off the branch in front of him.

"Do you still think about her?"

"Not much."

"Did you love her?"

"I liked her a lot, but I don't think it was love," he said, chewing on the stem of the leaf.

"No, I mean did you—did you do it? Did you get naked together?"

"What? NO!" He bit off the stem, then spit it out because it was bitter. "When we. . .I couldn't. . .It—it just never came up." He spat again to get rid of the aftertaste of the leaf and he felt Winnie shake with laughter.

"What's so funny?" he asked, then sputtered, "Aaaahh."

"I couldn't help it," she said. "It was your choice of words."

True, but she had been too quick on the uptake. And he had to wonder what kind of things were going on in her mind right now.

"Did you want to?" she continued.

"Want to what?" He didn't look back at her, but watched her hands as she pulled nervously on her fingers.

"You know," she said, and he heard one of the joints crack.

"Do I have to answer that?"

"Yes," she insisted.

"I guess."

"Then why didn't you?"

"For reasons I'd rather not explain—." Then he told her anyway—partly. "Because, I couldn't let Jennifer see me naked."

"What about me? Would it bother you if I saw you naked?"

"No." He shook his head to emphasize this.

"How come?"

"Because you already have—seen me naked that is."

"When?"

"When we were five years old"

"Oh, good grief, am I supposed to remember that?"

"I remember it," he said, squeezing her closer by taking hold of her wrists and giving a gentle downward pull. "I thought it was pretty special."

"Get out," she said, rubbing the top of his head with her knuckles.

"Tell me—. That night under the cliffs at Land's End." He watched the leaves on the branch in front of him shake as she shifted her position. "What happened? I mean, I know you had an erection, but—."

"Don't say that," he groaned, cutting her off.

"Why not?

"It isn't decent."

"Can't we be honest with each other and not be indecent?"

He turned his face up toward a patch of sky that showed through a hole in the leaves at the top of the tree and made a silent plea for help. "Yes. Mostly. It's just that some stuff is better left unsaid."

"Look I just want to know if every time a boy kisses a girl is there some kind of switch that turns on. Is it all a matter of tension and nerves; or does the boy have to be attracted. Does he have to like the girl or is it just a physical thing?"

"Whoa, slow down." Her thoughts seemed too disjointed for him to follow.

"I guess what I'm trying to say is that when we were out there under the cliffs, face to face, and we kissed, what happened. . .other than the obvious."

"Jeeze!: he moaned, and shook his head in dismay.

"Oh, shut up." She cursed, then swung her arm up and put his head in a stranglehold. "All I want to know is—did that thing down under come to life all by itself or did it take something from in here to make it work," she said, releasing his neck and poking at his heart with her extended thumb.

"If you mean does kissing cause a guy to . . . to. . . Yeah, I guess that happens no matter what. But if you're asking about Jennifer and what happened between us—that is between you and I. What I feel for you— what I felt that night at Land's End, that's about as different as the moon from the sun."

Winnie reached under his chin to tip his head back, then kissed him on the forehead and when she pulled away she was smiling.

"What are you smiling about?" he asked.

Nothing," she said, and her smile grew wider. Then she moved suddenly to join him on the same branch, but instead of facing forward the way he was, she came down as if she were mounting a horse and let her legs swing freely on either side of the fat tree-limb. She put her left hand around his waist and used the other to hold the branch in front of him so that she wouldn't roll off.

"You asked me a few minutes ago if I was happy and I kinda brushed it off. Happiness is a new thing for me, and I guess I'm not all that comfortable with it."

"That's okay."

"No, it's not okay; not when it comes to you."

"What d'ya mean?"

"When I'm with you my feelings get all mixed up—or as Em puts it: I get all pixilated."

"What the heck is pixilated?"

"I'm not sure. Lovesick?" he spouted in a quick breath."

"Isn't that a contradiction?"

"Maybe."

"Can't you just tell me flat-out what it is that has you so *pixilated.*

"I'm in love with you," he said, in a rush, relieved that he'd finally gotten the words out. "Not the wild, silly infatuated kind of love, that I felt for Jennifer, but the kind that goes so deep it makes your bones ache."

"It's about time," she said. Then, letting go of the branch in front, she grabbed him around the neck and kissed him hard, which nearly knocked them both out of the tree.

Once they righted themselves, Sam began to speculate about the future: "We've been friends as far back as I can remember. Probably since the day we both climbed out of the crib. And other than the last few months there's hardly been a day when we didn't do something together or at least call each other to say hey. Those weeks you spent in New Hampshire were the loneliest. . ."

"For me too."

"One day I'll go off to college and you'll go off to college and then what?

"You could write?"

"I'm not a letter writer," he said rubbing her shoulder.

"What if one of us meets someone else?" she asked with a frown.

"It could happen," he said, with a shrug.

"It wouldn't bother you?"

"Of course it would bother me. I can't imagine loving anyone more or settling for anyone who loved me less," he said, deliberately pacing his words.

"Oooou, I think that's the nicest thing you've ever said to me—the most romantic at least."

She reached out with both arms and he called out a warning: "Don't let go," but it was too late and this time they did fall to the ground. They were on one of the lowest branches, and the grass was tall and thick, so it only knocked the wind out of them. As they sat up and shook off the impact, they heard a roustabout shout out to them: "Hey, what are you kids doing?" He started toward them with a large wrench in his hand, looking angry and menacing. Sam scooped up his shirt, and he and Winnie took off together, racing down Blue Bogg Road.

They stopped when they realized he wasn't chasing them.

"I thought that guy was after us," Sam said, wondering if he'd been chasing them at all or if he'd just imagined it.

"Me too," Winnie said huffing, then bent forward and grabbed her knees sucking in the air to catch her breach, and Sam, hands on hips, paced in front of her trying to do the same.

"All that talk back there," Sam said, waving his hand up the road. "about going away and finding someone else. I guess what I was trying to say is that it took a long time for me to understand my feelings for you and now that I do I desperately want to hold onto those feelings—I guess I want us to last forever. And when I think of all the years ahead and all the things that could get in the way. . ."

"Well, we can't ever lose what we already have," she said. "And for the next few years we're pretty much free to do whatever we want."

"That's what scares me," he said.

"How's that?" she asked and her posture straightened as if she expected the proverbial ax to fall.

"You asked me earlier about Land's End. About what happened out there and I got all anxious and jiggy.

"Yeah, you do that a lot."

"Only when you get to the personal stuff."

"So, I can't get personal?"

"No, but it would help if you'd sneak up on it instead of jumping in with both feet.

'I can do that."

"Ever since that night when we kissed under the cliffs, I've been possessed—well, maybe not possessed. But if it hadn't been for the tide I think we might have. . .well, I mean if we'd had more time. I suppose it's as much about curiosity as anything, but there's this little war going on inside my head and it's hard to tell who's winning. Sometimes I think if would be so easy to let go. When I catch the smell of your soap, or taste the dry salt on your cheek or hear that little *stck* and pop you make when you kiss, it's enough to make me want to explode. Jennifer put me through this craziness too, but I don't think I was ever in any real danger. It's a matter of trust; and you and I have oodles of trust, which is why I'm afraid that—that we—and I don't want that to happen. Not because of what someone might think, and not because you" have to see things that I'" ashamed of—I just don't want to end up like my mother."

"What are you talking about?" she asked, her face contorted.

"I don't want to end up married too young, and for the wrong reasons."

"Who said anything about marriage?"

"Nobody. But the way I feel about you I'd like to think that someday—you and I—that we might get married—and I'd like to think that you felt the same way."

"I do—I would—" she said, sounding a little flummoxed, by his backdoor proposal.

"But not now," he cautioned.

"Relax Sam. I'm not in a hurry to grow up. Not like that anyway."

Sam took Winnie's hand, felt that same perfect fit when her fingers slid between his and they crossed Beachwood Road. Once they were clear of the cottages they walked down the beach leaving clear prints in the wet sandy flats and now and then the wash from the ebbing tide crept up to surround their ankles.

A Gift Once Given
A Novel by
Robert O. Barclay

IN JUNE of 1957, on a hot and sultry summer's afternoon, Michael looks up and sees a young girl walking along the beach. At sixteen he's had little experience with girls, but from the very beginning he is attracted to her and studies her unashamedly. It's not that she is incredibly beautiful, but there is a dauntless air of self-assurance that sets her apart from the other girls he knows This is a story of innocence and coming of age in an era when people only talked about sex in euphemisms like "doing it" and "in a family way".

"It's been a long time since any story has touched me so deeply or made me feel as happy inside as this one did. And what a pleasure it was to . . .lose myself in the world of Linda and Michael and Ocean Bluff. Their story reached beyond the cynicism I too often fall prey too and put me back in touch with my own innocence."

Barbara Cockrell, author of "Gateway to the Heart"

Beaver's Pond Press, Inc • 952-829-8818
www.Beaverspondpress.com

• Order Number ISBN 1-931646 -19 -8

Also available at bookstores or at these websites:
Amazon.com • Borders.com •
Barnesandnoble.com